Holbrook Stepped into an Alley and Waited in the Darkness

The alley appeared deserted. Staying close to the buildings, he hurried to his front door.

Waiting for the lift, he wondered why it seemed to be taking so long.

The lift arrived. He stepped into the cage—and froze. *It took as long to come down as it takes to go up because the lift was on my floor. And my flat is the only one on my floor.*

He got out and cautiously began walking up the stairs, stopping to listen at every landing. No noise. When he got to a point where he could see his own door, he was surprised to find . . . nothing.

"You're a neurotic horse's ass," he said out loud, and plodded up the rest of the stairs.

He fumbled for the key to the bolt lock, put it in. But the key didn't turn. *That's funny. I guess I didn't double lock it. I guess I just forgot. But I never forget.*

He turned the other key and the door swung open. His flat was pitch dark. *Goddammit, the timer didn't turn the lights on. But it's brand new. And it worked yesterday.*

His mouth went dry. He took a step backward. There was a flash of light. And then there was an explosion . . .

Books by Jeffrey Robinson

The Pietrov Game
  (*formerly titled:* Pietrov and Other Games)
The Plutonium Conspiracy
  (*formerly titled:* The Ginger Jar)

Published by POCKET BOOKS

THE PLUTONIUM CONSPIRACY

(formerly titled THE GINGER JAR*)*

JEFFREY ROBINSON

POCKET BOOKS

New York   London   Toronto   Sydney   Tokyo

First published in Great Britain as *The Ginger Jar* in 1987 by New English Library

POCKET BOOKS, a division of Simon & Schuster, Inc.
1230 Avenue of the Americas, New York, N.Y. 10020

ISBN: 0-671-64252-9

First Pocket Books printing March 1988

10 9 8 7 6 5 4 3 2 1

POCKET and colophon are trademarks of
Simon & Schuster, Inc.

Printed in the U.S.A.

to
Constance and Jack
many fêtes
and love

THE
PLUTONIUM
CONSPIRACY

Prologue

THE DATE WAS Monday, April 21.

The place was the U.S. Navy's nuclear submarine base, cut into a cove along the Kyle of Tongue on the very northern tip of Scotland.

The time was late at night.

And it was raining.

Really raining.

Pouring down.

The kind of rain that makes you wonder if it's ever going to stop.

And it was windy too.

Really windy.

So windy that the sea was covered with whitecaps and waves banged the rocky shores.

In the middle of all this rain, and in the middle of all this wind, a cream-colored van was being loaded at a one-story cement warehouse, lit by huge spotlights.

Just there, inside the cove, a pair of shiny black submarines huddled close together.

Just here, under those spotlights, Marine guards stood back-to-back, heavily armed, soaked by the rain, as a large lead crate was tied down inside the cream-colored van, as the doors were locked, as the alarm systems were activated, as the shipment was judged to be secure.

After a while the cream-colored van pulled out of the spotlights, away from the warehouse. With windshield wipers at full speed, it moved slowly toward the heavy electric gates where more Marine guards looked out of their rain-beaten shack.

First they checked the coded orders attached to the shipment.

Then they checked the van's license plate against a written set of orders that hung on a graffiti-covered clipboard.

Then they checked the driver's papers.

Then they checked the papers of the Navy guard riding shotgun.

And only after they were convinced that everything was in order, did they open the gates and wave the shipment through.

The rain and the wind never stopped.

The cream-colored van disappeared into the night.

Chapter One

ON FRIDAY AFTERNOON, April 18, Richard Holbrook, a highly trained forty-one-year-old career Naval officer who had graduated nineteenth in his class at Annapolis in 1967 and third in his class at the U.S. Navy Basic Flight School in Pensacola the following year, sat at his desk with nothing much to do except sort through his APO mail.

There was one copy of *Sports Illustrated* and two letters.

Darryl Strawberry was on the magazine's cover, giving the world a very toothy grin. I'll save you for the weekend, he told the Mets' star outfielder, and shoved Strawberry, face up, into his attaché case. Then he ripped open the first letter. It was from American Express. They had screwed up yet another bill on his credit card and were insisting that he pay for some items he knew nothing about. How many times must I tell them that I have never in my life bought either a genuine Italian espresso machine that makes regular coffee plus hot chocolate, or a complete set of stainless-steel gardening hoes good for a hundred jobs around the house? A bunch of idiots, he groaned, and tossed it aside. The second letter was from Millicent's lawyer. Please understand, Commander, that your failure to take this matter as being of the utmost importance is merely serving to compound the fact that late child-support payments and an increased alimony to meet inflation . . .

A pain in the ass. He tossed that aside too.

That evening he went to Happy Hour in the Officers' Lounge, where besides drinking good whiskey for 50 cents a glass he could talk about baseball . . . Yeah, well, Junior Jim Gilliam was the best second baseman who ever played the game and Pee Wee Reese was one of the best shortstops who ever played the game and together they were much better than Rizzuto and MacDougal. Are you trying to tell me that Moose Skowran was as good a first baseman as Gil Hodges? Who? Orlando Cepeda? You're out of your skull. He talked baseball and got quietly drunk.

On Saturday morning, April 19th, he ran some errands . . . or at least he tried to. Oxford Street was much too crowded to get them all done. Actually the only thing he managed was to fight his way into Selfridges' basement to buy a timer switch so that the living room lights would go on every evening at five and snap off automatically at midnight. He was tired of coming home to a dark apartment. We have two models, the clerk announced in that specially smarmy way, which told Holbrook that the kid was on a commission. He could always tell the difference. The ones on commission were smarmy. The ones on salary were asleep. There's the standard conventional model at £10.95. It turns any lamp on and off at set times. And you can choose up to four set times if you want to. But then there's the deluxe model at £22.50 which is the one I highly recommend because it's digital and you're not limited to the number of times on or off. That's good if you want to create a special effect in the house, like having the lights go on and off every other minute. But the best feature of the deluxe model is that it runs on batteries so that if you should have a power failure the timer will still work. Holbrook nodded. I do like the special effect of lights going on and off every other minute. Kind of a disco feeling. The clerk agreed. But tell me, if we have a power failure, what lights will the battery-operated deluxe model still be able to turn on? The clerk handed him the £10.95 model and said, uninterestedly, sorry, it only comes in one color.

Back in Oxford Street, fighting his way through the crowds, Holbrook decided that the best way to opt out of the Saturday rush was by opting in to The Courageous Dutchman.

Standing at the far end of the long wooden bar, he found

himself next to a fellow who listened to him order a beer, then asked, are you a Yank, mate? Holbrook said yes. The fellow smacked his lips in such a way as to say, that's the right thing to be. Holbrook smacked his lips too and bought the fellow a beer. What's beer like in the States, mate? Not like this, Holbrook said. The fellow smacked his lips again, as if to say he was happy to know that not all Americans thought everything in America was better than everything in England. So now he bought Holbrook a beer and the two of them stood there, hardly speaking at all, but smacking their lips a lot, until the publican showed them the door an hour after official closing time. The beer might not be as good in the States, Holbrook said, but at least they give you time to drink it. The fellow smacked his lips again . . . right you are, mate . . . and walked away. And at least beer in the States is cold, he wanted to say but by then the fellow was all the way down the block.

With nothing else to do, Holbrook went home to sleep off the beer.

When he woke up it was nearly 6 P.M. Ah Christ, he mumbled, because now it was too late for his weekly telephone call. Six here is one there and I'm sure they're all out somewhere by now. But then he figured, maybe I'll get lucky, and what the hell, and he dialed Florida anyway.

There was no answer.

On Sunday morning, April 20, he lay on his bed watching a Game of the Week video that he had borrowed from the office. A new taped game came in every week. But he couldn't have cared less about the Mets and the Expos. The Game of the Week was only something to do until two o'clock when he could call Florida again.

This time Millicent answered. "Oh, it's you. You were supposed to call yesterday."

"I couldn't," he said without bothering to make any explanations. "How are you?" She said, fine. "What's new?" She said, not a lot. "Weather all right?" She said, getting hot. "It's been raining here so much that I'm thinking about building an ark." She said, really? "Well, okay, nice talking to you. Would you please put David and Chrissie on."

Now she said, "Sorry, fly-boy. They expected your call

yesterday. Eventually they got tired of waiting so they went out to live their lives.''

"Where are they now?"

"David's at Tony Scrudato's house. And Chrissie's at her friend Samantha Love's house. Does that tell you anything?''

Two o'clock here minus five hours . . . "It's only . . . what . . . nine in the morning. They know if I can't call them on Saturdays I always call them on Sundays. Why would they leave the house so early when they know. . . ?''

"They didn't leave the house this morning," she said. "They left the house last night. Seems we all had plans of our own.''

Oh. Now he understood. "I see. Everybody gets to have a pajama party.''

"Don't worry," she told him right away. "It's nobody you know." There was a long pause. "Did you get that letter from my lawyer?''

"Yes, I got the letter." What else was there to say? "I'll try to take care of it this week.''

There was another pause and now she said softly, "I spoke to Barbara yesterday. Did you remember to call her? You know, it was two years ago today.''

Two years ago today? She's right. April 20th. Two years already? He could hear it as if it were playing in stereo right now. Okay, Bean Bag, straighten 'em out . . . gear is down . . . and locked . . . you're doing fine . . . level off now . . . you're high left . . . bring it down just a skosh . . . okay, you're doing fine . . . hang in there, buddy . . . coming in straight . . . keep your nose up . . . nose up, Bean Bag . . . nose up. Bean Bag . . . get your fucking nose up. Bean Bag!

Millicent broke into the silence. "Just thought you might give her a call. As for Chrissie and David, try again next Saturday. Same time. Same station.''

"Okay," he said. "Yeah. Okay. Bye, Millicent." She said, "Bye, Richard." And they hung up.

Two years already? He just couldn't believe it. April 20th. Yeah, two years ago today. He thought about phoning Barbara. Maybe I should. Just to say hello. Just to ask how her kids are. Just to tell her I'm thinking about her.

Instead he found a gin bottle and poured a drink.

Okay, Bean Bag, straighten 'em out.

Then he poured a second drink.

Hang in there, buddy . . . coming in straight.

Then he poured a third drink.

Somewhere in his head he reminded himself, it was two years ago today.

His *Sports Illustrated* went unread.

Nose up, Bean Bag . . . nose up.

Sunday dissolved into his glass.

Monday never happened.

The next thing he realized was that his phone was ringing and it was 4:57 in the morning.

Chapter
Two

ON MONDAY, APRIL 21, men and women, but mostly men, from at least nine countries filled the small room on the third floor of Bonhams Auction House in Cheval Place, in Montpelier Street, off Knightsbridge just a block from Harrods.

"Lot number two hundred *and* forty-three," the young auctioneer announced, affectedly drawing out the *and* with his practiced Etonian accent, as he sat high in the podium at the front of the room, wearing his best dark-blue pinstriped suit, grasping a small mahogany gavel head in his left hand which he could slam down the instant the bidding was done. "A Ming cup," he added just before a fellow in a white smock hoisted the cup into the air and called out, "Showing here, please." Immediately the young auctioneer started the bidding. "Two hundred pounds, thank you. Two-twenty . . . two-forty . . . two-sixty . . . two-eighty . . . two hundred *and* eighty pounds . . . selling now for two hundred *and* eighty pounds . . ." He surveyed the faces staring back at him . . . surveyed them all hoping to spot a nod or a wink or a twitch of a nose. "Two hundred *and* eighty pounds . . ." He slammed down his gavel . . . Bang! . . . then whispered the name of the buyer to a young woman at his side who recorded the sale results. And without any ceremony, the auction continued. "Lot number two hundred *and* forty-four."

Some of the people in the room sat on metal folding chairs facing the podium, making the place look like a kind of gospel hall lacking only a wooden Jesus, but with plenty of parishioners anxious to answer the rallying Gospel of the voice that boomed out to them from the pulpit. Some of them stood in the doorway, partially blocking the way for anyone wanting to come in or go out, so that you had to say, "Excuse me," or "Pardon me," or "May I get by, please," as you made your way through the crowd. And some of them wandered around just beyond the doorway, in the hall, in front of the lift that brought more people up to the third floor where in their haste they didn't always close the cage behind them.

"Lot number two hundred *and* forty-four," the auctioneer called out while the fellow in the white smock held up a pair of blue and white export serving plates. "Showing here, please."

Christopher Li'Ning hurriedly squeezed past the people in the doorway and quietly asked someone sitting just there what lot was being sold. The person sitting just there pointed to it in his catalog and Li'Ning then made his way to the rear corner of the room to wait.

The auctioneer bounced a bid off an empty chair. He said, one hundred pounds, thank you, then turned to the wall and said, one hundred *and* ten. Then he said, one hundred *and* twenty to the empty chair and one hundred *and* thirty to the wall. Then it was one hundred *and* forty, one hundred *and* fifty, and then one hundred *and* sixty. He got all the way up to one hundred *and* sixty pounds without a single legitimate bidder in the room, so he sold the pair of plates to the empty chair. No sense lingering too long on such an item because momentum is money and the first thing any auctioneer learns is that the more excitement he can pour into the sale the higher the prices will be. One hundred *and* sixty pounds. Selling now for one hundred *and* sixty pounds. He banged down his gavel, then whispered to the girl on his right. Shire, he said, pretending that there was someone in the room named Shire who had wanted the plates, even if everyone in the room knew the plates had been bought in.

He followed it with lot two hundred *and* forty-five. Showing here, please. Four thousand pounds . . . now four thousand five hundred . . . now five thousand . . . and five thousand five hundred . . . the bid is against you, sir, at five thousand five hundred pounds. He paused for only a moment before warning them. I am selling now at five thousand five hundred pounds. And true to his word he banged down the gavel head. First he jotted down the result in his notebook and then, knowing that he must keep up a fast pace to give the next lot some excitement, he called out right away, lot number two hundred *and* forty-six, and someone else called out, just as quickly, showing here, please.

The men in the room, and the women in the room as well, were almost all dealers. And dealers always made it a point of showing how blasé they were about this sort of thing, about how they had mastered the art of the auction and had become skillful matadors at the *mano a mano* needed to survive when you are fighting for the lowest price against fifty or sixty or seventy other dealers who all know the good from the bad, the high prices from the bargains, while all the time the auctioneer at the podium is being paid to wring out the highest price he can get from them.

The only non-dealers in the room were the half-dozen Bonham's employees, and of course, Li'Ning—a smallish, lean man in his late thirties, impeccably dressed in a gray silk suit, pale-blue shirt and pink tie, with perfectly trimmed black hair, manicured fingernails, and large squarish glasses which he wore during the week to make his eyes look less Oriental.

The auctioneer sold lot two hundred *and* forty-seven, then two hundred *and* forty-eight, and with the same speed he sold lot two hundred *and* forty-nine. Now he proclaimed, "Lot number two hundred *and* fifty."

"Showing here." The young man in the white smock held it up very carefully in both his hands.

And now Li'Ning nervously shuffled his feet.

The catalog description of Lot 250 was spread over an entire page, with a color photo just opposite.

An Exceptionally Rare And Very Large Late Ming/Early Transitional Ginger Jar. In deep cobalt blue (certainly of the imported *hui-ch'ing* variety) and cracked ice white, painted on one side with two panels, both showing a mythical beast standing on rocks surrounded by stylized waves, the reverse with two other panels showing "the hundred antiques.'' With original cover. 36.25 cm with six character mark in underglaze blue of Cheng-te on bottom of both jar and cover.

Below that was a note from the auction-house experts which read:

The rarity of this jar is not only its size but also the sheer clarity of the figures drawn by the Cheng-te craftsmen. Only two other examples of this size and quality are known to exist. One is the "Burchard" jar in the British Museum collection, having been shown at the Berlin Chinese Art Exhibition of 1929 and acquired by the Museum at the liquidation auction sale of the Dr. Otto Burchard and Co. Collection, auctioned on 22 March 1935. The second example, referenced by Willett, Medley, Sato, et al. including and most importantly by Bonnier, is held by a private collector in the United States.

The estimate at the end of the description was £10,000–£12,000.

The auctioneer took a drink from a glass of water on his podium, then bothered to inform everyone in the room, "May I point out, please, that this particular ginger jar is from the collection of Major-General Sir Alexander P. G. Thistlethwaite, DSO, and is being sold by his estate. Because of the quality of this particular item, I already have several commission bids and therefore must begin the bidding at eleven thousand five hundred pounds."

A slight murmur ran through the audience.

The curtain was up and this was the main attraction.

"Eleven thousand five hundred pounds . . ." The auctioneer hesitated only a second before nodding. "On my right, thank you . . . now . . . twelve thousand pounds . . ."

A man seated in the third row—who happened to look something like the American actor and film director Carl Reiner—motioned discreetly to take the bid at twelve thousand five hundred. A woman standing in the doorway—who happened to look something like the French writer Marguerite Yourcenar—said yes to thirteen thousand. The Carl Reiner look-alike agreed to thirteen thousand five hundred. The Marguerite Yourcenar look-alike accepted fourteen thousand. The Carl Reiner look-alike nodded okay for fourteen thousand five hundred. The Marguerite Yourcenar look-alike hesitated, then said all right to fifteen thousand.

Suddenly a large bearded man—who didn't actually look like anybody famous except perhaps a little bit like a young Raymond Massey when he played a young Abe Lincoln—fought his way inside the room from the corridor and said, "Sixteen thousand." The Carl Reiner look-alike said seventeen thousand, the Marguerite Yourcenar look-alike said eighteen thousand, the large bearded man said nineteen thousand and the Marguerite Yourcenar look-alike said, "Twenty thousand."

Now the auctioneer tried, "Twenty-one thousand?"

But now there was a pause.

The auctioneer glanced toward the Carl Reiner look-alike who hesitated, then shook his head and dropped out of the bidding.

"Twenty thousand pounds," the auctioneer said. "It's the lady's bid at twenty thousand pounds."

In the back of the room Li'Ning knew he had to pick his moment. The auctioneer waited. "Twenty thousand pounds."

He was in no hurry.

The auctioneer couldn't hide his determination to try to get more. "The lady's bid . . ."

But timing is everything in an auction room. Li'Ning had learned that lesson from experience. The expensive way. A bid too soon could cause someone to bid back in anger. A bid too late could mean the jar would be sold. Twenty thousand pounds. His eyes darted round the room. Twenty thousand. The bid was stuck there. Twenty thousand.

The auctioneer said, "Selling now for twenty thousand pounds . . ."

And that's when Li'Ning said in a loud, clear, and supremely confident voice, "Twenty-one thousand."

Everyone in the room turned to look at him.

Even the auctioneer was surprised, although he did his best not to show it. "Twenty-one thousand. A new bidder at the rear."

And now there was another long pause.

It was easy to see that the Marguerite Yourcenar look-alike hadn't expected anyone else to come into the game this late because she was mumbling to herself, obviously trying to answer all the questions which had come suddenly into her mind. Will this new player stay? Will he drop out? How far is he prepared to go? She looked at the notes in her catalog while the auctioneer reminded her, ''The bid is against you at twenty-one thousand pounds.''

There was another moment when nothing happened.

Then the auctioneer threatened her. ''Selling now to the gentleman at the rear of the room for twenty-one thousand pounds.''

The woman in the doorway stared at the auctioneer for a very long moment.

''Selling now . . .'' The auctioneer raised his hand.

And with an almost characteristic feisty Gallic style, the Marguerite Yourcenar look-alike called out, ''Yes.''

Just as quickly Li'Ning also said, ''Yes.''

''Twenty-two thousand in the doorway and twenty-three thousand again at the rear of the room.'' The auctioneer instantly moved the bid back to the Marguerite Yourcenar look-alike. ''Twenty-four thousand to you?''

There was another long pause.

Christopher Li'Ning waited without moving a muscle.

Everyone in the room was waiting for the Marguerite Yourcenar look-alike to do something . . . to say something . . . but when she saw their eyes on her, she simply turned on her heels and walked away.

His deadpan never faltered.

''Twenty-three thousand in the rear of the room.'' The auctioneer was greedily trying to get another bid. ''Selling now for twenty-three thousand pounds.''

Li'Ning stared straight at him.

''Twenty-three thousand pounds . . .''

And then, bang!

With a businesslike nod to the auctioneer, Christopher Li'Ning hurried out of the room, purposely avoiding the glances of anyone who might be wondering to themselves, who is he and why would he pay such a price for that jar?

The auctioneer announced, "Lot number two hundred *and* fifty-one. A pair of blue and white Phoenix dishes." And the fellow in the white smock called out, "Showing here, please."

Once he was out of the room, far enough away from all those people and heading down the stairs, Li'Ning finally let out his breath and allowed himself a tiny smile.

"Excuse me, sir." A young woman raced up to him.

He quickly erased the victorious smile. "Yes?"

"Hello." She was carrying a notebook and pencil. "That's a really wonderful ginger jar you just bought. May I ask if it's for your own private collection?"

"I'm sorry?" He didn't know who she was.

"This is for the *Antiques Trade Gazette,*" she said as if he should have been able to guess that. "They ask us to keep them informed about our sales. May I ask if you've bought the ginger jar for your own personal collection? I mean, excuse me, but you are Mr. Li'Ning." She said that more as a statement than a question. "Did I pronounce it right? You see, they always like us to tell them what lots fetch prices far beyond the estimates . . ."

"Oh." He wanted to be polite but there were reasons why he didn't want this in the papers—at least not yet. "I see. Well, if you have to say something perhaps you could just say that this particular ginger jar was purchased by the Mandarin Commerce Bank of Hong Kong. That's really all."

"Mandarin . . . Commerce . . . H. K. . . ." She jotted that down. "Can I say it was bought by you for the bank?"

"I would prefer if you didn't. After all, I'm not a dealer." He grinned, trying to charm her. "I think perhaps just the bank's name would be suitable."

"But you are a collector, aren't you? I mean, you have bought with us before and I thought . . ."

"Just the bank," he said. "Really, this is only for the bank."

"Well . . . okay. Thank you."

"Quite all right." And he hurried down the stairs and outside to his chauffeured Jaguar before anyone could ask him anything else.

Chapter Three

SUNDAY DISSOLVED INTO HIS GLASS.

Monday never happened.

The next thing he realized was that his phone was ringing and it was 4:57 in the morning.

Lying perfectly still, spread-eagle on his back, one pillow on top of his face, the other draped across his chest, he told himself, I think I'm awake.

His legs felt like they each weighed a ton.

He told himself, at least I'm alive.

His head was throbbing.

He told himself, I don't want to be awake.

The phone kept ringing.

In the middle of the dark room, in the middle of his monologue, from under the pillows he heard that terribly annoying ring of the modern British telephone—the high pitched wavering ring that always made him think of a screaming lamb being led off to slaughter.

He assured himself it would stop.

It didn't.

Then suddenly, like some sort of delayed action, he sat bolt upright, throwing the pillows off, scared, looking around the dark room, turning his aching body toward the phone and lunging for it.

"Commander Holbrook," he whispered hoarsely.

"Sir," a crisp, wide-awake voice came out of the receiver

at him. "Sir, this is Chief Petty Officer Charles. The admiral wants you to report to his office a.s.a.p."

"The admiral?" He tried to get his bearings. "What time is it?"

"Zero four fifty-seven, sir."

Zero four fifty-seven. Not sixteen fifty-seven. Not four fifty-seven in the afternoon. But three minutes to five in the morning. Monday morning. Is it Monday already? It must be. But he didn't dare ask. Instead he mumbled, "Right. I'm on my way."

He put the phone down, waited a few seconds, and with a hugely exaggerated groan forced himself out of bed. But as soon as he stood up a queasiness overtook him. He stumbled through his bedroom, tripping over clothes, breathing deeply until he got to the bathroom. He thought he was going to puke. He stared into the toilet bowl for nearly a minute. When nothing happened, he figured the next best thing was an ice-cold shower. He turned the shower head so that a sharp stream of water poured on top of his face. He stood there, with both his arms stretched out, holding the walls for support until the throbbing in his head finally began to subside. It's raining, it's pouring, let's make this shower less boring. Millicent used to sing that whenever they took a shower together. He'd stand that way, with his arms stretched out like he was being crucified, then she'd kneel down and sing that song . . . It's raining, it's pouring . . . Now he put his face up to the shower and the pressure behind his eyes began to fade away. It's raining, it's pouring . . . After a few minutes, when the water was so cold that he couldn't stand it anymore, he decided, I think the patient is going to live.

Wrapping himself in a bathrobe, he went back into the bedroom and yanked open the drapes.

A thin drizzle was falling past the orange streetlights three floors below.

He said out loud, "So what else is new."

Making his way into the kitchen, he found his light-timer switch still in the yellow Selfridges bag, and two used gin bottles sitting empty on the counter. He pushed them aside, reached for a jar of instant Choc Full O'Nuts, boiled some water and made a cup of coffee. Opening the fridge to look for some milk, all he found was a package of Mallomars—he ate them all—one peach melba yogurt and half a box of Twiglets.

Then he did his vitamins. Mixed into the peach melba yogurt he swallowed one multi, one E, one special fiber, one cod-liver oil, one hyper-C, and one special iron.

He ate the Twiglets like a chaser.

In the living room he tried to plug the light-timer switch into a tall floor lamp with a beige shade. But that lamp was plugged into a small round three-bolt socket and the light-timer switch was for a large rectangular three-bolt socket. He wanted to scream. England has got to be the only country in the world where appliances are sold without plugs because they have so many different types of sockets. Sometimes two or three or even four kinds in the same house. It's enough to drive a sane electrician to drink. What do you mean there's no plug? he'd asked the blank wall that time he carried a portable TV set home from Selfridges and found that he wasn't able to plug it in. How come there's no plug? he demanded when he stormed back to the store. The clerk there gave him the standard answer—I'm sorry, sir, but that's the way we've always done it. You see, sir, because there are so many different types of outlets in this country we never supply plugs except as a separate item. I suppose you call it tradition, Holbrook said. No, the clerk explained, tradition is all those blokes on horses, wearing funny hats, playing "Hello, Dolly" music at 11 every morning in front of Buckingham Palace. The lack of a plug on the end of your television cord is good business for the plug manufacturers. Oh. There was nothing else Holbrook could say. Just, oh. No plug. He couldn't get used to that. Radios. Televisions. Clocks. Toasters. I wonder if that espresso machine that American Express keeps asking me to pay for comes with a plug. Shit. I want to use my light-timer where I want to use my light-timer. The quality of life is judged by the number of choices you have. Poor people have fewer choices than rich people. Well, I want to plug my light-timer switch in where I want to plug it in and not just anywhere because this country can't get its socket-and-plug act together.

In the end he had to put the light-timer switch onto the

lamp in the window that looked down to Duke Street. At least I can see it on from the street and maybe if there are any burglars around they'll see it too. Once that was fixed, he went to the front door where two copies of the *Herald Tribune* were lying just inside the mail slot.

Holy shit, he cursed the moment he saw the top one.

It was dated Tuesday, April 22.

He picked up the papers and tossed them onto a chair.

How the hell can it be Tuesday?

He hurried into a clean uniform, fumbled with his name tag and his gold Navy wings, checked himself in the mirror, took his raincoat, put a rain cover on his hat and left the apartment.

Duke Street was empty.

The wet streets and the orange lights made it look like a movie set—as if some Hollywood director had built London in the back lot at Universal and then decided at the very last minute to turn on the sprinklers because everyone knows that London before dawn only really looks like London before dawn if it's wet.

A lone taxi circled Grosvenor Square.

When it passed, there was no noise at all—except for the rain and the click of Holbrook's heels on the wet pavement.

A few lights were on at the U.S. embassy.

Two obviously very bored uniformed British policemen leaned against the barricades that were supposed to keep the demonstrators away from the Embassy's front door. Last week there had been several thousand. But there were no demonstrators now. Just those cops . . . two hours on, four hours off . . . armed discreetly under the coats, waiting for something to happen. Except nothing would happen. Not now. Not at this hour. Not in this weather. Pro-Gaddafi. Pro-Khomeini. Always anti-USA. Keep your missiles out of Britain. Send the F-111s home. You are the murderers. The blood of Tripoli is on your hands. Washington Fascists. Imperialist Pigs. Down with Reagan. Up with the Holy War. But not now. Not in the pre-dawn rain. After all, protesters may be a nuisance but they aren't crazy. They all know that, in the final analysis, very few causes are actually worth the risk of double pneumonia.

He walked to North Audley Street, turned right, and went into the door marked U.S. Navy.

Two Marine guards waited just inside the door, armed, on special alert since the bombing of Tripoli. They checked his ID and let him pass. Another Marine guard lit only by a blue light at the otherwise dark security checkpoint also looked at his ID. Then he sorted through a stack of numbered security badges, handed him one, buzzed him through the locked bulletproof door, and Holbrook headed for the elevator.

The dark linoleum along the corridor of the top floor was highly polished. All militaries are big on highly polished linoleum. Our side. The other side. Everyone's. And the walls there, painted off-beige, were lined with framed posters of ships and planes. Militaries are big on off-beige–colored walls. And those kinds of pictures too. The difference between our hallways and their hallways is that in ours you also find large bulletin boards with notices such as, "Looking for higher interest? Your Credit Union Needs You."

The only light in the hallway came from the far end, from the admiral's office. And when he got there he could hear voices.

He left his rain gear in the outer office and walked into the big room just behind it. "Good morning, sir."

Three men were there.

Admiral Y. C. Roth stood in front of his desk, with his jacket unbuttoned. A short, wiry man and Commander-in-Chief, U.S. Naval Forces in Europe—CINCNAVEUR, for short—Roth was almost entirely bald and that made him look slightly older than his fifty-three years. He had four stars on his shoulders. On his chest he wore pilot wings and a submariner's badge. Under that he had only two rows of ribbons. Most officers who had more wore more. But not Roth. It was a kind of reverse snobbery because the few ribbons he wore were ribbons that counted, like the Silver Star and the Navy Cross and the Bronze Star and the Purple Heart, and there were oak-leaf clusters on his Legion of Merit.

Seated on the leather couch that ran along the side wall, just under a dozen framed photographs, was Rear-Admiral Martin M. Foster, U.S. Naval Attaché in Great Britain, a tall, blond cowboy from Oklahoma who had earned his reputation coordinating the fleet's tactical activities in the Gulf of Tonkin during the final years of the Vietnam War. Sitting on the window ledge, with his back to the venetian blinds which cut off the view from Grosvenor Square, was Captain Robert A. Wagner, a stocky, dark-haired man who served as Staff Security Officer.

Roth returned the salute. "Dad, we've got a problem." He handed Holbrook a TWX.

The yellow slip of paper was stamped in tiny letters "Top Secret." It was dated Monday April 21 and timed at 22:45 hours Zulu. The message said in a difficult-to-read dot matrix print, "Alert CCR. Shipment D-17 Grand Pin two hours overdue. No contact last checkpoint."

Holbrook simply muttered, "Ah, shit."

"You can say that again," Wagner volunteered. "Sierra, hotel, India, tango. Put 'em all together and they spell more bad-assed trouble. But like I keep telling the admiral, my people can handle it all with no fallout effect."

"I got the TWX last night," Roth said. "I left word to be called every two hours if nothing turned up. They're now eight hours overdue."

Holbrook wanted to know, "What was their last checkpoint?"

Roth motioned him to look at the road map of Great Britain that was spread across his desk. "The van left the Tongue area on time and this was the route, down the A836." He pointed to a series of roads with his finger. "Checks at Altnaharra, here, and another at Rhian, here. The third check was supposed to be just the other side of this lake called Shin, here, at the village of Lairg. But the van never made it to Lairg."

Staring at the map, Holbrook noted, "That's the middle of the Scottish Highlands. It's the middle of nowhere."

"The base at Tongue followed procedure and sent a car along the route. Nothing showed up. I've ordered an air search out at dawn." Roth looked at his watch. "Just about now, I suppose. They might come up with something in the next few hours." He paused. "Let's hope like hell they do. But in case they don't, we could have one helluva problem on our hands."

Wagner cut in. "Skipper, you know how I feel about it.

And I reiterate that the more people who are aware of this, the more we put our entire security operation at risk. My people can handle this. There's no need to call any amateurs in.''

"I wonder . . ." Holbrook said, knowing full well that Wagner's remarks had been aimed at him. "Sir, looking at the map, there aren't all that many roads feeding off the A836. I mean, according to this, it looks like the van couldn't go any other way except up or down the highway.''

"Unless," Wagner suggested, "someone pulled it sideways.''

Holbrook asked Roth, "British know yet?''

"Not yet.''

"Well . . . if something's happened to that shipment we have to tell them right away.''

"Eventually," Wagner interjected. "Or maybe eventually. But not right away. And not unless we absolutely have to. It's our goddamned shipment which means it's none of their goddamned business.''

"That might have been true two weeks ago," Holbrook reminded him, "but not since Tripoli." He turned to Foster. "Does the ambassador know yet?''

"No," Foster said. "No one outside this room knows yet.''

Holbrook looked at Roth. "Sir, I'm afraid we really have to liaise with the British. And I think the sooner we do it, the better.''

Roth said nothing for several seconds. He paced the floor, then dropped down into his chair and kicked his legs on top of his desk. His shoes crumpled the map. "The search parties only know that a van is missing. They don't know what's inside the van. The air search may turn up something. If, however, it doesn't, we've got to be ready to do something. But whatever happens it's got to be kept quiet.''

"I couldn't agree more," Wagner said. "And it can be done. Tripoli has nothing to do with it. I said all along we could have pulled that off without anyone in this country knowing where those planes were coming from.''

"Tripoli has everything to do with it," Holbrook said. "The host country has to be kept informed. Can you imagine what would have happened if they found out the F-111s came

21

from here? The same shit will go down if they find out about this before we tell them.''

"And the same shit will happen here that always happens if we don't tell them,'' Wagner mimicked his voice. "Ever know that a few years ago 385 kilos of PuN disappeared on route from Ohio to St. Louis? It showed up nine days later in a crate at Logan Field in Boston. Didn't hear about that, did you? How about the theft of some PuN in 1981 from the Rosyth Dockyards? Didn't ever hear about that one either, huh? What I'm driving at is that those two scenarios prove these things can be kept quiet if we work at keeping it quiet. I'm sure you all remember the reaction we got in Spain a long time ago when a B-52 inadvertently lost some nuclear weapons on a beach. The Spaniards went berserk. Made us look like a bunch of incompetent jerks. We sure as hell don't need an instant replay of that.''

Foster said, "Of course not.''

But Holbrook insisted, "If we keep this quiet and the Brits ever find out this came down . . . I mean we're talking about less than one week after the world started giving them shit because of us . . . they're going to toss our asses outta this place.''

"Nonsense,'' Wagner said.

"Point is,'' Foster chimed in, "the PuN is still missing and whether we tell the Brits or not, we've gotta find it. And fast.''

Holbrook wondered, "Did the van have a beeper system?''

"Sure it did,'' Wagner answered, as if that was just about the dumbest question he had ever heard. "Everything was the way it was supposed to be, for Christ's sake. And we've been listening for six hours but there's nothing happening on any frequency.''

"That's pretty empty country,'' Holbrook said. "There can't be a lot of places where that van could go. I mean, if God forbid someone did try to hijack it . . .''

"What do you mean, if?'' Wagner demanded. "I say it's dollars to donuts that someone grabbed that van. We're dealing with people who know precisely what the hell they're doing. Real pros.''

"They'd have to be real pros,'' Holbrook said ironically.

"That stuff is self-protecting. You can't just put it in your pocket and walk away with it. If the radioactivity doesn't kill you, just breathing the dust will. On top of that it's not as if there are all sorts of intersections where the van could have been stopped. It would have been moving pretty fast. It wouldn't be easy to grab because . . ."

"Problem is," Foster cut in, "if someone did go after the van then they know what to do with it. Anybody who goes after a shipment of plutonium nitrate knows what it can do and what they can do with it. I'm talking about, you know, Gaddafi's guys."

Holbrook raised his eyebrows. "With all due respect, Admiral, this is England. Maybe it could happen in Italy or Greece. But the scenario of Libyan terrorists stealing plutonium nitrate from the U.S. Navy and then somehow getting it out of this country . . . I'm not saying it's totally impossible, but I think there could be some other, more logical options to work with. Yet no matter what's happened to the van, we're getting away from the point. We've still got to inform the British."

"How's the IRA grab you?" Wagner smirked, somewhat pleased with himself for having come up with the idea. "I'll bet my damn butt you never thought about those bastards, did you?"

He hadn't thought about them. "Okay. The IRA is a possibility." Holbrook gave up the point because he didn't want to lock horns with Wagner. "I'm just not so easily convinced that anyone could actually hijack that van. To grab it they'd have to know about the shipment, its route and all the times involved. That stuff always varies with every shipment. Except for some of the roads we have to use because there aren't any others, no two routes are precisely the same. We shake them up as much as possible. Then they'd have to know how to get into that van without setting off any of the alarm systems. Don't forget that even the drivers can't open those doors without bells and sirens and radio signals going off loud enough to be heard all the way to Tijuana. Then they'd have to be damn-well certain that they were handling the stuff properly. They'd also need some way to get it safely out of England and into wherever . . . Northern Ireland . . ."

23

"Christ," Wagner stopped him. "You make it sound like they're the Boy Scouts. Don't forget that they made that damn racehorse disappear. He weighed a ton, could bolt if they spooked him and anyway was probably high-strung nasty enough to kick their balls off just for the sport of it. A couple of kilos of PuN won't even click click click on a goddamned Geiger counter as long as they keep it under wraps. Listen, Holbrook, I'm telling you that damn van's been hijacked."

You won't lay off me, will you, he thought as he stared at Wagner. "Frankly, Captain, it would weigh more than a couple of kilos."

"It still weighs less than a fucking horse."

It was useless arguing with the man. So he looked back to Roth and Foster, paused for a second and tried another tack. "If the van has broken down somewhere, and we've told the host country all about it, well, then nothing's lost. We've kept them informed and that's what we're expected to do. But if there has been a hijacking, we'll be forced into playing the game by their rules anyway. Not telling them from the word Go could mean a lot of unnecessary flak coming in our direction."

"And I say, Skipper, that right now it's none of their goddamn business." Wagner was sticking to his ground. "It doesn't concern them until we decide it concerns them."

"Okay," Roth said, holding up his hands to show them the debate was over. "I appreciate your input. Now . . ." He waited a moment, then nodded as if he was finally sure of what he wanted to say. "From where I sit this is not merely a military decision. It also has to be a political one. Marty, when would you want to brief the ambassador?"

"I can do that any old time," Foster said. "And, Y. C., don't you worry 'cause it won't be much of a problem for me to hold it off for a while if you want. Anyway, I agree with you about the politics of this. They've got elections coming up in this country soon and we don't want our nuclear force here to become any more of an issue than it already is. It's already gotten outta hand. The damn Socialists would just love to get us the hell outta England. Bastards forget pretty damn fast who their friends are. But it's not only them that worries me. It's also the damn bureaucrats. You know as well as I do that bureaucrats are dangerous. British, Americans, I don't care who you're talking about. As soon as civilians get involved, we're up Shit's Creek without a paddle.''

Wagner couldn't agree fast enough. ''Right, sir. Last guys in the world we want in on this. The less any civilians know, the better off we'll all be. Bastards make headlines out of everything. And I'm not just talking about the F-111s now. Look at what they did to the Air Force and their damn coffee machines. I always say that the less any civilians know the less any civilians can leak.''

I don't believe this, Holbrook thought. A truckload of plutonium nitrate is missing and Wagner is trying to cover it up like some sort of cost overrun on percolators. ''Sir?'' He knew he simply had to talk his boss into telling the British right now. ''If that shipment has been hijacked, then the Ministry of Defense guys and the Atomic Energy Authority's Constabulary are going to have to be called in. No matter what, the press will get wind of it eventually. When they do hear about it, they won't just write that a van-load of fissile material has gone missing, they'll also play up the story that we tried to keep the British out of the picture. I really think that all the rules of the game got changed here last week. The way I see it, we might already be in a no-win mode. I honestly don't think it's a good idea to wait until this hits the papers and we find ourselves holding an open can of worms.''

''Christ,'' Wagner snapped, ''of course we have to keep this out of the papers. But getting the Brits involved now should be one hundred ten percent out of the question. It's too soon. The less said to them, or anybody, the better. And you mark my words, Admiral''—he pointed to Roth—''telling the British authorities about this would be like buying ads in the newspapers. Don't forget that their goddamned Official Secrets Act has more holes in it than Swiss cheese. Remember Greenham Common? Remember the logbook of their damned submarine in the Falklands? The civilian bastards in this country can't keep their mouths shut.''

''I think Bob's right,'' Foster said. ''You can't trust civilians in America because of the press. Over here it's even worse because most of them are Liberals or Socialists. I say we take our chances and try to find the van ourselves. Then, if we really strike out bad, then and only then, as a last resort, we pow-wow with the MoD at the highest uniformed levels. They'll think the way we do and no one will ever be any the wiser.''

"But civilians have copies of the shipment orders," Holbrook reminded them. "By reg, we have to file everything with the MoD. They send it over to the Constabulary. And those guys are outside of MoD channels. No matter what we do, sooner or later, someone is going to find out that this shipment never arrived. Then they're going to see that we never bothered to tell them anything was wrong. Some civilian in the chain is going to get real pissed off at us. One phone call to *The Times* or the *Guardian* . . . " He glanced at Foster. "Or even the ambassador . . . then it's too late. There'll be no way to keep this out of the press once they get wind of it.''

"Right," Wagner said. "Proves my point, exactly. That's why we don't tell any of the bastards anything. I mean, Commander Holbrook here has got to figure out sooner or later that we know more about this than he does.''

Holbrook tried to keep cool. "Let's say," he took a deep breath, "let's say, for the sake of argument, that the Brits never find out. Then let's say we manage to locate the van and the PuN is still there. Okay. All's well 'cause it ends well. But let's say we never find the van. Or we find it and the PuN isn't there. Then let's say maybe the IRA has something to do with this. And let's say you're right, Gaddafi is tied in somehow. Let's also say that the police in Belfast get wind of it and they tell Scotland Yard and the cops here start asking questions. What do we do when every newspaper in the world starts phoning? How do we explain that we forgot to tell our host nation that somebody stole enough of our PuN on their soil to make nuclear weapons? There's just too much that can go wrong. Too many scenarios that wind up with us neck deep in pig shit.''

"Pig shit . . . horse shit!" Wagner waved him off. "If and when the time comes to tell the Brits we can see that the story gets killed. They have that D-Notice law here. None of that free press or freedom of information and right-to-know crap. By God, we'll pull all the strings we have to in order to make sure they use that D-Notice. Should have goddamned insisted they use it last week. And of course I know damn well that if we don't keep this quiet those Socialists will pick up on it and make a big-deal issue out of it in Parliament."

Now Roth asked Foster, "How long do you think we have until the Brits should be called?"

"My ambassador first. Brits second," Foster said. "And there is time. Might even be able to tell the ambassador and still keep it from the Brits. But if the Brits find out first, then the old man is going to have someone's scalp because he wasn't in the light. Don't forget, Y. C., ambassadors are civilians. They don't think like us. However, I guess what I'm saying is if you can keep it from the Brits, then I can cover for you across the street."

"Okay." Roth looked at Wagner. "Bob, how long?"

"Plenty of time where the Brits are concerned. If at all."

"Okay." Finally Roth turned to Holbrook. "Dad . . ." But instead of asking his opinion, the admiral told his special assistant, ". . . we'll wait until the air search comes up with a definite yes or a definite no before we worry about the ambassador. And even if we tell him I think it's best if we keep it from the Brits until I decide they need to know."

Wagner smiled triumphantly.

Holbrook merely nodded. "Yes, sir."

"Okay." Roth pointed toward his secretary's office. "Maybe you could fire up the java machine, Dad. You look like you could use a cup."

You're making a huge mistake, he thought. But all he said was, "Yes, sir." And then Richard Holbrook, a highly trained forty-one-year-old career Naval officer who had graduated nineteenth in his class at Annapolis in 1967 and third in his class at the Navy Flight School in Pensacola the following year, went to make the coffee.

Chapter Four

MATTHEW BOSTON PREFERRED to be called Buster—a not so common nickname for an Englishman, but when he was a child his mother thought he looked like Buster Keaton, and while he was growing up all of his boyhood friends called him Buster, and anyway he never really liked the name Matthew. He had been named after his mother's cousin's husband, a sea captain who, Boston recalled, always smelled of rum, spat when he spoke and, according to family legend, supposedly died when his ship sank in a storm. Although the family rumor—carefully whispered so that none of the children would ever know—was that the sea captain had jumped his own ship somewhere in northern Brazil because he had fallen in love with a native woman and ended his days fathering fifteen half-caste kids.

No, he did not particularly care for the name Matthew. He much preferred Buster. But then anything would have been better than being named after someone in Brazil who stank of rum and spat when he spoke.

On that Tuesday morning, Buster Boston walked up to the newsagent's in the station at Farnborough, change in hand, ready to buy his morning newspaper for the trip to London. But as soon as the woman behind the counter saw him— before he even had a chance to say anything, like his usual monotone, "Morning"—she gave him a fleeting apology. "Sorry, luv." He thought to himself, what on earth, and asked, "Sorry about what?" And she said, "No *Telegraphs* today, luv."

"No *Telegraphs?*"

"Yes, luv," she said, using a positive to enforce a negative.

"How can there be no *Telegraphs?*"

"Sorry, luv." She moved her attention away from him and on to customers who were spending money for newspapers and sweets . . . that's 23p, luv . . . Amazin' Raisin Bar? Sorry luv, we don't stock them—what's that, luv, turn it over so I can see the cover. *Health and Efficiency?* Harry," she shouted loud enough for everyone in the station to hear her, "how much is *Health and Efficiency?*"

Boston reminded her, "But I buy the *Telegraph* from you every morning."

"That's right, luv." She took change and handed over newspapers to the constant stream of customers. "Don't suppose you'd want the *Mirror* or the *Guardian,* would you, luv?"

"Heaven forbid," he mumbled, as people pushed past him . . . the *Times* . . . two *Expresses* please . . . a packet of crisps and a can of carbonated Ribena.

"Sorry, luv, but I don't suppose you'd mind stepping aside so that I can serve these other people."

He reluctantly settled for the *Mail.*

However, just in case anyone should think that he regularly read a tabloid, as soon as he paid for it he rolled it up under his arm. Then, instead of giving it a cursory glance on the platform, he avoided peeking at it while he sat in the waiting room impatiently listening for his train to enter the station. When it did arrive he made a dash for his usual carriage.

Once he got settled into his usual seat, he had the oddest feeling that the other commuters in his usual carriage were looking unusually askance in his direction. My *Telegraph* didn't come in this morning. He felt the need to explain it all to them. So what's a man supposed to do? Not the first time this has happened. Problems with the unions, I suppose.

Of course, the moment he looked back at any of those commuters who were looking at him, they immediately looked away. In the end he didn't have to make any explanations at all. Then again, he knew very well, if he had said something to them it would have been frowned upon because one doesn't speak when one commutes.

It has always been the unwritten rule of British suburban commuting that one neither welcomes nor encourages conversation. Undoubtedly, there are always certain people who make attempts at idle chat while they travel on a train. Foreigners, for example. But then foreigners also stand on both sides of escalators instead of keeping to the right. Other people who speak casually on trains are Day-Savers and all those people on OAP fares. But when one holds a regular first-class ticket, the way Boston had for years, a nodded hello on the platform is about as far as one dares to go. Perhaps a quiet "Good morning" while getting into the compartment. However, it would be an outrageous violation of an Englishman's privacy if someone in the compartment were to launch out on any subject. Politesse is confined to a quiet greeting and a final "Good day." In this changing world, there aren't many places left where decent reticence counts the way it does on British Rail. At least in first class.

He read the *Mail* quickly, then stuffed it onto the overhead rack only to discover his hands blackened by newsprint. He went to the loo and washed them. The tabloid experience had definitely not helped to put him in a better mood.

When the train pulled into Waterloo, he quite deliberately stepped into the bookstall to ask for the *Telegraph*. The young Indian girl behind the cash register pointed to all the newspapers. "It must be there, mister." And it was. Hah, he exclaimed. A whole stack of *Telegraphs*. Hah. He took one and assured himself, the day is not entirely lost.

Because there was a queue at the till he lingered for a moment at a table covered with books at special sale prices. He wasn't necessarily looking for anything but his eyes hit upon a title and when he realized what it was, he let out a rather pronounced, "Hah!"

Syd—The Official Biography of Sydney Francis Barnes, the Greatest Test Bowler of All Times.

He couldn't believe what he was seeing. "Hah." He put his newspaper down and eagerly thumbed through the book. It's about time. Someone has finally done him justice. Wait till Nigel sees this. He'll go mad. The book was filled with pictures, even though some of them were slightly out of focus. There were also several pages of statistics. Apart from Barnes' autobiography, this was the first book Boston had ever seen entirely devoted to the man he too considered to be the finest cricketer of all times.

And it's reduced, he noted—which pleased him no end— so I'll get one, read it today and then send it to Nigel. Instantly his spirits picked up. The 1984 Ashes would never have been lost had Barnes been bowling for England. He studied the top copy, then checked the others in the stack to see if he could find one that was mispriced. A long time ago he accidentally stumbled across the fact that shop assistants frequently made mistakes and put a cheaper sticker on some copies. Ever since, he had made it his business to look for what he liked to call bargain bargains. But all the *Syd*s were priced at £4.99, so he took the least soiled one off the bottom of the stack and queued for the cash desk.

He was crossing Westminster Bridge in the bus before he even realized that he had left his *Telegraph* back on the book counter.

Thanks to *Syd,* the *Telegraph* almost didn't matter . . . although when he got into the office he did ask the commissionaire at the front door if he wouldn't mind sending out for one. Then Boston went to the mail room, took an official MoD envelope, and addressed it to Nigel. Once that was done, he checked his morning post, sorted through whatever messages had accumulated overnight, and decided that nothing was of any importance. It was all routine. It could all wait for *Syd*. I'll read it now so that I can send it to Nigel. He told Mrs. Fitzgerald, his secretary, "No calls," and shut his office door. Then he leaned back in his chair, settled his feet on his desk, and opened the book.

There is no doubt at all, that Sydney Francis Barnes, a marvel from Staffordshire, was the greatest Test bowler of all time . . .

Boston's office was in 7 Storey's Gate, where the sign on the front door downstairs read MINISTRY OF DEFENSE. The sign on his own office door, on the top floor of Chappell House, read SPECIAL COORDINATOR. That's all. But he couldn't have cared less what the sign said.

He was more concerned with the view.

Once upon a time he had the best view of Westminster Abbey that anyone could ever have hoped for. Big Ben and the Palace of Westminster too. Then they built the Conference Center across the street and now all he had was a view of glass and steel and concrete. This is what you call progress, he'd explain to anyone who sat in his office long enough. Gresham's Law. Bad views will drive out good views. In response, and true to bureaucratic form, his bosses argued that if everyone in the MoD insisted on having a good view, there wouldn't be enough good views to go around. After all, we must first and foremost consider those very senior people whose rank warrants a good view. And yes, we agree that the world is filled with bad views, but someone has to get them. Be grateful. Don't forget that some people in government service go through their entire career without any view at all. But, he argued, I used to have a great view and now I've got a horrendous view and that means I'm going backward. It's tantamount to a *de facto* demotion. Well, they pondered that one and finally said, all right, tell you what we would consider. We'll try to get you office space next to the Constabulary and we're certain that once you get the lie of the land there and maneuver yourself around, you'll requisition yourself an office with a great view, or at least a decent view. Some offices there look onto the Haymarket, you know. No, he told them, thanks but no thanks. To work in the AEA offices would be even worse than keeping his Conference Center view at Chappell House. So his bosses at the MoD merely shrugged, then you'll just have to take the view as you've got it. Of course after nearly two years of having suffered with the Conference Center's construction—two years' worth of lorries and cement mixers and jackhammers—he was so glad when the place was finally finished that at least to begin with the lack of noise made up for the lack of an occasional peek at the Abbey. Then again—although he rarely admitted it—there were other benefits to Chappell House. Besides the convenience of being near Waterloo and also having a decent selection of inexpensive restaurants and pubs in the area, the best perk of all was that MoD Headquarters was far enough up Whitehall that no one ever bothered him. They left him alone to get on with his job which was to coordinate whatever military nuclear fuel traffic took place in the U.K., to inspect it and to make certain that the tens of thousands of pieces of paper that came across his desk every year were properly logged, filed, copied and passed along to the proper agency for logging, filing, copying and passing along yet again.

As far as Boston was concerned, it was a dream job.

He had rank. He had status. He had authority. He had a pension. He had a small expense account. And he also had all the time he wanted to read about Syd Barnes.

It was the 1913–1914 season in South Africa. A summer to remember. For that would be the summer when Barnes would immortalize himself. For that would be the summer Barnes would take 49 Test wickets . . .

The intercom sounded. He flinched, shaken out of his concentration, annoyed that Mrs. Fitzgerald hadn't obeyed his orders not to bother him. "Yes, what is it?"

"Your wife, sir."

He took the call. "Hello dear."

"Buster . . ." She spoke very softly. ". . . I can't speak now so I'll ring you later."

"Why did you ring me then, dear?"

"It's because . . . I don't want Mary to hear. But she's stealing from us again."

He asked calmly, "What is it this time?"

"I can't find my blender. I think she's stolen my blender."

A week ago it was Nigel's old portable typewriter. The week before that it was a glass bird-shaped ashtray. "Perhaps I should have a chat with Mary when I come home tonight. Now," he asked, "how are you feeling?"

"I don't feel very well, Buster. I think it's all this rain. Did you remember to take your raincoat this morning? Is it raining in London? It's pouring here."

"Yes," he said. "I took my raincoat. Now . . . don't forget you have an appointment with the doctor today. Mary will take you. And I'll speak with her about it this evening. Goodbye, dear. I'll probably ring you later."

"Goodbye." She hung up and he went back to his book. His intercom sounded again.

"I thought I said no calls," he reminded Mrs. Fitzgerald.

"It's Assistant Chief Constable Wooldridge on line two," she said. "I told him you weren't taking any calls but he said I should buzz you anyway so I did."

He put his book down and mumbled, "Thank you," then clicked the button to line two. "Boston here."

"Wooldridge here," came a voice sounding exactly like someone imitating a sergeant-major. "Trouble here, too, I fear. Could you come over right away?"

"Trouble?" Not in the middle of my book, he wanted to say. "What kind of trouble."

"Can't discuss it on the phone, I'm afraid."

"Woolley, I'm very busy. I'm in a meeting," he lied. "Can't you even give me a hint?"

"All right. Here's a hint. It's the Navy."

"The Navy?"

"Yes, the Navy."

"What about the Navy?"

"I keep telling you that I can't discuss it on the phone. But I'll give you another hint. It's not our Navy. Buster, it's the American Navy."

"Oh God." He suddenly understood. "Not again. You mean the planes? When? Last night? This morning? You mean they've done it again? Where this time? Tripoli? Benghazi? There's been no message traffic across my desk."

"No, no, nothing like that. And not on the phone. I've said too much already. But it's trouble. Or could be. Just heard it on the grapevine. Nothing official yet. Let's call it potential trouble. If you could get here right away."

He sighed, "Oh all right, Woolley. All right. I'm on my way." He hung up, and slammed *Syd* down onto his desk. "I knew I was in for something like this today," he said out loud. I knew it was going to be this sort of day. Right from the moment when they didn't have my *Telegraph*.

Chapter
Five

HE MADE THE COFFEE.

The four of them sat around drinking it.

And nothing else happened.

By 7:30 the admiral's secretary arrived at work, and so did his ADC—a likable, if otherwise too-timid, commander named Camille Parrot whose pet project was sponsorship of the "Let's Help Cut Costs" Navy Suggestion Program which invariably wound up, each six months, bringing in letters from throughout the command saying that the best way the Navy could save money was to do away with the Suggestion Program.

"Good morning, sir," Parrot reported in.

As if that was his cue, Roth announced, "We'll call it business as usual until we hear about the air search."

Foster, Wagner and Holbrook took the hint and got up to leave. But Roth asked Holbrook to stay. He waited for Parrot to deliver the morning's read file, to check on some duty rosters and to go over the day's appointment schedule. Then he motioned for Parrot to leave them—and once they were alone Roth said to Holbrook, "What happened to you yesterday, Dad?"

Holbrook tried to shrug it off. "I wasn't very well."

But Roth wasn't going to let him get away with that. "If you feel a problem coming on," he said sternly, "I want you to head it off. Get yourself some help."

"Yes, sir." There was a long pause. "This weekend was the second anniversary . . . you know . . . Mike Sawnders."

"I see." Roth's tone softened. "Okay. Just don't go it alone if you need some help." He folded his hands behind his head. "Maybe you need something to take your mind off other things. Tell you what. With this van gone missing, what do you say we take a thorough look at all our fissile material movements throughout the Command. Maybe we're getting too lax. Maybe it's time to check our barn doors before we start losing the whole damn stableful of horses."

Sure, why not. What else have I got to do with my life. It's called pencil whipping. The Navy's perpetual answer to everyone's personal problems. "I'll get right on it, sir."

"I want a report as soon as you can. With recommendations wherever it looks like we're vulnerable." Roth half saluted and the meeting was over.

Holbrook strolled back to his office, a small, windowless room with a gray metal desk, a brown metal swivel chair, a gray metal filing cabinet and two gray metal armchairs facing his desk. He had a lamp and a phone, and a brass nameplate sitting on the front of his desk so that anyone who walked into his office could tell right away that it belonged to Richard Holbrook, Commander, USN. Two framed aerial photographs hung on his walls. But that was all. The rest of the room was empty. He tried several times to stick some sort of big green plant in the corner to make the room more cheerful, but plants don't like rooms without windows. Neither did he. All plants, and all people too, deserve sunlight. Every ficus, and every man, needs a room with a window.

"What you heard in there this morning stays in there." Wagner poked his head into Holbrook's office. "Get my drift? I want to make that very clear. This is Command's business." Wagner pointed a finger at him. "I know what you're thinking 'cause I can read you like a book. I've always been able to know what you're thinking before you even think it. So you better understand that when the time comes to tell the Brits, if it ever does come and I doubt like hell it will, then I'll do the telling through my channels."

Holbrook glared at Wagner. "I hear what you're saying, Captain. Just get off my case."

"Your case?" Wagner sneered. "Holbrook, I don't make no bones about what I think. 'Specially what I think about you. I didn't like you in Hawaii. I didn't like you in SEA. And I sure as shit don't like you in this goddamned place. You got penciled in on the wrong page in my book a long time ago. You and your dead buddy. But it wasn't until you played chicken-shit and refused to fly and then you came crying to the old man for a job on his staff that you finally got inked in." And just like that, Wagner walked away.

First Holbrook took a deep breath, held it for a while, and let it out. Then he shook his head. "Bean Bag, why the hell did he have to catch you screwing his wife?" Then he got up and went to the admin office. "I need some files out of your safe."

The chief there, a jovial, good-drinking guy named McIntyre, asked, "Which ones?"

Holbrook said, "Everything you've got on nuclear fuel shipments throughout the Command. Naveur 6648/Gs and DoD 3093s. And any NATO forms . . . whatever you've got."

"Tall order," the chief said, dialing open the large wall safe at the far end of the office and making a whole series of proper entries in the safe's logbook. "Sounds to me like a pencil-whip."

"Don't rub it in." Pencil-whip. Look busy. Stay busy. Make the work fit the time allotted to it. Don't finish too soon or someone will find you another job to do. Uncle Sam needs you.

"Let's see. How about, co-op shipments, DoDs and U.K.-onlies?"

Holbrook said, "Everything."

"Everything? Weaponry too?"

"Yeah. Weaponry too."

"How far back you want me to go?"

"Dunno. Couple o' three years."

"That could take hours." The chief grimaced.

And Holbrook sighed, "I've got hours."

Chapter
Six

"NAME'S SAWNDERS," PROCLAIMED the lanky, blond-haired kid in the ill-fitting suit, moving into the room late in the summer of 1963, kicking a duffel bag while at the same time struggling with a suitcase covered in decals from places like Niagara Falls and Yosemite National Park. "S-a-w-n-d-e-r-s. Not Sanders. Or even Saunders. It's Sawnders with a *w* between the *a* and the *n*."

"Holbrook." He put down his newspaper and extended his hand. "Richard Holbrook. I'm from San Diego, California."

"Mike." He let go of the suitcase just long enough to shake hands. "I guess I'm from Atlanta, Georgia, except I was born in Battle Creek, where the cereal comes from in Michigan, but I went to high school in Dayton, Ohio, 'cause my dad traveled a lot. He sold heavy earth-moving equipment. Like Caterpillars. Except it wasn't Caterpillar. But no one ever heard of the company he did work for. It was called Fortunato and Gongora. You know, F and G. But like I said you never heard of it, no one ever did, so I always say Caterpillars. And my mom is from Cleveland although we lived in Atlanta where my dad is from, up until two and a half years ago."

Holbrook stretched across the unmade bottom bunk. "I think I'm sorry I asked."

"Want to know how I got accepted here?" He never gave Holbrook a chance to answer. "I got in through Georgia. My mom has a distant cousin on her mom's side who's married to Congressman Bob Dalton. The one from Georgia, not the one from Oregon. There are two guys with the same name in Congress now. Although the other one is actually Robert Dalton and this one calls himself Bob. He's a Democrat, well, they both are, but this one is on the Ways and Means Committee so he knows all the right people.''

"Gee, I'm sure glad you told me that." Holbrook held up his hands to stop him, or at least to slow him down. "Right." He thought to himself, this could be a long year. "Now . . . ah . . . what do you say we toss for top bunk?"

"Actually, if I had my druthers, I'd take the bottom bunk."

"It's all yours," he said fast, before Sawnders could change his mind, because he knew enough to always choose the top bunk and Sawnders obviously didn't. That's one of the first things every kid learns when he goes away to camp. Too bad for Sawnders.

"I know that the bottom bunk is the worst bunk," Sawnders said, walking out of the room then reappearing with his arms wrapped around a huge shapeless red form. "I know that if you sleep on the bottom bunk and the fellow on the top bunk is a bedwetter, it's like living under Niagara Falls. But I figure they wouldn't let a bedwetter into the Academy."

"What the hell is that?"

"Neat, huh?" Sawnders dropped the shapeless red form onto the floor and sank into it. "My bean-bag chair."

Terrific. I get stuck in a room with some whacko who comes to Annapolis with his very own bean-bag chair. "Didn't you read the regs? Didn't you see the list of what you're allowed to bring with you?"

"Nobody said anything about not bringing a bean-bag chair. And anyway, this bean-bag chair goes with me wherever I go. I even used to take it to high school with me until my guidance counselor—this was at Dewitt Clinton—well, he told me if I brought it into history class ever again they were gonna throw me and the bean-bag chair out of school together. You see, I transferred into Dewitt Clinton in my sophomore year. That's when we left Atlanta. That's when they gave me this. It was the guys at my school there who gave it to me like a going-away present . . ."

"PLEBES!" someone with a booming voice screamed. "PLEBES!"

Sawnders stopped. "That mean us?"

Holbrook was about to say, "I guess so," when a midshipman in a spanking white uniform stormed into their room.

"PLEBES," he screamed at the top of his lungs.

Sawnders and Holbrook looked at each other in bewilderment, then Holbrook leaped off the bunk and shot to attention. Sawnders quickly got up to stand at attention as well.

"PLEBES!" the midshipman barked in their faces. "When a senior midshipman makes his presence known to you, the first thing you do is call the room to attention. Then you stand braced and wait to find out what it is the senior officer wants. And when the senior officer calls out plebes, he's talking about you, the lowest form of life in the United States Navy. You are the lowest form of life in the . . ." The midshipman stopped and glared at the bean-bag chair. "What in the name of holy creation is that?"

Sawnders happily explained, "It's a bean-bag chair."

"SIR!" The midshipman put his face right up to Sawnders' and said, "It's a bean-bag chair, sir."

"Yes . . . sir," Sawnders replied. "It's a bean-bag chair, sir."

Now the midshipman asked in a semi-scream, "Is that a regulation U.S. Navy bean-bag chair?"

Holbrook started to laugh.

"What are you chuckling about, mister?" The midshipman spun around to him. "Did somebody say something especially funny?"

"Ah . . . yes, sir. It's the idea of a regulation U.S. Navy bean-bag chair."

Sawnders also started to laugh.

And now Holbrook was having a very hard time keeping himself together.

"It is not funny," the midshipman yelled. "Nothing is funny unless I say it is funny. And I haven't said that anything is funny. Is that clear? So, what's your name, mister?"

"Richard Holbrook."

"No, it is not," the midshipman said.

Sawnders chimed in, "That's what he told me it was."

"A couple of wisecrackers?" The midshipman glared at both of them. "Well, what do you say we get a few things straight around here. When I ask you your name, mister, the answer is Richard Holbrook, sir. Got that? You call me, sir. Now, I'll ask again and we'll see if you get it right this time. What's your name, mister?"

"Yes, sir. Richard Holbrook, sir."

"You are a fast learner and I like fast learners." He looked at Sawnders. "And what's your name, mister?"

"Michael Sawnders, sir," he said. "S-a-w-n-d-e-r-s. That's with a *w* in between the *a* and the *n.*" He paused and glanced out of the corner of his eye toward Holbrook. "But, sir?"

The midshipman asked, "What is it, Mister Sawnders, with a *w* between the *a* and the *n?*"

"Well . . . you see, sir, my friends all call me Bean Bag."

That was finally too much for Holbrook. He doubled up laughing. "Bean Bag Sawnders?"

That in turn triggered off Sawnders.

The pair of them laughed until tears came out of their eyes.

But the midshipman didn't think it was funny. "PLEBES!" he screamed. "PLEBES!" He was furious.

And neither Holbrook nor Bean Bag laughed again for the next six weeks of their freshman year at Annapolis.

They stayed roommates for their entire four years at the Academy. Although the bean-bag chair wound up spending its four years there in storage. Several times a year Sawnders actually went to visit the chair because he liked to study on it before a really big exam. He said it brought him luck, even if that meant studying in a warehouse surrounded by smelly old suitcases. When he went on leave, he always checked it out of storage so that he could take it with him. He even dragged it onto the beach every day when he and Holbrook went to Fort Lauderdale on a spring leave in their junior year. That's where Bean Bag met Barbara Fox. She was a freshman at "Old Miss" and had hitched down with two other girls to Easter-party in Florida. Before the week was over, Bean Bag and Barbara announced their engagement. Barbara said her father had been in the Navy so a midshipman was perfect. Bean Bag said she wanted to marry him because she was into doing things on bean-bag chairs. Holbrook decided they were both telling the truth. Sixteen months later Holbrook was their best man in the Annapolis Chapel, the day after graduation, when he and Bean Bag were commissioned ensigns in the U.S. Navy with orders in their pockets to the Naval Air Station at Pensacola Mainside for pre-flight and primary flight instruction.

They roomed together in flight school—Barbara was back in Mississippi, finishing college—and this time the bean-bag chair lived with them. This time there were no senior midshipmen to bark at them and no Mickey Mouse regs about official U.S. Navy issue furniture.

They roomed together too at NAS Saufely Field in Pensacola during basic flight training, when they learned how to fly the T-34 Mentor. They both opted for the jet pipeline and roomed together for the first few weeks at NAS Meridian, in Mississippi. But then Barbara quit school so that she and Bean Bag could be together.

Holbrook lived alone in the Bachelor Officers' Quarters, although he ate dinner almost every night at Bean Bag's and Barbara's, and sometimes even brought girlfriends there to sleep in the spare room with him because, he said, the BOQ was hardly the right atmosphere for serious seduction. "It's all that furniture made at Leavenworth," he claimed. "What the hell," Bean Bag argued, "you'd screw some girl in a car with license plates made at Sing Sing, wouldn't you?" Holbrook argued, "It's not the same." Bean Bag said, "Sure it is." And Barbara just objected to the whole idea of Holbrook using their guest room as a brothel. But Bean Bag said that he and Holbrook were like brothers. In fact they were even closer than brothers. He said that Holbrook was his third great love. Barbara insisted in knowing who the first two were. So Bean Bag said that his first great love was Barbara and his second great love was stock-car racing. Holbrook then informed Barbara that in all the years he and Bean Bag had roomed together, Bean Bag had never once mentioned stock-car racing. But Bean Bag insisted he had been a stock-car racing fan since he was a little kid, and faithfully followed A. J. Foyt's career. In fact, he suggested, seeing as how he was such a great fan of A. J.'s, why didn't they climb into Holbrook's car that very night and drive down to Daytona because the 500 race was on and maybe they could meet A. J. and maybe even get passes to watch the race from his pit. Holbrook said this was one of the dumbest ideas Bean Bag ever had. But Barbara proclaimed them the three mouse-keteers and said that if her husband wanted to watch the Daytona 500 from A. J.'s pit, the mouseketeers owed it to him. So they piled into Holbrook's car and drove all night across the top of Florida and down to Daytona for a weekend of stock-car racing.

Saturday, during the time trials, the Speedway was hot, crowded, dusty, noisy and the air smelled of exhaust fumes.

They never got within half a mile of A. J. Foyt.

Sunday, the day of the race, the Speedway was hotter, more crowded, dustier, noisier and the air totally reeked of exhaust fumes.

It was the perfect place to stand around and drink beer.

Holbrook, wearing bermudas and a Snoopy Flying Ace T-shirt, was just on his way to a beer tent when he spotted a girl carrying three beers, making her way through the crowd, wearing a bright yellow sundress and no bra. He couldn't believe how pretty she was. He watched her coming toward him, waited until she got close enough, then moved in with his most subtle line. "If I said you had a beautiful body, would you hold it against me?" She smiled, looked him straight in the eye and told him, just as subtly, "Blow it out your ass, cowboy."

"Cowboy?" He couldn't believe such a great-looking girl could have a mouth like that. "We don't have cowboys in San Diego." He ran after her. "Hey, wait a minute."

"Sit on it." She wouldn't have anything to do with him. "Pack it in your ear."

Never one to give up that easily—any girl who looks that sweet and talks like a fighter pilot and drinks three beers at a time is my kinda lady—he watched her until she rejoined a group of other girls where she handed over two of the three beers. Oh well, he said out loud, she still looks damn good and talks damn good. I want some of that.

He ran off to find Barbara and Bean Bag and persuaded them to wander over in the girl's direction. It was all part of his "Operation Pick Up By The Numbers."

Listen, guys, he first explained it to them back in basic flight school once he discovered that the best way to pick up a girl was with another girl. Just go down the list like a pre-flight check. Follow the numbers, step by step. Kinda like painting by the numbers. Now, Barbara makes the first contact. She recces the primary target. Chit-chat. Girl talk. Directions, like how do you get to the ladies' room. Or, nice dress. That kinda stuff. Step two, Bean Bag circles nearby, then comes in for a landing. Step three, Lt. j.g. and Mrs. Bean Bag prepare the target by making her laugh. Step four, the conversation moves on to fighter jets and flying, with words casually thrown in, like extreme danger, dog fights and missions over North Vietnam. Step five, Barbara mentions in a relaxed way that a lonely fly-boy friend is hovering around somewhere. Step six, Bean Bag radios me with a secret tug on his ear. Step seven, I walk up with a severe limp and quietly move into the conversation. Oh, by the way, Miss Primary Target, this is Richard, and Richard, this is Miss Primary Target. Step eight, within a few minutes Barbara and Bean Bag prepare for takeoff and vacate my air space. Step nine, I refuse to talk about my war wounds. Step ten, flight plan is filed for trip into Happy Valley. Operation Pick Up By The Numbers. It's even better than painting by the numbers because instead of winding up with a picture of fruit on a table, I could get laid.

"Are you really a flyer?" the bra-less girl in the yellow dress asked suspiciously over all the noise of the race and the huge crowd packed close together under the hot Florida sun. "Honest, now, are you really a Navy jet pilot?"

"Yeah," he shouted back. "A real live Navy jet pilot."

"That's what they all say."

"Ask nice and I'll show you my wings."

She stared at him for the longest time, then tilted her head and wanted to know, "What else you got to show?"

He looked at her. "What else you want to see?"

She opened her eyes wide and started to laugh.

"Oh yeah?" Holbrook laughed too.

Ten minutes later they were in her car looking for the first motel they could find with a vacancy sign.

"I love motels," she told him early the next morning when

he said he really had to get back to his base. " 'Specially seedy motels. How many seedy motels do you think there are in Florida?''

"No idea."

"Maybe a thousand?"

"Maybe more."

"How long do you think it would take us to do them all?"

"How much time you got?"

"Weekends."

"Worth a try," he said.

"Fly-boy"—she moved close to him—"I have this funny feeling you're gonna be late for work."

Two months but merely nine motels later, right after she graduated from Florida State, they were in Panama City, about a hundred and twenty miles east of Pensacola, staying in a motel there for the weekend—Bean Bag and Barbara were there too—and as they sat around the swimming pool drinking gin and tonics that first afternoon, Bean Bag asked, "How come you guys don't get married?" She said, "Okay, sure, how come?" And Holbrook said, "I don't know." So they did. The next morning they found a Justice of the Peace who charged them an extra $25—cash, no checks or credit cards, strictly cash—because otherwise they would have had to wait until Monday to file the proper papers and Holbrook and Bean Bag had to be back at the base by Sunday night. Barbara was the bridesmaid. Bean Bag was the best man.

Millicent became Mrs. Richard Holbrook.

And now the three mouseketeers became the four mouseketeers.

They lived next door to each other in Beeville, Texas, while Holbrook and Bean Bag were there for advanced jet training, gunnery and carrier qualification. They ate dinner together and spent weekends together, and the two girls got themselves jobs together at a furniture store selling sofas and recliners to other young married couples.

Then Holbrook and Bean Bag got orders again. Exactly twenty-three months after they first went to Pensacola, they were sent back to Florida—this time wearing the gold wings of Navy flyers—to join RVAH-3 at NAS Sanford where they started flying RA5C Vigilantes and learning all about the business of being a reconnaissance pilot.

Because the Vigies were two-seaters, Holbrook and Bean Bag were teamed up with a couple of guys who were to fly as their Radar Attack Navigators. They were the fellows who actually took the reconnaissance photos, navigated and also handled the electronic countermeasures necessary to protect the plane from enemy attack. Holbrook drew a pimply faced kid named Patrick Murphy III from a town called Chittenango in upstate New York. Murphy III told him he went to Syracuse and originally wanted to go into computers but when he failed to find a graduate school he applied for Navy OCS. It was just what Holbrook didn't want to hear. Listen, man, I don't want a failure in my rear seat. You better learn your trade real good 'cause I have a wife and someday I'm gonna have kids and I don't want to find some SAM getting stuck up my tailpipe. Murphy III quickly learned to stay out of his pilot's way. Bean Bag flew with a guy from Little Rock, Arkansas, named Billy Joe Douglas. And those two did get along. But Holbrook had already decided that the four mouseketeers were going to stay the way they were, as four, and not become the five mouseketeers or the six mouseketeers for anybody named Billy Joe, or anyone with pimples and a III after his name. I don't even know where the hell Chittenango is and I never trust people who come from places that aren't on my Texaco gas station road map of the Continental United States. Four is real fine with me.

It was fine with the other three as well.

Barbara and Millicent found themselves jobs at a local garden center, selling geraniums and picket fences to retired sailors and their wives. The Holbrooks and the Sawnderses lived next door to each other and ate together and drank together and played Bingo together every Thursday night at the Elks Lodge. Once in a while they'd wander off to some seedy motel together. It was a game they called "X-Rated Weekend." The guys would each take a room while the girls, all whored up, would stand around the motel's bar chatting with other men. Holbrook and Bean Bag would come along, mosey up to the two girls and buy them drinks until the girls finally agreed to go back to their rooms with them.

Then Bean Bag and Billy Joe got orders to join a carrier squadron out of Hawaii.

Holbrook was furious.

Barbara and Millicent both cried.

Bean Bag swore he hadn't put in for the assignment, that he didn't know how his name came up. Millicent begged Holbrook to get transferred to Hawaii too. But Holbrook tried and couldn't manage anything more out of his skipper than, we'll see what we can do. It seemed as if that would be the end of the four mouseketeers until Bean Bag remembered Congressman Bob Dalton. He rang his mother and she rang Dalton.

Ten days later Holbrook and Millicent, with Murphy III in tow, also had orders to Hawaii.

The boys spent four months there flying around the islands. Most of their days were spent practicing carrier landings—a very tricky task with the Vigies because of the way the planes wobbled and wallowed at low speed. Some of their nights were spent trying to take high-altitude recce pictures of couples screwing on the beach. Millicent and Barbara found jobs together at the base library, loaning books to dependent children. They did their best to pretend that their men would be there, with them, for a full-year tour. But Holbrook and Bean Bag had other ideas. Their first week in Hawaii they met a Navy captain named Roth who told them he started out as a recce pilot. One afternoon, during Happy Hour at the Officers' Club, the three of them got drunk together and Roth announced that he was taking over a carrier command out of the Philippines. He invited them along. The two of them replied that it was a good idea because they were the best recce pilots in the U.S. Navy and only another recce pilot could know just how good the best truly was.

Their orders were cut. And the day quickly arrived when it was time to leave.

It was the Fourth of July, 1970. Honolulu was closed. Wherever you went there were parades and flybys. The Hickam AFB Officers' Wives Club organized a shindig that they labeled "The world's largest weenie roast." The NCO Wives Club at Navy Terminal titled theirs, "The world's biggest picnic." Wherever you went, swimming pools were mobbed, and kids played softball. Wherever you went, portable radios blared baseball games and snappy jingles for Coppertone.

Barbara and Millicent stood alone at NAS Ewa Beach, sweltering just inside the doorway at Base Ops, both of them crying, as Holbrook and Bean Bag, with Murphy III and Billy Joe in the rear seats, took off and wiggled their wings goodbye, on their way to join Roth and the aircraft carrier *Kitty Hawk* as part of Task Force 77 on Yankee Station in the South China Sea.

Holbrook and Bean Bag called themselves the dynamic duo.

Barbara and Millicent called themselves scared.

The guys roomed together on the *Kitty Hawk*—a spanking new bean-bag chair came with them. Batman and Robin, their crews called them. The best recce pilots in the Navy, they told their crews. Billy Joe and Murphy III also roomed together, and also flew every mission with them, but as far as Holbrook and Bean Bag were concerned, those two were only along for the ride. Sure, Billy Joe and Murphy III had an important job to do, but they were RANs, not recce pilots. And recce pilots were a special breed of cat. Not even fighter pilots could measure up to recce pilots, Holbrook loved to say. Even Roth used to say that recce pilots do two things better than any other kind of pilot and both begin with the letter F. Flying is one of them. Football, frisbies or french fries ain't the other.

Their first two months on the *Kitty Hawk* were days of hotshot flying and nights of lucrative poker-dice. But then their pal Ketchup Medley got killed taking daytime pictures of Haiphong Harbor. Two weeks later Medley's replacement 'Bama Rattray never returned from a nighttime mission over the Mekong Delta. One month after that Roth got his two stars. Medley was dead and Rattray was dead and Roth was kicked upstairs, onto the Task Force Commander's staff. And now when the Dynamic Duo went to their airplanes all they wanted to do was fly their missions, take their pictures and one day soon go home.

R&R came up, halfway through their tour. The two of them couldn't get off the carrier fast enough.

The girls met them in the Philippines.

It was just after Christmas.

Manila was teeming with Americans in those days because it was closer than Hawaii and there were dozens of flights back to SEA so that you could easily hitch a ride, and anyway Hong Kong and Sydney were both much tougher getting into and out of without spending a fortune. So Holbrook and Bean Bag had the girls meet them in the Philippines for a two-week fling. They ate together and drank together and slept together in one big high-ceilinged room—it was the only room they could get—in an old colonial hotel just outside Manila called The Conquistador. Bean Bag and Barbara moved their bed to one side of the room and Holbrook and Millicent shoved their bed to the other side of the room. And the four of them each promised not to look. Or listen.

Sometime around midnight on New Year's Eve, Barbara and Millicent both got very pregnant.

By May 1971 Holbrook and Bean Bag both had orders. Once again, they were going to be assigned together—this time to a recce squadron out of Newport News, Virginia.

And then there was only one week left on the *Kitty Hawk*. We're FIGMO. They made sure everyone knew. FIGMO. Nothing counts no more until we get the hell off this floating runway and back to dry land. FIGMO. Fuckit I Got My Orders. Home is in sight. Wives too. No more pictures of Haiphong Harbor. No more gooks. No more pals getting killed because they flew too low inside the coastline and some commie bastard gook ran a SAM up their ass. FIGMO.

One week left.

Warm up the coffee, Mama, 'cause I'm coming home.

The pair of Vigies were catapulted almost simultaneously off the deck and into the air. Holbrook flew lead. Bean Bag sat on his wing. They banked left together, then climbed to 29,000 feet, and paralleled the coast toward the port city of Vinh, 320 kilometers north of Hue.

"Wake me when breakfast is served," Bean Bag said over the radio as the dawn sun glared off their green visors.

Holbrook looked across at the blue-and-white helmet that looked back at him, "Keep your eyes open, will ya? I'm about to become somebody's father."

"As long as Barbara's not the mother," he replied.

Puffy white clouds dotted the sky below them. Their radar screens were clear. Holbrook checked in with Da Nang Center as soon as they were in the area and Da Nang told them, "The sky is yours."

"Air Force still asleep?" Bean Bag wanted to know.

"Night shift," Da Nang answered. "Just got home."

Not quite two hundred miles into the Gulf of Tonkin, Bean Bag asked Holbrook, "What do you say we start looking for some tit to teethe on."

Holbrook said to Murphy III in the seat behind him, "Find us something to drink, will ya?" And Murphy III got on the radio to call for the tanker.

The Vigies midair-refueled on schedule, and with great ease.

"Big smile now," Bean Bag called to the refueling master who watched him through a tiny window at the back of the tanker as he slipped away from the cone at the end of the hose that dangled down in front of his Vigi's nose. "Say cheese."

The refueling master pressed his face against the glass and gave Bean Bag the finger. "Cheese."

Bean Bag aimed the nose camera and ordered Billy Joe, "Get the SOB's mugshot . . ." And then he told the refueling master, "This is *bon voyage*, Kimosabe. We're FIGMO. Catch your act next war."

"You-all take care," the refueling master said. "Send me the picture."

"Hell with all you guys," Holbrook said. "Let's race."

"Balls to the wall," Bean Bag shouted, snuck under the tanker's belly and hit his afterburner. His Vigi shot out in front. Now Holbrook hit his afterburner and raced up to Bean Bag's wing.

The two planes, flying at Mach 1.6, sped through the air, staying wing to wing, until Murphy III announced to Holbrook, "Company."

"You smell 'em too, Bean Bag?" Holbrook asked.

"Shit man," Bean Bag said. "Billy Joe got 'em ages ago. They're high. Not locked in on us. Let's bring it down and lose 'em."

On the radar screens in both Vigies, two blips were coming

from somewhere over North Vietnam. Murphy III plotted their position. They might not have seen us. Holbrook called over to Bean Bag, keep the faith, then started diving sharply, bringing his Vigi into clouds at 11,400 feet, following Murphy III's set course for Vinh.

The blips fell off the scope.

"Lost 'em," Bean Bag radioed from somewhere out of sight.

"Better keep it quiet," Holbrook said.

Suddenly Murphy III told Holbrook that more blips had just popped onto the radar. He counted half a dozen of them, and they were coming out of the west.

"Oh shit," Holbrook said. "Let's go." He banked left, coming closer to the coastline, knowing that they would soon trigger bells in the ground-to-air missile sites which protected Vinh.

"How much time?" Holbrook asked.

Murphy III calculated, "Three, three and a half minutes."

Then they both heard Bean Bag say, "I've got traffic high at eight o'clock."

"Doesn't matter if they stay with us for a while. They're not locked on . . ." That's when a soft tone began whistling in his earphones. "I take it all back."

"I'm loaded," Murphy III said.

"Here we go," Holbrook announced.

The Vigi screamed through the sky.

Holbrook made a supersonic sweep of the area while Murphy III activated the cameras and also operated the electronic countermeasures equipment. A SAM was fired at them from somewhere off to the port side, but it never had a chance. By the time it was ready to lock on them, they were long gone.

"Two minutes," Murphy III called out. Then it was, "One minute." Then it was, "Thirty seconds." Then it was, "Let's go . . . now."

They made a first sweep, then Holbrook swung around for a second sweep while Murphy III monitored the on-board computer as it kept snapping pictures. "We got 'em," Murphy III said. "Textbook job." So Holbrook nosed the Vigi eastward, toward the sea and the carrier. "Heading home. Bean Bag, wherever you are, see you in the showers."

But then Murphy III screamed, "MiGs. Fast. Three o'clock."

"Shit." Holbrook saw half-a-dozen blips making steady progress toward them. Unarmed, the best he could do was outrun them. But the Vigi's huge two G.E. J79-2 engines gave off a lot of heat and a barrage of heat-seekers from the MiGs could eventually find their way up his tailpipe. "Hang on," he called back to Murphy III, and arced the huge jet due west. "Keep your eyes on our ass."

Murphy III yelled again, "More. Above us. Where the fuck did they come from?"

Above and just slightly behind, a pair of MiGs shot out of the sky toward the Vigi.

There was cannon fire.

"Stupid mothers, they can't hit us with cannons." Holbrook dived for the ground, then banked sharply to his left and climbed, rolling over on his belly at the top of the arc, then swooping down inside the MiGs' turn. The MiG trying to stay on his tail fired a missile but it went far astray. "That's right," Holbrook said, "missiles. Not cannons. Where the fuck did you learn to fly?" Murphy III in the back seat had his hands full keeping his ECM signals steady, watching the radar and telling his pilot, "A pair closing at 275 . . . a pair at 275 . . ."

Now Holbrook dived for the ground again as two more heat-seeking missiles followed his exhaust fumes. "Hang in there." He aimed straight down, racing for the ground, waiting for the very last fraction of a second before jerking the Vigi out of the nosedive, careening along the coastline, trying to make an end-run out to sea. "Enough of this bullshit . . . Oyster . . . Oyster . . ." he called on his emergency radio frequency, looking for any Navy fighters that might be in the area and could come to his assistance. "Tyke one one . . . heavy MiG pursuit . . . squawking SIF, if you read me . . . this is Tyke one one, squawking SIF . . . Oyster, Oyster, Tyke one one under fire."

In the middle of his cry for help a pair of MiGs came at him from his port side.

Another air-to-air missile was fired at them.

Suddenly something shot past his Vigi, on his port side, diving with such a force that it rattled him.

"Tyke one one . . . it's Bean Bag to the rescue . . ."

Screeching between Holbrook's plane and the pursuing MiGs, Bean Bag first dived for the ground, then went into a high yo-yo, looking exactly like a plane about to attack.

Holbrook swung seaward.

The MiGs turned with him.

Bean Bag rolled at the top of his arc.

Now diving, now climbing, now swerving to keep out of missile range, Holbrook headed for the carrier.

"Tyke one one," came a radio call, "this is Oyster. We've got you a flight of four Phantoms on their way."

Holbrook only had enough time to call back, "Roger, Oyster, Tyke one one," when he had to swerve again because Murphy III was shouting at him, "Christ, more Gooks at six o'clock, high."

A pair of MiGs came at Holbrook from above. But just as suddenly, they broke off. "Spooked 'em," Bean Bag radioed with glee, turning inside them like a fighter on the attack.

At such high speeds the MiG pilots couldn't tell that Bean Bag's Vigi wasn't armed, and by the way they tailed home it looked to Holbrook as if they weren't going to take any chances.

"Worked once," Bean Bag said over the radio, "so it might just work again. Stay steady on your course and don't look now, Satchel Paige, there are four more of them gaining on you."

"With the cavalry on the way," Holbrook told Bean Bag.

"I've got 'em," Bean Bag shouted like a kid at a party.

Holbrook had to laugh. "Shit-head, you're taking Polaroids, not shooting a six-gun."

"Oh fuck," Bean Bag said. "Hope they didn't hear you." He made a long, wide turn, looped at three-fourths throttle, somehow managed to sneak below the flight of the four North Vietnamese MiGs, carefully inched out from under them, and then, in a totally crazy stunt, he full-throttled, nose up, and started his arc about five-hundred feet directly in front of them.

The four MiG pilots pursuing Holbrook didn't know what the hell was going on.

"I just scared the shit out of four Gooks," Bean Bag shouted, rolling high.

It gave Holbrook the second or two he needed.

He broke loose to his port side.

At the same time Bean Bag faked port and ran starboard. The four MiG pilots hesitated.

And then from on high, four Air Force F-4Ds swooped down on the MiGs. There was more cannon fire. And Sidewinder missiles. And now the hunter was the hunted.

Holbrook and Bean Bag joined up wing to wing for the last forty miles back to the carrier.

The pictures they shot during that mission—close-ups of North Vietnamese MiGs in action against a pair of unarmed Navy recce jets—have sometimes been called the best aerial photos taken during the entire war. Holbrook's year on the *Kitty Hawk* got him the Navy Commendation medal. But Bean Bag's flying that FIGMO day won him the Legion of Merit. The LOM—the love of Mike, the sailors called it. Nah, he preferred, the love of Bean Bag.

In the fall of 1971, David Charles Holbrook and Michael B. B. Sawnders Jr. were born in Virginia, in the same ward, at the same Naval hospital, six days apart.

In the fall of 1974, Bean Bag got orders to Miramar NAS in San Diego and Holbrook got orders to teach flying in Pensacola. Bean Bag reminded him, those who can, do, and those who can't, teach. But Holbrook wasn't laughing. He pulled all the strings he could to get a flying job. None of them worked. Dalton was out of Congress, a victim of the 1972 Nixon routing of the Democrats. The best the Holbrooks could do was watch Bean Bag and Barbara leave for the west coast, wave goodbye and promise to keep in touch.

All four of them cried.

Over the next eight years, they both got promoted to commander, they both had daughters, they phoned each other every couple of days, the two families spent their leaves together, and even from afar, they all stayed the best of friends. For a while Bean Bag phased into Phantom RF-4Bs and did a tour in them. Holbrook worked his way out of teaching and into a Crusader II RF-8G squadron.

Then in 1981 Vice-Admiral Y. C. Roth took command of the U.S. 6th Fleet in the Mediterranean. Immediately Bean Bag orchestrated a campaign to get a new job. It took the better part of a year, but he and Holbrook simultaneously applied for cross-training into TARPS-equipped F-14 Tomcats . . . swept-wing, twin-tailed Grumman-made fighters with something called a "tactical air reconnaissance pod system" mounted on the fuselage. It meant the F-14 was a fighter that also carried three recce cameras.

Holbrook and Bean Bag spent four months, together again, getting qualified in the F-14s. At the same time they contacted Roth who, after a lot of friendly badgering, brought them to Italy. But then three months later Roth got his fourth star and moved up the ladder to take over the Navy's big European Command.

We come to visit, Bean Bag told him, and you move the hell out. We're starting to take it personal.

It was Roth's last night with the 6th Fleet and the three of them got drunk together. Just like old times, Roth said.

Yeah, Holbrook reminded him, another YCR Going Away Party.

Fully operational in F-14s, they were not only recce pilots, they were also fighter pilots—gunslingers—and so now they called themselves Wyatt and Doc.

Millicent and Barbara, with kids in tow, lived next door to each other, in semi-detached officers' quarters, on the base at Naples.

Holbrook and Bean Bag shared a room on the aircraft carrier *John F. Kennedy.*

Billy Joe and Murphy III had been lost along the way, years ago. But like the Vigies the Tomcats were also two-seaters so they were teamed up with another pair of RANs. Bean Bag got Lt. Teddy DiBenedetti—they called him Bear—and Holbrook wound up with Lt. Oscar Hammerstein Shaugnassy.

"What the hell kind of a name is that?" Holbrook and Bean Bag both wanted to know.

"My mother loves Broadway musicals," he told them. "Me too. Kinda runs in the family. My brother's name is

Richard Rodgers Shaugnassy. And my little boy's name is Marvin Hamlisch Shaugnassy.''

The four mouseketeers were now the four mouseketeers plus four mini-mouseketeers, and everything looked almost like old times until one training mission in April 1984 when something went wrong in Bean Bag's cockpit, and Bear punched out in a panic to save his own life, leaving Bean Bag alone in the crippled plane.

Holbrook saw the flash.

"Bean Bag!"

Bear smashed through the canopy and was gone.

"Christ," Bean Bag screamed on the radio. "Holy shit . . .''

"Bean Bag, straighten it out . . . what the hell happened? . . . level off . . . Bean Bag.''

"I can't see.''

"What happened?'' he called to Bear. "What happened?'' But the radio in Bear's helmet must not have been working and by the time Holbrook saw a chute open they were a mile away. "Bean Bag!'' He said to Shaugnassy in the rear seat, "Mayday home. Get help.'' And now he asked Bean Bag again, "What happened, man? Nose up. Straighten 'em out. What happened?''

"I don't know. I don't know. But I can't see. I'm blind. The son of a bitch punched out on me. But I can't see.''

"Hold 'em level, Bean Bag. Hold 'em level. I'm coming up on your wing.'' Holbrook pulled up to within thirty feet of Bean Bag's plane, and saw him sitting in the cockpit. Smoke was starting to fill it up. Bean Bag was shaking his head. "I can't punch out. I can't blow the canopy. The fucking thing just won't blow. I've got hydraulics. I think she's flying. I don't know what that explosion was. But I can't see a thing, man. It blinded me. I'm blind.''

Holbrook knew he had to keep his voice as calm as possible. "Let's see you pull your nose up . . . okay . . . now nose her down . . . now let me see you wiggle it . . . okay . . . you just keep flying it, Bean Bag, and I'll get you down . . .''

By now Shaugnassy was clicked onto the carrier's emergency frequency. Holbrook told them, "Popeye, Mayday.

Mayday. There's been an explosion in the cockpit of Olive zero four. We've got one man in the water, marking my position now . . . marking now . . . about two miles behind me. I had a visual of his silk. But the pilot is still in the plane. He's hurt. He's reporting damage to his eyes. We're wing to wing. He can't blow his canopy so it might be the ejection seat. However, he's got full hydraulics.''

"We're scrambling ASR . . .'' There was a short pause and then the carrier's radio officer came back. "Olive zero four, this is Popeye . . . Olive zero four?''

Bean Bag didn't answer.

Holbrook tried, "Bean Bag, can you read Popeye?''

"No, man, I can't read a thing but you. I can't see a thing. I think I'm filling up with smoke in here. I can't blast the canopy . . .'' His voice was getting shakier. "I don't know what the hell happened, but I can't see a thing and I think I'm bleeding. I just feel like I'm bleeding inside . . .''

"Hold tight, Bean Bag. Start singing . . . take me out to the ball game . . .'' He told the carrier, "Popeye, you clear the decks and I'll talk him down.'' He called back to Bean Bag, "Come on, sing. Take me out to the ball game, take me out to the park . . .''

"Roger Olive zero three, we've scrambled assistance now.''

A flight of four more F-14 Tomcats were catapulted off the deck of the carrier within seconds, afterburners blazing, flying at twice the speed of sound to help Holbrook and Bean Bag.

"Buy me some peanuts and Cracker Jacks . . .'' Holbrook did some fast calculations. "Bean Bag, we're on course. But we gotta get out of these clouds so we're coming down to 15,000 feet . . .'' He told the carrier, "Popeye, this is Olive zero three. We're moving down to 15,000.''

Now another voice came on the frequency. "Olive zero three, this is Misty zero one. Hang in there, good buddy, cavalry's on the way.''

"You hear that, Bean Bag? Four Tomcats farting fire. Come on, sing . . . buy me some peanuts and Cracker Jacks . . .''

"Nothing, man.'' Bean Bag slipping into a panic. "I can't hear anything but you and I can't see anything at all . . .''

"Sing. Take me out to the ball game . . .'' Holbrook shouted to Bean Bag and told Shaugnassy to patch Misty zero one onto the frequency with Bean Bag. "And it's root, root, root for the home team, if they don't win it's a shame . . . Bean Bag, sing."

He wouldn't. "I'm blind. I can't see. I can't see a fucking thing, man . . ."

". . . one, two, three strikes, you're out at the old ball game . . ."

Within four and a half minutes of the F-14 scramble, all four of the Tomcats were pulling up alongside Holbrook and Bean Bag.

"Hey, old buddy," the Tomcat leader called over to Bean Bag. "Y'all doing fine."

"I read you five-by," Bean Bag called back. "I read you. But I can't see, man. I'm bleeding and I can't see."

"Where's your little back-seat boy?" Misty zero one asked.

"I'll kill the fucker," Bean Bag said. "I'll kill him."

Now Holbrook radioed to Misty zero one, "You guys pave the way. I'll talk him down."

"Roger," Misty zero one said. "Hey, Bean Bag, why the hell don't you punch out. We've got ASR on the way to pick up the back-seat boy. Get you two rides for the price of one."

"I can't, man," Bean Bag screamed. "I can't. Don't you understand that? The fucking canopy won't go. I can't make it work. Something's jammed in there. Don't you understand that? I'm bleeding inside. And I can't see a fucking thing . . ."

"Come on, Bean Bag." Holbrook needed to calm him down. "We're okay. We're gonna be okay. We're heading home. You just keep it together and I'll get you down on the deck."

"Bean Bag," another voice came on the radio. "This is Poker Face. Shit, man, when I heard it was you I jumped in Misty zero two and got my black ass here as soon as I could. Need your money at poker-dice so we're all here with you, buddy. We're gonna get you home."

The flight of six planes continued toward the carrier, where the decks had been completely cleared for the emergency landing. One of the Air Sea Rescue helicopters reported that they had contact with DiBenedetti while others hovered off the port side of the *JFK*. Crash crews and fire crews and medical crews were all on alert, all waiting in place on the deck, all looking skyward for the first sight of Olive zero four.

Holbrook stayed on Bean Bag's wing. The other four F-14s formed a ring around the two of them. They came down from 15,000, slowly to 10,000 and then just as slowly to 5,000. "Nice and gentle, Bean Bag. Easy does it. Coming home." Within ten miles of the carrier, Holbrook guided Bean Bag down to 4,000 and then to 3,000 and then to 2,000 and then to 1,000. And now he lined Bean Bag up on the glide scope and asked that the F-14s get the hell out of the way so that he could have enough space to get Bean Bag safely onto the deck.

"Okay now, you're right on the scope . . . just keep 'em steady . . . Bean Bag . . . bring your gear down . . . let it down and I'll check that it's locked . . ."

"I'm bleeding . . . I can feel it . . ."

"Get your gear down, Bean Bag . . . come on . . ." They were two miles out, approaching the carrier at just above stall speed. "Bean Bag, get 'em down . . ."

"I'm trying," he shouted back. . . . "For Christ fucking sake, I'm trying . . . now . . . now . . . are they down?"

Holbrook watched Bean Bag's underbelly as the hold opened and the landing train clicked into place. "Okay, Bean Bag, you've got 'em down. They're down and locked."

But Bean Bag called back, "I'm bleeding bad, man. I can't see a thing and I'm bleeding bad."

"You're doing fine . . . just keep your wings steady . . ." The carrier deck was getting closer and closer . . . "I'm right next to you . . . I'm right here holding your hand . . . just keep 'em steady . . . nose up a little . . . come on . . . now bring your speed down just a skosh . . ."

"I'm not gonna make it, man . . ."

"Yes, you are, Bean Bag . . . come on, I'm right here . . . you're gonna make it . . . you're gonna be fine . . ."

"I'm not gonna make it . . ." He was slipping back into a panic again. "I'm bleeding bad and I can't see a thing . . ."

"Bean Bag, you are gonna make it . . ." The carrier was a thousand feet away. Shaugnassy counted off the distance and altitude in Holbrook's earphones while Holbrook never took his eyes off Bean Bag. "Keep 'em steady . . . Okay, Bean Bag, straighten 'em out . . ." Five hundred feet. "Bring it down, level off and bring it down . . . you're doing fine . . ." Two-fifty feet. "Level off now . . . you're high left . . . bring it down just a skosh . . . okay, you're doing fine . . . hang in there, buddy . . ." One hundred feet. "Coming in straight . . . keep your nose up . . . nose up, Bean Bag . . . get your fucking nose up. Bean Bag!"

Olive zero four hit the side of the deck with its nose too low. The plane careened left, missed the guy wires, snapped its landing gear like a chicken's wishbone and skidded across the entire width of the flight deck. The crash sent sparks into the fuel tanks. Foam jets opened on the plane instantly. Somehow the force of the landing jolted the ejection seat loose. But the canopy never blew. The pilot was exploded into the canopy, then through it, just as a billow of black smoke and a ball of fire consumed the entire plane.

The day after Bean Bag's funeral Holbrook put in for a transfer.

He never wanted to fly airplanes again.

Chapter
Seven

WHENEVER CHRISTOPHER LI'NING was in London, which over the past five years averaged three to four months a year, he arrived at the Mandarin Commerce's office every morning at 7:55.

Some of the people who worked for him thought he came in at precisely the same time every morning because it gave him a chance to speak with Hong Kong before they closed for the day. The time difference meant that 7:55 A.M. in Threadneedle Street was 3:55 P.M. in Central District. Obviously it was sound banking strategy to be in direct touch with the Asian markets—mainly currencies and gold—before the action swung from the Pacific to the City. The right information together with a good nose for spotting the trend could be the difference between leading the London market for a few hours and making money, or spending the rest of the day following it and perhaps losing money.

It made sense. But it wasn't the reason.

A few of the bank's employees, those close to Li'Ning like Peter Kan, knew that he had a special pre-dawn passion. Every morning that he was in London, at precisely 6:30, he'd leave the bank's executive flat on the twentieth floor of the Barbican's Shakespeare Tower, ride the lift down to The Bard's—a private and extremely expensive health club in the Tower's basement—and play one hour's worth of squash. His opponents were either fellow members, or his guests, or when he couldn't find anyone for a game, he would just as happily take a court alone and spend that hour working on his backhand. Then at 7:30 he'd go upstairs to the flat, shower and shave, have one cup of lotus tea, dress, and within twenty minutes be getting into his waiting car for the five-minute drive to the office.

That logically accounted for his prompt 7:55 arrival.

But it still wasn't the reason why he always got there before everyone else.

The truth was that as a young man, in 1970, just out of Stanford and starting work for his father at the bank in Hong Kong, someone gave him a copy of a book called *Up the Organization*, by Robert Townsend. He was mesmerized by it. He found it remarkable. He deified Townsend for preaching a commonsense philosophy of sound management tactics that he believed could not fail to help him become a modern manager in the midst of the otherwise very traditional Anglo-Sino Hong Kong banking community.

For instance, Townsend wrote, if you're not in business to have fun and make money, then what the hell are you doing in business?

The Townsend philosophy, however, was not necessarily one which pleased Joseph Li'Ning. Business, he claimed, especially banking, was never meant to be fun. The only fun in his life were his passions for racing and cricket. You become a banker to make money. A banker who wants to make money has to be a leader. And a leader, whether he be a banker or a general, has to lead from the front. That means you don't sit down to break bread with the soldiers. You stay aloof and lead them into battle. If you're too familiar, they will question your orders. If your mouth is filled with their food, you may not be able to bark commands at them when the enemy begins to fight. Joseph Li'Ning was very much from the old school. He believed that putting yourself on an equal footing with the employees, which is the way he saw Townsend's philosophy, would merely breed contempt. When that sets in, the employees will take advantage. Discipline, like respect, will totally break down. The Founding Chairman's rank, much the same as a War Lord's, meant total respect, final authority, ultimate responsibility and limitless privilege.

Having had his head filled with a California education, and seeing that severe changes would come to Hong Kong banking in 1997, like it or not, Christopher Li'Ning wanted to make his father understand where the future lay. It was not, he argued, in mourning Britain's abandonment of the Colony to the Chinese—a particular point Joseph Li'Ning simply could not rationalize—but rather in being able to foresee China's need for monetary outlets through genuine capitalist forward-thinking westernized banks which could at the same time stand on their own two feet under a communist system.

While his father bemoaned his fate, Christopher shaped his philosophy around Townsend's. However, as long as Joseph Li'Ning was alive, Joseph Li'Ning would manage his business his way. A Chinese son, even one with a California education, would never argue that point. It just wasn't on.

Joseph Li'Ning died in his sleep in February 1983.

By March, Christopher was making serious changes at the bank.

He also announced that he wanted to open a branch in Beijing.

The guru wrote that one of the first requirements of a good manager was the ability to create a good working environment. So Li'Ning deliberately set out to do just that. He had all the bank's offices redesigned. Walls came down. Flexible working hours were established. He computerized everything. He had kitchens installed on every floor. He had a gym built in the Hong Kong office.

Then he began a worker's cooperative profit-sharing plan that, at least on the surface, looked more benevolent than anything of its kind in any other Hong Kong bank.

The guru wrote that being a sensitive leader did not necessarily mean you got all the privileges simply by virtue of your job title. And Christopher Li'Ning was especially fond of the guru's thinking behind the remark that no one should have a reserved parking place, especially the boss. Townsend wrote, if you want the best parking space, right in front of the office door, then arrive at work before anyone else has a chance to park there. With offices in Hong Kong, London,

New York and Zurich, any parking spaces at all were generally out of the question. But Townsend's reasoning was sound. So right from his very first day—even though he was the boss's son and heir apparent—he made it his business to be the first one in to work. In London, a lot of the bank's currency dealers straggled in at eight. He decided, if they come in at eight then I want to be here at 7:55. In Hong Kong some employees showed up at 7:30. When he was there, he moved his morning schedule ahead by thirty minutes.

Everybody who worked for him knew that he was always the first in—and more often than not, the last out—which was why on Tuesday April 21, when some of the employees of the Mandarin Commerce Bank in the City of London came to work at 8:15 and discovered that Christopher Li'Ning was not yet there, one of them remarked that this was the only morning they could ever recall that happening.

Instantly, a rumor ran through the office that something was amiss. That something had happened to Li'Ning. A secretary rang his flat. There was no answer. That fueled more speculation. Someone suggested Li'Ning might have been kidnapped. No one took it seriously, but it gave them something to talk about. When Peter came to work at 8:30 he phoned The Bard's. The club manager said that Li'Ning had not made his morning appearance, but added that he wasn't surprised as Li'Ning had the night before canceled his standing court reservation. Ever calm, Peter then rang the phone in Li'Ning's car. The driver, an Englishman named Terry, explained that he and Li'Ning were at the India and Millwall Docks on the Isle of Dogs in East London. What on earth for? Peter wanted to know. Terry answered, he's having breakfast on a ship. It didn't make a lot of sense to Peter, but it certainly quashed the kidnap theory.

When breakfast was finished—lotus tea and steamed dumplings in the captain's cabin—Christopher Li'Ning came down the gangplank of the small Chinese freighter called the *Dragon Empress,* got into the car and told Terry, "Bonham's Auction House."

"The office wanted to know where you were," Terry said.

Li'Ning asked, "And what did you tell them?"

Terry started the motor. "I told them you were having breakfast."

Li'Ning said, "Good," and sat back into the rear seat as the Jaguar pulled away from the docks.

Commercial Road was crowded.

The West End was mobbed.

At Bonham's, he paid for the ginger jar, held it in his hands to take a very close look at it, nodded that he was extremely satisfied, surrounded it in clear plastic bubble-wrap, put it in a large carrier bag, got into the car and gave Terry an address off the Mile End Road, again in East London. Terry remarked, "We just came from there." Li'Ning told him sharply, "And now we're going back there."

Traffic was hardly any better, against the rush hour. It took them nearly forty minutes to fight their way eastward. Then they got lost. When Terry finally found the place it turned out to be an old stable with a sign on the door which read, "Seafarers—Packing and Shipping."

Inside, the large open room stank of damp and freshly cut wood. It was filled with crates and boxes of all sizes, and a carpenter's bench covered in saws and hammers and nails, and a long table covered with cord and rope and tape.

"Have you got it ready?" Li'Ning asked.

A funny little man with a mustache and gnarled hands, wearing a filthy white smock and with an unlit pipe dangling from his teeth, looked up from the bench. "You the bloke I spoke to on the phone? Didn't sound Chinese to me. Sounded English. You English or Chinese? You look Chinese."

"I'm from Hong Kong." Li'Ning tried to be polite. "Now . . . is everything ready?"

"You said you wanted it for this morning," he replied, "so you've got it for this morning. But if the measurements are wrong it isn't going to be blamed on me. Are you sure the measurements you gave me are correct?"

"I'm sure," Li'Ning said.

"Then if you're sure, I'm sure." He reached for the ginger jar. "This it?"

"Please be careful . . ."

"If you're careful, I'm careful." He brought it over to the

long table, took it out of the carrier bag, unwrapped it and put it down. "This is worth how much money?"

"Quite a bit," Li'Ning said.

"How old is it?"

"Very old," Li'Ning said, then asked, "May I see the crate?"

The funny little man nodded. "You're paying for it, you can see it." He reached across his workbench to lift up a wooden tea chest. "It works like this." He took off the top and yanked a wooden slatted crate out from the inside. "The jar gets covered in bubble-wrap and fits in here." He motioned for Li'Ning to look. "I've built in enough room so that you can cover it with plenty of bubble-wrap to make it fit snug. You want it to fit snug. It's going to fit snug. Then this inner crate is suspended inside the tea chest. See? It's padded. It's a cocoon suspension crate. That's what we call it in the business. I've built a thousand of them. You said you didn't want anything to happen to your jar, so I've built a cocoon suspension crate for you and believe me, they can kick it, drop it, or stand on top of it. Nothing can happen to your jar."

"Let's see the fit." Li'Ning lifted the ginger jar and carefully laid it inside the slatted crate. "Good," he said, because surrounded by that clear plastic bubble-wrap the ginger jar would still be almost entirely visible. It could be inspected without being unwrapped should the need arise. Then he slid the slatted crate into the tea chest. The bubble-wrap on the tea chest's inner walls made the fit good and tight.

"See, no movement at all." He was proud of his work. "When we seal the top, the inner crate is like a baby in the womb."

"What about the lining I asked for."

"It's under the bubble-wrap on the inside walls of the tea chest. Just the way you wanted it. Of course, it's none of my business, but why on earth . . . ?"

"To make it seaworthy," Li'Ning explained. "It's got to be totally watertight."

"Well"—the funny little man pulled his pipe out of his mouth for the first time since Li'Ning walked in—"you want it watertight, so you've got to make it watertight on the outside. I can't guarantee it will stay watertight lined like that on the inside. Probably won't. So heavy it might not even float.'' He chuckled. "Who knows what it will do. You know what? I never made a crate like this one. A cocoon suspension, of course, but exactly like this one, no, never.''

Li'Ning paid him, thanked him and carried the wooden box stuffed with the crate and the ginger jar back to the car. Terry spotted his boss coming out of the workshop and jumped out of the car to open the trunk.

Li'Ning told him, "I'll put them on the rear seat with me.''

"That looks like it weighs a ton. How come?'' Terry wanted to know.

"It's special,'' Li'Ning told him. Then to make certain that Terry wouldn't bother asking why it was special, Li'Ning said, "Let's go. I'm late.''

Chapter
Eight

"BECAUSE I SCREWED UP," he said softly.

"Oh . . . shit!" Millicent yanked herself away from him. "You're feeling so sorry for yourself that none of the rest of us matter." She picked her robe off the floor, tied it around her waist and went to the mirror to straighten her hair.

"Come back."

But after a while when she didn't he began to feel foolish lying there like that, so he grabbed the sheets and covered himself and pulled them over his head too.

I screwed up.

He kept his eyes open and stared up at the colored percale.

I screwed up.

That's all he could say.

It was six weeks after Bean Bag's funeral and two weeks since he filed his formal request to transfer out of aviation. Bean Bag was gone. And the only answer he had from Admiral Baker was to report to his office this morning at 0830. Shit. I wrote the letter according to Navy regulations and sent it through channels. Baker's endorsement should be automatic. All he has to do is write *I concur*. That doesn't take two weeks. That doesn't need a meeting.

He heard Millicent leaving the room, then coming back.

I screwed up. He wanted her to understand.

But he didn't say it.

And when he couldn't think of anything else to say he threw

the sheets off his head, walked past her and went to take a shower.

Millicent busied herself, getting the kids ready for school.

He stayed under the cold water for as long as he could stand it.

Breakfast was quiet.

Millicent told Chrissie and David that Daddy had a migraine.

Holbrook told Chrissie and David the truth, that he missed Bean Bag very much.

He dropped them at school, then made his way to Baker's office.

The secretary said the admiral would see him in a few minutes. Holbrook sat down to wait.

I concur. That's all he has to do. Just write those two words and sign on the bottom line. If he doesn't, I'll put in my papers. I'll put my cards on the table and tell the Old Man that if he refuses my request, I'll quit.

The voice inside his head wanted to know, what will you do?

He told the voice, I don't have the slightest idea.

"Come on in." The slightly overweight, gray-haired Rear-Admiral Holly Baker motioned from his office door.

"Good morning, sir." Holbrook stood up and saluted.

But when he stepped into the admiral's office he was surprised to see who else was there.

Sitting on the couch was the Reverend Carlton Mueller, thin, balding, a Navy captain and the command chaplain. Leaning against the windowsill and smiling was dark-haired Dr. Alex Angelides, also a Navy captain and one of the command's flight surgeons. Holbrook nodded. "Good morning." Mueller returned the nod. Angelides waved, "Hi."

"Take a load off your feet," Baker said, closing the door.

It was obvious where he was supposed to sit—in the middle of the room on a chair that was already turned to face both the couch and the admiral's desk.

The chaplain tried to make small-talk.

Holbrook said politely that the kids were fine and Millicent was fine and that everything was fine. Except he knew that they knew everything wasn't so fine. I don't know why you're here, he thought, but I think I'm glad you're here because you'll both be on my side.

"When I saw this"—Baker took Holbrook's request off his desk and waved it about—"I had to ask myself what would be best for the Navy and of course for you."

"Yes, sir." He held his breath. And when the admiral didn't go on, Holbrook decided to remind him, "These matters are generally straightforward, sir. I trust you'll endorse it."

Now Baker put the request down. "Taking you out of aviation is the Navy's loss. You're a damned fine officer."

I'm out. Holbrook suddenly felt very relieved. Just like that, it's over. "Thank you, sir."

"So I'm not."

And just as suddenly his heart sank. "You're turning me down?"

"Nope. Not refusing you either. I reckon the best thing for all of us is for you to just take this back and I'll make the rest of the paperwork disappear. Deep six the whole business."

He couldn't believe it. "I'm sorry, sir. I won't take it back. I want out of aviation. I screwed up and . . ."

"No, you didn't screw up. That's why I won't accept this. None of us here believe you screwed up. Commander Sawnders' death was one of those accidents that take place on an all-too-regular basis at sea. Flying's a dangerous business and unfortunately men die. But anyone who knew just how close you and Sawnders were can understand why you're taking it this hard. Now I'm not gonna lecture you about how the Navy spent half a million bucks getting you into a cockpit and keeping you there. And I'm not gonna insult your intelligence with smarm about how good recce pilots aren't born every day, even if they're not. Of course I could concur. And if I didn't give a damn I probably would. But I do give a damn. Granting your request is not the best thing for the Navy—or you. By the same token, refusing your request means this will live in your file forever. So you take this back and I'll see that all the other paperwork disappears and no one will ever have to know about this, especially when you come up for promotion."

"Sir . . . I filed my request as a standard procedure in line with Navy regulations . . ."

"Commander," Baker said sternly, "if you're trying to tell me there are other ways outta flying, I know all the tricks you do and a bunch you never even dreamed of." His tone softened. "Anyway, I'd be damned disappointed if an officer as fine as you took any other route besides standard procedure."

Holbrook knew precisely what the admiral was implying. There were lots of do-it-yourself ways out of flying. The simplest was to purposely miss the line on a few landings and spill a couple of planes into the water. That would get you sent ashore before you even had a chance to dry off. It cut through the red tape and was super-efficient. It also happened a lot. I've lost my touch. He's lost his nerve. I can't do it anymore. Ship him out. But Holbrook didn't think he could ever go through with anything like that. Missing the line was easy. Living with yourself afterward was the hard part. "I put in my request according to the regulations . . ."

Baker wasn't giving in. "All right. Let me try a bribe. A transfer anywhere you want, as long as they've got airplanes. Will that convince you to take the request back?"

"I'm afraid not, sir."

The admiral took a deep breath, walked around the side of his desk, fell heavily into his chair and pointed to Angelides. "You try."

"Sir . . ." The flight surgeon shrugged. "I don't have the foggiest notion of how to talk him out of it." He turned to Holbrook. "Except maybe to tell you that what happened to Bean Bag wasn't your fault. Although I don't know how to help you understand that. I'm no psychiatrist. My thing is tummies and tushes. Of course if the admiral wants my medical opinion I'll swear you don't have piles."

The admiral laughed.

So did the chaplain.

Holbrook didn't.

"The real problem," Angelides went on, "is that you were born stubborn. And the longer you hold out, the tougher it's going to be when you do go back to flying. And I happen to know you well enough to know some day you will."

"No," Holbrook said. "It's finished."

"You're running away from something you're going to have to face one day or another. Someday you're going to have to get it through your head that what happened to Bean Bag wasn't your fault. He's dead. He got killed. But you didn't kill him." The flight surgeon moved away from the windowsill, looked for somewhere to sit down and finally decided on the arm of the couch. "You know, I guess it was around the third year of medical school, when you have to take all those courses in psychiatry . . ."

Holbrook cut in with, "Alex, please . . . just leave it alone." But what he really wanted to say was, you son of a bitch, you're supposed to be on my side.

"Hear me out. What you're experiencing, all this pain you're feeling and the way you're reacting to it . . . it's very new to you, but any third-year med student would recognize it right away."

"What am I supposed to do, pretend I've gone around the bend? To swear in front of a medical board that I'm seeing things and hearing things and talking to myself? Christ, man, I am!"

"I've sailed with you. I've also played liar's dice with you. And if you try to get out of flying by claiming you're crazy, I'll swear you're no more crazy than anyone who flies airplanes off carriers. Or regularly bets on a full house when he doesn't even have a pair under the cup."

"And anyway," the chaplain intervened, "Christ had nothing to do with this. Mustn't blame him this time."

"Maybe you're on my side," Holbrook said, looking at Mueller.

"Certainly I am," Mueller answered right away. "We all are. And maybe me more than anybody else because I'm seeing this from the spiritual side. I understand your grief and I understand your fears. That's why I believe in the bottom of my heart that the admiral is right. Taking you out of aviation won't solve the problem."

"On the other hand," the flight surgeon suggested, "getting you back into the cockpit will change things. It's a question of confidence in yourself and that's the first step in coping with this. That's the first step on the road to convincing your-self that what happened to Bean Bag wasn't your fault.''

"Tell me something," the admiral said. "Your boy play baseball?" He didn't wait for an answer. "Probably does. So what do you do when your kid gets hit by the ball? Or, I don't know . . . what do you do if he falls on ice skates? Or he takes a tumble on skis, or something like that? You send him right back into the game, don't you? He gets hit by a fastball and the next time he's up you make him stand right there in the batter's box, face that pitcher and take whatever the guy sends down the pike. If you don't, that kid will never go back. Letting him quit while he's still hurting, well, that's about the most unfair thing I can think of doing to him.''

"This is not the same thing." Holbrook tried to make them understand. "Not at all. This isn't the fifth inning. This isn't the Little League. This is my life. What's important here is whether or not someone should be flying airplanes when he himself feels he can't. And the Navy's usual answer to that question is, no, he shouldn't.''

"This is not the Navy's usual situation," the admiral hammered on. "No one is saying you shouldn't have time to work out your problems. We'll give you that time. But quitting aviation won't solve the problem, it will only create a whole mess of bigger ones. So I want you to take this request letter, tear it up and give the Navy a chance to help. That's best for everybody.''

"I agree," said the chaplain. "And I'm certain Bean Bag Sawnders would agree too.''

Holbrook could still hear it all so clearly. Coming in straight . . . keep your nose up . . . nose up, Bean Bag . . . get your fucking nose up . . . Bean Bag! The voice inside his head wouldn't stop playing it back to him. Keep your nose up . . . nose up, Bean Bag.

"You two . . .'' He shook his head at Mueller and Ange-lides. "Did you rehearse this before I got here? Work it out between yourselves? Funny, because when I walked in and saw you both I was sure you'd be on my side. At least I hoped so. But it strikes me that you've got . . . well, let's call them, higher priorities.'' And now he said to the admiral, "Sir, I screwed up. I don't want to fly anymore. If you don't endorse my request I'll put in my papers.''

The admiral sighed. "I truly hope that won't happen. You're too fine an officer for the Navy to lose you.''

"Sir, I feel that strongly about it.''

"Well . . .'' The admiral picked up Holbrook's request. "I sincerely hope to God you don't. Because I feel just as strongly about this.'' And just like that he ripped the letter in half, then in half again. "I'm telling you from experience that this way is much better for everybody than turning you down.''

"Okay, sir,'' Holbrook said without any hesitation. "I'll file my separation request papers this afternoon.''

Mueller jumped up. "No, he won't, sir. If you'll give me some time to counsel Commander Holbrook . . . another day or so . . .''

The admiral agreed. "All right, Chaplain. But let me warn you that if you don't talk him out of resigning his commission, I'll personally see you transferred to some unit, like the Israeli Navy, where they've got nothing but Jews.''

"I don't need another day,'' Holbrook said flatly. "Will that be all, sir?'' He stood up. "If you'll excuse me, sir.'' He just wanted to get out of there. He nodded to Mueller and Angelides. Sons of bitches. The admiral watched him leave.

Bastards, Holbrook kept mumbling under his breath as he hurried out of the building. Goddamned sons of bitches.

Angelides rushed up to him in the parking lot. "If the padre doesn't talk you out of resigning, I'm coming by your quarters tonight to beat the shit out of you. Then I'll stick you in my hospital and keep you sedated till you change your mind.''

Holbrook really wasn't in the mood. "You could have helped but you didn't. Just keep out of my way.''

Now Mueller grabbed his arm. "Don't even think about resigning.''

"Leave it alone. And leave me alone too. Both of you could have helped and all you wound up doing was kissing Baker's ass.'' He started to climb into his car.

The chaplain wouldn't let him go. "Use your brains. Of course you were set up. Do you think either one of us wanted to be there? We were ordered to be there. Attendance was mandatory. But you've still got a card to play. Pick up the phone and call Y. C. Roth.'' Mueller reached into his pocket and pulled out a dime. ''Here. I'll even pay for it. You wouldn't want to see me preaching to the Jews, would you?''

''Fuck off, both of you.'' Holbrook pulled himself loose and went home.

''I'm going to quit,'' he said to Millicent as soon as he walked in the front door. ''The bastards set me up. Everybody's speech was rehearsed. Well, I told him if he didn't take me out of flying I'd file my papers. He sat right there and ripped up my request. Tore it up in front of me. Fuck it, I'm getting out.''

''I don't know who you're babbling about,'' she said, ''but if you're thinking about tossing all these years out the window, you'd better think again, mister. What about your retirement? Just what do you think Chrissie and David and I have gone through all this bullshit for? So you can throw your retirement out of the window? We sit home alone while you're out playing cowboys and Indians with your toy jet planes, and God knows what else, like screwing every teenaged Italian girl in Naples, and you think I'm gonna let you flush away what little security we've got or might ever have!''

''I'm getting out.''

''Yeah, well, as far as I'm concerned you'd better start adding up what this is gonna cost us because you're not qualified to do anything but fly those goddamned planes. Life in the States is no picnic anymore. Just where do you think you're gonna find a job?''

He told her, ''I don't know.''

''You got that right.''

''Maybe you'll find a job.''

And she told him, ''But you got that wrong.''

He took a deep breath and after a long pause he said quietly, ''Millicent, I've gotta get my head straightened out.'' She stared at him. He watched as her eyes began to redden. For a second he thought about asking, where did we get blown off the track? He almost said, where did it go sour for us? He wanted to say, how come everything with us is like a record playing at the wrong speed? He even almost told her, I wish we could go back to square one and start all over again. But suddenly she blurted, "I can't handle any more of this shit," shoved her hands into her pockets and stormed out of the room.

The moment to speak to her or ask her anything or even tell her what he was thinking . . . that moment was gone.

That night he lay in bed and thought about what he wanted to do.

He lay there looking at the ceiling, his eyes wide open as he listed all his options.

The next morning it was clear in his mind.

I need some time on my own.

He reassured himself, Millicent will survive. The kids . . . well, they'll just have to survive too.

Chrissie and David went off to school. As soon as they were gone Holbrook called his CO and said, "I won't be in for a while." Then he sat down for breakfast. It was the first weekday morning in years that he was still in his pajamas and bathrobe at 9 A.M.

Millicent started putting the house in order.

Funny, he thought, she hasn't even asked me if I'm going to work today.

He stayed in the kitchen, hovered over a bowl of cornflakes until he had rehearsed his speech a dozen times. I've gotta get my head straight. And I've gotta do it by myself.

Then he reached for the phone to ring Admiral Roth in London.

He told Roth what had happened. "I killed Bean Bag." He told Roth, "I want out of flying."

Roth said, "Okay, Dad, I'll see what I can do."

When he hung up, Holbrook turned toward their bedroom door and called out to Millicent, "I think it's time we split up for a while."

Chapter
Nine

ON PAPER, THE U.K. Atomic Energy Authority's Constabulary is a police force.

When you ask for an official description you are told that the Constabulary is trained along the lines of and has powers commensurate with any of the Home Office police forces.

But in practice they are more than just a police force.

They are empowered to protect civilian nuclear installations, atomic power stations and shipments of atomic fuels in the United Kingdom, at all cost.

The key words are "at all cost."

Housed in a faceless building just off St. James's Square, they display no signs outside to tell you whose offices you are walking by. There is nothing in the tiny entrance to tell you what goes on upstairs. And although the plainclothes security guard who glares at you when you walk through the door immediately says, "May I help you," he really means, "What the hell do you want?"

Boston dashed through the rain, and into the tiny lobby.

"May I help you." The heavy-set, thick-necked security guard said it more as a statement than question.

He shook water off his coat. "Assistant Chief Constable Wooldridge, please."

The security guard wanted to know, "Is he expecting you, sir?"

"Of course he's expecting me. Would I come out in weather like this if he wasn't expecting me?"

The security guard didn't so much as flinch. "Just a minute, sir." He went to the small wooden desk in front of the lift and opened a plastic folder with a typewritten list of phone numbers in it. "You did say Assistant Chief Constable Wooldridge didn't you, sir?"

"I come here once a week and that's who I always ask to see."

"I wasn't on duty last week, sir," the security guard mumbled as he dialed . . . got the wrong number the first time, and nothing at all the second time. After a third attempt he managed to get through to a secretary who told the guard, "Send him up straight away."

"It's all right," the guard told Boston. "Sign the logbook, please, and wear this badge in a visible position at all times that you are in the building. You will have to surrender it to me when you leave."

"You did hear me say that I come here once a week to see Assistant Chief Constable Wooldridge."

But the guard would have none of it. "You will still have to sign the logbook and still have to wear this badge in a visible position at all times when you are in the building."

"That's not what I meant."

"That is what I meant." The guard pointed toward the logbook.

Boston let the matter drop. I can't win. It's not worth pursuing. He filled in the logbook entry and clipped his visitor's badge onto his jacket. "Here, sir." The guard pushed the lift button for him and announced, "Fifth floor."

Wooldridge was waiting for him by the time the lift finished its agonizingly slow climb.

"Could be very serious," he said, pumping Boston's hand. "This time we could be in for serious problems. I'm glad you could make it. Terrible weather, this."

"You really must do something about the guard downstairs. A most chilly personality. Not very bright, I'd say. Hardly worthy of your office."

Wooldridge said, "Yes, of course," and went on mumbling about the weather.

Constabulary officers working in London wear civilian clothes.

Like senior policemen throughout the country, a standard off-the-peg basic drab men's suit is the norm. Basic drab green or basic drab gray is the preferred choice. But Assistant Chief Constable Derek Greystone Wooldridge was just a little different because in addition to basic drab he always wore a fresh carnation in his lapel. Today it was white. Most of the time it was pink or red. When anyone asked why he wanted to call attention to himself that way, why he couldn't dress like everyone else in the Constabulary, he'd proudly exclaim, "RHIP." Rank has its privileges. Of course it didn't actually mean anything, but it stopped most people from asking any further questions.

"I've a busy morning on," Boston lied, following Wooldridge into his office. "Can't stay too long. What's up?"

"It's the Americans." He closed the door and motioned for Boston to sit down. "I'm afraid it's serious." Wooldridge's large, imitation wood but basically metal desk was littered with folders and papers and a bank of five telephones. "Tea? Coffee?"

"No thanks." Boston waved him off. "Just tell me what this is all about? You said on the phone it was the Navy. Nothing at all to do with last week?"

"I'm afraid they've lost some fissile materials."

"What?" Boston froze.

Wooldridge fell into his own chair. "There is fissile material missing."

Dear God, he thought, the day has turned truly nasty. "When? How?"

"In other words, you don't know anything about it?"

"Of course not," he said immediately.

"I'm afraid, Buster, that's the heart of the problem. You see, neither do we."

He stared at Wooldridge. "What do you mean?"

"I mean we know that they're looking for something they've lost and we're certain it's fissile material, but we don't know exactly what or where. We think it might have been plutonium nitrate."

"Oh, my God." He was suddenly short of breath. "How can you be certain?"

"The most logical way," Wooldridge said, as if it should have been obvious. "Because I have learned for a fact that they're looking for it."

"Logical," Boston had to agree. "Have you begun following up on any incomplete coordination forms."

"I have someone working on it right now. I thought I'd ring you in the meantime and suggest that you might start by checking with your contacts at the U.S. Navy."

He tried to think of a way out of that. "Woolley, I can't just ring over there and ask if something is missing. It doesn't make sense. It isn't the way we do things. I can't accuse them of not playing by the rules, like that. I mean . . . these are the Americans we're talking about."

"Oh." Wooldridge thought about that for a while and agreed. "Yes. Of course not. You're perfectly right. These are the Americans after all."

"Right," Boston said, thinking he might have hit on a way to keep Wooldridge from acting too hastily. "It's not as if we're treating matters with the French. Hah. I'd never trust them. And neither would you, Woolley. But the Americans are our best allies and we can't just start prying into their affairs on the hunch that something might be amiss."

"Yes. Yes." It must have made sense to him. "Of course we can't."

"Of course. Especially after last week. Everybody's down on them."

"Quite an episode, last week, eh?"

"Discretion," Boston said confidently. "That's the best way. Discretion. Tell you what we should do, Woolley. You check your files and I'll check mine. Then if there is an incomplete form we can make some rather discreet inquiries."

"Good." Wooldridge nodded. "Discretion it shall be. After all, we owe the Americans a lot. Falklands and all that."

"Indeed we do." Boston hurried to stand up. Too many potential problems were now running through his mind. "Discretion. I'll ring you as soon as I've had a chance to look through my files. We'll talk again in a few hours. I'll ring you. Or you can ring me. Whatever. In a few hours.''

Wooldridge escorted him back to the lift. "Good of you to stop by. And I think you're right. Our motto on this one must be discretion."

"Discretion," Boston repeated with the lift doors closing.

But on the way back to Chappell House, he berated the Americans.

How could they do this to me? How could they put me in a position like this? They're required to coordinate through me. If something's amiss, I could have headed it off before it ever reached Woolley's ears. What have I ever done to them to deserve this kind of treatment? Well, I'm not going to stand for it. My God, don't they understand how serious this could be?

Mrs. Fitzgerald had several messages for him the moment he walked into his office. "A Mr. Benjamin Katzman rang no less than three times. It's about something called Las Fontanas. He said you'd know what that meant."

Oh no, he thought. The salesman about the condominium in Spain. "I can't talk to him now." Why would he phone me today of all days? "If he rings back, tell him I'm out for the rest of the week. Tell him I've got the papers . . . no, don't tell him anything except to ring back next week. Tell him, yes, no, yes, to ring next week."

"All right," she said and went on to the others. "A Mr. H. Goodman who said he's ringing about a magazine subscription and a Mr. Follett who says he's the mechanic from the garage where your son's car is being repaired. Also, there was a Mr. Samson who says he is from a life insurance company . . ."

"No," Boston threw his hands into the air. "No calls, No magazine subscriptions. No insurance policies. None of them. Not now. Please."

"And Mrs. Boston."

He shooed her out of the office and shut his door.

A few seconds later she buzzed him on the intercom. "Your wife wanted you to ring her."

"Not now," he said. "Not now." He went to his filing cabinet and rifled through the drawers until he located the folders on U.S. Navy shipments. His copies of the forms were filed by reverse date with the earliest on the bottom. And the very first one, the most recent one, didn't have any completion information.

This could be the one, he hoped. It was for a shipment of plutonium nitrate from their nuclear submarine base in the Kyle of Tongue to a secure U.S. Navy storage depot on Merseyside. Hah. If this is the one we're all right. If this is what all the stink is about, we're fine.

He grabbed his phone. "Woolley, I think I've found it. Check your files under order number 4224 SJ 06."

"Right, let me look at that." He repeated the order number, put the phone down and left Boston to hold on for nearly ten minutes.

This must be the one, Boston assured himself. He tapped his fingers on his desk and when he grew weary of that he started tapping his feet on the floor. This has to be the one.

"You still there?" Wooldridge came back on the line. "We've got the file and yes, I think you may be on to something. Nothing complete on my form either. All my others show completions. Does that ring true to you too?"

"Yes. Yes it does. So . . ." He dared, "So that's that, eh?"

Wooldridge's voice dropped. "I'm afraid it only seems to be."

"What do you mean?" He didn't like what Woolley could be implying. "What does that mean . . . it only seems to be?"

"I say it only seems to be because we've not confirmed anything with them."

"But if that's the only one, then that's the only one," Boston said. "That's really the only one you're worried about?" He said it first as a question and then repeated it as a statement. "I mean, that's the only one you're worried about, isn't it? Just one shipment."

"Well, yes," Wooldridge said, slightly confused. "Just one. Why? Did you want there to be more?"

"No." Boston forced a nervous laugh. "No, certainly not. I was merely wondering if this might have had to do with us. You can understand, I am more than just a little concerned."

That's an understatement, he thought. What if someone at MoD hears about this and decides to take a long look at current procedures? What if there is a complete overhaul of the system? What if the U.S. Navy PuN has been hijacked and the MoD gets involved at a level above my head and they want to take a very close look at the entire system of checks and balances? I can't let them do this to me. I have to keep this in-house. I can't just let someone walk in and take over my office. I can't let this get out of control. "I'd better get on to the U.S. Navy right away. But why on earth didn't they alert me? By regulation they're supposed to go through my office."

"I know," Wooldridge said. "Chain of command and all that. Although in this case the problem is that there is no chain of command. Your office knows nothing about it which means they haven't alerted your office, as they are required to do. Therefore, my office knows nothing about it. And that leads me to believe that if this shipment has indeed gone missing, our American allies are trying to pull one over on us."

He didn't like the sound of that. "I'll ring them. I'm certain there's a simple answer. Probably something silly like a missing form. Or the computer. Yes. That's it. Of course. It's always the computer, isn't it, Woolley." He forced a chuckle. "It's always the computer except when it comes to adding a few zeros to our pay slips, eh? Oh well, Woolley, not to worry. I'll straighten it out and get back to you."

"Buster?" Wooldridge said quietly. "If there has been some sort of hijacking . . ."

"Woolley . . . no. That would be unthinkable." He wanted to get off the phone. "It's nothing more than a breakdown of communication. I'm certain that's what this is. It couldn't be anything more than that. I'll ring you back after I've checked with my contact."

"Discreetly, of course."

"Of course." He hung up, then rang the U.S. Navy at 7 North Audley Street. An operator answered and he asked for, "Commander Holbrook, please."

They spoke for only a few minutes.

There was no small talk.

Boston went straight to the point.

Too much was at stake for him to beat about the bush.

Don't they realize how serious this could be?

When he hung up with Holbrook he dialed Woolley again. "Boston, here. I've just spoken to the Americans."

"And? What did they say? Breakdown in communication as you suspected? Probably right . . . the computer . . . I've been thinking about that . . ."

"Well," Boston cut in, "not quite."

"What do you mean, not quite? Don't tell me . . . oh my God, gone, is it? Did they *tell* you that some PuN has disappeared?"

"Actually, no." Boston shook his head. "No. Not at all. My contact there didn't say anything of the kind." He knew he had to be careful the way he phrased this. "You see, I told him that we'd heard some PuN was missing. I felt it best to take the direct approach. So I told him. And straight away he denied knowing anything about it."

"Denied it? So . . ." Wooldridge seemed relieved. "Then there's nothing to worry about, is there?"

"But Woolley, that's exactly what *he* said. Nothing to worry about. You see, he denied everything." Boston paused. "Which, frankly, I think means that something very serious has happened."

"Serious? Like a hijacking?"

"Now that you mention it, Woolley . . . Yes, I'm afraid it might be."

Chapter
Ten

RICHARD HOLBROOK SPENT the rest of the morning trying to read through all the reports and forms and files that piled up on his desk as the admin chief located more.

There were hundreds of Naveur 6648/Gs, hundreds of DoD 3093s, hundreds of NATO forms B-35.7 and B-35.8, a whole series of Dutch forms which had to do with the delivery of cruise missiles in Holland, and several volumes of British MoD and U.K.-AEA forms, including the entire 49-Series, both A and B files, which was the British equivalent of the Naveur 6648/Gs.

He wanted to go through all of them if possible without having to beg favors off the computer guys downstairs. Asking them to sort through this mess will only land me with more paperwork because they'll make me fill out a dozen forms before they'll even consider my request for their help with these forms.

He tried to read as many of them as he could but he kept hearing Wagner's voice and he kept thinking about Bean Bag, and finally he reached for the phone to call Barbara.

The number rang three times before a man picked it up and in a sleepy voice said, " 'Lo?''

Holbrook couldn't believe it.

" 'Lo?'' the man said again, clearing his throat, then finally managing a full ''Hello?''

Holbrook hesitated, then almost as if he was afraid to be found with the phone in his hand, he quickly hung up.

A man answered.

He sat there, staring at the phone, trying to convince himself that it was a wrong number. I'll call again. This time Barbara will answer. I'll call back. But he didn't.

A man answered.

He sat there staring at the phone, thinking about Bean Bag.

Then the phone rang. It broke into his thoughts. It startled him.

He flinched, then picked it up. "Commander Holbrook."

"Good morning, Commander," came a crisp British voice. "Boston here from the MoD. I'm afraid we've got an important matter to discuss."

Holbrook mouthed the word, shit!

Boston asked about the missing van.

Holbrook told him there was no missing van, that there was absolutely nothing to worry about.

Boston seemed to accept that.

But, Holbrook told himself, he accepted that too easily.

"Shit!" He slammed down the phone. How the hell could they have found out? Son of a bitch. Now what do I do? Should I tell the old man or do I try to contain it? Maybe the MoD guy believed me. Maybe Boston was just taking a poke in the dark. Maybe he'll forget all about it.

And maybe Chicken Little was right.

He argued with the voice inside his head. Why should Boston believe me? He knows. They've found out. Maybe I should call him back and try to work something out. I'll tell the old man that the Brits are on to us. We'll brief the ambassador and use his office to cover our tracks. Christ, what happens if the papers get a hold of the story? I warned the old man that we could get into trouble.

McIntyre, the admin chief, announced, "Delivery," and came into the room carrying an armload of forms together with the office copy of *The Times*. "I got these damn things coming out of my whazoo." He half-shoved, half-dumped the papers into Holbrook's hands. "Makes you damn-well know why God invented computers. And you'll be delighted when I let you in on my little secret. There's more to come."

He surveyed the growing pile of papers on Holbrook's desk. "It sure is wonderful for an enlisted man to see an officer actually doing something useful . . . sir. Of course, if all else fails there's always the crossword puzzle in the newspaper." He raised his eyebrows, grinned and walked away.

Holbrook dropped the forms into a heap on his desk, mumbled, "Shit," and hurried to Roth's office. "I've got to see him right away," he said to the admiral's secretary. "Can you get me in there, please?"

She was a heavily built, overly made-up English woman named Cecilia Archibald. Miss Cecilia to those officers she favored and nothing short of Ma'am to everyone else. She had been working for the U.S. Navy in London since the mid-1950s, and "Admiral Roth," she often bragged, "is the seventeenth admiral I've had." Although she never understood why some people snickered whenever she announced that.

A small plaque on her desk reminded anyone who doubted her authority that she had served a total of sixty-two stars.

But then no one ever doubted her authority. Or if they tried to once they never dared to a second time.

Miss Cecilia sat fiercely behind her desk, plunked down almost right in front of the admiral's door, making certain that no one got in to see him without her approval. She had been brought up in a world where executive secretaries protected their bosses and she ruled her executive-secretary roost like someone who had long ago forgotten that there was a difference between her rank and the admiral's. "Sorry, Commander. It's one of those by-invitation-only meetings."

"It's important," he said.

"Sorry." She was immovable.

"Where's Commander Parrot?"

She pointed, "In there."

"Would you call him out, please?"

"Sorry, Commander." She shook her head. "They'll be finished by twelve forty-five because the admiral has a luncheon."

He knew enough not to argue with her for anything less than all-out nuclear war. He feared being "Cantonized."

Legend had it that she once ran up against a certain young Lieutenant named Canton. It was the story every long-time officer on station told to every newly arrived officer when he reported in for duty. How much of it, if any, was actually true, Holbrook didn't know. But the way the story was currently being told, one day this Lt. Canton made a joke about how English women were the obvious victims of English society because English men all went to boarding schools where their value system and social status was based on comparing penis sizes.

Miss Cecilia didn't care for that at all. She flew off the handle, ranting after Canton, "There's nothing wrong with anyone's penis in this country." When Canton dared to suggest, "You must be talking from experience," he instantly hit the top of her list. For the next eight months, until he transferred back to the States, his name was on every extra-duty assignment issued out of the admiral's office. His TDY expenses never came through on time. His housing allowance was stopped and he was forced to move into government quarters. And just for good measure, when he transferred back to the States—to a very junior desk job in a sonar training school—his household goods took five months to arrive.

Just in case the story was even half true, Holbrook made it his practice to stay as far away from her as he could. "How's twelve-thirty then?"

"By the way, I'm told you brewed the coffee this morning." She gave him a stern look. "Well, Commander, next time you make coffee, I do not want to discover that you've tossed the used filter into my straw wastepaper basket. Soggy coffee filters go in the lined bin under that table."

"Ah. The soggy coffee filter." He tried not to take it any less seriously than she did. "Lined bin under the table. Sorry, Miss Cecilia. I wasn't thinking too straight at that hour. Lined bin not straw bin. Roger."

"As long as we've got it clear." She nodded. "Be back here at twelve-thirty and I'll get you in before he leaves."

"Thank you." He returned to his office muttering, lined bin not straw bin. Why don't I put out a contract on her life? I could take up a collection. Lined bin not straw bin. I bet the admiral would be the biggest contributor.

He sat down at his desk, took a deep breath and asked himself, now, do I ring the MoD guy or not? If I can contain it with a phone call so much the better. On the other hand, if it blows up in my face . . . ?

He started fidgeting with the several hundred forms that had collected on his desk. Naveur forms. DoD forms. MoD forms. NATO forms. Someday, he thought, the Russians will forget bombs and simply invent a kind of micro-worm that they'll drop into our file cabinets. The worm will eat paper, breed more worms that eat paper, and before too long the file cabinets will be empty. Then the Russians won't have to attack. They'll simply walk ashore and take over because no one will have the correct paperwork to issue the orders to fight back.

So . . . do I call the MoD guy or not? Come on, make a decision. Heads or tails. Or do I wait and let the admiral worry about it? Pass the buck. Sure. That's the Navy way. Sorry, sir, not my table. I guess I'll wait for the admiral.

With nothing else to do, he divided the forms by category. One for each issuing command. Then he arranged those piles by dates. From there, he reconstructed the piles, this time matching all the forms for the same shipment. He even thought he was making progress, getting the stacks down, when Chief McIntyre showed up at his door yet again.

"You wouldn't believe how sloppy the filing system is on these things. Found them in the archives. Go way back to the early '70s. I thought I'd ask you how come they've never been coordinated. But it looks like they're getting themselves coordinated right now." He dropped the forms on Holbrook's desk. "Should keep you busy."

Holbrook grimaced. "You got a sailor who can help me with this?"

"No, sir. I got me two boys on leave and one on sick call. Anyway," he pointed, "I never let my sailors play with officers who don't wash their hands." With that he chuckled and left.

Glancing down, Holbrook saw the tips of his fingers on his right hand were black with ink. "Ah shit." He went to the men's room to wash. Then he returned to his office and sat down again.

Alice in Wonderland.

He stared at the pile of forms.

That's who I feel like. Alice in Wonderland. Or maybe it wasn't Alice herself. Which character was it who had to run twice as fast just to stay in the same place?

His phone rang.

He thought of picking it up and saying, the Mad Hatter here. Instead he answered, "Commander Holbrook."

An American woman's voice said softly, "If you take me to a movie tonight we can sit in the back row and smooch."

Oh Christ, he thought. When it rains it pours. "Hi."

"Where you been, sailor? Another port, another girl?"

"Sorry," he said. "I've been tied up."

"Mmmm, sounds wonderful."

"That's not the way I meant it."

"Too bad," she said. "Anyway, I'm serious about tonight. You know who is out of the country for three whole days. He says it's business but who knows for sure. Anyway, the nanny is sworn to secrecy."

"Gee, I'm really kind of snowed under . . ."

"Playing hard to get?"

"No. It's just been a tough week."

"It's only Tuesday. A movie will do you good. Come on, sailor, I don't bite."

He almost said, yes you do. "What's playing?"

"Dunno. I never emasculate my men by making decisions like that. Got a newspaper handy? If not, get one quick-like and commit yourself right now before I start thinking about much younger men."

He took a deep breath. "Okay. Wait a minute." He held the phone between his chin and his shoulder while he half-heartedly searched for the newspaper he knew was buried somewhere under the disarray of his desk. He found it, then fumbled with it to locate the films page. But nothing jumped out at him. Nothing caught his eye. Eventually he simply decided to tell her, "Listen . . . I don't think I want to go to the movies. I'm sorry. I got called before dawn this morning. Maybe we should do this another night."

"Early to bed and early to rise . . . if you know what I'm saying. In fact, that's a better idea. I'm glad you suggested it. I'll bring a pizza or something. See you at your place at say, six?"

He didn't want to bother but after a long pause he said, "Yeah. Okay." It was easier than trying to make her go away. "Okay. Six."

He put the phone down, tossed the newspaper aside, and then noticed that his hands were black with ink again. "Enough's enough. That's twice in five minutes." He went back to the men's room. Goddamned newsprint in Great Britain is so cheap it comes off all over you. He washed his hands and dried them. But as he stood with the roller towel in his hands he thought to himself, newsprint is one thing, but government forms shouldn't do that too. Not U.S. government forms.

Out of sheer curiosity, he started sorting through the forms on his desk, first looking for smudges and then rubbing his finger along the fronts of those forms, waiting for some of the ink to come off again on his finger. He started with the NATO forms. Nothing. Then the Naveur forms. Nothing. Then the MoD forms. Still nothing. Then the DoD forms. And now his finger occasionally picked up a lot of ink.

What a sloppy job, he decided. Imagine the Department of Defense accepting substandard work like that from the Government Printing Office.

He took a Kleenex and wiped the ink off his finger. But now he was intrigued by the poorly printed forms. So he rode the elevator down to the second basement.

Because he had never been down there before, Holbrook had to ask where the supplies store was. A Marine, on his sweaty way back from the small workout gym they nicknamed Iwo Jima, pointed to it.

Opening the door, Holbrook poked his head inside, and said, "Hello? Anyone home?"

No one answered.

He stepped up to the long wooden counter that separated a few square feet of blue linoleum from the large, dingy, windowless storage area where dozens of floor-to-ceiling shelves were covered in blank forms, typing paper, and scores of other administrative supplies. A sign on the counter in front of a bell read, "Please Ring Only Once."

He rang the bell once and waited.

When nothing happened, he rang the bell again.

"Didn't you see the sign, sir?" A woman's voice came from somewhere toward the rear of the room. "The sign says, please ring only once."

"I did," he said, waited for a couple more minutes, and when nothing happened he rang the bell a third time. "I'm kind of in a hurry," he announced.

"Everybody always tells me that," came her voice. "All right. All right. But I heard the bell the first time. So everybody says they're in a hurry. I hear that a hundred times a day." A tall, big-shouldered, dark-haired WAVE appeared from around the corner of a shelf, moved up to the counter and leaned next to the sign. Breathing noisily through her mouth, she stared at him like a bartender waiting for a drunk to pay for his beers.

Holbrook looked at her and realized, I've never seen this person before. Jeezus, this building could be filled with people I've never seen before, like her, hiding down here, below decks, like moles on a ship. Like Aquaviva. The guy they found on the *Kitty Hawk*. Poor bastard. His paperwork had gotten lost somewhere along the way and he lived below decks for five or six years without ever coming up for air. No one even knew he was there until the ship's shrink accidentally stumbled across him in the NCOs' chow line, saw a strange look in the man's eyes and bothered to ask what his billet was. Mole fever. They had to drag Aquaviva outside into the fresh air and then evac him off the *Kitty Hawk* in a strait-jacket. Mole fever. Once you've seen the special look of it you never forget it. And now here's another case of it in the middle of downtown London . . .

She broke into his thoughts. "You rang the bell, Commander. You rang the bell more than once even though the sign says . . ."

"Oh, sure." He snapped back to the moment. "Yeah . . . you got any DoD 3093s?"

She nodded. "Yep."

He waited for her to do something. When she didn't, he said, "Can I have some? Please. Say, ten?"

"Yep." But she didn't move.

"Today?"

"Yep," she said, now rubbing the top of the sign. "As soon as you hand me a DoD 101. Or even a Naveur 101."

"Why? I mean, what's a 101?"

"It's what you need. A DoD 101 or a Naveur 101. See, you can't requisition a form without a requisition form. So, if you want DoD 3093s, then I want a DoD 101 or a Naveur 101, whichever you prefer."

"A 101? I see." He shook his head. "A requisition form to requisition other forms." I ring the bell more than once so now she's going to prove who can do what to whom. "Well, how about if you give me the 3093s now and I send the 101 back down to you as soon as I get one from my office?"

"I have a better idea," she said. "How about as soon as you get a 101 from your office and fill it out properly and send it down here to me, I'll send the 3093s up there to you."

"Okay. Well . . ." He thought fast. "I have another idea. How about loaning me a single 101 for thirty seconds?"

"Why?" She showed that she was on to his scheme. "So that you can use that to order the 3093s? Sorry, that would mean my inventory is out by one 101. And my inventory can't ever be out, not even by a single form."

"No, no, no," he said, "I wouldn't want your inventory to be out, not even by a single form. I promise not to order a 3093."

She looked at him suspiciously. "All my forms have to be accounted for and if there's one missing . . ."

"Trust me. I just want to borrow a 101 for thirty seconds. Please?"

She pointed to the sign. "All day long people come down here and I ask them nicely to please ring the bell only once but they pound on that bell because they don't care about other people's feelings and at night when I go to sleep all I hear are bells . . ."

"I understand . . . and I apologize . . . I really do. But please . . . a single 101 . . . just to borrow."

"Every form's got to be accounted for," she warned before reaching under the counter and coming up with one form-requisition form.

"Thanks." He took a pen and filled out that 101, requesting two 101s.

"Two?" She didn't understand.

"Right. But now you only give me one of them. We'll count the one you've already loaned me as one. See? One and one makes two. Your inventory will work. *Capisce?*" Then he filled out the second 101 as a request for ten DoD 3093s. "And with this I'll take the forms I originally came down here for." He pushed that 101 across the counter toward her. "Thank you."

Back upstairs he inspected the new 3093s. He rubbed his fingers across them. He even licked the tips of his fingers and scraped them over the tops of the ten forms.

Nothing smeared.

Taking one of the slightly smudged 3093s, he compared it with a new 3093. The two seemed identical. The headings were the same. The spaces to be filled in were the same. On the bottom of each there was writing and a date. In the lower left-hand corner it said in tiny print, "DoD FORM 3093" with "Jan 1983" under it. Next to that was "Replaces Sep 74 Edition." In the lower right-hand corner was "☆GPO: 1983-337-459." The smudged forms were exactly the same as the new forms.

Just a poor printing job, he decided.

But why would the ink come off some and not the others?

The government printing office screwed up.

It probably isn't the first time.

How often have I heard someone say, close enough for government work?

He shrugged.

Yet the more he looked at the forms the more he found himself thinking that the government printing office isn't supposed to screw up like that. This isn't a British tabloid newspaper operation. This is the United States Government Printing Office, for Chrissakes.

He laid one form squarely on top of another, turned his desk lamp toward him, and held the pair up to the light. By overlaying the letters of the Department of Defense heading on both forms, then aligning the paper with the date on the bottom of both forms, he could check to be certain that the forms did indeed match letter for letter.

With a smudged 3093 on top of a new 3093, they seemed identical. But when he put the smudged one on the bottom, he noticed something very strange.

The letters in "Department of Defense" were just a fraction of an inch closer together on the new form than they were on the smudged form.

Nor did the two forms line up totally straight. The smudged form was just off-center.

He tried it again with a second copy of each form.

Everything was right except the spacing and the paper alignment.

Then his eyes lit on the bottom right-hand corner. "★GPO: 1983-337-459." First he looked at the smudged forms. Then he checked the new forms. The asterisk was different. On the new forms it was an open five-pointed star. On the smudged forms it was a closed five-pointed star.

Chapter Eleven

"I WILL NOW tell you the secret." Christopher Li'Ning took off his jacket and handed it to a young Chinese girl who draped it over her arm while she wrapped a starched blue and white apron around his waist. "Always begin with a very, very hot wok."

"A very, very hot wok?" A flashy, middle-aged, poorly toupee'd man named Joe Tyler poked his elbow into the side of the more tastefully dressed but otherwise starkly serious younger woman next to him. He tried to make a joke. "You must begin with a very, very hot wok. That's what the whactress said to the whishop."

The woman, whose name was Frances Pommeroy, forced a nervous chuckle.

The young Chinese girl, whose name was Han, went to hang up Li'Ning's coat.

Li'Ning himself merely gave Tyler a polite smile.

"Do you blokes really eat things like elephant trunk?" Tyler asked as Li'Ning lit the stove in the open kitchen that took up nearly a third of the small dining room. A low red Chinese table was set for three with a large bowl, a smaller bowl, a crystal wineglass, chopsticks and a linen napkin at each place.

"It's a great delicacy," Li'Ning said, putting the heavy, dark steel wok directly on top of the burner, adjusting the flame to exactly the right height, and then wiping the wok clean with a large brush. "So is bear's foot."

"So is rat." Tyler made a face. "Uch! And monkey's brain. And I hear you blokes even eat praying mantises. Or is it praying mantae. Chocolate-covered bugs. Thanks anyway. I'll stick to bangers and mash."

"The joy of Chinese cuisine is in the pursuit of texture, color and flavor." Li'Ning turned to Frances Pommeroy. "The important thing is to eat with all your senses and none of your prejudices."

Tyler tried to make another joke. "I thought you said the important thing was a very, very hot wok."

"So I did." Li'Ning smiled politely yet again. "So I did." He waved his hand across the Chinese frying pan to see if it was hot enough. Then he reached over to a work surface for three blue and white ceramic serving plates filled with food, all chopped into small pieces. "Chicken with cashews." He showed them. "Scallops with ginger. And stir-fried mixed vegetables. I think they're always referred to as monk's vegetables on Gerrard Street."

"Looks super," Frances Pommeroy said.

"Looks even good enough to eat." Tyler finished his Scotch and motioned toward Han that he'd like another. She filled his glass while he said, "Imagewise, would you rather see yourself as a Chinaman banker who cooks great or a great Chinaman cook who also banks?"

"I happen to be a Chinese native of British Hong Kong." Li'Ning decided the wok was finally hot enough to add the peanut oil. "We don't usually call ourselves Chinamen."

"Ah." Frances Pommeroy made an obvious attempt to cover her boss's *faux pas*. "Tell me, where did you learn to use a wok? At your mother's knee? It can't be all that easy to cook with."

He poured the chicken pieces into the oil and they sizzled wonderfully. "A wok's beauty lies in the fact that it spreads the heat evenly over all the food you're cooking. You would hardly think it to be revolutionary. However, because it comes from the East, it has been marketed by men—and women, I add—in the West as something strangely exotic. Yet, isn't that what marketing in the West is all about? Exotica. Imagine that. Oriental fantasies in the shape of a frying pan.''

"Wish we had the account." Tyler poked Pommeroy again. "Eh, Frances? Wish we had landed the Chinese frying-pan account?"

There was a single knock on the door and a young Chinese man poked his head inside.

Li'Ning saw Peter and motioned to Han to take over. "If you will kindly excuse me. I will be right back."

In the hallway Peter explained, I just received a call from the Gerrard Street Association to say it's fine for May 8. They were worried about the costs but I assured them we were paying everything. Li'Ning was pleased. He asked, what else. Peter read from a list. J. A. Lin has been trying to reach you about Wainwright Tokyo. Also, Mr. Risdey at Hill Sam, Mr. Schoop at the Royal Bank, and Mr. Gresham from Lloyds of London. Gold is down three cents, the dollar is steady on thin trading, the pound is falling for the third consecutive day against the deutschmark. Where's the yen? Li'Ning asked. Peter quoted the figures. Anything else? Yes, you've got a meeting at two o'clock to talk about the Sao Paolo and Tokyo issue. Also D. F. Lee and R. Lee both want to see you as soon as the two o'clock meeting is done. Li'Ning said, thank you, and went back into the dining room. "I'm terribly sorry."

"Quite all right." Tyler gestured. "But Frances here says the suspense is killing her. So it looks as though I'm the one elected to ask. Did you, in the end, get that ceramic thing you wanted to buy? I told Frances obviously you must have because you said you had to speak to us right away. So, am I right? Did you buy that ceramic thing?"

"The ceramic thing?" Li'Ning moved up to the stove, checking to see if the rice was steaming, and surveying Han's stir-frying technique. She dropped the cashew nuts into the wok. And again there was a lot of sizzling. "Lovely odor, isn't it?" He added a few drops of soy sauce. "Please, Mr. Tyler, it isn't just any ceramic thing. It happens to be a rather ancient and extremely beautiful ginger jar.''

"That's what I meant," Tyler said. "I'm sure there's a difference and believe me, Mr. Li'Ning, Frances and I are going to learn absolutely everything there is to learn about ceramic ginger jars. We always do our homework at the agency. I always say, there is never a substitute for solid research. Now, this ceramic ginger jar that you just bought, was it expensive? I'll bet you really went first-class. What did you have to pay for it?''

"It was . . ." Li'Ning thought about how he should phrase it. "It was pricey, yes. However, considering the excellence of the piece, no, I would not say it was over-priced. I was . . . or rather, my bank was prepared to pay a great deal more for it than we in fact did. Even to the point of perhaps paying too much. I was totally determined to buy it.''

"How about a peek at it?" Tyler rubbed his hands together in expectation. "Let's see what this pricey thing looks like.''

"In due course. In the meantime I've had my secretary type a slightly edited version of the auction house catalog description.'' He took an envelope off the counter and deliberately handed it to Frances Pommeroy. "This will give you an idea of what it is.''

Han lifted the wok off the stove and poured the stir-fried chicken and cashew nuts onto a serving plate. Li'Ning asked her in Mandarin to serve some rice while he began cooking the scallops in fresh ginger. "Sorry," he apologized for having lost his train of thought. "Cooking always distracts me. Perhaps that's why I love it so much. What were we talking about? Oh, yes. Next week, once I've seen your rough draft of the news release, I'll arrange to have you inspect and photograph the ginger jar. Naturally that will have to be done here as I am reluctant to let it out of my hands.''

"Of course.'' Tyler volunteered, "Frances will take care of the photographer. And she'll get you a draft of the news release by . . . how's Friday?''

The phone rang.

"Excuse me.'' He lifted the extension and moved away from the wok so that Han could finish cooking the scallops.

It was the man who handled the bank's foreign exchange activities in London. They spoke Mandarin. It looks as if the Bank of England is just now coming in to support the pound against the deutschmark. Our position is too long in DM. I'm getting us out of there and also want to start heavily shorting the yen.

That will be fine. Keep me posted. Li'Ning pushed the button to terminate the call, then dialed Peter's extension. Still in Mandarin he said, "Cancel that two o'clock meeting. Tell Bernie Loomis that D. F. Lee informs me the B of E is coming in to support the pound against the DM. We said £11 million for that Sao Paolo issue. But if interest rates climb half a point, we can do better elsewhere. Tell Loomis I want him to either renege on our part of it, or pass it off to someone else. Do it right now, this very minute, because if the B of E is indeed coming in, everyone will know about it in the next ten minutes."

Peter said he would take care of it immediately. Li'Ning started to hang up. But Peter caught him just in time. "Oh, the *Daily Telegraph* rang. Their Arts and Antiques correspondent. They wanted to know if they could photograph the ginger jar."

"How did they hear about it?"

"I have no idea."

"Find out. And when you do, tell them no photos yet. Don't mention anything about May 8th, but hint to them that something will be happening soon and we'll see that they're kept informed. I really do not want this publicized too soon."

Li'Ning returned to the wok. "Please excuse the interruptions." He stirred for a few seconds. "It looks to me as if the scallops with ginger are ready." All that was left to do was the vegetables, but Han was managing well so he didn't interfere. He lifted a bottle of Rosé d'Anjou out of an ice bucket, opened it, invited them to the table and poured them each a glassful. "Please," he toasted. "To your health."

"To your ginger jar." Tyler sat down. "Kind of low, isn't it? Probably kill my back but the food smells great. Anyway, is that all you want us to promote for you? I have to confess that neither Frances nor I quite understand exactly what kind of publicity you're looking for. I mean, if you just want some diary mentions, you know, in the Sunday papers and maybe a picture placed somewhere to show the world that you've bought this ceramic ginger jar . . . ."

"Not quite," Li'Ning said. "No. We want something very

important in the way of press coverage. But it all has to happen at just the right moment. Timing here is paramount."

"So, it ties into a certain date?" Tyler asked.

Li'Ning said, "Yes."

"Well, I'm afraid I've got to tell you," Tyler confessed, "if it's less than three or four months away, forget it. We'll never get the magazine coverage. Can't be done."

"Perhaps I should qualify what I've said." Li'Ning directed his comments to Frances Pommeroy. "Consider this for your own background information." She nodded okay. "Now, you are of course aware that in 1997 the colony of Hong Kong will revert back to the People's Republic of China. Needless to say, as a Hong Kong–based bank, we have more than just a passing interest in what will happen. We are more than just a little concerned about the future of Hong Kong as a major financial market. The ginger-jar is therefore a gift from my bank to the people of China. You might even call it an offering. Perhaps the approach we would want to take in our publicity is that we're trying to show our good intentions by helping, in a small way, to repatriate some of the nation's treasures."

"I was just thinking." Tyler raised his eyebrows and winked at Frances Pommeroy . . .

"Excuse me." Li'Ning turned to Han and said to her in Mandarin, "You may serve us now."

She did.

Li'Ning continued, "We are planning to make a formal presentation of the ginger jar at a street banquet—you know, a Chinese street party—on the eighth of May. It's very important that we keep to that date and just as important that no one knows about this too soon. We're going to take over Gerrard Street . . ."

"I was thinking," Tyler interrupted. "It sounds to me like the truth is more along the lines of you're a pretty shrewd capitalist who is paving his way toward a friendly welcoming handshake the day the communists take over."

Li'Ning reached for his chopsticks. There was no polite smile this time. He let Tyler's remark slip by. *"Bon appetit."*

Chapter
Twelve

THE UNITED STATES Government Printing Office takes up the entire block along North Capitol and H Streets in Washington, D.C.

Providing printing and binding services for every department of the federal government—from farm reports on how to control the boll weevil to children's literature, from the Congressional Record to all of the approximately 162,300 different forms in use at any given time by the various branches of the U.S. military—it is in volume of output, in printing machines operated and in printers employed, the largest, most important printing works in the world.

Using a DoD line patched through the U.S. Embassy across the street directly to the Pentagon, Richard Holbrook asked to be connected with the main switchboard at the Government Printing Office. When the operator answered, he explained that he wanted some information about a DoD form. The operator gave him the Public Information Office.

"I'm ringing from CinCNaveur in London," he said. Immediately, the secretary at the Public Information Office asked him to hold on. After nearly a minute she came back on the line to say she was having the call transferred to the Public Affairs Office. When they heard who he was, they had the call transferred to the Navy Liaison Office at the GPO. An ensign there said his boss wasn't in yet . . . "It's only just after 0800, sir, and he doesn't usually get in until

0815 or even sometimes 0820 . . .'' But to be helpful he told Holbrook he'd have the call transferred to the DoD Liaison Office. After speaking to three people there, Holbrook's call was finally taken by a man who introduced himself as B. Grant Farmer, Lt.-Colonel, USAF.

"Air Force?" Holbrook asked. "I'm sorry, Colonel, I think I want the DoD liaison . . ."

"In case you forgot," Farmer replied, "the Air Force happens to be part of the DoD. So that makes me the DoD liaison officer. Now, what can I do for you?"

"Well . . ." He felt exasperated, having been passed along to so many people. "There's a form we use at CinCNaveur that's called DoD 3093."

Farmer cut in, "This isn't something we should be discussing on the telephone."

"It's all right. I'm not looking for any classified information. I'm only asking about a blank form that is not classified . . ."

"I will neither confirm nor deny that the form in question is a classified form, but I would advise you to put your query in writing. Anyway, Commander, I shouldn't be talking to you for two reasons. The first is because of security. The second is because of the chain of command. You should address your query to the Navy Liaison here, and if it concerns the DoD . . ."

"Hey, Colonel? Colonel, listen. It's a very simple question I have. Really, if you'd just hear me out . . ."

Farmer said, "I'm sorry. I can't be giving out information like this over the phone. I have no idea who you are. I have no idea what you want. For all I know you could be a Russian spy trying to get classified information. I mean, get serious, how do I know you are who you say you are?"

"Colonel, how many Russian spies phone you at eight in the morning your time to talk about a printing job?"

"I'm sorry, Commander. It's got to be in writing." Click. Just like that, B. Grant Farmer, Lt.-Colonel, USAF, hung up.

Russian spies. Holbrook thought for a moment. That's the way to handle this. What would a Russian spy do? He grabbed the phone again and asked the Embassy operator to get him back to the Government Printing Office switchboard. I'll show them Russian spies. When the Government Printing Office operator answered, Holbrook told her, "Quality control." It was worth a shot.

"Quality control?"

There must be an office called quality control. Every government department has a quality control office. All governments are very big on quality control. It's offices like that which keep loads of people employed. "That's right," he said in his most authoritative voice, "quality control. Military forms. This is CinCNaveur in London calling."

"Yes, sir," the operator said. There were some clicks . . . a phone rang . . . and a woman answered, sure enough, with, "Quality Control, DoD, Miss Spangles speaking, may I help you, sir?"

This one is for all the Russian spies. "Holbrook here," he said in that very official-sounding voice. "CinCNaveur. Who's in charge?"

"Miss Jimenez, sir."

"Get her on the line, please."

Miss Spangles said, "Yes, sir," and an instant later another woman came on the phone to say, "This is Juanita Jimenez."

"Holbrook here. CinCNaveur in London. What's going on with your DoD 3093s? Quality control, indeed. Miss Jimenez, this has got to stop."

She dared, "What has got to stop, sir?"

"The forms smudge." He knew how to handle her. He knew that no one ever challenges authority. That's what Russian spies would do. "Can you hear me? Is the connection clear enough? They smudge."

"Smudge?"

"Roger. I repeat, smudge. S-M-U-D-G-E." He tried to think back to his high-school Spanish. "Smudge as in . . . no, I can't remember what it is in Spanish."

"Tiznar," she answered curtly. "But I do speak English."

"Okay, smudge as in tiznar. Now . . . what I want to know, Miss Jimenez, is this—are DoD forms supposed to smudge?"

"Why would you . . . ? Oh, no, I get it. Is this some sort of joke?"

He wondered what he would think if someone called him at eight in the morning and asked the same kind of thing. "No, this is not a joke. Miss Jimenez, this is deadly serious. The ink has come off on my hands . . ."

"Sir, this would be the first time in the twenty-seven months that I have been assigned to this office that anyone has complained about . . . about smudging forms . . ."

That's what he wanted to hear. "I see. Well, I'll send you the forms and a complaint through channels." It struck him as an official-sounding thing to say. What a Russian spy would say.

"Yes, please," she said. "If you can locate GPO Form 1206 D . . . that's D as in . . ."

"Tiznar?" he asked.

"No," she said. "D as in December."

"GPO 1206 D as in dog. Or D as in delta. Never D as in December. Roger. I'll get it right away and forward it on through channels."

"In triplicate please," she said.

"Yes. Triplicate. Of course. Thank you. Now . . . next item. The copyright star in the bottom right corner. Is it an open star or a closed star?"

"Is it what?"

"Open or closed," he said with just the right touch of annoyance in his voice. "Is the star open inside or closed inside? I mean, should there be a white space in the middle of the star or is it always filled in with ink?"

"I don't . . ." She paused. "Is this Jim Ritchie? Jim, is that you playing a joke . . ."

"No, this is not Jim Ritchie," he barked. That's the way the Russian spies would do it. "This is an official call from CinCNaveur and I need an official answer a.s.a.p. about the copyright star in the lower right hand corner of all DoD forms."

"Yes, sir," she said. "If you'll just wait a moment I'll check." She put him on hold. If someone called me at eight in the morning asking questions like this, I'd have hung up on them a long time ago. "Sir?" she came back on the line several minutes later. "I've checked on your query about the copyright star. On all DoD forms issued after May 1979 the star is standard."

"Well, Miss Jimenez, does that mean open or closed?"

She told him, "Always open."

He said, "Thank you very much," and hung up.

So much for being a Russian spy in search of information.

Tiznar. To smudge. Not the kind of word that used to pop up on high-school Spanish vocabulary tests. But it's probably worth a good score in Mexican Scrabble.

It took hours to spread the forms out wherever he could find a place for them. He covered his desk, all three of the chairs in the room, and even the top of the filing cabinet. Then he arranged the forms by date. Then he collated them by specific shipment. Each shipment had a code number to identify it, but that number was in a different place on each different form. It took a lot of time just trying to find those numbers. Then, depending on the issuing authority of the form, there were various prefixes and suffixes surrounding the numbers. Some shipments were only Naveur and NATO. Some were DoD, Naveur and MoD. Some were NATO and MoD. Some shipments came from the States, passed through the U.K. and then went on to NATO members like Holland or Belgium. Some came from Germany, through England, on their way back to the States. He grouped each shipment separately, paper-clipping all of the pertinent forms together, and piled them out of his way on the floor. Little by little he worked through the masses of paper scattered around his office.

He didn't realize how late it was until Bob Wagner stormed into his office. "Are you out of your fucking mind!"

Holbrook flinched. "What?"

Wagner threatened him with a pointed finger. "I'll have your ass for this. You really screwed up this time. The admiral is furious."

"What are you babbling about?" Suddenly he remembered his twelve-thirty appointment. His watch said 4:40. The admiral. "Ah shit." His phone rang.

"I spotted you as a wash-out the first day you arrived on station," Wagner went on.

Holbrook picked up the phone.

"Hey," Camille Parrot said. "You better get into the old man's office right away. He's livid."

"Listen, I'm sorry I forgot my twelve-thirty appointment . . ."

Wagner was still speaking to him. "It's because you forgot your brains. Because you clued the Brits in about the missing PuN van when you were specifically ordered to keep your trap shut."

At the same time Parrot explained, "The ambassador just got a call from the British Foreign Office. It seems the Ministry of Defense has asked them to file an official complaint and the admiral has just gotten flak from the ambassador about it. He's up a wall."

Wagner continued, ". . . because you blatantly disobeyed orders . . ."

"I'll be right there," Holbrook said to Parrot, hung up, then demanded of Wagner, "Get off my ass." He came from behind his desk, tripping over some papers on the floor, shoving Wagner out of the way before hurrying down the hall.

Miss Cecilia pointed to the admiral's office. "You had a twelve-thirty and I covered for you. It won't happen again. This time you're expected."

He stepped inside and saluted. "Sir."

Roth, alone in his office, glared at him. "Dad, what the hell kind of bullshit is going on here?"

"Admiral, I don't know. Camille Parrot just told me . . ."

Now Wagner arrived, with Parrot fast on his heels. "Sir"—Wagner saluted—"I knew this would get out of hand. I could have told you that this morning."

"Admiral," Parrot interrupted. "The ambassador would like a full briefing in twenty minutes. His office if you don't mind, sir."

Roth looked sternly at Holbrook. "I've got twenty minutes so you've got ten."

"Sir . . . I have not told the Brits anything about the missing PuN van."

"Yeah, well, someone clued them in," Wagner said. "In this very room, this very morning, there were only two flag officers, me and you. They didn't do it. Camille here didn't know anything about it until a few minutes ago, so he couldn't have done it. I know I didn't. That, sonny boy, leaves you sucking hind tit. And I'm sure the admiral will remember that you were specifically ordered not to inform them, which means you blatantly disobeyed those orders."

"Admiral," he appealed to Roth, "you know me better than that. Yes, I think we should have told them this morning. But no, I do not disobey orders."

Wagner wasn't going to let up. "You wanted to tell them. You tried to convince us to tell them. I stood right here this morning and watched you. Damn, Admiral, I knew this was going to happen."

Now Roth asked Holbrook, "Who is Matthew Boston?"

"Boston?" It's hitting the fan, Holbrook thought. He answered, "Mr. Boston is my contact at the MoD, sir."

"Did you speak with him at any time today? And if you did, what did you tell him?"

Holbrook took a deep breath. I blew it. I got caught up with those forms and I blew it. "He rang me, sir, and asked if there was something happening. The gist of the conversation was that he suspected something was wrong and wanted me to confirm it. I absolutely denied it."

Roth said, "And you kept that conversation to yourself?"

Holbrook told himself not to turn away. He told himself not to look down at the floor. He told himself, stare right into the admiral's eyes. Brief him straight. Don't look guilty. Stand tall. Defend your turf. "Yes, sir."

"Have you spoken to anyone else or said anything else to your MoD contact? Do you have any reason to believe that anyone else might have known about the missing van or suspected it?"

"No, sir," he said. "I repeat, sir, my MoD contact phoned me, asked me if there was anything wrong, I told him no, and that was all."

"Why didn't you inform me?"

Do I say, I tried to get in to see you but Miss Cecilia blocked the way? Do I say, I forgot that I was supposed to be here at twelve-thirty. "I didn't think it was important, sir. And by the time I realized . . . I'm sorry, sir. You went out shortly after I got the call and I've been tied up until just now."

There was a pause.

Wagner filled the void. "Admiral, this never would have happened had we done this thing the proper way. My people could have contained it. Instead it's about to become a diplomatic incident . . ."

Roth motioned to Wagner to wait. Then he said to Holbrook, "I'll deal with you later."

Holbrook stood where he was. It's Wagner. This is Wagner trying to get to me. Goddamnit, why didn't I keep my ass covered? That's the first thing you learn in the Navy. Watch your ass. "Yes, sir."

Roth saluted.

Holbrook left the admiral's office.

"Damnit," he said loudly as soon as he was in the hallway. Fucking bastard Wagner. I should have kept my ass covered. I should have known that Wagner would jump on me the first chance he got. Son of a bitch. Goddamned fucking son of a bitch!

He went downstairs, disregarding anyone he passed in the hallways who nodded hello. He had nothing to say to anyone. He just wanted to get the hell away from there and be alone. He handed his badge in at the Marine guard station and went to the building's front door. Shit. It was still raining outside. Shit. I left my hat and rain gear upstairs. He looked at his watch. The fucking pubs are still closed. Goddamnit. But there was a covered area outside where he could stand without getting soaked. So he went there, moved off to a corner and leaned against the wall. Goddamned fucking Wagner.

The rain was steady. Traffic in North Audley Street was snarled, the way it always snarled in London every time there was any rain. People hurried by, hunched down, hands on their hats to keep them on, carrying umbrellas, sidestepping puddles along the curb where they tried to cut across the street.

I'm gonna get even with him. The bastard. Someday.

Somewhere. Somehow. I should have protected my ass. Don't look back 'cause someone might be gaining on you. Satchel Paige, you was wrong. If you don't look back, they'll run one straight up your tailpipe.

After a while he got annoyed with all the people walking past him, in and out of the building, always stopping to ask, you all right, Commander? Anyway, he decided, he was hungry. So he went downstairs to the cafeteria. Do me a couple or three eggs scrambled, with crisp bacon, please. Sorry, the man behind the counter said, no breakfast after eleven-thirty. Only hot dishes and sandwiches. All right, Holbrook tried, give me a scrambled-egg sandwich with bacon and hold the toast. Sorry, the fellow said, that only works for Jack Nicholson. Holbrook stared at the man. What are you talking about? *Five Easy Pieces,* the man replied. Remember? Jack Nicholson. Hold the toast. Shit, Holbrook said out loud. He bought a cup of black coffee with extra sugar and went back to his office. He slammed his door shut—they'll all think I've gone home—before reaching into the bottom drawer of his desk to bring out a bottle of dark Jamaican rum. He poured a healthy shot into the too-sweet black coffee and drank it all in one hot gulp.

The coffee burned the back of his throat. Then the rum got to his head. For a few seconds he felt dizzy. He shut his eyes.

Eventually Wagner and Roth and Parrot and everyone else simply melted away.

Eventually he went back to sorting through the forms.

After he had them all arranged, he started checking the DoD 3093s, looking for open stars and closed stars. He had DoD forms going all the way back to 1976. But the new 3093s only came into service in January 1983, so he decided, at least for the time being, to disregard everything logged before then.

A shipment dated 16 June 1983 was the first one where the DoD 3093 had a closed star.

He set the file aside.

The following shipment had an open-star 3093 but the next two had closed-star 3093s.

By the time he got through all the shipment files, there were nine forms with closed stars.

Putting all the others aside, he concentrated on those.

He took a Kleenex, licked it and started smudging the forms. Every one of them smeared.

On a pad of yellow legal paper, he listed the points of departure for the PuN runs and the warehouses where they had been stored and the points along the route where they had passed out of American hands and the points where they had come back into American hands. He also listed all the figures on all the forms . . . shipment numbers, codes, shipment weights, volumes, every possible number or amount that could mean anything.

Then, using a secure phone line, he called every nuclear safety officer at every station named anywhere on those nine closed-star 3093s. When he got each of them on the line he asked them to confirm all the dates and figures from their file copies. He wrote down all the information they fed back to him. It took a couple of hours, but two dozen calls later he had several pages covered in numbers.

Adding. Subtracting. Cross-checking. Backtracking. He wanted to see that everything matched perfectly.

He wanted to be certain that in every case, the times and dates of departures and arrivals matched the information on the closed-star DoD 3093s.

He wanted to be certain that in every case, the amount of PuN shipped by the originator matched the information on the closed-star DoD 3093s.

He wanted to be certain that in every case, the amount of PuN received at the end of the shipment matched the information on the closed-star DoD 3093s.

Adding. Subtracting. Cross-checking. Backtracking.

Everything seemed to be in order.

But something felt wrong.

His gut feeling told him something wasn't quite right. So now he took all the separate figures and started combining them, playing with the totals, moving numbers around, adding up totals shipped and then matching that with totals received.

The first time he did it his sums were off by 270 grams.

My mistake, he reasoned. So he did it again. This time he used his pocket calculator and scrupulously went through the figures, comparing the long columns on his written notes with the amounts taken directly off the original DoD 3093s.

And again, he was wrong by 270 grams.

I don't get it. He went over the figures a third time. But the result was the same. He listed the figures another way—horizontally this time, not vertically—so he could compare the subtotals per shipment. And now he could see that there were thirty grams missing per shipment. My math is right. Something else is wrong. Thirty grams. Just a shade over an ounce. Thirty grams. On shipments of from six to twenty-four kilos, not counting the heavy lead containers, thirty grams is a negligible amount. But added together that means somewhere along the line, just about half a pound of plutonium nitrate has gone astray.

No, he decided, it's got to be my arithmetic. I copied something wrong.

He did it a fourth time, just to be absolutely certain. The answer was still 270 grams. Then he started checking back to the DoD 3093s that were open-starred from June 1983. In every case other nuclear materials were being accounted for, including cruise missiles into Greenham Common. The closed-star DoD 3093s were all PuN-only runs. These are nine shipments of only plutonium nitrate. These are the only nine forms that smudge. Each of these nine PuN runs had at one point or another passed out of U.S. Navy hands and through foreign hands before coming back to the U.S. Navy.

He sat back to think about that.

An ounce at a time.

Acceptable losses.

Materials lost in transport.

A small enough percentage.

Jesus H. Christ, he said. Thirty grams. No one would ever think twice. The way these forms are arranged, no one would even notice it unless they were looking for it.

Except he noticed it. Thirty grams missing per time. An ounce for every closed-star DoD 3093. And only on closed-star DoD 3093s. And only on closed-star DoD 3093 shipments that have at some time or another passed through foreign hands.

And in every case, in every single one of those nine shipments, the foreign hands have been . . .

Now he understood.

Oh my God, the British are stealing it.

Chapter
Thirteen

A HIJACKING, BOSTON SAID to the picture of Syd Barnes staring back at him from the cover of the book as it sat in the middle of his otherwise neatly arranged desk.

There's been a hijacking of nuclear materials on British soil and the United States Navy is trying to cover it up.

Syd Barnes didn't seem to care.

Boston's initial reaction was anger.

Hah. I won't let them get away with this.

But when he thought about it, he knew that he wasn't angry for any of the obvious reasons. He was angry because this had happened at the worst possible time. Why now? he wanted to know. Why couldn't that lorry have been hijacked six months from now . . . or six months ago?

As he thought about it his anger turned to determination. I'm not going to let the U.S. Navy get away with this.

He looked at the already addressed envelope next to *Syd*.

Nigel will have to wait. I'll finish the book tonight and send it off to him in the morning.

Tonight. I wonder if Nigel can meet me. He rang his son. "If I stay in town this evening, can you come and dine with me?"

"Dine?"

"That's what I said. Dinner."

"In London?"

"Of course, in London."

"Tonight."

"Yes, tonight." He said to Nigel, "I'll be at the Reform. Meet me there at, say, seven-thirty."

"Seven-thirty?"

"Yes. Meet me at the Reform. You've been there before so don't ask me where it is. Seven-thirty. All right?" He didn't give his son a chance to say anything more. "I'll see you this evening."

Switching lines, he got a dial tone and called home. It rang engaged. Come on, he said out loud, get off the line. He pushed the "R" button so that the number redialed automatically. It was still engaged. Damn repeater button never works. He buzzed Mrs. Fitzgerald, "Would you please be kind enough to get my wife on the line. Thank you."

She said, "Right away, sir."

He reached for the copy of *Syd* so that he'd remember to take it with him. I'll show it to Nigel but I won't let him have it until I finish it, no matter what he says . . . and just that quickly Mrs. Fitzgerald buzzed. "Your wife for you on the second line."

Shaking his head—it's a British Telecom plot—he took the phone. "Hello dear, how do you feel?"

"Hello, Buster." His wife slurred her words slightly whenever she was tired, the left side of her face never having recovered. "I'm not very well just now. I was better this morning. Is it raining in London? It's raining here."

"Yes dear, it's raining here too."

"Buster, I rang you because I had to find out, did you take your raincoat this morning?"

The medication made her forget things. "Yes, dear."

"Well, Buster, remember to wear it when you come home tonight. Don't leave it in the office again . . ."

"About tonight, dear." He didn't want to upset her, but staying in town and seeing Nigel was a good idea. "That's just it, dear. I don't think I can get home tonight. Something has come up at the office and I shall be at the club. And I've invited Nigel to join me for dinner. That will be nice, won't it?"

"But Buster, you promised you'd be home tonight. That's why we told Janice and Warren that they could bring the children tonight. You know I can't handle them when you're not here . . .''

Our children. And their children. "Yes, dear, I know I did . . ."

"I even baked. I made a lemon tart this morning. Mary had to help me peel the lemons, but I did all the rest of it myself."

He really didn't have the time to worry about this now. "I'm sorry, dear, I truly am. Something has come up. You can always ring Janice and tell her not to come. She'll understand. And as for the children . . . Denise dear, they are only two and four years old. Frankly, they don't have to understand anything. It might be best too if you rested this evening. You sound tired to me. Now, I really must go. I'll ring you tonight. Please put Mary on, will you?"

"All right, Buster." She sounded very disappointed. "Just a minute."

Mary took the phone and said, "Mr. Boston? Will you be home for supper? Mrs. Boston baked a tart for you and your daughter and her husband and your grandchildren."

"No," he said. "I can't come home tonight." Why did he have to make so many explanations. Didn't anybody else realize what had just happened. "Mary, tell me, how is Mrs. Boston today?"

"She baked a lovely tart for you," Mary said.

"Oh, no." He knew the code. "Is she giving you a hard time again? Well, she has to go for her treatment and that's all there is to it. So that's why she baked the pie and that's why she's upset that I can't come home tonight. That's why she told Janice to bring the children over so she can get out of going to her treatment. Is that why?"

"Yes, Mr. Boston," Mary said. "A really lovely tart."

"All right." But he had other things to worry about. "Mary, when she takes her nap ring me back. I'll be at the office all day. Ring me back here and I'll ring Doctor Kettlestone." Why today, he wanted to know, why is this all happening to me today? "I have to go. Ring me later when she's taking her nap."

Mary said, "Yes, Mr. Boston. You have a nice lunch. 'Bye now."

As soon as he hung up he realized he'd forgotten to ask Mary about the electric blender. Oh well, they must have found it or Denise would have told me.

He rang the Reform Club to reserve a room. "Oh, and a table for two in the dining room at eight."

"Yes, sir," said Martin, the on-duty assistant manager. "By the way, sir, there is some post just arrived for you."

"Post?" Hah. Finally. "One letter or two?"

"I believe there are two items. I'll check for you sir . . . yes, it's one letter, sir, and one large envelope."

"Thank you," he said, knowing what those letters were, and thinking to himself, they certainly took long enough. For the life of me I can't imagine why first-class post should take that long. It's totally unreasonable. The mail has got slower and slower as the transport used to carry it has got faster and faster. In the days of horses and stagecoaches, a letter across town took half a day. Now with jumbo jets and the Concorde it takes four days. "Thank you, Martin, I'll pick them up this evening."

Martin said, "Very well, sir." And Boston said, "Thank you," again. And Martin repeated, "Yes, sir, very well."

Boston finally hung up. I'll be here all day if I don't because Martin is much too polite to ring off before a member does.

Now he rang his boss at the MoD. "Sir Donald, please."

"Sorry," the secretary said in that silly, girlish voice Boston always found so particularly annoying. "I'm afraid that Sir Donald is in a meeting. I'm afraid you'll have to ring back."

"How much longer will he be?"

"Sorry," she whined. "I'm afraid I don't really know."

I can't believe she always speaks like that. Would she dare sound so foolish when she's out with her boyfriend? What would she sound like if someone woke her in the middle of the night, before she remembered to put on that appalling voice? Some of the girls at the MoD used to think it was smart to have a foreign accent. Now they think it's smart to whine. And why is she always afraid? he wondered. "I'll come right over. It's rather important."

"Sorry," she said for the third time, "I'm afraid you may have to wait to get in to see him."

"Please tell him I'm on my way."

"Yes, sir," she said. "I'll tell him." And just as he was about to be polite and say, "Thank you," she hung up. Just like that, she put the receiver down and the phone clicked in his ear.

Hah. All MoD secretaries should be sent for their training to Martin at the Reform. Martin would teach them a thing or two. He'd whip them into shape. But then Boston changed his mind. No, it might not be such a good idea after all. Bad manners drive out good. An all-too-likely result might be that Martin would begin to preface everything with, "I'm afraid . . ." while at the same time the MoD secretaries would start to think of themselves as civilized. Life at the MoD would instantly become insufferable. It was horrifying enough to imagine Martin speaking like an MoD secretary. But the possibility of being subjected to whatever greater-than-usual delusions of grandeur that would surely run wild through the MoD typing pools . . .

Good God in heaven, he said. Perish the very thought.

He couldn't get the girl's terrible whining voice out of his ears.

I'm afraid . . . I'm afraid . . . I'm afraid, he said to the picture of Syd. Why is she always afraid of everything? Why are working girls always so afraid?

Still mumbling, he stood up, took his raincoat, left the office and walked through the rain up Whitehall to the MoD.

The Ministry of Defense is in the center of Whitehall, on the site where King Henry VIII's palace stood until it burned to the ground in 1698. Matthew Boston came in through the south portico, under the old Air Ministry insignia, showed his pass and headed directly toward Sir Donald's office on the eighth floor.

Next to a bank of lifts, a large yellow Know Your MoD sign caught his eye. It was stapled onto a bulletin board, with the words "Did You Know . . ." in dayglo green. "Did you know . . . that the 3000 people who work here handle some 200,000 items of mail every week, and fill more than 1000 sacks of wastepaper in the same period?"

Under it, someone had inked in the words, "So that's what we do here."

Boston raised his eyebrows. That someone had defaced government property displeased him. That the MoD would bother counting sacks of wastepaper and then brag about it was hardly to his liking either. But the thing that truly irked him was that he had to admit, graffiti sometimes made a point.

He stepped into Sir Donald's outer office. "Is he available?"

The secretary with the awful voice looked up from a paperback novel she was reading. "I'm afraid he's tied up in a long meeting."

"I'll wait," Boston said, sitting down on the couch next to her desk. If it got too long he could always insist she interrupt.

She shrugged—"If you like"—and went straight back to her book.

Two minutes later, Sir Donald's flat, balding head appeared from behind his door. The girl instantly hid her book. He told her, "I'm out of there now," then spotted Boston. "Buster? Lovely surprise. Should ring first. Do come in." He mentioned to his secretary, "No calls."

A long meeting, indeed. Boston went into Sir Donald's room. "I did ring."

Sir Donald didn't seem to care. "Tea, old boy?"

"No, thanks," Boston said, looking jealously at Sir Donald's view of the Thames. "I popped by because we've got a serious problem."

"Not before lunch."

"Sorry to say it's so." And he proceeded to explain about the missing U.S. Navy van and the possible cover-up.

"Serious indeed," Sir Donald said, now leaning on the window ledge. "Lovely view, what? Never get tired of it. Helps me think. Too bad there isn't more barge traffic along the river. Always like watching barges. I envy the German Defense Minister. He's got a view of the Rhine. Wonderful barges along the Rhine. Too bad about the Thames."

"I used to have a view of Westminster," Boston reminded him.

"Oh, yes." Sir Donald nodded. "Pity about that. Now . . ." He reached across his desk to check his appointment book. "We shan't let the Americans take advantage of us like this. No need for my Minister to get involved. Being new and all that. Still has so much to learn. Needn't worry, though, I'll send him a memo. But I can see straight away this isn't his kind of problem. Prefers heavy equipment like ships and tanks. Very good with tanks. I'd say they were his favorite. I'd say they were everyone's favorite since it's still bad form around here to play with helicopters, eh, Buster? But this sort of business . . . no, it's not him. Pity really that these things pop up before lunch. I'm due out in a few minutes. Tell you what, old boy, why not let the F.O. handle this one? Good idea, what? No sense getting one's hands muddied. After all, the Yanks are on our side. These sorts of things have a nasty way of coming round again to haunt one. What do you say we let the F.O. boys have it so that, you know, just in case anything goes awry they can take the blame?" He reached for his phone and dialed a number. "Toppy? Donald here. Sending my man Boston over right away. Serious matter. Should protest and all that. See you Sunday on the first tee, no doubt. Right." When he hung up he jotted a note and pushed it across the desk to Boston. "Harold Topping. You know him, don't you?"

"Topping? Why, yes," Boston said. "Knew him in Hong Kong. Played against him. Used to be a decent spin bowler."

"That's him." Sir Donald grinned. "Of course. Good old Toppy."

"You know, I hit a six off him once." Boston remembered Topping very well. "He worked at Government House when we lived there. That's right. I hit a six off him. Yes, quite a decent spin bowler."

"Handy with his mid-irons these days. Though not much around the greens." Now Sir Donald stood up. "Tell him what you've told me and he'll arrange something. Probably nothing more than a slap on the wrist. But it's better if it comes from them instead of us just in case the Yanks slap back."

"Donald, you realize, of course . . ." Boston wanted to make certain that someone was going to take the responsibility if this buck-passing backfired in their faces. "I mean, after all, we're talking about a possible hijacking of nuclear materials on our soil."

"Of course." He escorted Boston to the door. "Serious matter. Better off without it. Must run these things through proper channels, you know. One mustn't forget that the Yanks do take care of us. They did cut us in on Star Wars. And everybody is still very sensitive about that F-111 business. What a rumpus, eh? Oh well, I suppose because it's the Yanks one can't be too harsh. It's not as if this happened with the French. Then one could really have got nasty. I'm off for lunch. Not to worry. Toppy will do whatever he thinks is best."

Boston nodded.

Sir Donald patted him on the shoulder. "Tuesday today. Steak and kidney pudding in the canteen if you're hungry." He led Boston out of his office. "Best staff canteen in government. Minister eats there all the time." He waved good-bye and left Boston standing in the hallway.

Steak and kidney pud in the staff canteen . . .

The mere thought of it made him feel queasy.

And anyway, there couldn't be a best staff canteen in government. The words *best* and *staff canteen* were contradictions. Throughout his entire career there was one steadfast rule he absolutely refused to break. No matter what. No matter who. He never ate in a staff canteen.

Nor did he particularly care to hear that the Minister himself ate there regularly. Least influential of all was Sir Donald's one-time left-handed praise that the food served in the MoD staff canteen was "bloody edible." No. Boston would not listen to anyone where staff canteens were concerned. One bad experience was enough to turn him off forever. And to prove how single-minded he could be, that one bad experience was in 1958.

He remembered it vividly. An Indian chef at the Home Office had served something he called creamed chicken on toast. It seemed all right at the time. But then a rumor ripped through the building that the chef had been seen that very morning bringing a sack filled with dead cats into work. Boston always believed anyway that Indian restaurants served cooked cats, so the creamed-feline-on-toast rumor made perfect sense to him. He became violently ill. His aversion to staff canteens was immediate, and final. As far as he was concerned—even after all these years—the only way he'd ever be seen eating in any government staff canteen was when the government hired the Roux Brothers to cook there. Absolutely nothing less would do.

As he walked out of the building he wondered, would Sir Donald have been so cavalier about the missing PuN van had he been told about it *after* lunch? The question amused him. He asked himself, what would the world be like today had the battle of Waterloo taken place before breakfast? And, did Cornwallis surrender to Washington on a full stomach?

He recalled that someone had written a book about the "what ifs" in history. He'd never read it, but he saw a review of it in the *Telegraph* and thought at the time how the idea appealed to him. It was based on questions such as, what if Brutus had missed and Caesar had lived? What if Christopher Columbus had made a wrong turn and landed in Ireland? How did that old joke go—what if Moses had turned right instead of left and the Israelis got the oil? But this wasn't a book of jokes, it was a serious treatise on history. What if Mao had drowned during his great swim? What if Truman hadn't stopped MacArthur from marching on to Moscow? What if Nelson had lost at Trafalgar? Even better, Boston asked himself, what if Nelson had exacted war reparations from the French, such as the annexation of Cannes? Wouldn't it just be lovely if Cannes were a British protectorate. At least then the waiters there would have to speak English.

He left the MoD building and made his way through the rain to the Foreign Office, two minutes down Whitehall, next to Downing Street.

What if England had Mediterranean weather?

What if Toppy decídes he too never handles problems before lunch?

Harold Topping's office was on the second floor, a private enclosure at the far end of a long, dark and dreary, neon-lit, narrow L-shaped corner room where the windows were too small to let in much light and where at least three dozen desks were plunked down in various positions. Some were at right angles. Some were facing each other. Some were back-to-back. Boston couldn't help but wonder if someone had laid out the route like that on purpose. Or if the desks had merely evolved. Darwin would have loved it. Desks grown that way, through natural selection. The place looked like Aintree.

"Buster." Topping marched up to grab his hand and shake it heartily. "Donald said you were stopping by." He led Boston into his office. "Buster . . . how long has it been? My God, man, I left Hong Kong in '65. Can it be more than twenty years already?"

"You look well," Boston lied, thinking that Harold Topping was once a handsome man but the years had been unkind. Now the deep lines in his face were valleys separating pouches that come with late middle age. Now the schoolboy's curly blond hair was yellowish, and somewhat unkempt. Now the sharp blue eyes were half closed with that overworked functionary's squint. "Yes, it must be."

"And you, dear boy." Topping took his coat. "Right. Now . . . do sit down. It's been too long. Tell me everything. Could the last time have been more than twenty years ago face-to-face across the crease?"

Boston reminded him, "I hit a six off you."

"A four," Topping corrected.

"A six. I'm sure." If Topping wasn't, he certainly was. I'm positive. It was a six, Boston recalled. I know it was. After all, it wasn't every day that I hit a six so I do remember all of them.

"Right. Now. A four," Topping said, putting an end to that. "You don't still play, do you? Not at your age?"

Not at my age? What does he mean by that. He's older than I am. And just look at him. I'm in better shape now than he ever was. "I stopped playing years ago. But I could still bowl a few overs if I had to."

"By God, Buster . . . I've often wondered whatever happened to you."

"Actually I work at Chappell House. In Storey's Gate."

"Fancy that," Topping was genuinely amused. "All these years and you're just a stone's throw away. When did you leave Hong Kong?"

"Late '67."

"Had a wife and two children, if my memory serves me."

Now Boston told him, "Yes. We had to leave. My wife was taken ill."

"Ill?" Topping flinched. "Nothing serious, I trust. Don't care much for illness, you know."

"I'm sorry to say it was serious. She . . ."

"Right. Yes. Now." Topping was obviously uncomfortable and wanted to change the subject. "Good old Hong Kong. Right. It will never be the same. Remember the night markets on Nathan Road? And I can tell you that every time I go to the races here I miss Sha Tin. Did you like to go to Sha Tin? The meetings there had a certain *je ne sais quoi*. Can't really compare with race meetings here. Ah, Buster, those were the good old days. Right. Now. To the good old days." He raised his hand in a mock toast.

That's what these blokes at the F.O. are really all about, Boston thought. WWII . . . those were the good old days. The Somme . . . those were the good old days. The Plague . . . those were the good old days. Everything was better in the good old days. If someone hadn't already invented the good old days, the F.O. surely would have by now. Hah. If it weren't for the good old days, they'd have nothing to do all day. "Did Donald tell you why I'm here?"

"Right. Now . . ." Topping leaned all the way back in his chair. "There's really nothing like it, is there?"

"Like what?" Boston asked.

Topping arched his right hand high over his head as if he was bowling. "The smell of the pitch. The sound of the ball snapping off the bat. It is England, Buster."

"Yes, of course," he politely agreed, then asked again, "Did Donald explain why I'm here?"

But Topping wanted to talk cricket. "It was only a four. I remember it very well now. You had just started playing for the MoD team. It was when you first arrived in Hong Kong . . ."

"Yes," he said, hoping that would end the conversation. "Yes, you're right. I recall it now, as well. Only a four."

"By God, it certainly is good to see you, Buster. It's been so long." He pointed to a large clock on the wall. "What say we have a spot of lunch. Staff canteen . . ."

"Sorry," he instantly begged off. "Another time perhaps."

"Beef on the trolley today," Topping tried to persuade him. "Yorkshire pudding?"

"Beef on the trolley and Yorkshire pudding in the staff canteen?" Steak and kidney pud across the street and the F.O. gets beef on the trolley? No . . . not even for beef on the trolley. He couldn't bring himself to do it. "Another time, perhaps."

"Lobsters on Fridays." Topping actually smacked his lips.

Boston forced himself to stop thinking about staff canteen food.

"Hah. Now . . . about this little matter with the Americans. We really can't let them get away with this sort of thing, you know."

"What sort of thing?" Topping looked at him.

He stared at Topping. "Didn't Donald tell you?"

"Tell me what?"

Boston sighed. What if all wars adjourned for lunch. "There's been a hijacking. A U.S. Navy van-load of plutonium nitrate has disappeared."

"My God. That's awful."

"It's worse than that. It's much worse than awful. The Americans have tried to cover it up. They are required to inform us immediately when an incident like this takes place. That's by treaty. Well, instead of letting us know, they've tried to cover up. Derek Wooldridge at the AEA's Constabulary is furious. But his hands are tied. Mine too. Donald thought the best solution would be a formal protest through F.O. channels. Something decidedly stern. Maybe even at ambassadorial level. I mean, after all, how dare the Americans think they can make up their own rules."

Topping interjected. "Indeed. You're quite right, Buster."

Indeed I am, he thought. "I don't have to remind you of the dire implications that surround such a matter. All the more so after we took so much stick for them about their planes being based here. A hijacking of nuclear materials on sovereign soil is horrendous enough. But for our own best allies to even attempt a cover-up . . . ."

"Right. Scandalous." Topping nodded.

"Undermining our authority." Boston was really going to lay it on thick. "That's what they're doing. They're undermining our authority. Our sovereignty. I consider this a very rude slap in the face. They need a rebuke. Something they'll never forget. My God, man, the Americans are treating us as if we were their poor cousins."

Topping shrugged. "But we are."

"Well . . ." Boston rubbed his chin until he could think of something else to say. "We mustn't let them get away with treating us like this."

"Right. Now . . . no, of course we can't. I'll see that the Minister files a formal complaint through ambassadorial channels." Topping stood up, went to his office door and called out, "Marks and Spencer."

Boston stared at him, slightly astonished.

Two young men came into the office. Topping introduced them as Gregory Marks and Freddie Spencer. "Just a coincidence," he added.

No, Boston thought to himself, the F.O. blokes are not like the rest of us.

"Right. Now . . . run upstairs to the Secretary's office," Topping ordered Spencer, "and get a hold of that new junior minister . . . whatever his name is—you know. Tell him we've got something on. Tell him that we shall need him to sign some papers in, say, half an hour. Don't let him disappear until I get the paperwork up there." Then he turned to Marks. "Right. Now . . . get out one of those sample formal complaint letters. You'll find them in the forms cabinet. Bring it in here and we'll fill in the blanks. Get it typed immediately with that junior minister's name on the bottom. You'll have to check your spelling. Then rush it up there for signature."

They both nodded and ran off to do what they had been told.

"Right. Now . . . let's see." Topping sat down at his desk, put a blank sheet of paper in front of him and readied his fountain pen. "The junior minister will sign anything we put in front of him, which speeds matters up immensely. All brand new junior ministers are like that. But this one has spots. Perhaps other offices think he might be contagious. We've found that he's so thrilled to be a part of government he might even be inclined to sign his own resignation if someone simply asked for his autograph.''

Boston smiled, then pointed to the sheet of paper. "I'll give you the details of the incident as I've got them and then we'll get Woolley on the phone and find what he's come up with.''

"Right," Topping said.

"Right," Boston said, and was just about to explain the incident when Marks reappeared with the letter. "You did want the standardized complaint at ministerial level, I presume.''

"Oh, yes, well done," Topping said. "Right. Now . . . let's see." He mumbled the first two paragraphs of the letter. "Usual bumf about to and from and re and of course this being in the name of Her Majesty. Hmmm. Let's see . . . here. Under my authority as Secretary of State . . ." He shoved it toward Boston. "Right. Now . . . this is the part where we explain that they've violated our authority.''

"Undermined our sovereignty," Boston suggested. "We should get the phrase, undermined our sovereignty, in there somewhere.''

"Right," Topping agreed, then turned to Marks. "Did I ever tell you that Boston here once hit a four off me. True, he was much younger then. But still, rather lucky of him, what?" He leaned over to tap Boston several times on the shoulder. "Good old Buster. I'll tell you," he said, shaking his head to show he approved. "Buster, the more I think of it the better I like it.''

"Think of what?" Boston asked.

"This business with the Americans. Undermined our sovereignty. I like that. Good choice of words. To the point. Direct. No room for misinterpretation. Right. Now . . . we'll fill this in and get it typed and get it signed and get it over to their ambassador this afternoon. Formal protest. For immediate action. His office will, of course, send a formal apology by return messenger first thing tomorrow morning. They're very courteous, the Americans, especially when they know that courtesy is expected. Naturally the matter will be quietly put under the carpet. After all, they are the Americans. God only knows, but they'll probably deny the whole business. Yet what I like about all this is that we might be able to hit a few sixes off them if we play carefully. You see, they'll know that we know. And we'll know that they know that we know. And that's always a good thing when it comes to dealing with the Americans. It's good for trading purposes. I've learned from experience that it's always a good idea to have something on the Americans because you never know when you can use it to bargain with them. Imagine how grateful they might be that we've kept such a matter out of the press.''

"Good thinking," Boston said, even though he couldn't believe what he was hearing. Who cared that highly toxic and dangerous nuclear materials might have been hijacked by some terrorist group intent on using the stuff to destroy half the kingdom? That wasn't the F.O.'s problem. The way the F.O. saw it, this was a marker to be called in some day in the heat of a diplomatic poker game.

Topping began filling in the blank formal protest form.

Hah, Boston reminded himself, the best defense truly is a strong offense.

God save the F.O.

After all, what could possibly be more offensive than blackmailing your closest ally.

Chapter
Fourteen

"THE BRITISH ARE STEALING IT," Holbrook said.

Roth furled his eyebrows while he continued studying the figures on his desk. "It isn't possible."

"The numbers don't lie, sir."

"Then I'll rephrase that, Dad, and say it isn't plausible."

"And I repeat, sir, the numbers don't lie."

Punching a button on his intercom, Roth summoned Wagner. "Bob, come and see me, now."

Almost immediately Wagner reported in to the admiral's office, gave a chilly nod toward Holbrook and asked, "Yes, sir?"

Roth handed Wagner the four handwritten pages that comprised Holbrook's report. "Take a gander at this."

Wagner sat down on the chair next to the admiral's desk and carefully read all the pages before he said, as if Holbrook wasn't even there, "I don't see how he can even dream that this is tied into the missing van."

"It isn't," Holbrook defended himself. "It has nothing to do with the van. But it does have to do with the systematic theft of American plutonium nitrate by the British. They've been stealing thirty grams per shipment over the past nine shipments."

"This is only a pubic hair short of insanity," Wagner exclaimed. "Who ever heard of such nonsense? Commander Holbrook has got to be joking." He looked at Roth. "I mean, for his own mental health, I hope this is a joke. To begin with, why would they steal our PuN? It's preposterous. Admiral, I can tell you right away there isn't anything in this. He's just a little late for April Fools' Day, that's all. I fear this is basically nothing more than Commander Holbrook's way of trying to make good on having screwed up by telling the Brits about the missing van this morning.''

''Excuse me, Captain.'' Holbrook didn't hide his anger. ''I'm standing right here. You don't have to talk around me. You could at least have the balls to try calling me an asshole to my face.''

Wagner disregarded him. ''Admiral, who's checked these figures?''

''I've been over those figures half-a-dozen times,'' Holbrook said.

''So, you've been over these figures half-a-dozen times.'' Wagner shook his head, as if to show Holbrook that it didn't matter to him how many times anybody added them up. ''So, I'm still a long way away from being convinced.''

Roth cut in. ''Tell Bob what you told me. The same way you told it to me.''

Holbrook reluctantly briefed Wagner, repeating almost word for word the speech he had given to the admiral. He explained everything. The smudged DoD 3093 forms. The minute difference in the lettering on those forms. How the PuN only disappeared on U.S. Navy shipments that passed briefly into British hands. The constant figure of thirty grams. The idea that a negligible amount, such as thirty grams, would hardly be noticed. That the missing amounts probably never would have been noticed if he hadn't happened to stumble across the inconsistencies on the 3093s. He told Wagner exactly what he told Roth. ''The numbers don't lie. The British are stealing it.''

Wagner tossed the four pages onto Roth's desk. ''Admiral, this is crazy. He's trying to get both of us to believe that our allies are stealing fissile materials from us. I'm sorry to say that I think the man is certifiable. Just think about it for a sec. The Brits can make as much PuN as they want and already have more than they need. For Chrissakes, if they ever needed more they could buy it from us.'' He looked at Roth and started to laugh. "I'm afraid our friend here has been under some serious stress lately, sir."

Holbrook challenged him. "Then how do you explain the missing amounts?"

"I don't," Wagner said. " 'Cause in reality there aren't any. It's only on paper. I'm surprised you never thought of it. The net-net is CCE. Constant Computer Error. Ask any nine-year-old kid who's ever programmed one of those toy computers and he'll tell you that all you need is one bit of bad dope in the beginning of the program and everything you ask for will come up consistently wrong." He shook his head to dismiss Holbrook's claim. "It's ridiculous. Admiral, if we were talking about one shipment, like this morning's PuN van, then I'd be alarmed. If we were talking about two or three, sir, I'd be in a panic. But nine shipments where the same figure appears throughout? Come on. That would be ludicrous enough if Holbrook here wasn't adding insult to injury and saying it's the Brits who are doing it. No, sir, all you have to do is audit the figures. Put them through the computer another time with a correction for the CCE and I'll give you dollars to donuts that everything will be fine."

"I don't care how many times you run it through your CCE-corrected computers," Holbrook said defiantly. "I don't think it will be fine."

Wagner appealed to Roth. "Admiral, we both know all about the stress and strain that Commander Holbrook has been under ever since he left carrier duty."

Holbrook decided he'd had enough. "Horse shit. Just what the hell does that mean? Who the hell do you think you are . . ."

Wagner said softly, "Calm down, Dick . . . I don't mean nothing personal."

"The fuck you didn't." Holbrook stormed up to the edge of Roth's desk to lean across it. "Sir, there is nearly half a pound of plutonium nitrate missing . . ."

"And a whole goddamned busload of it disappeared this morning," Wagner bellowed. "That's what worries the hell out of me. That and the fact the bloody Brits found out and now they're making a stink."

Roth stopped them. "Knock it off, both of you. Enough."

He said it loudly to show them he meant business. "We'll handle one thing at a time. Now, this two-seventy grams of PuN. I know that CCE has in the past produced exactly these kinds of bugbears. So, before we run off accusing the British of stealing anything, I think we should check our own back-yard and see if there are any weeds." He turned to Wagner. "You go ahead, Bob, and take the report and have the whole thing run through the computer."

"I'll get on it first thing in the morning, sir."

Roth said, "All right. Good night."

Holbrook stood where he was.

Wagner left with Holbrook's report.

"Now you, Dad." Roth took a deep breath. "I don't know why he's on your case like that. Fact is, I don't much care. But if something besides personalities is bothering you, I want to know about it."

"He's a vindictive son of a bitch."

"He's a professional United States Naval officer and if I thought, for even one second, that there was any sort of breach of his duties due to personal attitudes, I'd not only have his ass shipped out of here, I'd have it shipped out of the United States Navy. But Dad," Roth warned, "I've also told you that if you're having problems, you've got to shape up and get them sorted out."

"Why can't I make you believe what's happening?"

"Because frankly I've got other problems on my mind. Or have you forgotten about that fucking van?" Now Roth's tone softened. "Telling me that the Brits are stealing our PuN is pretty far-fetched. CCE is the logical answer but Wagner's in charge of security and I'm not going to override his authority just because you've been under some stress lately. In fact, I sincerely think you ought to have a talk with the padre."

"I don't need to have a talk with the padre. And I also don't need to take any shit from Wagner. I did not screw up. I did not tell the British about that missing van. The guy called and I lied to him. I denied anything was wrong when I knew there was a hell of a lot that was wrong. Remember me, I was the fellow who begged you to tell them right away. But I got overruled. No sir, I did not screw up. And what's more, I did not come in here to report that two hundred seventy grams of PuN are missing thanks to CCE. Admiral . . . you've got to believe me. I checked my figures and they're right.''

Roth stood up, came from behind his desk and put his hand on Holbrook's shoulder. "Do me a favor, Dad, have a talk with the padre. Let's get a few of your personal problems out of the way before we get too bogged down with anything else. Let Wagner do his thing. And don't worry about him.''

"I did not screw up," he said again.

"Listen, I got hell from the ambassador this afternoon. He got a pretty stern note from the Brits and it's splashed a puddle of mud on us. Marty Foster believes whatever Wagner's been telling him. He figures you're responsible so he's got the ambassador saying to me he wants your ass for this. Now, just so you understand where I am, I don't think I'm gonna let either of them have you on a platter—least not yet.'' He smiled. "Bean Bag would never forgive me if I did.''

"I did not screw up," Holbrook insisted for the third time.

"Someone did," Roth said. "But you let me worry about that. Go on. It's late. Now I'm gonna catch hell from the old lady for not making supper. And you gotta have something better to do than stand here talking to me.'' He pushed Holbrook toward the door. "Why don't you ring your kids? Tell them you love them. Use a WATS line. Put the call on Uncle Sam's bill. But just this once.''

Holbrook saluted and went down the hall.

I did not screw up, he told the voice inside his head. But the voice didn't answer.

He yanked the bottle of rum out of his desk drawer and poured some into an empty styrofoam coffee cup. Then he plopped himself into his chair and took a long swallow.

I did not screw up, he said to the voice again. But still the voice didn't answer him.

He poured himself a second shot.

He liked the way the rum burned his throat. And softened the edges around everything.

I didn't screw up, he was trying to convince the voice.

This time the voice inside his head answered him, sounding just like the admiral . . . ring your kids . . . tell them you love them . . .

Why the hell not, he decided, and called Florida.

No one answered.

Shit. He checked his watch. Seven-twenty minus five hours. They're still at school. Maybe I'll call them at school. I don't know the number. He hung up. Or I'll wait. I'll sit here and wait until they come home from school.

He poured a third shot of rum.

I'll sit here and wait till the kids come home from school.

Before he poured a fourth shot, he tried Florida again.

This time Millicent answered.

"Oh, it's you. Hi."

"It's not Saturday," she noted.

"Nope. I think it's Tuesday. I just called . . ." He laughed. "Hello, my name is Little Stevie Wonder and . . ." Now he started to sing, "I just called to say I love you . . ."

"You never could carry a tune. And drunk you're even worse than usual."

"Drunk?" He took a deep breath. "Yeah, I guess I am. A little. Not a lot. Just a little. You see, I got myself into heavy shit today, Millicent. I don't even know how. I never saw it coming. Right down my tailpipe. I didn't protect my ass when I should have and some son of a bitch ran one right up there."

She said, "It must be serious if you have to phone me."

He didn't understand.. "Why?"

"Why?" She forced a laugh. " 'Cause you haven't talked to me or shared anything with me or told me anything about what's in your head for five years. So all of a sudden you get drunk 'cause you're in trouble and you've got no one else to talk to, so you ring me. Yeah, fly-boy, you really must be in one big pile of shit."

He thought about that for a moment. "What do you mean I haven't shared anything with you for five years? You walked out on me nearly two years ago—"

"I walked out on you? Funny how there's always two sides to the same story. Seems to me, you did the walking."

"Well," he said, "yeah, I did, but not really. I didn't really walk out on you 'cause in your head you left a long time before me."

"In my head? No, fly-boy, you've got it backward. I was the one who sat home telling your kids, don't worry, your daddy still loves you but he's got to be away so much because he's the best aviator in the United States Navy. I was the one who kept a home ready for you whenever you decided to stop by. Whenever you decided it was time to put your toy jets down and play with your wife and kids for a couple of days.''

"Millicent," he said, "I never meant to—"

"Your dime, you listen. You say I left you?" She wasn't going to let up. "The hell I did, fly-boy. I raised your kids because you never had the time. I lied to them when you and Bean Bag were out catting. Don't think I didn't know. I always knew. I always knew and I always hurt. But I wouldn't let your kids see that hurt. So I lied to them that everything was peachy dandy and that they should be real proud of their daddy 'cause he's such a brave man. Do you hear me? I lied to your children so they would never stop loving you.''

He shut his eyes.

"Funny how life works out," she went on. "You and I meet, and one hour later we're fucking. You remember that? Or was it a record thirty minutes? Christ, we couldn't get enough of each other. Then you and Bean Bag go flying off into the sunset and what was I supposed to do? Well, you want to know what I did? You probably won't believe it—"

"I didn't call to argue—"

"But I'm gonna tell you anyway. From that very first day we met until long after you sent me and the kids packing back to Florida, what I did was what you never dreamed I'd do. I kept my panties pulled up tight. My jeans stayed on. For you. I could have been dropping them every twenty seconds. Every horny pilot in your squadron was trying to pull my legs open. But believe it or not, I clamped them shut because that was only for you. You didn't know that, did you? You thought I was just like all those other horny wives." She sniffled.

He wondered, could she be crying?

"Something else you don't know—"

"Please, Millicent . . ."

"Just listen," she insisted. "There's a lot you don't know and maybe it's time you heard it. Like how Bean Bag came home drunk one night. He found Barbara in bed with someone. Does that shock you? She was the one who was fucking her brains out. I was the one who used to babysit for her kids while she was getting it on behind the officers' club. How's that make you feel? So Bean Bag came home drunk one night and found her shacked up with some guy. And you know what he did? He started laughing. He sat right down on the edge of the bed and laughed. The guy she was with grabbed his pants and tore ass outta there. But Bean Bag just laughed. When he stopped laughing he told Barbara the reason it was all so funny was because you and he had been fucking every other guy's wife and he figured it was only a matter of time till the rest of the world got even."

"It's not true," he said. "It's just not true."

"You trying to make me believe you kept your pants on?"

"No," he admitted. "But I've never lied to you about that."

"You never lied because I never asked." She wasn't sniffling now. "Come on, fly-boy, you never lied because I never gave a shit about whatever bitches you found in faraway ports. That's all part of the Navy. I knew what I was getting into when I signed on. But I also knew what was going on. And I hurt. I really hurt. I hurt because I couldn't miss it. You want me to start naming names? You want me to go down the list at every base? You want me to tell you how some of the wives got drunk one afternoon and started comparing notes, started comparing sizes? You want to know where you ranked?"

"Please stop it," he begged her.

"I left you, huh? Bean Bag got killed and you had no one else to play with so you had to come home. But I wasn't as much fun as he was."

"That's not true, Millicent."

"No, you never lied to me and I never lied to you. But I did worse. I lied to your children."

"Millicent," he spoke slowly and gently, "please . . ." He paused for a moment and then told her, "Millicent, I'm sorry."

"So am I." Now she was crying. "But I'm sorriest of all for you."

He told her, "It was never the way you thought it was. It really wasn't."

She asked softly, "Does it even matter anymore?"

"I guess in a funny way . . . in a funny way it does."

"Why?" she wanted to know. " 'Cause you're sitting around, drunk, feeling sorry for yourself and there's no one else to talk to? No more Bean Bag to play with. Is that why?"

He wondered how he could say it. "No. Not for that. I think it's for something you said just now. That you lied to the kids for me."

There was a long silence. "I did."

He told her, "Thank you."

There was another long silence.

He finally said, "I guess I'd better go. I think I've sobered up. Tell the kids I called, will you, please. I'll call on Saturday. As usual. Tell them I love them." He thought about what else he might say. "And Millicent?" He settled for, "I'm just trying to get my head together."

She said, "Let us know when you do."

He said goodbye and she said goodbye, and after he hung up he played the call over again in his head. Like a tape, he ran it back and listened to it.

The rum had worn off.

He grabbed his rain gear and walked out of the office.

The rain was still coming down.

He looked at his watch and couldn't believe that it was already eight-thirty.

Maybe I'll go to Franco's and have a bowl of spaghetti with clam sauce.

He changed his mind. Naw. Maybe I won't.

Maybe I'll go home and try to fall asleep.

He walked along Grosvenor Square, across Duke Street and went the half a block to his apartment. He let himself into the main door, found the lift just there and took it to the fourth floor.

As soon as he got out of the lift he remembered . . . whatshername.

Tied to the handle was a pair of silk panties. And written in lipstick across the front of the door in huge letters was the word BASTARD.

Ah shit. He untied her panties from the handle so he could unlock the door.

The light-timer switch had snapped on the lamp in the living room so he wasn't coming home to a dark apartment. He said out loud, I like that.

But he didn't like the way she left messages—goddamned stupid bitch—and he used her silk panties to try to rub out the lipstick on the door. It smeared. Idiot woman. He'd worry about it later. He tossed her panties into the wastepaper basket with last week's newspapers.

Locking the door, he threw off his clothes, put on the television and sprawled across the couch.

It didn't matter what program was on because the voice inside his head was screaming too loudly.

You've got it backward. You left. I was the one who sat home telling your kids, don't worry, your daddy still loves you.

The voice shouted at him.

I was the one who kept a home ready for you whenever you decided to stop by. Whenever you decided it was time to put your toy jets down and play with your wife and kids for a couple of days.

The voice inside his head wasn't going to let him be.

I raised your kids because you never had the time. I lied to them when you and Bean Bag were out catting. Don't think I didn't know. I always knew. I always knew and I always hurt. But I wouldn't let your kids see that hurt. So I lied to them that everything was peachy dandy and that they should be real proud of their daddy 'cause he's such a brave man. Do you hear me? I lied to your children so they would never stop loving you.

He lay on the couch, staring blankly at the television until the voice inside his head had its say. He was too tired to fight back. The BBC droned on. The voice grew fainter and fainter. After a time he was just too weary to listen.

He slept on the couch, in the glow of the TV.

It was the breakfast show's musical theme which woke him. He opened his eyes. His body felt as though he'd just gone ten rounds. He hurt. His mouth tasted bad. His head was filled with cobwebs. But the voice inside his head was silent. He told himself, I'm gonna live. He struggled off the couch, stretched, snapped off the television, and glanced outside to see that the rain hadn't stopped. Maybe I'll build an ark and stock it with two stewardesses, two Waves, two chorus girls, two go-go dancers . . . or maybe I won't.

He washed out the inside of his mouth and padded into the kitchen.

There was nothing in the flat to eat.

Improvise, he decided. So he showered—a long, cold shower which woke him up—then shaved, brushed his teeth, dressed and improvised his way across the street to the Marriott.

Their dining room wasn't open yet.

He made his way through the rain to the Britannia on the other side of Grosvenor Square.

They weren't open for breakfast yet either.

That's the main problem with Europe, he told himself. Breakfast. Can't get a decent breakfast early in the morning anywhere in Europe. Not like you can in San Diego or Galveston or Atlanta. He tried to think of the best breakfast he'd ever had. New York? That time with Millicent in the Plaza, and room service brought up a huge tray filled with breakfast goodies and Millicent worked it out so that they could eat it together in the bathtub. No, he remembered another one. That Sunday brunch at the Bolling Air Force Base Officers' Club. He and Millicent and Bean Bag and Barbara went through a dozen Bloody Marys before they attacked the eggs Benedict. A dozen Bloody Marys. No, I guess that shouldn't count either. How about . . . yeah, he decided, that time in Los Angeles. Millicent and Barbara wanted to see a movie star so he and Bean Bag sprang for breakfast at the Bel Air Hotel. Now that was a great breakfast. The eggs were perfect. The bacon just crisp enough. The toast was lightly buttered. The coffee never ran out. And Millicent spotted Cliff Robertson. There's whatshisname, she said, excitedly, tugging on Barbara's arm. You know, come on, he was in that film . . . Bean Bag turned to stare at Robertson, caught his eye, gave him a wink and a smile which got him a wink and a smile in return. Then Bean Bag looked at the girls, and swore, "I'd recognize him anywhere. Seen all of his films." Millicent wanted his autograph. Barbara said she'd go ask for it if Millicent came with her. Bean Bag got up his courage and said,

"I'll go." By the time they agreed that all three of them would go, Robertson was gone. "Oh well," Bean Bag said, taking a menu and writing down the date and the time. "An official sighting is hereby logged. One movie star." But, Holbrook wanted to know, what's his name? Bean Bag said, "You know . . . ah . . ." Barbara and Millicent joined in, "Come on, it's ah . . ." Then Holbrook got the bill. Their four-minute sighting of a movie star, with eggs and bacon and toast and coffee thrown in, cost $45, not counting the tip. "It's nothing," Bean Bag calculated. "Only works out to $675 an hour. Cheap at twice the price. And I just remembered his name." They wanted to know what it was. Bean Bag gloated in triumph. "Dale Robertson."

That was a terrific breakfast, Holbrook remembered.

Then he reminded himself, I guess we did have some fun.

Going back to North Audley Street he mumbled, third time lucky. First prize is a week in Philadelphia. Second prize is two weeks in Philadelphia. Last prize is breakfast in the Navy snack bar.

If nothing else, it was open for business.

He stood with his tray at the end of the line and the cashier told him, "$2.25." He took what change he had out of his pocket, thinking it was American, but it turned out to be a handful of British coins. "Goddamnit," he said to her. "This carrying two wallets is driving me crazy. I never remember to take them both." He reached into his back pocket. "I hope this is American." It was. He handed her a $5 bill to pay for breakfast, but cursed himself for having forgotten his English folding money and his American change.

He took his tray and found a table off in a corner. But just as he started to eat his waffles with maple syrup and a side of bacon, a tall redheaded man put a breakfast tray down on his table. "Howdy, Dick. Mind if I join you?" The man was probably in his fifties, although he looked at least ten years younger. Red hair does that, Holbrook thought.

"Sure." He motioned for the man to sit down. "The boss phone you last night or this morning?"

"Last night," said the man with big hands and a smiling face. He wore a Navy uniform with captain's eagles on one side of his collar, and a small silver cross on the other. His name tag read, "Brothers." "Thought we should have a chat. Figure it might be time you started thinking about flying again."

Holbrook said right away, "I can't."

"Well"—the chaplain gave him one of those paternal smiles—"the way the boss explained it to me, you've been under some stress lately and it's been getting in the way of your work. How about leave? Why not take some time, maybe go back to the States and see your kids. Does a man good."

Holbrook ate his waffles and chewed on his bacon and sipped his coffee. "What's the best breakfast you've ever had?"

"The best breakfast?" The chaplain obviously couldn't see the relevance of the question. "Gee, I don't know. Why?"

"I ever tell you what we had to do when we were plebes at the trade school?" Holbrook was finished and pushed his tray aside. "We had to stand on a chow line every morning. Now, we could have anything we wanted, but in order to get it we had to shout it out to the cooks when we got to the front of the line. Okay, you've got to picture this. The first guy in line is at parade rest until it's his turn to grab a tray and move up to the counter. So he snaps to attention. Well, the rules were that you had to do whatever the man in front of you did. When that first guy snaps to attention, the whole chow line behind him—like a hundred guys—they all go from parade rest to attention. Then the guy with the tray moves up to the counter and gets his breakfast, while the guy who is now first in line moves up to the stack of trays and shouts out whatever he wants. Seven eggs scrambled, six slices of bacon, five toasts. Get it? Then he goes to parade rest and so does everyone behind him until there's room for him at the counter. That's when he snaps to attention, and so does the rest of the chow line. That guy moves up to the counter and the next guy calls out his breakfast order before going back to parade rest. And all of this happens at a breakneck speed so there are always guys snapping to attention and other guys going to parade rest and then back to attention again. And there's always somebody shouting out, four eggs, three bacons, two sausages, eight toasts. And you know what you learn while all this is going on, Padre?" He didn't give the chaplain a chance to answer. He simply pointed at the man's breakfast. "You learn that you never order scrambled eggs in the Navy. You see, they use powdered eggs for everything when they can. Except sunny-side up. We can put a man on the moon but we can't figure out how the hell to make eggs-over-easy out of powder." Now Holbrook stood up. "Have a nice day." He left the chaplain sitting right where he was, suddenly not wanting his eggs.

Holbrook went to his office and with nothing else to do he started going over the paperwork one more time. He checked his figures. I know I'm right. But he also knew that he had to convince the admiral. If I don't, Wagner wins. If Wagner wins, I'm the big loser. So I better grab a few more cards off the table and have them in my hand when he asks me to play.

The card he decided that he needed had a Union Jack on it.

Now he picked up the phone and rang Matthew Boston.

"Good morning . . . I'd like to come and see you if I can. As soon as possible. Preferably this morning . . . well, sir, it's important . . . no, no, it's not about a certain vehicle gone astray . . ." He didn't want to say much more than that. "No. And it's not something we should be discussing on the phone." Holbrook tried to couch his interest in vague terms. "I need some information about certain forms . . . well, I'd rather explain it all when I see you. Can I come this morning? . . . yes, eleven is fine." Then he figured, what the hell? and suggested, "Look, just to save time, Mr. Boston, could you please have handy whatever files you maintain on our joint treaty shipments as detailed on our DoD form 3093 . . . Thanks."

For a brief few seconds, some doubt crept into his head. Maybe I should tell the admiral that I'm going to speak to my MoD contact.

But he quickly talked himself out of that because he knew that the admiral would probably say, don't go. He'd probably send Wagner instead.

Holbrook put on his raincoat, took a copy of Boston's address, and went to find a taxi.

Then he remembered he didn't have enough British money. Back at the front entrance he asked the Marine guard if anyone with a car was going toward Westminster and could they drop him off.

The only person who had a car scheduled for that morning came down looking for his driver.

Wagner gave him a big smile. "Need a lift, Commander?"

And Holbrook said, "Matter of fact, I do."

Wagner motioned. "Follow me."

They both climbed into the rear seat of the dark blue Chrysler. "Where to?" asked Wagner.

Holbrook told the driver, "Westminster Abbey."

Wagner wanted to know, "What's up?"

And Holbrook told him, "I'm going to pray."

Chapter
Fifteen

MATTHEW BOSTON SUDDENLY felt better than he had all day.

On the way back from Topping's office, he dropped into a pub for a plowman's lunch and a lager. He still couldn't get over the fact that the F.O. staff canteen served beef on the trolley. Then he went upstairs to his own office and assured himself, the situation is contained.

He spent the rest of the afternoon reading *Syd,* although he didn't finish it in time to take it to Nigel.

Before leaving for the day, he decided to ring Topping's office. "I was curious. I trust everything was signed, sealed and delivered through the proper channels."

"Indeed," Topping said. "And you can imagine what has hit the fan. You've done us a great service, Buster. The Americans are right red-faced about this. Showed them a thing or two."

Contained, Boston grinned at Syd's face on the book cover. Contained, indeed.

It was an easy walk from Chappell House to the Reform Club.

A porter in a dark jacket said, "Mr. Boston, good evening, sir. I understand you'll be staying with us this evening."

"Good evening. Oh, my son will be here for dinner some time around seven-thirty. Please show him into the library when he arrives . . ."

The porter said, "Certainly, sir," then handed him a large

manila envelope and a small white envelope. ''There's the post for you, sir.''

''Thank you.'' Boston went up the stairs, left his coat in the cloakroom and stepped into the main hall.

Men and women, but mostly men were milling about the ornate atrium.

He moved past them, going into the large, wood-paneled library where he found a winged armchair next to a pair of women dressed in white silk shirts with ties, and blue pin-striped jackets over long blue pinstriped skirts. They were sipping sherries and seemed—as best he could hear—to be discussing the stock market.

He stared at them—until they caught him looking—then he smiled a modest hello, and turned away.

Blue-pinstriped women talking shares and bonds. The only thing missing, he decided, were cigars.

Of course there have been women at the Reform for nearly ten years now. Not that Boston minded. He was, in fact, relatively proud that the Reform had been one of the first of the older, more established clubs in London to welcome fe-male members. He was even among the men who defended the women a few years before when, at the annual general meeting, one of the long-standing members—Alistair Wright-Pike, well known in some circles for a series of letters to *The Times* blaming the drought and subsequent bankruptcy of his salmon farm directly on Mrs. Thatcher—had the temerity to ask for a vote on the revocation of female memberships. There was a rather startling backbench-type uproar from those as-sembled which many people found upsetting. As some of the members later explained, this isn't Parliament, it's a haven for gentlemen. With little or no effort, several of the more loquacious members skillfully argued down Wright-Pike's motion. Boston stood up to remind his fellow Reformers, ''Women have a place in our club. That is, as long as they are the right women.'' It didn't hurt his standing among the older male members, but it didn't do much for his standing among the younger female members. Anyway, the Wright-Pike motion was quashed and Mr. Wright-Pike immediately announced that this vote of no confidence would force his resignation. No one insisted he stay. So he left. The question of female membership was never raised again.

But blue-pinstriped women smoking cigars . . . Boston didn't know what he'd do if they lit up.

A waiter standing at his elbow cut into his thoughts. Would he care for a sherry? Boston said, yes, thank you, and waited until the waiter was gone—until he was certain to be alone —before he ripped open the large manila envelope.

Las Fontanas, the cover page of the contract announced, a little taste of England in a tasteful little corner of Spain.

He thumbed through the fifteen typed pages, checking to see that the price and method of payment was still as agreed . . . £47,000, payable in pounds sterling by bank transfer to an account in the Isle of Man.

The waiter reappeared. "Your sherry, sir."

Boston tucked the contract away. There'll be time to read the full sale agreement later. He signed the chit and when the waiter walked away he opened the small white envelope.

The stationery heading read, Alexander Gwynne-Peters, Doctor of Medicine. The address was Harley Street.

My Dear Mr. Boston:
  Further to our conversation of the 14th, I have consulted with my associate, Dr. Emilio Vargas, at his clinic in Tortosa, Spain, and he informs me that satisfactory regular treatment equivalent to that which Mrs. Boston is now receiving from the National Health Service will run in the neighborhood of £12,000 per annum. This sum does not include any additional English-speaking nursing staff as you may require. However, I am assured that English-speaking nursing staff is contractually available through Dr. Vargas' clinic. I hope this has been some assistance to you. Yours sincerely . . .

The scribbled signature was illegible.
Twelve thousand pounds. And that doesn't include nurses.
He sipped his sherry.
I'm surprised Gwynne-Peters didn't send me a £20 bill just for this letter.
He peeked inside the envelope just to be sure.

Now he sat back and went over the figures. The £100,000 in Switzerland will pay for the house and provide nearly enough in tax-free income to pay for the nurses. My pension will pay for the treatments. When we sell the house here . . . we'll have to sell the house here . . . anyway it's too much bother and we won't be using it . . . so when we sell the house . . . yes, we should have just enough to get by.

Now he added, thank God.

She'll be out of this weather.

We'll be together.

Everything will be all right.

The porter murmured in his ear, "A telephone call for you, sir."

"A what?" He snapped back to the moment. "Oh. Thank you." He got up to take the call. "Boston here."

"It's . . . it's me," Nigel said.

"Is that you?" Boston demanded, checking the time to see it was just after seven. "Where are you? I'm expecting you here for dinner."

"I . . . I can't make it," Nigel apologized. "I'm sorry. Truly I am. But I can't."

"And why not? I've already reserved."

"I can't . . . you see, I'm still at work. I'm ringing from Harwell. I'm sorry . . ."

"You should have left there an hour ago." Now Boston was curious. "What's going on? Anything serious? I mean," he asked cautiously, "nothing . . . you know . . . nothing?"

"No, nothing."

"Hah. Well . . ." Relieved, he shrugged. "Except I did reserve a table for us. And I've just received the contract for Las Fontanas. I thought you'd like to see it."

"Yes. I would have . . . but I'm sorry . . . I really am."

He wondered if he should tell Nigel about the hijacked U.S. Navy van. But then he thought, not over this phone. "Well . . . do you have to work late? Will you be staying at Harwell all evening?"

"Yes . . . well . . . I mean, not all evening. Just a little while longer . . ."

Suddenly Boston decided, he's meeting someone. He's had a better offer for dinner than joining me. "I'll speak with you soon," he said, in a slightly offended way. "Call your mother, will you. I think she'd like to hear from you."

"Yes . . . I'm sorry . . . I really am . . ."

They hung up.

So . . . he's had a better offer.

Boston went back to the library to finish his drink and order a second one.

At least, he thought to himself, I hope it's a girl. Odd that we never see Nigel with any girls. He never brings any girls home to meet his mother. I hope . . . I mean, if he doesn't want to have dinner with me that's one thing. But . . . well . . . I simply hope it's a girl.

Other possibilities flashed through his mind.

Just as quickly he pushed them out of his mind.

It is a girl, he assured himself. Of course it is.

He started thinking about other things.

He dined alone.

Afterward he rang his wife. But Mary said that Mrs. Boston had already gone up to bed. I thought she was having supper with the children. She canceled it, Mary said. I just remembered that I was supposed to ring the doctor. That's all right, Mary explained, Mrs. Boston made an appointment for tomorrow morning. All right, he said, I'll ring her when she wakes up. Good night. Good night.

He slipped into bed and left a wake-up call for nine.

He read the Las Fontanas contract from cover to cover before falling asleep. And glanced through the *Daily Telegraph* from end to end over breakfast the next morning.

Then he walked through the drizzle to Chappell House and was in his office before ten.

Mrs. Fitzgerald buzzed him as soon as he had settled in behind his desk. "It's Commander Holbrook from the U.S. Navy."

Oh no, he thought, not this early. He took the call. "Good morning, how are you? . . . This morning?" He tried to think of an excuse. "I'm not sure I can this morning . . . Yes, I'm sure it is important, but . . ." He really wanted to find some way to stall Holbrook. "Look, Commander, if it's about, you know, the matter we discussed yesterday, about a certain vehicle gone astray . . . It's not about the van?" He didn't understand. "Information about certain forms?" Boston dared, "Which forms in particular?" Now he mumbled, oh my God. "Yes, yes of course. I'll see you here at eleven."

Oh my God.

He hung up.

Holbrook knows.

He looked at his phone again, started to reach for it, hesitated, then dialed a number. It rang engaged. He punched the R to repeat it automatically and it rang engaged again. I have never got a number with that silly R contraption, he mumbled. All it ever does is redial the engaged tone. He dialed it himself this time and got a crossed line.

I can't believe it. He slammed down the phone and sat fidgeting for a few minutes until he tried again.

When a man answered he announced, "It's me, Boston. I had to ring you. We have a problem . . . Well, it's that someone knows . . . Of course I'm certain. I'm so certain that I'm ringing you to tell you . . . He's an American. My liaison with the U.S. Navy here . . . his name is Holbrook. He's Commander Holbrook of the U.S. Navy . . . At Grosvenor Square . . . Of course he might be dangerous. Why the hell do you think I'm ringing you?" What a stupid question, Boston thought. "What does he know? He knows about the forms. He must know because he's coming here at eleven this morning and he wants to see my files. I knew this would happen. It was too simple by half. What? . . . For God's sake, what kind of a question is that? How do I know if he always wears a uniform? What possible difference could it make anyway? . . . Identify him? What for? What are you going to do? . . . What does that mean, you'll handle the rest? Handle what? I said, what are you going to do?"

The man on the other end said goodbye and hung up.

Boston thought of ringing him back.

He pushed the R button on his phone but the number was engaged.

Now what? He stood up and tried to think of how to handle Holbrook. Maybe I'm making too much of this. Maybe he doesn't know as much as I'm giving him credit for. Maybe there's nothing at all to worry about. Boston was still trying to work it out in his mind when Mrs. Fitzgerald buzzed to say that the American was on his way up.

Checking to see that his desk was orderly, he straightened his tie, and tried to reassure himself. Maybe there's nothing at all to worry about. Keep calm. Put the ball in his court. Maintain control. The best defense is a strong offense. Don't be too friendly. Stay businesslike.

He met Holbrook at the lift with an uncharacteristically chilly greeting. "Commander. This way please." He led Holbrook into his tiny office. "I have a bone to pick with you."

"Oh?"

"You lied to me yesterday," Boston said. That's right. Take the offensive. Set the mood so he knows exactly where we stand. And now throw him totally off guard. "Tea?" A little charm to give him a false sense of security. "Or would you prefer coffee?"

"Coffee, thanks. Light milk."

Now go back on the offensive. "My superiors at the MoD have since sent the matter to be dealt with at ambassadorial level." He matter-of-factly asked Mrs. Fitzgerald to bring in two coffees. "Of course I had no alternative but to forward it to them. After all, I quite clearly asked you if there was a PuN shipment van missing and you told me, just as clearly, no. I therefore feel an obligation to alert your superiors to the fact that we find ourselves facing a serious problem of, how shall I put it . . . confidence."

"The missing van incident has been out of my hands from the very start. I've never been privy to anything more than an initial briefing . . ."

"The coffee first." Boston stopped him, sat down behind his desk, smiled and folded his hands to wait. Good, he thought. This is going just right.

"Are you a cricket fan?"

"What? Oh, this." He glanced toward the Syd Barnes book. I really must finish it and send it off to Nigel. "Yes." He looked back at Holbrook. So you want to be friends? Okay. I'll play your little game. For a few minutes anyway. "I just started reading it. It's about the finest player the game has known. Ever heard of Syd Barnes?"

"No. Can't say that I have."

My God, you Americans are parochial. Why do you all think that the sun rises and sets on Kansas? "Syd Barnes? You must have. He was as world-famous as your Joe Di-Maggio."

"Ever heard of Junior Jim Gilliam?"

Where do they get such names as Junior Jim. "Who?"

"He played second base for the Brooklyn Dodgers."

I take it back. The sun rises and sets on Brooklyn. "Oh. I see."

The coffee arrived.

"Sorry there are no biscuits," he said. Now, enough stalling. Now it's back onto the offensive. "I must be totally frank and say that you've put me personally in a most awkward position." He sipped his coffee. "I'm certain you can see that from where I view the situation, there has been a grave breach of trust."

"I hear what you're saying. But that's got nothing to do with the reason I'm here. I'm here because I want to do some routine checking on some DoD 3093 forms as they've gone through the system."

"Well"—Boston put his coffee down—"I'm certain we can arrange something." He knew he should try to change the subject but he figured he'd take a small risk in order to find out what Holbrook knows. "Are you looking for anything in particular?"

"Not necessarily. If I could just check your files."

The Americans are always so bloody transparent when they lie. "Unfortunately, at this moment in time, I'm afraid it won't be possible."

"What do you mean? How can it not be possible?"

That's good. Get angry. If you lose your temper you've lost our little game. "It won't be possible just now for several reasons. Amongst them is the fact that the files you're looking for are not kept here."

"Well, then let's go to where the files are kept."

Boston smiled. "If only life was so easy." Believe you me, Commander, I'm not going to make anything easy. Not for you. Not for anyone. "You see, the files you're talking about are kept with various agencies, depending on the type of shipment involved. The U.K. Atomic Energy Authority's Special Constabulary has some. Various MoD offices have others. It would take quite some time to gather the ones you want.''

''We've always been led to believe that the files were maintained by your office. After all, you're the liaison . . .''

''Ah yes . . .'' Damned Americans. Whenever they want something they think they can have it just as soon as they want it. Well, I'm going to show this one it just isn't so. ''Ah yes,'' Boston stammered until an excuse popped into his head . . . ''They have at times been kept here but reorganizations . . . you know, every time a new minister comes in, he wants things done his way . . .''

''You mean that there's nothing here regarding any of our shipments? None of our DoD 3093s wind up here?''

Hah. The last thing that I'm going to do is allow myself to be bullied by him. ''Commander, I don't come into your office and suggest that you don't do your job properly. I said at the outset that I've got a bone to pick with you and I think it's only fair that we clear the air about that before we go on to other matters. After all, you must realize the particularly sticky position you've put me in. That an officer of the United States Navy would lie to a duly authorized representative of Her Majesty's government about a matter as sensitive as the possible hijacking of U.S. Navy nuclear materials on British soil . . .''

''We still don't know that it was a hijacking.''

''No? A van filled with nuclear materials disappears off the face of the earth, you try to cover it up and you want me to congratulate you for your cooperation and sense of fair play?''

''That notwithstanding, it is of the utmost importance that the United States Navy be permitted to properly audit every step of the accounting procedures concerning our nuclear shipments. Now, I would sincerely hope that we could handle this amicably on our level. But if need be . . .''

''Just a moment.'' Boston flew off the handle. Who does he think he's trying to shove around? ''Is that a threat to go above my head? I've told you, Commander, that the information you're seeking will have to be gathered from various repositories. That will take time. It's a lot of extra work for me and I can tell you frankly, I've got other things to do. In the meantime, I should remind you that the U.S. Navy has seriously breached our bilateral agreements concerning nuclear substance shipments in the United Kingdom.'' Time for my lecture. He stood up, went to a filing cabinet, yanked it open, pulled out some papers and returned to his chair. ''Would you mind terribly if I read the regulations to you, to illustrate precisely what our agreements say about material accountancy.''

''Mr. Boston, the point is . . .''

''Please have the courtesy to hear me out.'' By God, what a terrific offense. The best-ever defense. ''Now. Listen to this.'' He cleared his throat, then read in a stern monotone. ''Safeguards will involve the applications of measures for material accountancy, supplemented by containment and surveillance.'' He looked up at Holbrook to emphasize that point. ''I'll spare you the technical definitions of material accountancy, containment or surveillance. But, the regulations go on to say . . .'' Turning the page, he ran down a long paragraph until he found what he wanted. ''. . . it will be the responsibility of the guest nation to inform the host nation of any and all incidents, suspected, imagined or actual, at the earliest possible moment when prevention of mishaps and containment of theft, vandalism, accident or terrorist acts might immediately take place.'' He put the paper down. ''Does that sound familiar, Commander?''

''Somewhere in there you'll find the letters MUF.''

Boston took a deep breath. ''MUF?''

''Materials unaccounted for. You know, the difference between book inventory and physical inventory. So as long as you brought up the business of material accountancy, we have reason to believe that there might be, let's call them 'minor discrepancies' in certain accountings.''

''Discrepancies?'' I've got to get him off this subject. ''You talk about MUF. But of course you also know the term LEMUF—limit of error of materials unaccounted for. It's not uncommon for there to be some differences between book and physical inventories. I've often found that instrumental uncertainties can be calculated accurately enough so that if the inventory difference is within this range it can be accepted.''

"Yes. But in cases of larger discrepancies, an investigation might be called for to determine whether or not nuclear material is missing."

Oh Christ. I've got to get back on the offensive. "What sort of numbers are you talking about?" Boston asked in a relaxed way in order to pretend that he wasn't needlessly worried. "Percentagewise, of course."

"A very small amount."

Hah. An opening. "Less than an allowable five percent?"

"Yes."

Now I've got him. "Less than two-and-a-half percent?"

"Yes."

"My God, man"—Boston gestured—"less than one percent?"

"That's not the point."

"Less than one percent? Hah!" Fifteen, love. Thirty, love. Forty, love. Game. "It absolutely is the point." He slammed his hands on his desk, accidentally shoving the Syd Barnes book toward the edge and nearly spilling some of his files onto the floor. "That is the whole point." He stood up to pull the book and the files back into the center of his desk. Then he reached for another book which was propped against his windowsill. "Here, Commander, let me read this to you." He thumbed through his copy of *International Atomic Energy Agency Safeguards* until he had the paragraph he wanted. "The reasons for MUF may be found in measurement uncertainties or other technical causes. If the size of the MUF is found to be beyond a value attributable to such identifiable causes, the possibility that a diversion has been made must be considered." He put the book on his desk and said to Holbrook almost mockingly, "Now are you going to ask me to file an official report on a LEMUF of less than one percent?"

"Yes, sir, I am."

"You must be joking." Except Boston knew he wasn't. "We'll both be laughed out of the business." He knew he had to make sure Holbrook did no such thing. "Of course it's your right and privilege to do what you like. But let me tell you this, Commander, such nonsense will not get past my desk." He pointed a finger at Holbrook. "Believe you me, I won't put my name to anything of the sort." He shook his head. "I won't."

"All right. All right. If you feel that strongly about it . . . I mean, you're probably right."

Now Boston stared at him. He's giving up? Just like that? "You simply have to understand that we do not answer to the United States Navy or the United States government." He's giving up without a real fight. "You must understand that you're talking to a British civil servant who is ultimately responsible to the British Parliament." He's quitting, just like that.

"I'm sorry. I've been under a lot of pressure lately. Personal pressures. Of course you're right. We're talking about LEMUF ballpark figures."

"Yes," Boston said cautiously. "Yes. Definitely LEMUF ballpark figures, to use your term."

"I shouldn't have wasted your time with this."

Could he really mean it? "I'm glad you've come to a proper conclusion." Perhaps he knows when he's beaten. That's it. He must know I've got him dead to rights. He must realize how silly we would both look if he filed a report and it went nowhere. And by God I'd make certain it went nowhere. So he's come to his senses because he doesn't want it to boomerang back into his face. He doesn't want any trouble. "It means we can go on to other matters. I trust you'll consider the MUF matter dropped."

"You're right. We've both got more important things to do. I only hope this won't go any further. What I'm saying is, I wouldn't want this to get back to my superiors."

"No," Boston said. "Of course not." He stared at Holbrook. Hah. He's finally seen that this could be trouble for him. He's like all of them. He just wants to skate through his twenty or twenty-five or thirty years and avoid trouble. It's the Achilles heel of all career military men. Toppy is right. You should always have something to hold over the Americans. Being able to bargain with this is my opening past any line of defense. I simply have to make sure he knows that I know. I've got to apply just enough pressure on him to make certain he clearly sees where we stand. "I should raise hell with you for putting me in such an awkward situation. But, I'm a reasonable man.''

"It's my personal problems which I've allowed to get in the way of my better judgment.''

"As I said, I'm a reasonable man.'' And now it's time to make my move. "So I'll tell you what. Eventually I've got to write a formal report about the missing van incident. If you forget about this MUF business, I'll see that your name stays out of my report.'' He looked directly at Holbrook. "I'll simply forget to mention your little white lie.''

"Thank you.''

I suspect we understand each other, eh? Boston shook Holbrook's hand. "I'm going out on a limb for you.'' Except, Boston assured himself, he's on the very tip of the limb and I'm holding onto the tree with a saw in the other hand. "I hope you understand that. But life is too short. So I'll stonewall my superiors and see that it goes no further. I'll see that you're protected.'' That's telling him. "How's that sound?'' He smiled. "Do we have a deal?''

"Yes . . . yes, we do.''

Holbrook left.

Boston watched the lift doors close, and when they were shut he allowed himself a great big smile. Hah. That's that. No more problems there. I've nipped it in the bud. He'll go away quietly and before too long there will be so much more paperwork on top of the other paperwork that it would take a dozen Holbrooks to dig their way out from under.

He went back into his office.

Nipped it right in the bud, he kept telling himself.

Then he spotted Holbrook's untouched coffee sitting on the edge of his desk.

And his imagination ran away with him . . .

Chapter
Sixteen

THE COMMISSIONAIRE POINTED to Mrs. Fitzgerald.

She took his raincoat and told him, "Fourth floor."

Stepping into the minuscule lift, Richard Holbrook pushed the button marked four. The lift groaned and rattled as it climbed. He leaned against the side of the cage and went over his tack yet again. *I don't know what he knows. He probably doesn't know anything. He'll almost certainly try to give me flak about the missing van. I can bank on that. I'll have to let him do his thing. Then I can come at him from the side. The oblique approach. The trick is to let him talk until he gives me an opening. The trick is not to jump in too fast. If he doesn't know anything and I spook him, he'll get too curious. If he knows and I spook him, he'll bolt and then it will be too late.*

The lift stopped.

And the door opened.

"Commander. This way please. I have a bone to pick with you."

So predictable. Okay. I'll let him get it off his chest. "Oh?"

He followed Boston into his office.

"You lied to me yesterday. Tea? Or would you prefer coffee?"

Go on. Get it out of your system. "Coffee, thanks," Holbrook said, then added quickly, "light milk." He had learned the hard way that in England the choice is either white coffee or black coffee, and that if you don't insist, there's never anything in between. Even worse is tea. In England, tea arrives as a sickly white fluid. You have to know enough to ask for it with lemon, or just plain. Why the Brits habitually killed their tea by flooding it with milk was beyond him. Weren't they, of all people, supposed to know better? Didn't they actually start a war for the sake of a few crates of tea dumped into a harbor in 1773? The least they could do these days is drink it properly.

"My superiors at the MoD have since sent the matter to be dealt with at ambassadorial level. Of course I had no alternative but to forward it to them. After all, I quite clearly asked you if there was a PuN shipment van missing and you told me, just as clearly, no. I therefore feel an obligation to alert your superiors to the fact that we find ourselves facing a serious problem of, how shall I put it . . . confidence."

If only he knew how much shit I caught for even suggesting that we should have informed the Brits. "The missing van incident has been out of my hands from the very start." He sat down in a chair facing Boston's desk and crossed his legs. "I've never been privy to anything more than an initial briefing . . ."

"The coffee first."

The coffee. Okay, Holbrook thought, if you want to play this kind of game, that's fine with me. He looked out of the window at the ugly building across the street. Then he casually inspected the papers on Boston's desk. None of them seemed to be from the DoD 3093 file. But there was a book . . . he spotted it sitting on a corner of the desk and he figured, maybe I can throw him off-guard by coming at him with another approach. "Are you a cricket fan?"

"What? Oh, this. Yes. I just started reading it. It's about the finest player the game has known. Ever heard of Syd Barnes?"

"No. Can't say that I have."

"Syd Barnes? You must have. He was as world-famous as your Joe DiMaggio."

World-famous? Why do people insist someone is so famous when other people have never heard of him. How can someone be world-famous if I don't know who he is. "Ever heard of Junior Jim Gilliam?"

"Who?"

"He played second base for the Brooklyn Dodgers."

"Oh. I see."

The coffee arrived.

Just in time, Holbrook decided as he took the cup and looked inside. It was much too milky white. He shook his head. What a country. They don't know a goddamned thing about coffee. They don't know a goddamned thing about tea. And they never heard of Junior Jim Gilliam. He put the cup on the edge of Boston's desk, stirred it politely a couple of times, and left it sitting right there.

"Sorry there are no biscuits. I must be totally frank and say that you've put me personally in a most awkward position. I'm certain you can see that from where I view the situation, there has been a grave breach of trust."

"I hear what you're saying." Holbrook could see his game plan being shot full of holes. "But that's got nothing to do with the reason I'm here." He reminded himself, if I let him talk around me now I'll never be able to get him back onto the track. No guts, no glory. He jumped way ahead of where he wanted to be. "I'm here because I want to do some routine checking on some DoD 3093 forms as they've gone through the system."

"Well, I'm certain we can arrange something. Are you looking for anything in particular?"

"Not necessarily," Holbrook lied. "If I could just check your files."

"Unfortunately, at this moment in time, I'm afraid it won't be possible."

"What do you mean?" He didn't like that at all but tried not to show his anger. Stay calm. Don't spook him. Don't let him get to you. "How can it not be possible?"

"It won't be possible just now for several reasons. Amongst them is the fact that the files you're looking for are not kept here."

Don't give me that crap, Holbrook wanted to say. "Well, then let's go to where the files are kept."

"If only life was so easy. You see, the files you're talking about are kept with various agencies, depending on the type of shipment involved. The U.K. Atomic Energy Authority's Special Constabulary has some. Various MoD offices have others. It would take quite some time to gather the ones you want.''

He's throwing out a lot of chaff. ''We've always been led to believe that the files were maintained by your office. After all, you're the liaison . . .''

''Ah, yes . . . ah, yes . . . they have at times been kept here but reorganizations . . . you know, every time a new minister comes in, he wants things done his way . . .''

It's all bilge. He's lying to me. I've somehow touched a nerve and now he's lying to me. ''You mean that there's nothing here regarding any of our shipments.'' He pointed to a filing cabinet in the corner. ''None of our DoD 3093s wind up there?''

''Commander, I don't come into your office and suggest that you don't do your job properly. I said at the outset that I've got a bone to pick with you and I think it's only fair that we clear the air about that before we go on to other matters. After all, you must realize the particularly sticky position you've put me in. That an officer of the United States Navy would lie to a duly authorized representative of Her Majesty's government about a matter as sensitive as the possible hijacking of U.S. Navy nuclear materials on British soil . . .''

Now he's purposely turned the subject around to me. ''We still don't know that it was a hijacking,'' Holbrook pointed out.

''No? A van filled with nuclear materials disappears off the face of the earth, you try to cover it up and you want me to congratulate you for your cooperation and sense of fair play?''

''That notwithstanding''—Holbrook assured himself that he was on to something—''it is of the utmost importance that the United States Navy be permitted to properly audit every step of the accounting procedures concerning our nuclear shipments. Now, I would sincerely hope that we could handle this amicably on our level. But if need be . . .''

''Just a moment. Is that a threat to go above my head? I've told you, Commander, that the information you're seeking will have to be gathered from various repositories. That will take time. It's a lot of extra work for me and I can tell you frankly, I've got other things to do. In the meantime, I should remind you that the U.S. Navy has seriously breached our bilateral agreements concerning nuclear substance shipments in the United Kingdom. Would you mind terribly if I read the regulations to you, to illustrate precisely what our agreements say about material accountancy?''

This is getting me nowhere. I've got to put the ball back in his court. "Mr. Boston," Holbrook tried to interject, "the point is . . .''

"Please have the courtesy to hear me out. Now. Listen to this. Safeguards will involve the applications of measures for material accountancy, supplemented by containment and surveillance. I'll spare you the technical definitions of material accountancy, containment or surveillance, but the regulations go on to say . . . it will be the responsibility of the guest nation to inform the host nation of any and all incidents, suspected, imagined or actual, at the earliest possible moment when prevention of mishaps and containment of theft, vandalism, accident or terrorist acts might immediately take place. Does that sound familiar, Commander?''

Familiar? I'll tell you what sounds familiar, Holbrook muttered to himself. What sounds familiar is that as soon as I get anywhere near the question of the DoD forms, you slipslide away. You can't really be so pissed off at us for bending the rules when we've made a habit of looking the other way every time *you* bend the rules. "Somewhere in there you'll find the letters MUF.''

"MUF?''

"Materials unaccounted for," Holbrook said. It's my turn again. "You know, the difference between book inventory and physical inventory. So as long as you brought up the business of material accountancy, we have reason to believe that there might be, let's call them 'minor discrepancies' in certain accountings.''

"Discrepancies? You talk about MUF. But of course you also know the term LEMUF—limit of error of materials unaccounted for. It's not uncommon for there to be some differences between book and physical inventories. I've often found that instrumental uncertainties can be calculated accurately enough so that if the inventory difference is within this range it can be accepted.''

Holbrook agreed. "Yes. But in cases of larger discrepancies, an investigation might be called for to determine whether or not nuclear material is missing.''

"What sort of numbers are you talking about? Percentagewise, of course.''

Shit. This is not where I want to be. He had to concede, "A very small amount.''

"Less than an allowable five percent?''

He saw that he had to get off this quickly or Boston would latch onto it. "Yes.''

"Less than two-and-a-half percent?''

Now he had to admit, "Yes.''

"My God, man, less than one percent?''

He's shooting from the hip and I'm getting plugged. Son of a bitch. "That's not the point,'' Holbrook tried to argue.

"Less than one percent? Hah! It absolutely is the point. That is the whole point. Here, Commander, let me read this to you. The reasons for MUF may be found in measurement uncertainties or other technical causes. If the size of the MUF is found to be beyond a value attributable to such identifiable causes, the possibility that a diversion has been made must be considered. Now are you going to ask me to file an official report on a LEMUF of less than one percent?''

"Yes, sir.'' This should upset him. "I am.''

"You must be joking. We'll both be laughed out of the business. Of course it's your right and privilege to do what you like. But let me tell you this, Commander, such nonsense will not get past my desk. Believe you me, I won't put my name to anything of the sort. I won't.''

Holbrook stared at Boston for a long time. Okay. Maybe this is my opening. I push. He pushes back. I've pushed again. Now it's his turn to push back. Maybe this is where I can bring him down with his own weight. "All right,'' he sighed. "All right. If you feel that strongly about it . . . I mean, you're probably right.''

"You simply have to understand that we do not answer to the United States Navy or the United States government. You must understand that you're talking to a British civil servant who is ultimately responsible to the British Parliament.''

Now give him plenty of rope. Look away. Feign contemplation. Nod a little. Agree with him. ''I'm sorry,'' Holbrook pretended. ''I've been under a lot of pressure lately. Personal pressures. Of course you're right. We're talking about LEMUF ballpark figures.''

''Yes. Yes. Definitely LEMUF ballpark figures, to use your term.''

More rope. Holbrook sat back in his chair. ''I shouldn't have wasted your time with this.''

''I'm glad you've come to a proper conclusion. It means we can go on to other matters. I trust you'll consider the MUF matter dropped.''

Okay, fella, let's see you hang yourself. ''You're right. We've both got more important things to do. I only hope this won't go any further.'' I push. You push back. I've pushed. Come on, goddamnit, it's your turn. ''What I'm saying is, I wouldn't want this to get back to my superiors.''

''No. Of course not. I should raise hell with you for putting me in such an awkward situation. But, I'm a reasonable man.''

Here it comes. ''It's my personal problems which I've allowed to get in the way of my better judgment.''

''As I've said, I'm a reasonable man. So I'll tell you what. Eventually I've got to write a formal report about the missing van incident. If you forget about this MUF business, I'll see that your name stays out of my report. I'll simply forget to mention your little white lie.''

Bingo. Holbrook forced a grin. ''Thank you,'' he said and extended his hand.

''I'm going out on a limb for you. I hope you understand that. But life is too short. So I'll stonewall my superiors and see that it goes no further. I'll see that you're protected. How's that sound? Do we have a deal?''

''Yes,'' Holbrook said, ''yes, we do.''

Chapter
Seventeen

STARING AT THE untouched cup of coffee, Boston's imagination ran away with him.

Holbrook didn't drink any of it.

Oh well, the man probably doesn't like coffee, that's all.

Or maybe, Boston thought almost as a joke, maybe Holbrook thinks I've poisoned it.

Hah. Some joke. Holbrook thinks I've poisoned his coffee. Hah.

Except as a joke it didn't seem very funny.

Holbrook didn't touch his coffee. Not at all. Good God, could he seriously think I was going to poison him? Could he seriously think I've somehow dropped a little strychnine into his coffee . . . or truth serum? What do they call that—sodium pentathol, that's it—could Holbrook seriously think I'd pour sodium pentathol into his coffee just to find out what he knows? Ridiculous. Pure fantasy. He couldn't possibly imagine for a moment . . .

Yet the more Boston stared at Holbrook's untouched coffee, the more he was bothered by it.

He didn't drink it because he didn't want it. Except, I quite distinctly remember asking him if he wanted coffee or tea and he said coffee. If he didn't want anything to drink, he would have said as much.

So Holbrook didn't drink his coffee because . . .

The reason he didn't drink the coffee was because . . .

Because . . .

The idea popped into Boston's head—because he's on to me and he thinks I know it.

For a few seconds that idea sent shivers down his spine.

Ridiculous. He tried to talk himself out of it. What could Holbrook know?

Nothing. Nothing at all.

But he didn't believe that for an instant.

All right, I will concede that he knows there's something wrong somewhere and that it's somehow tied into the DoD 3093 forms. Hah. I warned that printer to be careful, to copy them exactly. I wonder if Holbrook has spotted a fault on the forms. No, there couldn't be any faults. I checked. Anyway, how many U.S. forms did I use? Not that many. Holbrook would have to sort through hundreds if not thousands of the real ones before he'd ever find one of the copies.

Boston went to his filing cabinet, unlocked the bottom drawer and reached into the rear of it to pull out a very full manila envelope. He yanked out a handful of forms. DoD forms. NATO forms. A set of forms used by the Dutch army. Another set, these sequentially numbered and used by British forces under NATO stationed in Germany. Hah. They all look fine to me. They all look exactly like the real forms. They are fine. The forms are perfect. Holbrook probably doesn't know anything. He suspects something but doesn't know for certain.

Just the same, Boston quickly came to the conclusion, this is no time to push one's luck.

He stuffed the forms back into the envelope, went downstairs to the mailroom, saw that he was alone, and shoved the forms through the shredder machine.

He sliced every form he had into a thousand little strips.

There. That's that.

He went back upstairs.

Now it doesn't matter if Holbrook does suspect there's something wrong with the forms he has because there are no more forms left to be traced to me. He can look all he wants but he won't find a thing. Anyway, I suspect he won't bother looking too far because I made him a good deal. He's a career soldier. The most important thing in his life is his retirement pension. He won't risk that. I made him a good deal and he took it. He thinks I've let him off the hook . . .

Boston fell into his chair.

. . . he thinks I've done him a huge favor . . .

No matter how he tried to reassure himself, Boston couldn't stop worrying.

The forms are gone and the amounts missing from the U.S. shipments are much too insignificant. Hah. If we launched official inquiries every time such a minuscule amount of U.S. Navy PuN went missing, they'd never have time for anything else.

No, he said out loud, it's over. Done. Finito.

He took the phone to ring home. The number was engaged. He tried the "R" button. The number still rang engaged. Oh well, I'll get back to her. Or maybe I'll just buy her some flowers and take them home with me tonight. Good idea. Then he dialed Mr. Katzman, the salesman for Las Fontanas. "It's Mr. Boston. I'd like to come to see you in your office tomorrow afternoon about the condominium."

"Tomorrow afternoon about the condominium," the salesman repeated.

"Yes. I'll arrange for a transfer of the funds, just as we discussed."

"Just as we discussed."

"Good." He hung up. There. That's done too.

Yes, he wrote himself a note, some flowers to celebrate. She'll like that.

Then he glanced toward Holbrook's untouched coffee again.

No . . . surely he couldn't possibly imagine in his wildest dreams . . .

He buzzed Mrs. Fitzgerald to take the coffee cup away.

When she did, he picked up *Syd*. If I hurry I'll be able to get it off to Nigel in this afternoon's post. So he opened the book and started reading.

Barnes continued to bowl until he reached the age of 57 and there are some estimates which put his lifetime wicket total at over 6000 . . .

He started reading but he couldn't concentrate.
It's over. It's finished. The problem is solved.
Except, in the pit of his stomach, he knew it wasn't.

Chapter
Eighteen

MUTTERING TO HIMSELF, what an old woman, Christopher Li'Ning reached for the intercom and asked Peter to come in.

"Find Sze. Tell him this is important." He grabbed a slip of paper, opened his address book and copied down, Chappell House, 7 Storey's Gate. "Here. A U.S. Navy officer named Holbrook will be arriving at this address at eleven. It's around the corner somewhere from Westminster Abbey. Sze will have to hurry because there isn't much time."

Peter took the address and started out of the office. "Oh. The fellow from the *Daily Telegraph* rang again. About the ginger jar."

"What does he want? Didn't you tell him yesterday? . . ."

"He said this was important. Maybe you should speak with him. He wouldn't say anything to me except that it was now very urgent. His name is Pantucci."

"All right," Li'Ning said. "Find Sze quickly."

He told his secretary to get the man from the *Daily Telegraph* on the line. When the call was ready she buzzed it through.

"Mr. Pantucci? This is Christopher Li'Ning from Mandarin Commerce. I'm returning your call."

"Oh yes," Pantucci said, "the Chinese fellow from the bank. Listen, it's about that pricey piece of ceramics you bought. I've been trying to get a photograph because we want to run it with a story tomorrow. Can I send someone over right away?''

"You've caught me at a very busy time." Li'Ning tried to put him off in the most polite way possible. "I'm returning your call because I thought this was something urgent."

"It is. I need it for tomorrow."

"Yes, of course. But . . ." He chose to try the subtle-bribe technique. That usually worked. "You see, letting you have the photo now puts me in a slightly delicate situation. If this could wait a few days . . . say, middle of next week? I would really appreciate it. On top of that I'm afraid we've got some currency problems on the burner. But if you'll do that favor for me, and hold off for a few days, then I'd be delighted to do whatever I could for you."

"Listen, Mr. Li'Ning, I don't want to cry on your shoulder, but you see, I've got this editor who hates it whenever we're second with a story. I just heard it's already down for tomorrow's *Antiques Trade Gazette.* So if I could send someone over straightaway for a photo . . . I mean, I'd look pretty foolish if I let some weekly trade rag come up with the story before I do."

"Someone is running the story tomorrow?" That was not what he wanted to hear.

"Yes. Hold on a sec. Don't go away." Pantucci put the phone down . . . there were voices in the background and someone fumbling with papers . . . then he came back on the line. "Here's what I've got of it." Pantucci read several paragraphs, most of it sounding as if it had been lifted word for word from the sale catalog. "Now, that would be fine except they're running it tomorrow which means in a few weeks it isn't a story, and anyway I understand there's more to it than just the jar's rarity and value."

Li'Ning simply said, "Oh?"

"Yes. I understand that this is not for your private collection."

"You do?" Then he recalled that he himself had made that very point to the girl at the auction house. "Well, let me just confirm what that report says. It's no secret, I bought the ginger jar on behalf of the bank."

"I've heard it's got something to do with a gift from your

bank to the Chinese government. If it's true, it's a pretty good angle for a story."

That stopped him. "Now where did you hear that?"

"Wherever," Pantucci said. "What I've been told is that you're on this big kick to help repatriate Chinese treasures, to return treasures like the ginger jar to the Chinese people. Of course, just between us, I suspect it has more to do with your opening a branch in Beijing. Am I close?"

Li'Ning thought fast. "Yes and no. The ginger jar is a gift from the bank." He knew if he didn't tell Pantucci enough, the fellow would worry more about his deadline than the truth. The trick was not to tell him too much. To stall him. "Actually we're in the midst of preparing a formal release about the purchase, but we hadn't planned on saying anything for a week or so, at the earliest. We'd like to have a formal ceremony to present it officially. It will be quite a party, I can assure you. In fact, I'd be delighted if you'd come to the ceremony. Better still, perhaps you would be kind enough to join me here at the bank for lunch one day next week and we can discuss it further."

"This parade and ceremony, you've set it for early next month, no?"

He couldn't believe word was already around Fleet Street. "It would be in early May, yes."

"Well, that's fine for you, but I don't think the story can wait that long for me," Pantucci said.

"I would hope," Li'Ning said, "that it could at least wait until it is a story."

"Problem is, if someone runs it first . . ."

"I understand your situation," Li'Ning said, trying to come up with a new way to get out of this because the subtle-bribe technique obviously wasn't going to work. "I'd love to know how you heard about our plans for the ginger jar."

"Like they say in the movies, I've got my sources."

"Well." Li'Ning reminded himself, stall for time. "I hope we might meet next week. In any case, why don't I have someone get back to you about it this morning?"

Pantucci said, "If you're saying that you'll arrange for the photo, that's fine. But it has to be this morning."

"I'll see that someone rings you this morning," Li'Ning assured him. "I'll take care of it, right away." He hung up.

Now, he wondered, where could Pantucci have heard about the ginger jar being a gift? And how could he have known about the date for the ceremony? Telling the world too much about this too soon could jeopardize everything. He thought about the story Pantucci had just read to him. It could have come from the Bonham's catalog. Or it might have come from the edited description he gave Joe Tyler.

He picked up his phone again.

Tyler's secretary said that he was in a meeting.

Li'Ning demanded, "Get him out of it."

She said she would try.

Instead of Tyler, Frances Pommeroy came onto the line. "Mr. Li'Ning, is that you? We must thank you for a splendid lunch . . ."

"Please put Mr. Tyler on the phone."

"I understand he's tied up with a client," she said politely.

He instructed her in a slow, very stern voice, "I want Mr. Tyler right now."

She couldn't have misread that tone, so she excused herself for a moment, and put the call on hold.

Music played, the music stopped, then "Hi," Tyler's voice broke into the line. "How's everything at the best chop suey parlor in London?"

"I will ask you once and only once," Li'Ning said. "Who else have you spoken to about the ginger jar?"

"Me? About the ginger jar? What are you talking about?"

"I made it clear to you yesterday that everything we discussed was just between us." Li'Ning could always tell when Westerners were nervous. "I have just received three phone calls about the ginger jar."

"Three?" Tyler seemed shocked.

"Yes," he lied. "The *Daily Telegraph*. The *Sunday Times*. And the *Standard*."

Tyler shrieked, "How the hell did the *Sunday Times* and the *Standard* get it?"

"That's what I thought," Li'Ning said. "Now tell me how the hell the *Telegraph* got it."

"The *Telegraph*? Yes, I meant . . . how did the *Times* and the *Standard* and the *Telegraph* get it."

Anyone could see that Tyler knew he had been trapped. "You guaranteed that no one would get the story in advance."

"I did . . . certainly I did . . . I can't imagine how they . . ."

Now Li'Ning told another lie. "He mentioned your name."

"Pantucci?"

It was easy, he thought to himself. Westerners in general, but the British in particular. Almost too easy. "You have seriously damaged certain plans about which you were not aware. First, please consider your work for this bank as terminated. Second, I shall seek legal advice and see if there is any action that we might take to extract damages."

"Wait a minute," Tyler yelled. "I know my job and when I leak information to friendly journalists it is always in my clients' interests. Whatever I discussed with Pantucci, I did with your interests in mind. I might have said something to Pantucci . . . but I did not discuss it with the *Sunday Times* or the *Standard* so I have no idea . . ."

"Goodbye, Mr. Tyler." Li'Ning dropped his phone back on its cradle.

He squeezed both his fists together tightly and held them up to the sides of his face, then tilted his head all the way back. He shut his eyes and held his breath.

Eventually his fury began to subside.

As it did, an old expression came to mind.

Before the river floods, there is a gently rising tide.

Peter stepped into his office. Li'Ning sat up straight. Peter told him, "Everything is taken care of. But you're due in a meeting."

He followed Peter to the conference room where he spent nearly an hour with the bank's senior foreign exchange dealers trying to get their overall currency exposure into line. The meeting ended without anyone coming up with a plan. Then he went into another conference, this time forty-five minutes with three brokers representing a German consortium interested in financing a £22.6 million real-estate project. He turned them down, annoyed because the brokers had not been up front with him as to exactly how much of the loan would be unsecured.

"Those brokers are no longer welcome here," he told Peter on their way back to his office. "I have better things to do with my time than put up with such amateurish attempts to pull one over on us."

His private line rang.

Grabbing it, he answered with a sharp, "Yes."

"It's me. Boston. That matter I spoke with you about earlier . . . you know, the interested third party . . ."

He shook his head. "Why are you being so vague? You're speaking, of course, about your U.S. Navy fellow named Holbrook. I told you I would take care of the problem."

"Well . . ." Boston sounded upset. "It's not really a problem. I mean, yes, he knows there's something amiss, or at least he suspects there is, but he doesn't know exactly what or exactly where. So . . . I was just thinking that perhaps we shouldn't press our luck."

He hated the way some Englishmen were so easily excitable. "If you mean you want out of our agreement, please just say so."

"No . . . well . . . yes. After all, it's been how long now . . . since your father passed away? Is it three years already? We agreed in the beginning it would only be once or twice . . . just enough for the house in Spain."

Li'Ning thought, he's holding something back from me. "I have the feeling that you are more worried than you let on."

"No . . . no, I assure you."

He's not telling me everything. "I can hear it in your voice."

"I'm simply being cautious."

"I must tell you that nervous people make me nervous."

"I am not being nervous. I am simply being extremely cautious."

Boston. Then the newspapers. Then Tyler. Then two wasted meetings. Now Boston again. "You've gone from cautious to extremely cautious."

"You don't seem to realize the situation I'm in." He was pleading. "You don't seem to realize what I've risked. We've been all right up till now. But with that American snooping around . . ."

Li'Ning leaned all the way back in his chair. My options must be narrowing, he told himself. Excitable people cause excitement.

Boston cut into his thoughts. "You have to understand what I've risked . . . Please . . ." There was an awkward pause. "Ah . . . perhaps we might discuss the other half . . . you know, the rest of our agreement."

Ah, this is why he's so very concerned. "Oh yes. Your Swiss account."

"Shhh. Please. There are some things that we mustn't discuss over the telephone. I've got to be cautious. I mean, there are all those crossed lines. It happens all the time. One simply never knows who might be listening. I'd feel better if we could meet. Yes, let's meet. As soon as possible. Say . . . tomorrow? At my club. That's always a good place. Do you know the Reform? Lunchtime. Twelve-thirty. I'll reserve a table."

What to do. Boston's nervousness is contagious. I need some time to think. Perhaps I shall pacify him. "Certainly."

"And you will have the . . . you know, the numbers with you?"

"Of course."

"Good. Excellent. I'm glad we can . . . well, that you can see my position. Maybe you're right. Maybe I am getting a bit too nervous. It's simply that he came here this morning . . ."

"I told you I would take care of everything. That I would handle Mr. Holbrook. Now, please excuse me, I really must go." Yes, he thought, the time has come to handle this. "Goodbye."

He tossed the telephone onto its cradle.

He shut his eyes for a moment and tried to list his options. Boston. Holbrook. Me. A chain will break at its weakest link. But if the chain is snapped first then the weakest link becomes meaningless. So, what part of the chain must I snap.

Boston. Holbrook. Me.

Opening his eyes, he told his secretary to call for Terry and have him come up to the office right away. While he was

174

waiting he rummaged through a stack of newspapers on the edge of his desk, found Lloyds List and checked the shipping column. A freighter called *The Year of the Ox* was due in from Taiwan. The *Dragon Empress* was listed as sailing at 1 P.M. for Rotterdam. From there he knew she was going on to Riga and Tallinn, before stopping back at London on May 8th for the return voyage to China. The timing would have been perfect. It still might, he thought, but just in case . . .

He jumped up and sorted through a shelf filled with books on the far wall. He pulled down a huge atlas, opened it and studied the page that showed the North Sea. Rotterdam would never do. It had to be somewhere in the British Isles. His finger followed the east coast northward. Hull. Newcastle. No. Too small. Edinburgh. Dundee. No. Then he came to Aberdeen. The North Sea oil port. A lot of traffic. Busy. As far away from London as you can get. Aberdeen it is. He took a piece of blank white paper . . . purposely avoiding bank stationery . . . and wrote a note in Chinese characters.

Terry knocked on his door. "You need me?"

"Yes." Li'Ning folded the note and stuffed it into a plain envelope. Then he wrote something in Chinese on the front of the envelope and handed it to Terry. "Do you remember the freighter yesterday morning? It's called the *Dragon Empress*. Can you find it again?"

"Sure I remember."

"You'll have to hurry." He started to hand him the envelope, but just to make sure Terry wouldn't make a mistake, he wrote the freighter's name on it in English. "There may be another Chinese freighter in port. So be careful. Give this to the captain of the *Dragon Empress* and no one else."

Terry glared at him. "You trying to tell me that you think all Chinese people look alike to us?"

"I didn't say that," Li'Ning answered. "But even to me all Chinese freighters look alike. Now get going. She's due to sail in about an hour."

Terry left with the note.

Before the river floods, there is a gently rising tide.

And Li'Ning knew the tide was rising.

Chapter
Nineteen

RICHARD HOLBROOK RODE down in the tiny lift, took his rain-coat, stepped out of the building at 7 Storey's Gate, and thought to himself, I have just been offered a bribe.

He walked toward Westminster Abbey, hoping to find a taxi, until he remembered that he had his American wallet with him and only a few British coins. He shoved his hand into his pocket and pulled out 65p. I wonder if John Paul Getty or Howard Hughes ever carried much more.

Looking around, he realized he wasn't far from the West-minster tube station. So he headed for the Underground.

Boston tried to bribe me. He tried to buy my silence. Hol-brook wanted that voice inside his head to play Devil's Ad-vocate. I have just been offered a bribe.

Of sorts, the voice chimed in. A bribe of sorts. Boston was simply putting his cards on the table.

He argued, you've got to be kidding. Boston as much as said that if I forget the business of the 3093s, he'd keep my name out of the missing van report.

At the corner of Parliament Street, he stopped to glance at the Houses of Parliament. The scaffolding was down and Big Ben once again looked like it did on the biscuit tins.

When he first arrived in England, Holbrook was surprised to learn that Parliament was a nineteenth-century building and not something straight out of King Arthur's days. What about the Knights of the Round Table and Robin Hood and

176

all those guys? Sorry, he was told, but British history isn't necessarily always as romantically medieval as Americans like to think it is. Well then, what about King George the Third, you know, Crazy George, and the American Revolution? Do your history books have blank pages for the years 1776 to 1812? And here, they said, you are referring to the illegal overthrow of the lawful British government by force and violence at the hands of colonial radicals. The what? Yes, they reminded him, there are, after all, always two ways of looking at everything.

I say it was a bribe, he argued with the voice. He doesn't want me going too deeply into those 3093s. That's the only thing it could possibly be. A bribe.

No, the voice reminded him, there are, after all, always two ways of looking at everything.

Holbrook went into the tube station, bought a ticket to Bond Street and only then checked the wall map to see that, in this case, the tube wasn't a very convenient route back to the office. Damnit, he mumbled, why can't everyone on earth use dollars. It would make life so much simpler.

Maybe I should just grab a taxi and find someone to lend me the money at the other end. But then, nah, he decided, I've got my ticket so the hell with it. It's too embarrassing at my age not to have enough money in my pocket for taxi fare. Anyway, getting a taxi in London when it rains is hopeless.

He waited for the eastbound train on an almost deserted platform. For a rainy day, he observed, there are surprisingly few people in the Underground.

At Embankment, he followed the signs to the Northern Line . . . down one set of steps, then down an escalator. Keep to the right. Excuse me, people said as they hurried down the left side of the moving steps. He turned to look at the people lined up behind him. Three women in cloth coats and rain bonnets. A young Oriental guy in a baseball jacket. Four American tourists with cameras and golf caps . . . and all four of them were standing on the left side of the escalator. He had to smile.

Signs at the bottom of the escalator directed him through a long tunnel—it reeked of urine—and finally to the platform.

A train pulled in. He sat down. But almost as soon as it

pulled out of the Embankment Station, it pulled into Charing Cross. So he got up and followed the signs there for the Jubilee Line.

He walked along another tunnel—this one smelled more like peanuts—and now he decided that each of the London Underground lines has a different smell. The Circle Line doesn't have the same odor as the Northern Line. The Jubilee Line doesn't smell like the District Line. Maybe they do it that way on purpose.

Where that tunnel ended there was another escalator down.

The train was nearly empty at Charing Cross. He was totally alone in the carriage. The doors closed and the train pulled out. Some people got on at Green Park, but so many people were waiting along the platform at Bond Street that he had to turn and sidestep his way through them. Why don't they ever move aside and let people out before they try to get in.

Handing in his ticket, he started to walk out of the Bond Street shopping arcade when he noticed that one of those jeans shops with loud music blaring had a huge banner in their window announcing a special sale of football jerseys. You mean, soccer shirts, he wanted to say. He went inside and tried to remember what sizes Chrissie and David would wear. The salesgirl wasn't very helpful. I'm afraid you'll have to know their size. Well, how about if I tell you their ages. I'm afraid I wouldn't know, she said, not even taking the trouble to hide her boredom. Yeah, thanks, he nodded and fumbled through the sweatshirt pile. The only size they had anyway was medium. Thanks loads, he said out loud. If they're too big they'll grow into them. The first one he took was Manchester United. Good. The next one was Everton. I guess. He stopped and wondered if he could find one for Queen's Park Rangers. Ah, what the hell, he shrugged and went off in search of the cash desk. My kids never heard of these teams anyway.

"You take plastic?" He paid for them with a credit card, then went out onto Oxford Street.

The HMV record shop was just down the block.

A thought ran through his mind.

He went into the record store, fought his way through the

crowds of kids, and found a copy of Stevie Wonder's "I Just Called To Say I Love You." There are more Oriental guys wearing baseball jackets in London, he thought as he pushed past one, than anywhere else on earth. He paid for the record—"You take plastic, don't you?"—and told himself, I'll put it in the box with the sweatshirts.

Walking along Oxford Street to Duke Street, he figured as long as he was passing his apartment, he'd drop off the sweatshirts and the record so he could pack them well before mailing them at the American post office in the Navy building. But first he stopped in the tiny supermarket on the corner. "Ali, I'll come back and pay you for this tonight." He took bread and orange juice and coffee and milk. He also helped himself to some spaghetti, a can of meat sauce, six cans of soda and two boxes of Twiglets.

Upstairs, he simply tossed everything on the couch. It can all wait till tonight. He wanted to get back to the office. So he locked the door and rode the lift down to the ground floor.

He crossed the street and walked past the front entrance of the Marriott Hotel.

Out of the corner of his eye, he noticed someone was standing just inside the door, staring at him.

He didn't think anything of it, until he got to the corner where he should turn right to North Audley Street.

That's when he realized that the person staring at him from inside the Marriott's front door was an Oriental guy in a baseball jacket.

Three in the same day.

A coincidence.

Or the same one three times.

The voice inside his head told him not to go straight back to the office.

The same one three times.

He crossed the street and walked into Grosvenor Square.

Paths in the square form an X as they go from corner to corner, with another path bisecting it so that you can walk from the statue of Franklin D. Roosevelt down to the Britannia Hotel. He strolled into the middle of the square and up to the statue, where he stood for a moment pretending to read the inscription.

All summer long secretaries from offices in the neighborhood brought their brown-bagged lunches here, and spread out on the lawn to take a few minutes of sunshine. All summer long the park was alive. But now in the rain it was deserted. There weren't even any Swedish nannies pushing prams filled with Iranian babies.

The square was empty.

He waited there pretending to look at the statue while he watched the Duke Street corner of the square.

Nothing happened. No one appeared. And after a few minutes he told himself, this is crazy. There must be thousands of Oriental kids in London wearing baseball jackets.

He moved away from the statue.

And there he was.

The guy in the baseball jacket was crossing the street toward the square.

Holbrook walked to the other side of the square, waited for the traffic to clear, crossed the street and went inside the Britannia Hotel.

As soon as he was far enough through the front doors, he turned around to look out to the square.

The guy in the baseball jacket was hurrying along in his direction.

Now Holbrook went down the long corridor toward the hotel's pub, past the florist, past the barber shop, past the newspaper shop, and out of the door there. He turned left into the alley behind the Britannia, edged along the Connaught into Mount Street, and walked quickly toward South Audley Street.

The same guy three times? He couldn't believe he was actually being followed. By whom? Why? It's a coincidence. All young guys have baseball jackets. Baseball jackets are sold in every shop on Oxford Street.

He stopped in front of a tailor's shop and pretended to be looking in the window.

By moving just a bit, by turning his right shoulder up to the glass, he could peek inconspicuously to see if . . .

He was there.

Way down the street, on the opposite pavement.

Without thinking, Holbrook stepped into the tailor's.

"Good morning, Commander." A tall, intelligent-looking man with a round, soft face walked up to him.

Holbrook moved all the way into the shop, then glanced back through the window. He watched as the guy in the baseball jacket came up the block, and ducked into the post office entrance. Was he Japanese or Chinese? He couldn't see the boy's face. He has longish black hair and a longish black mustache. He's following me. But why? And where did he start following me. Boston's office? My office? Should I confront him? No. We're supposed to play it cool and notify security. I've got to lose him. I've got to get rid of him and then report this.

"May I help you, Commander?" the man asked.

"Ah, yeah." Holbrook glanced around the shop. Clothes. "You take credit cards, I guess. Listen, I want to buy a pair of pants, a shirt, and some sort of jacket."

"You do?" The man grinned. "Commander, I'm sorry to say that I think you might have come into the wrong place."

"Why? Don't you sell clothes?"

"Not exactly. But I ah . . . perhaps I could make you a suit."

"Oh." Holbrook glanced around the shop again and this time he understood. "I'm sorry." He looked through the window toward the post office and wondered how he could get out of there without being seen.

"That's quite all right," the man said. "How about a cup of tea as long as you're here?" He motioned for Holbrook to sit down on the leather couch that took up a good part of the middle of the shop. "Or coffee perhaps."

Holbrook shook his head. "No thanks."

"I was in the Navy myself. Ours, that is. Not yours. National service. Enjoyed it a lot, too. I was on an aircraft carrier for a couple of years."

Holbrook nodded. "Me too."

"No kidding." He smiled and extended his hand. "My name is Doug Hayward. You're stationed at the U.S. Embassy, I take it?"

"Yeah, sort of, just down the block." Holbrook shook his hand.

"Do you fly?"

"Yeah." He kept glancing out of the window. "I used to."

Now Hayward asked, "Ah . . . is something wrong?"

Holbrook faced him, took a deep breath and decided to tell him the truth. "I'm being followed. Have you got a back way out of here?"

"No, I'm sorry. But who's following you? Been a naughty boy, have you?"

"It's the fellow out there, standing in the post office doorway. The Oriental. In the baseball jacket. Look, I've got to get out of this uniform because it's much too conspicuous. I'm certainly willing to pay for anything . . ."

Hayward thought for a moment, said, "I'll tell you what. Come with me," hooked Holbrook's arm and took him to the rear of the shop, to the small changing rooms. "I have an idea. What size are you?" He held open Holbrook's raincoat. "About a 42 regular?"

"Good guess," Holbrook said.

"Professional guess." Hayward nodded. "Take that off and wait here." He handed Holbrook a hanger, then fumbled through some racks of clothes. "Can't let the Navy down, now can I?" When he found what he wanted he exclaimed, "This will do nicely," and took a suit off the rack. "Get out of that and see if this fits."

"Listen," Holbrook said, slipping out of his raincoat, "I really appreciate this."

"Not to worry. You change. I'll go see if the bloke is still there. Just like in the movies, eh?" Hayward walked back into the main part of the shop and peered out of the window. "Not there now," he called back to Holbrook.

"No? Are you sure?"

"Positive. Now he's standing in the doorway of the pub on the corner. Chinese. About twenty or twenty-two years old. Hard to tell. But not much older. Maybe even a year or two younger. Dark blue baseball jacket. Just standing there as if he's waiting for someone."

"Waiting for me." Holbrook got into the slacks. They fitted pretty well. He pulled off his tie, opened his collar and tried the jacket. "I think it will do fine."

Hayward came to see. "Not a bad fit. Of course if I had made it for you the shoulders would be . . ."

"I'll be back for a second fitting," he promised. "Another time."

"I'll get you a shirt." Hayward took one off a shelf and tossed it to Holbrook. "That should do."

"Can I pay you with plastic?"

Hayward started to laugh. "Let's just call it a loan. From one sailor to another. As long as you can return it in a couple of days before the fellow who owns it comes to fetch it . . ."

"You sure? I appreciate it. My name is Richard Holbrook. I'm over at Navy Europe Headquarters . . ."

The shop door opened.

Both of them spun around.

A smiling red-haired woman came into the shop. "Hi."

"Hi." Hayward grinned, then said to the woman, "Do me a favor, will you, Marce?"

She asked, "You're trying to tell me we're not going out for lunch."

"Not at all." Hayward pointed to an umbrella. "Take that. Hold it low. Walk out together." He looked at Holbrook. "I saw it once in a Michael Caine film. Marce will go with you and bring the umbrella back. You can return the suit and pick up your uniform any time. If you go out together dressed like that, half hidden by the umbrella, maybe even arm in arm, he may think the naval officer is still in here. If he follows you, come back and we'll try something else."

Marce demanded of Hayward, "What on earth are you talking about?"

"Just do this for me, luv, please."

"Thanks." Holbrook extended his hand to Hayward, and offered his left elbow to Marce.

"Would someone please explain . . ."

Hayward said, "Don't be too long, we've got reservations."

Holbrook promised, "She'll be right back. And thanks for the loan."

"Loan?" Marce wanted to know, "Who's he loaning you?"

"He'll tell you all about it later." Holbrook led her out of the shop.

They walked away from the pub, back along Mount Street toward the Connaught, then left up to Grosvenor Square.

Holbrook checked to see if the guy in the baseball jacket was following them.

He wasn't.

"Thanks. I'll be all right now." He handed her the umbrella. "Please tell your friend I'll get the suit back tomorrow."

"What is this all about?"

"Something he once saw in a Michael Caine movie." He left her standing under the umbrella in the middle of Grosvenor Square.

Back at the office he went to find Wagner to report that he'd been followed.

But Wagner wasn't there. Nor was Roth. Nor was Parrot. Word was that the van had been found.

Chapter Twenty

THE MARKETS HAD just closed in London and the bulk of the world's merchant banking business had swung to New York —gold currencies, financial futures, they all followed the sun —when the guard at the front desk rang through to say that there was a young Chinese gentleman downstairs who refused to give his name, who had long black hair, a straggly black mustache, was missing one of his two front teeth, was wearing a baseball jacket and was insisting that he be allowed to see Mr. Li'Ning.

One of the secretaries passed the call to Peter who told the guard, yes, it was all right to send the young man up.

He met Sze at the lifts and escorted him into Li'Ning's office.

"Why won't the round-eyed guard let me come upstairs on my own?" Sze demanded in Mandarin. "The round-eyed guard downstairs doesn't like Chinese. I can tell." He spotted the ginger jar sitting on the coffee table in front of the couch. "Hey, look at that. Terrific." He went to touch it.

Peter stepped in his way.

"I just wanted to see it," Sze explained. "How much did it cost?"

But Li'Ning had other matters to discuss with Sze. "What are you doing here?"

Sze shuffled his feet and dug his hands deep into his jacket pockets. "Peter told me to report back to you."

"He meant by phone." Li'Ning glared at Peter.

"Yes . . . well . . . so I came here instead." Sze kept trying to peek at the ginger jar. "But how come the round-eyed guard wouldn't let me come upstairs on my own?"

"Because," Peter answered, "you're not dressed like a banker."

Sze made a face. "Who would want to dress like a banker?" He pointed at the ginger jar. "Can't you tell me how much it cost?"

"Never mind that." Li'Ning was anxious to know. "Did you find the American?"

"Oh yes." Sze smiled, flashing the space between his teeth. "No problem. He wore his uniform so it was easy."

"And?"

"And I did like Peter told me to. I followed him from the address in Westminster. It wasn't so easy to find, you know. No one said exactly where it was. But I got there just in time. I saw him going inside and I waited for him to come out. I had to wait in the rain. Then, when he came out I followed him all the way to Mayfair. He went to Mount Street."

"And?"

"And in Mount Street he went into a shop."

Li'Ning asked for the third time, "And?"

Sze obviously couldn't think of what to say. "And . . . ah . . . it was a tailor's shop."

"And then what happened?" Li'Ning didn't hide his impatience. "What happened after he went into the tailor's shop?"

"And . . ." Sze shrugged. "He never came out of the tailor's shop."

Li'Ning demanded, "What do you mean he never came out of the tailor's shop?"

"It's not my fault. I followed him to a tailor's shop in Mount Street and waited across the street for a really long time but he never came out. And after a really long time when I walked up close to the shop window, he wasn't there."

"He never came out?" Li'Ning thought about that . . . studied Sze standing in front of him . . . and quickly realized what must have happened. "He never came out. What you mean is that you never saw him come out. That means he spotted you following him. He must have known you were waiting across the street. So the reason he never came out of the tailor's front door was because he went out through a rear door or something like that.''

"I don't know," Sze said. "I did the best I could. I don't know if he saw me. He didn't look like he saw me. Maybe he always goes in at the front door and out of the rear door.''

"Yes," Li'Ning said sarcastically, "most people do." He walked away from Sze to stare out the window. To watch the traffic along Threadneedle Street. To tell himself, if the American knows that he was followed, and if the American starts asking himself why, and if the American somehow learns that Boston is involved . . .

"If he went out of the rear door," Sze insisted, "it's not my fault. I can't watch the front door and the rear door . . .''

To tell himself, it would be a critical mistake to underestimate what the American knows or what the American might learn if he makes it his business to find out.

". . . I can't be in two places at the same time, you know.''

Now Li'Ning had to make a decision. "Where is Yuan?''

"Yuan? He is where he always is." Sze laughed. "Playing mah-jong. He's always playing mah-jong. That's all he ever does, is play mah-jong.''

It would be a critical mistake to allow the American to somehow connect me with Boston. "Find Yuan," Li'Ning ordered Peter. "Find Yuan and tell him I need him. Then you"—he pointed to Sze—"you find out where this American Navy officer lives.''

"Where he lives?" Sze grinned victoriously. "But I think I already know where he lives. I saw him taking groceries into a building.''

"Make certain that's where he lives.''

"How do I do that?''

"You begin by looking in the telephone directory." Li'Ning said, "Peter will write his name down for you. No, better still, Peter will check the telephone directory. Then you'll go to that address and check the names on the letter boxes or the doors. Maybe there's a card with the American's name and flat number. Or perhaps a letter addressed to him. You've got to find out exactly where he lives. Which floor and which flat. When you know, ring Peter . . . don't come here . . . just ring Peter and he will tell Yuan.''

"And then?" Sze's eyes lit up.

Li'Ning motioned to Peter that the meeting with Sze was over.

"Come with me," Peter said, taking Sze's arm and leading him out of the office. "I'll look in the directory right now and you can go there to make sure about the address."

Alone, Li'Ning peered out again at Threadneedle Street.

Before the river floods . . .

Traffic was at a standstill, backed up along the street the way it always backed up in the City in the rain.

Before the river floods . . .

Most of the cars in Threadneedle Street at this hour were taxis. He stared at every one of them. There wasn't a single taxi that had its orange For Hire light on. A Rolls and a Mercedes were stuck in the middle of a line of black cabs. A post office van was stuck there too. The only thing moving was a motorcycle messenger who swerved in between the cars and onto the pavement to get along the street.

Before the river floods, there is a gently rising tide.

Making the decision to call for Yuan was easier than he thought it would be. But having made that decision he realized he now had to keep all his options open.

My options. Hedging my risk. A basic banking principle.

He went to his office cupboard, picked up the tea chest and put it on the floor next to his desk. From the shelf in the cupboard he pulled down a roll of plastic bubble-wrap and a roll of padded cotton. He took the ginger jar off the coffee table, and lined the inside of it with two layers of the padded cotton. Then he loosely bubble-wrapped the ginger jar and slipped it inside the slatted crate. The fit was perfect. But once the ginger jar was snug inside the slatted crate, and once he suspended the slatted crate into the cocoon of the tea chest, he purposely didn't seal either. He left it so that he could still easily get to the cover of the ginger jar.

He reached for his phone and called the marine operator. "I would like to speak with the captain of the freighter *Dragon Empress* en route from London to Rotterdam."

The marine operator asked if he knew the radio call sign

for the freighter. Li'Ning apologized that he didn't. The marine operator said he would ring back. Li'Ning gave the marine operator the number of his private line.

Peter walked into the office. "Sze is sometimes a little slow."

Li'Ning didn't care about Sze. He was more concerned with his own problems. "Get me a seat on the first Concorde tomorrow to New York."

"That would be the ten-thirty, I guess. What about the return?"

"I'll take care of it from New York."

"What about your appointments tomorrow and Friday?"

He thumbed through his appointment book, letting his eyes run right past his lunch date with Boston. "I won't know if I'm going until tomorrow morning. If I'm not here by ten-thirty, cancel them. Otherwise, don't worry."

Peter said all right. "Where can I reach you in New York if I have to?"

"I'll reach you," Li'Ning said. "Did you find the American's address?"

"Yes. And Sze has gone there to find the flat number. I've rung around and I think I've found Yuan. He'll ring back."

Li'Ning checked his watch. "I'll need to speak with Yuan as soon as possible. If anyone calls for me, tell them . . . I don't know, tell them anything. Tell them that I've been called away to New York."

Li'Ning's private line rang.

He nodded to show Peter he wanted to take the call alone. So Peter walked out of his office, and Li'Ning answered the phone.

The conversation lasted less than one minute.

Li'Ning and the captain of the *Dragon Empress* spoke Mandarin except for one word.

That word was, Aberdeen.

When he hung up, Li'Ning looked through his atlas again, and saw that from Aberdeen an overnight sailing would get him into . . . his finger landed on Copenhagen. That was as good a place as any. He dialed the London office of Scandinavian Airways to ask them about their daily flights from Copenhagen to New York and from Copenhagen to Hong

Kong. They gave him the times and flight numbers . . . he copied it all down . . . then rang Air Canada to ask about their daily flights from Copenhagen to Hong Kong via Montreal. They suggested the connection might be better via Toronto, so he wrote that down as well. When he called British Airways they told him there were seven flights a day from Heathrow to Aberdeen. He copied down all the times, then phoned Dan Air and they gave him the times of their two daily Gatwick to Aberdeen runs.

He checked his watch. Where was Yuan?

What else? He knew he could get to the bank vault any time during the day, so that wouldn't be a problem. His own safety deposit boxes were in a corner of the vault so emptying them wouldn't be a problem either. No one could see him unless they actually came into the strong room with him. The guards might wonder why he was carrying the ginger jar and a crate into the vault, but he never felt compelled to make explanations. Certainly not to them. Yes, he decided, access to the vault would be all right. Except, he realized, if he had to get into it over the weekend. What about the weekend? It might be best if I had everything with me over the weekend. He wondered about keeping the ginger jar in his flat, stuffed the way it would be, with seven small lead tins about the size of cigarette packs. As long as the lead does what it's supposed to, it will be all right, he assured himself.

Before the river floods . . .

He was simply keeping all his options open.

Every option he could think of.

Although the next morning when he saw the *Daily Telegraph* he realized his options had instantly narrowed.

Chapter
Twenty-one

THE NEWS WAS all over the building.

The van had been found.

According to Miss Cecilia, a low-flying Navy helicopter equipped with heat detectors, metal detectors and infrared cameras located the van tucked into a ravine, off the A836 near Loch Beannach, just about halfway between the villages of Rhian and Dalchork. British police teams had now reached the scene, secured it and reported that the van appeared to be intact. But there were no signs of the driver or the guard.

According to Miss Cecilia, Admiral Roth was in a meeting at the embassy with British Defense Ministry and Foreign Office officials, Captain Wagner was on his way to head the investigation at the scene, and Camille Parrot was tied up with the Navy's Public Affairs Officer and the embassy's press staff.

I've been followed, Holbrook wanted to tell someone. By Navy regulation he was required to report the incident. But no one was home. I've been followed by someone and I don't know why.

It was like having a secret with no one to tell.

He asked Miss Cecilia if he could get in to speak with the old man as soon as he came back. She said she'd try to arrange it, but that before he saw the admiral he might put on a uniform, or at least find a tie.

Back at his office, he stood in the doorway looking at the mess of papers scattered all over the room.

So . . . I'm offered a bribe. And I'm followed. At least I think I was offered a bribe. But I'm certain I was followed.

So . . . the question has to be, why? The answer is, I don't know. The bribe, if it was a bribe, came from a Brit. But I was followed by an Oriental. Maybe there's a connection. Maybe there isn't. I don't know that either. Okay, the next question is: when? It all started when I stumbled across those DoD forms. All right. Now back to why. I guess because by stumbling across those forms I've somehow tripped a warning signal that went off somewhere. I've somehow worried someone by accidentally discovering a deliberate misaccounting on nine shipments of plutonium nitrate.

So . . . he now wondered, why were those DoD forms used only on plutonium nitrate shipments and nothing else?

He didn't know. But he thought he might know a way to find out.

Walking down to the third floor, Holbrook went in search of the Command's Nuclear Safety officer, a captain named Mike Redd. Instead he found Redd's deputy, a tall, well-built black lieutenant wearing a submariner's badge, named Patrick Ben.

"Mike's out," Ben said, putting a book down. "The van," he added, as if that should explain everything. "In the meantime, I'm the resident expert. Gee, nice threads." He motioned for Holbrook to sit down. "VFR." He pointed to the book. "Gotta pass the test before they let me solo. Funny how they try to keep you from crashing into bridges."

Holbrook looked at the book. *A Manual For Flight—Visual Flight Rules.* "Submarine sprout wings?"

"Flying club. Just a little Piper but they said if I learn real good they'll let me do practice loops in a jumbo with five hundred passengers on board. Hey, you fly." He opened the book to the page he had been reading. "Maybe you could just help me with this navigation . . ."

"I don't fly," Holbrook responded.

"Oh. Okay." He must have understood. "Maybe another time." Closing the book, he asked, "What can I do for you?"

"An instant course in plutonium nitrate."

"The abridged or the oversimplified version?"

"I want to know what it looks like."

Ben stared at him. "You've never seen any? I thought that was part of your act here, shipping it all over the earth."

"Nope. I just ship the paperwork all over the earth."

"It's a metal," Ben explained. "Hard and brittle in its pure form. Kind of like cast iron. But it can be molded or melted. You can machine it or alloy it with other metals so that it's soft and can be drawn into wire or rolled, like foil. You can also combine it with non-metallic elements to form stable compounds."

"What about PuN?"

"Comes in several forms. The most common is liquid and that's brownish. A little darker than me, I guess. It gets mixed in with a lot of nitric acid to keep it clean. As opposed to me. I use Palmolive soap. The solid is a kind of crystal powder called plutonium nitrate hexahydrate. Looks like muddy brown rock-salt. We like the solid flavor because it packs smaller. For some reason we think it's easier to protect. But try asking the van driver and the guard if they agree. On the other hand, the Brits tend to prefer the liquid variety. They call it liquor. Makes for a great mixer with tomato juice and a twist of lemon. They think the liquid is easier to handle and in a way they're almost right. The problem with the solid is that it has to be kept in what's known as a geometrically safe situation. That means well sealed with no moisture nearby. But we've had the packing problems knocked for years. The wonders of lead. I don't know, maybe we stick with the solid for traditional reasons. Nice to think we're finally into the age of nuclear traditions."

"Is one safer than the other?"

"Not really," Ben said. "Hide it in lead and you're okay. But the particular problem with PuN is that it's highly toxic. Radiotoxic is the official terminology. It emits alpha-particles which won't do too much damage outside the skin. But if you breathe it in, or drink it or swallow it or get any coming in through a cut, something like that, it stays there for a hell of a long time. It doesn't get passed out the way some radioactive materials do. It tends to stick to your ribs, like mom's oatmeal."

"Solid packs smaller. It's easier to protect. Easier too, I suppose, to hide." Holbrook thought about that for a moment. "What about the Brits?"

Ben mused. "If only they spoke English."

"How much have they got?"

"They've got enough to meet their own needs. And they're making more every day. But exactly how much? Offhand, no idea. I guess we could find out. That sort of stuff is published. A few years ago they went through one of those purge things. Exorcised themselves. They called it the Sizewell B public inquiry. Took more than a year and filled thousands, literally thousands of pages of testimony. I read through the reports when I first came aboard here and I guess all the numbers are in there. Except the only thing I remember is some cat telling the world that the Brits don't ever do any physical stocktaking. That no Pu is ever weighed against audited records. The guy said that because every grocer in the country backs up his audits with an annual stocktaking, Britain's nuclear industry executives shouldn't be trusted to run a grocer's shop. God, how I love European logic."

"Is that true?" Holbrook was astonished. "They don't do physical stocktaking?"

"Sizewell B witness said so." He made a face. "But who knows? Witnesses these days aren't what they used to be. Actually the best bit was that misaccounting happens all the time. There are pages upon pages of misaccounting nightmares."

"You mean, lost PuN?" Holbrook paused to think about that. "Let's say you could get a hold of some of that missing PuN. Accumulate small amounts over several months, not a lot each time but enough so that it started to add up. What would you do with it once you got it?"

Without any hesitation Ben answered, "Build a bomb."

Holbrook took a deep breath. "And I guess the more PuN you've got, the bigger the boom."

"Oh yeah," Ben said. "But don't forget, first you have to separate the Pu from the N. That's not the simplest of acquired skills. Nothing easy like making the perfect soufflé. Yet if you looked around you might find some guys in India or Pakistan or Libya or China or . . ."

"China?" Holbrook flashed back to the guy in the baseball jacket.

"Yeah. They're probably far enough behind in the bomb race that we don't have to worry about them for another five or ten years. But they started their nuclear research program in the late '50s and actually exploded a nuclear device in 1964. That's twenty-two years ago. Our best guess says that they haven't yet acquired enough plutonium to get a fast breeder into full swing. But you can bet your ass they're working on it."

A Chinese guy in a baseball jacket. "Say the Chinese were in the market . . . liquid or solid?"

"That's not how it works. You start with reactor grade. You put that into your fast reactor and if you know what you're doing, eventually, out the other end pops weapons grade. It's kinda like yogurt. You need the bacteria to make the bacteria."

"All right, then how do they get reactor grade?"

"Well . . . you see, the world is divided into two categories. There are the haves. And there are the have-nots. The role of the haves is to purposely make it as tough as possible for the have-nots to ever become haves. It is the divine duty of all haves. It also keeps prices high. And this theory applies to everything from reactor grade plutonium nitrate to bank credit to pussy. Now, our little yellow brothers are currently in the PuN have-not column because us haves—like America, like the Brits, like the French, even like the Russians in a certain respect—we've all agreed not to sell it to them. A by-product of that is therefore a worldwide black market for the stuff. I'd guess the Indians or the Pakis might be willing to flog some to the Chinese. Or the Libyans, if they've got any. Otherwise, the Chinese would have to make it themselves. Except that if they don't already have enough reactor grade they can't hope for much weapons grade with a fast reactor. You have to start with enough plutonium to breed more. If you can't buy any, well, then, I guess the only other way is to steal what you can."

"Except," Holbrook pointed out, "the Chinese are already a nuclear power which means they must have some supplies of plutonium."

"Obviously," Ben agreed. "But what grade? And how much? We don't know a lot about their capabilities except that they've tested weapons. And also that they don't yet have breeder capability. At least we don't think so. I, for one, seriously hope not."

"Now tell me this." He leaned toward Ben. "Let's say I've got half a pound of the solid stuff. How much do I need to build a bomb?"

"The example they always give you in school is that to build yourself a credible nuclear device—"

"A credible nuclear device?"

"Yeah," Ben said. "Nice way of putting it, huh? Well, for something credible, you know, to make the other side sit up and listen, you'd probably need seven or eight kilos of plutonium, reactor grade. However, if you've got a fast reactor and you peel some stuff off the core blanket, well, that would be weapons grade and there you'd only need a couple of kilos. Call it four-and-a-half pounds. At the moment your 50-pence bag is four quid short."

"What kind of volume is half a pound?"

"Probably fill half a cigarette package."

He held his hands a few inches apart. "That much?"

"Maybe twice that with the lead wrappings."

"Easy enough to hide." Holbrook stood up. "Thanks."

"Any time." He winked. "Send me the address of your tailor, will you?"

Holbrook started to leave, then stopped to ask, "Who was the best second baseman ever?"

"Pete Rose, Cincinnati, 1963."

"Pete Rose?"

"No?" Ben tried, "How about Rod Carew, Minnesota, 1977?"

Holbrook mumbled, "I'm glad I asked," and walked away.

He went back upstairs to see if the admiral had returned.

Word now around the office was that two bodies had been found a few hundred yards from the van. They had been shot at close range. The skipper of the sub base on the Kyle of Tongue had reached the scene and positively identified the bodies as the driver and the guard. He also confirmed that the van appeared to be intact, with the PuN shipment secure.

But complicating matters, the van was at least one mile from any road making it appear almost physically impossible to have driven it from the A836 to that point in the ravine.

Holbrook went downstairs to the snack bar and bought himself a sandwich.

He sat far off in a corner, with his back to the rest of the room just in case the chaplain should appear.

As he chewed his way through a tuna and lettuce with mayonnaise on whole wheat, he tried to sort everything out in his mind.

If the Brits are stealing it, tell me why? The voice inside his head answered, to sell it to the Chinese. If the Brits are selling it to the Chinese, why steal ours? The voice answered, I have no idea. It doesn't make sense because they've got enough of their own. They've also agreed not to sell it to the Chinese and they wouldn't go back on their word. Or would they? No, the voice decided, at least probably not where that's concerned.

He started all over again. Let's say the Brits are stealing our PuN and the Chinese are getting it somehow.

He stopped. No, I'll try it backward. Let's say the Chinese are on the receiving end. Where are they getting it from? The voice inside his head answered, the Brits.

Oh shit.

He put the sandwich down.

Now he saw the answer.

No, he told himself, it's not the Brits.

Chapter
Twenty-two

ON THE TRAIN home to Surrey, Matthew Boston sat in his usual seat, in his usual compartment, with his usual group of fellow travelers.

They read the *Standard*.

He tried to finish *Syd*.

It was his concentration that kept getting in the way.

"In his declining years, during those last few seasons . . ."

Boston stared at the words.

It's over, he told himself.

". . . as his reactions dulled and the speed of his bowling slowed . . ."

It almost went too far. It came that close to going too far. But now it's over.

". . . as younger players came up, staring at him from across the crease, younger players who had grown up to the legend that had been Syd Barnes . . ."

Tomorrow I'll have the money and we'll exchange on the house in Spain and even if Holbrook thinks he is on to something there won't be anything left for him to find because by tomorrow it will all be over.

At Farnborough he bought a large bunch of flowers, before driving home.

Mary met him at the door. "Mrs. Boston has gone to sleep. I'm afraid she wasn't feeling very well this afternoon."

"I forgot to ring the doctor," he muttered. "Did she go to the doctor?"

"Yes, sir, she did. I made her go. Doctor Kettlestone gave her an injection because she was having terrible pains. Then she came home and got very dizzy so I put her to bed and now she's asleep."

He nodded and took off his raincoat.

"Aren't they pretty," Mary said. "Do you want me to put them in water for you?"

"No," he said. "Not yet." He kept them wrapped and carried them upstairs, then quietly opened the bedroom door and peeked inside.

The room was dark.

He was about to close it, to go away, when Denise said, "Buster? Is that you, Buster?"

"I didn't want to wake you," he whispered. "Are you asleep?"

"No, Buster, I'm not asleep."

"Hello, dear." He leaned over and kissed her forehead. "I brought you some flowers."

Denise pushed the flowers away. "Why didn't you give them to Mary to put in water?"

"All right, dear. I'll do that in a minute."

"I went to the doctor today."

"Yes, Mary told me. He gave you an injection."

"No, he didn't. That's what I said to Mary so I could be alone. Buster," she leaned across the bed to whisper to him, "Buster, I think she's stealing from us. I think Mary is stealing everything we own."

"Stealing?" He realized she had forgotten their previous conversation. "Do you think so?"

"Yes, Buster. Remember that electric blender I used to have? Well, yesterday, when I was baking, I tried to find it and it was gone. I think Mary stole it."

He said to her very gently, "I shall have a talk with Mary this very evening. I'm certain that I can get to the bottom of it for you."

"Good, Buster. She must stop stealing from us or we won't have anything left."

"You know that you can count on me, dear." He nodded

THE PLUTONIUM CONSPIRACY

several times and squeezed her hand. "Will you be coming downstairs for dinner?"

"No," Denise said. "I can't tonight."

"Why not?"

"Because I don't feel very well. I told the doctor that my entire left side was killing me and he said it was only because of the rain. It rains so much these days. Every day for a week, Buster. It hasn't stopped raining."

"I know, dear," he said.

"Buster"—she looked up at him—"when can we go to where it doesn't rain all the time? When can we go to where it's sunny? I promise I'll feel better where it's sunny. But the rain here . . . Buster, I can't take the rain anymore."

"I know, dear." He moved closer to her. "Soon. I promise. We shall go to where it's sunny very soon."

Chapter
Twenty-three

IT'S NOT THE BRITS.

Now he knew the answer.

He left his lunch where it was and rushed back to his desk.

Still standing, he compiled a stack of forms for each of the nine smeared DoD 3093s. He wanted to see all the other forms that somehow related to those nine shipments.

Why didn't I think of this before?

Under each of the nine DoD 3093s there were five other forms. That made fifty-four in all. So he grabbed a couple of sheets of blank paper and listed separately every name that appeared on each of the forms. Was that the same as a Venn Diagram? College math, he recalled. Ever-entwining circles. Names. Places. Dates. Some would appear in one or two or three circles. Some wouldn't appear more than once. Fifty-four forms. Names. Places. Dates. Fifty-four lists for each. That times three. One hundred and sixty-two lists in all.

He spread papers further and further around his office.

Ever-entwining circles.

But where to begin?

He started with places.

Could there be one storage site where each of these thefts took place? He went through all the forms. Fifty-four lists later, he saw there wasn't. In fact there seemed to be five different sites where those nine shipments of Navy PuN had been stored. No pattern here, he decided. Shit. He was disappointed. That could have pinpointed anyone on the site who might be involved.

He looked at dates. And now he had a hunch. He didn't care about actual shipment dates, he was interested in variations of those dates. Each of the shipments had been sent into storage for a requested period of days. The length of storage was noted on the forms both in dates and numbers, logged in and out with a shipment number on at least two different forms. Could there be a differential between requested lengths and actual storage time? The first day in was counted as a day of storage. But the last day of storage, which would be the day the shipment went out, was not counted as a day in storage. So here he tallied the days requested and the actual days on site, and in each case there was a difference of two days.

He told himself, I could have bet on it.

Just to check, he grabbed some other forms, other shipments where nothing had gone missing, and counted a handful of those.

They were perfect.

But these nine were each two days off.

He went through them again.

Five different sites. He asked the voice inside his head, how could the PuN have disappeared out of five different places? The voice inside his head answered, not easily. All right, he agreed with the voice, then what about those extra two days? There was a long pause before the voice asked him, could those two days have been spent shipping the PuN to just one site?

He went through the forms a third time.

And now something popped up at him.

Why didn't I see that before?

The log numbers.

Checking the forms attached to the smeared 3093s, he saw that the log numbers in didn't match the log numbers out. But when he picked up a handful of other shipments the first thing he noticed was that the log numbers there did match. Each shipment had a number. The shipments on the smeared 3093s had two numbers. One in. Another out.

He let the voice inside his head play with that for a few minutes.

One in. Another out.

Two days' difference.

The voice inside his head told him, it's obvious. Is it? Yes, it is. How? Easy. Then tell me. All right, the shipment comes in from the Navy with one set of numbers. The Brits send it out with that number. When they bring it back in they've got to give it a second number in order to properly log it. So it gets returned to the Navy with that second number. But because those numbers are on two different forms, no one would ever think twice about checking them. Anyway, those numbers don't make any difference to the Navy. As far as you're concerned that's just British bookkeeping. And as far as the Brits are concerned, they're dealing with two different shipments. But they can be purposely made to look alike by taking the extra paperwork out of the middle.

Sure, he agreed. That's it. Okay. He nodded. Now the names.

He started searching for names on the first list that were missing from any of the others. Then he worked his way down the second list. Then down the third. When a name failed to show up even just once, he crossed it off all the name lists.

Eventually only one name was left.

There it was.

One person had signed every form.

There you are, he said.

And just because he felt like it, he screamed, "Gotcha!"

No. It's not the Brits. Gotcha, you son of a bitch. It's *one* Brit. One Brit with access to the PuN. One Brit who could fudge the DoD 3093 forms. One Brit who managed to get U.S. Navy PuN out of several storage sites and into a single site where he was somehow able to steal small amounts of PuN and then send the rest back to the main storage sites before anyone realized it was missing. Not the Brits. Just *one* Brit. His name was on every form.

Now he grabbed the phone and called the first of the five different storage sites. This one was less than half a mile from St. Pancras station in the heart of London. He asked for the duty officer, introduced himself and said he was merely trying to do a routine check on some forms. "One of our shipments in was dated 28 September 1982 and your log number on it is sierra sierra two, fiver, niner, niner, x-ray hotel bravo. The second shipment out is dated 7 October 1982 and your log number there is sierra lima, three, three, niner, three, x-ray, hotel, bravo. Can you track them and give me the date out and destination for the first one and the date in and source of the second?"

The duty officer hesitated. "I'm not certain we should be doing this on the phone."

Holbrook gave him the Navy's phone number. "You can always call me back here if you've got any doubts."

"Well . . . ah . . . hold on a moment, please." There was a very long pause before the duty officer came back and gave Holbrook the information he wanted.

"Thanks." He copied it down, then asked matter-of-factly for the name of the authorizing official. The duty officer read it to him as it was signed on the forms.

He grinned and mumbled, one down, eight to go.

It took the better part of an hour but he phoned every one of the five sites and checked on every one of the nine shipments.

And each time he got the same answer.

Gotcha!

Two missing days.

Shipments out to Harwell.

Shipments back in from Harwell.

Shipments authorized by the same person whose name appears on every form.

Boston.

He ran straight to the admiral's office.

But the admiral wasn't in.

Holbrook waited until eight o'clock.

Parrot never returned to the office.

Nor did Wagner.

Nor did Roth.

Boston.

That's why he tried to bribe me. He wanted me to forget

the whole matter, or at least he wanted to slow me down enough that he could cover his tracks.

It's Boston.

And like a total idiot I sat down with him and maybe tipped my hand. Now I've got to state my case to the admiral. I've got to make certain that someone else understands how Boston maneuvered this.

But tonight there was nobody to tell.

High on himself for the first time in a long while, Holbrook left his office, took the lift downstairs and almost walked out of the front door.

Then he thought twice about that.

The Chinese guy in the baseball jacket. Maybe he's out there. Maybe he knows I work here. He saw me in my uniform so it wouldn't be hard to figure out where I work. Maybe he already knows where I live. Still, if he doesn't there's no sense in helping him find out.

Now he wondered, how is he tied in to Boston? Would the Brits hire a Chinese guy to follow me? First he said, why not? Then he changed his mind. Probably not. So maybe he isn't directly tied in to Boston. Could Boston be selling the PuN to the Chinese?

Wait till I tell the admiral.

I can't wait to see Wagner's face.

Just to be on the safe side, Holbrook went down to the first basement, then up a rear stairway to a back door where the Marine guard there took his badge and saluted goodnight.

He stepped into an alley and waited until his eyes adjusted to the darkness, to see if anyone was there.

The alley appeared to be deserted.

Staying close to the buildings, he followed the alley around to the side of the Marriott Hotel, and finally into Duke Street.

All the time he kept looking to see if he was being followed.

All the time he kept trying to see if somewhere in the night there was a Chinese guy in a baseball jacket.

He crossed Duke Street and hurried into his building's front door. The lift wasn't there so he pushed the button and waited.

From upstairs he could hear the lift mechanism click as the cage started down.

He waited for the lift. It took a long time. He stood there wondering why it should take so long. He stood there telling himself that it seemed to be taking as long to come down as it usually took to go all the way up to the top floor.

The lift arrived.

He stepped into the cage, shut the gate and pushed the top button.

The mechanism clicked and the lift started up.

A vision of the Chinese guy in the baseball jacket went through his mind.

Immediately he pushed the STOP button.

And the lift stopped.

It took as long to come down as it takes to go up because the lift was on my floor. And my flat is the only flat on my floor.

Now he listened for any noises in the building.

The lift was on my floor.

He listened. But he didn't hear anything. So after a couple of minutes he pushed the button to go back to the ground floor.

He got out, waited again, heard nothing and cautiously began walking up the stairs. He got to the first floor and stopped.

No noise.

He stopped on the second floor.

Maybe I'm being silly, he told himself. But then maybe I'm not being so silly.

He stopped on the third floor.

He listened for anyone who might be waiting in front of his apartment door, just there, just above his head.

Not a sound.

So now he very slowly started up the last part of the stairs, looking upward, always listening . . .

And when he got to a point where he could see his own door, he was almost surprised to find—nothing.

No one was there.

You're a neurotic horse's ass, he said out loud, and plodded up the rest of the stairs.

He fumbled through his pockets for his keys.

At least this time there's no lipstick or panties.

Putting the key in the bolt lock, he went to open it . . .

But the key didn't turn.

That's funny, he thought, turning the key back to hear it lock. Oh, well, I guess I didn't double-lock it when I stopped by this afternoon. He shrugged and unlocked it again. I guess I just forgot.

Then he put the second key in the Yale lock and opened the door.

But I never forget to double-lock it.

The door swung open.

And his flat was pitch dark.

Goddamnit, the timer didn't turn the lights on and if there's one thing I hate it's coming home to a dark apartment.

But it's brand new.

And it worked yesterday.

The Chinese guy in the baseball jacket.

He froze where he was.

The lift was on my floor.

The bolt wasn't locked.

The lights aren't on.

His mouth went dry.

Oh, Christ.

Ever so slowly he stepped backward, down the few steps to the landing.

He waited there, staring at the darkness beyond his open door.

Someone is in there.

The Chinese guy with the baseball jacket.

Someone is waiting inside my apartment.

He took one more step.

And that's when it happened.

There was a flash of light.

And then there was an explosion.

Chapter
Twenty-four

MATTHEW BOSTON WALKED up to the newsagent's in the station at Farnborough and the woman behind the counter said, "Morning, luv," then automatically handed him the *Daily Telegraph*.

"Hah." He was pleased. "Thank you." He paid her.

"Ta," she said to him and then looked at the man behind him, "Sorry, luv, no *Mirror*s today. They didn't come in."

Boston smiled triumphantly. Serves a tabloid reader right.

He waited inside the station, staying out of the drizzle, until the train pulled in. Then he hurried to his usual compartment.

After hanging up his raincoat and laying his umbrella carefully on the overhead rack, he nodded hello to his usual fellow-passengers, settled into his usual seat and opened his usual newspaper.

He scanned the front page.

He expected to see something about the missing U.S. Navy van or at least the F.O.'s protest to the American ambassador.

But there was nothing.

Hah. He was pleasantly astonished. How do they ever manage to keep such things out of the papers? Shows what they can do when they put their mind to it. Thank God. Fleet Street would have had a field day with this one.

He turned to page two and folded the paper so that he could

give the page a look without flopping the newspaper onto the man next to him.

It is absolutely brilliant, he decided, that in this day and age the government still manages to keep such matters out of the press. God bless the Official Secrets Act. And God help all of us if those Alliance characters ever come to power and force a Freedom of Information policy down our throats. Just look what that sort of nonsense has done in America. Anybody can find out anything about themselves. Like police records. But why should a citizen with nothing to hide need to know what the police think about him? Like immigration department records. It's only illegal immigrants who would love to discover what the Home Office knows about them so they can avoid further prosecution. Like school records. A good student has nothing to worry about. Like official government memos and transcripts of discussions between ministers. I mean, what good does it do the government to keep secrets if just anybody can come along and find them out? This government couldn't function without secrets. Look how bad things get every time one is revealed. Who should bloody care that the *Belgrano* was sailing away? I say we bloody well need the Official Secrets Act. After all, how else is the government supposed to protect itself from prying journalists with newspapers to sell and the everyday nuisance of the general public.

He turned to page three and spotted a familiar face.

His eyes nearly popped out of his head.

There was a thumbnail archives photo of Christopher Li'Ning. Next to it was an auction house photo of a ginger jar. And the headline above the photos announced, "Hong Kong Banker Buys Rare Ceramic—£23,000 Plan To Appease Chinese."

The story began: "A very rare, late Ming/early transitional ginger jar was purchased this week for £23,000 by Mr. Christopher Li'Ning, Chairman of the Mandarin Commerce H.K. Bank, a Hong Kong–based merchant bank with offices in London, New York and Zurich."

Boston thought to himself, how unlike Li'Ning to seek such publicity.

The article went on to describe the jar and to suggest, according to reliable sources, that Li'Ning was planning to offer it to the Chinese government in a lavish street-party ceremony along Soho's Gerrard Street in early May. "It is believed by those close to Mr. Li'Ning that the gift of this ginger jar to China coincides with negotiations currently under way between the Chinese government and Mandarin Commerce concerning the opening of a Mandarin Commerce branch in Beijing for later this year."

Still, Boston thought, I'm surprised that Li'Ning would have allowed this, especially with his picture.

Then his eyes lit upon a paragraph further down the story.

"However, the export of such a rare and valuable example of Chinese ceramics should not be without controversy. Mr. Li'Ning's commercial and political motives aside, the sale of this ginger jar to Mr. Li'Ning and its eventual export to China is yet another example of the foreign pillaging of our heritage. According to HM Customs and Excise, Mr. Li'Ning will be notified within the next week or so that he will be required to apply for an export license before the jar will be permitted to leave this country. On paper that seems to be a step in the proper direction. But in the past such export licenses have been mere rubber-stamp formalities."

What a controversy, Boston said to himself. Didn't Li'Ning know what he was letting himself in for when he gave this interview? He shook his head. No, it's not like him at all to—

Now he saw the final line of the story.

"Mr. Li'Ning was in New York yesterday, unavailable for comment."

New York?

He read that a second time.

How can he be in New York? I spoke to him yesterday. He was here. He couldn't be in New York. We're supposed to have lunch. He's supposed to meet me this afternoon and give me the numbers . . .

Boston couldn't think of anything else for the entire journey into London.

It must be a misprint.

He can't be in New York.

The train pulled into Waterloo, and for the first time in ages Boston headed for the taxi rank.

At Chappell House he rushed past the commissionaire with only a brief nod, hurried by Mrs. Fitzgerald and went straight to his office. He grabbed the phone and dialed Li'Ning's private number.

It rang twice.

And Li'Ning answered.

"Oh." Boston fumbled with his words. "You're there. I thought . . . it's me, Boston. But the papers said . . ."

"What are you talking about?" Li'Ning wanted to know.

"I'm talking about what I just read in the paper. The interview you gave . . . The *Daily Telegraph*. The paper. This morning's *Telegraph*. It said you were in New York. There was a big story all about your ginger jar and some trouble with the museums . . . and all I know is that it said you were unavailable for comment because you were in New York."

"The *Telegraph* this morning? About the ginger jar?" Li'Ning seemed to be upset by that. "I've got to go." Boston heard Li'Ning muffle the phone with his hand across the mouthpiece and call to someone, "Get me the *Telegraph*. Quickly." Then Li'Ning came back. "I'm sorry. I must go."

"Ah . . ." Boston tried to interject, "I mean, we're still meeting at twelve-thirty. At the Reform. As we planned. As you promised."

"Yes. As planned. Of course," Li'Ning said. "I must go." And just like that he rang off.

He says we're meeting as planned. All right, Boston reassured himself. That's fine. Then there's nothing to worry about. He says we're meeting as planned so I shall be there as planned.

Mrs. Fitzgerald arrived with a cup of tea, the morning mail and the overnight messages. He hurried through the messages, pushed the mail aside, and left the tea.

After a while Mrs. Fitzgerald poked her head into his office and reminded him about her dental appointment. What dental appointment? I told you about it yesterday, she said. No, you didn't. Oh, but I did. No, you didn't. Yes, I did. He waved his hands to send her away. All right. It doesn't matter. Have a good time. At the dentist? Yes, yes, go on. It's all right. She wanted to know, is there anything for the post? Hah, he remembered, *Syd*. He turned to his desk . . . where the bloody hell is *Syd*. Oh damnit. I took the book home with me last night and left it there. I must go, she said. Yes, yes, go on. She went to the dentist. He asked himself, how could I have left that book at home when I wanted to post it off to Nigel.

He looked at his watch. It was ten-thirty.

He rearranged the papers on his desk.

He asked himself, is there anything at all in the office that could connect me to those DoD forms?

He assured himself, nothing at all.

He flipped through the mail and messages a second time.

There was absolutely nothing there about the missing Navy van.

He remembered that he wanted to ring Woolley. Then he remembered he also wanted to ring Dr. Kettlestone. He searched for Kettlestone's phone number but Mrs. Fitzgerald had it filed somewhere and he didn't know where it could be so he told himself, I'll do it later.

He thought about calling that Mr. Katzman at the Las Fontanas sales office, just to confirm that they would be meeting later. But then he told himself, no need, he'll be there.

He looked at his watch. It was ten thirty-two.

He forgot about ringing Woolley.

Checking the weather outside he saw it was still drizzling. No matter, he said, and went downstairs. He grabbed his raincoat and umbrella and started out of the office. Then he decided he really should leave word for Mrs. Fitzgerald with the commissionaire at the front door, but the commissionaire didn't seem to be anywhere in sight, so Boston penned a note and left it on the table in front of the lift. "Gone to the Reform for a lunch meeting." He stepped outside, turned right and went down to Victoria Street.

He looked in every shop window.

He went into the Army and Navy and browsed through the book department, then noticed there was a sale on computer chess games. Large Reductions, a sign said. He liked the idea of that and started sorting through the stack of different games to see if he could find one that might be mispriced.

None of them were.

I'll buy one anyway, he said to himself, then wondered if

he could ever learn how to make it work. And there were so many to choose from. He knew that if he asked any of the sales assistants they'd only point to the most expensive one.

He decided to ring Nigel and get his advice.

Where's a phone? he asked one of the salesgirls. I'm afraid I don't know. Where might I find a telephone? he asked another. I'm afraid you'll have to inquire at that desk over there.

Eventually someone sent him off in the proper direction. But then he had to get some change. I'm afraid this cash desk is closed. I'm afraid you'll have to ask over there. I'm afraid we're not allowed to give change for the telephones.

He finally came across a woman at a cash desk who reluctantly agreed to change a pound. Then he returned to the phones and dialed Harwell.

"I'm in a coin box in the middle of a shop, and I've just seen some of those computer chess games, they're having a sale, and I was wondering which one you'd recommend."

Nigel said, "I . . . I don't really know . . . I'd have to . . . to see them myself . . . I really couldn't say which . . . which one."

"I mean, there must be one that is better than all the others."

"I don't . . . I don't know."

"Oh." Boston had hoped for more help than that. "I suppose that means I don't buy one. I thought it would be nice for all of us. You and me. You know, in Spain . . ."

"Yes . . . yes . . . I think it . . . it would . . . it would be . . ."

"Oh well . . . too bad you missed dinner the other night. I had a book for you. Syd Barnes. Did I tell you about it?"

"Yes . . . yes . . . I think . . . I think you did."

Now he was curious. "Where did you go the other evening?"

Nigel said, "I was . . . I was . . . I was out."

"Some girl?" he hoped.

"No . . . no . . ." Nigel paused, "I . . . I went home . . . home . . . to see . . . Mother."

"Home? No one told me you went home. You went home for dinner? You were supposed to meet me. I had a table reserved and everything."

"I . . . I . . . I know," he said. "But . . . but Mother baked a lemon tart and you weren't . . . you weren't going to be there and . . . I didn't . . . I didn't want her to . . . to think no one cared."

"I see." He took a deep breath. "Well . . . I suppose that was the right thing to do. Odd that she didn't mention it."

"I . . . I asked her . . . asked her not to. I didn't want . . . didn't want you to think I was . . . playing . . . playing favorites."

Now he felt embarrassed. "I know. You'd do anything for your mother, and so would I."

"Yes . . . yes, we . . . we both would."

He changed the subject. "Perhaps I'll think about the computer chess game for a while. If you happen to see any, jot down the name of a good one."

Nigel promised he would.

He still had some coins left so he rang Wooldridge. "Boston here."

"Buster," Wooldridge sounded pleased. "I've just rung you myself. No answer at your end. Out on the town already? Celebrating, what?"

"Celebrating?" What was there to celebrate? "Woolley, I just rang because I didn't see anything in the papers this morning and wanted to . . ."

"To tell me the news," he interrupted. "But of course I should have got back to you yesterday when I heard it. Sorry about that. Good spot of luck, eh, Buster?"

"What are you talking about? What news?"

"The Navy van. Come on, old boy, you must know. They've found it. Came across it yesterday. Totally intact. Nothing at all missing."

"They've found the van? And absolutely everything is intact?"

"Yes, yes. Afraid that the driver and the guard were both killed, though. That will create a bit of a mess for the Home Office. They suspect a Libyan connection. But as far as we're concerned, our bookkeeping is up to date."

"Two men killed?" He didn't like the sound of that at all. "Could cause quite a scandal, I suppose."

"Hardly," Wooldridge said. "Serves the Yanks right too.

They'd do anything to keep it quiet now because they tried to keep it quiet right from the beginning."

"Yes . . . yes, I suppose you're right." He paused. "So . . . that's that, then?"

"That's that, then," Wooldridge agreed.

He thought for a few seconds before asking, "Woolley . . . of course there will be some sort of inquiry?"

"Routine. Merely routine. Some paperwork to file. But it's now a Home Office problem. Foreign Office too if they find a connection to Gaddafi. But nothing for us to worry about. The police report should cover most of it. Good show, by the way, getting the F.O. to file a protest. Heard about it all on the grapevine. Well done. Must ring off now."

"Yes," Boston stammered, "yes, yes, of course."

"Glad that's that, then."

"Yes," he kept saying. "Yes, yes, very glad."

Wooldridge said goodbye. Boston said goodbye. And they hung up.

So that's that, then. He grinned widely. The American Navy has their PuN. If there is any reporting to be done it will simply get filed away and forgotten. Holbrook will leave off because it's in his interest to . . . and I think I might just walk over to the Reform right now to be certain that Li'Ning and I will have a good table for lunch.

He left the Army and Navy feeling considerably better than when he came in.

That's that, then, he kept saying to himself.

He took the steps up to the Reform two at a time, deposited his raincoat and umbrella in the cloakroom, and immediately reserved a table for two far off to the side. Corner table, thank you. Yes, fine. Good. It's where we can talk.

A waiter asked if he would like a sherry.

A bit early, he said, but in an hour from now, yes, that would be fine, thank you.

He went into the reading room, took the *F.T.*, the *Times* and the *Wall Street Journal* off the long table in the center, found a comfortable winged armchair along the far wall, and settled down to read the papers.

At noon he ordered his sherry.

At 12:15 he went to tell the porter that he was expecting a guest for lunch.

At 12:30 he checked his watch and wondered if Li'Ning was going to be late.

At 12:45 he told himself, it must be the traffic.

At 1:00 he started to worry.

At 1:15 he told himself, perhaps I should ring the bank just to be certain that Li'Ning hasn't been delayed somewhere.

At 1:30 the porter came to say that his luncheon guest had arrived.

Now he stood up and turned around.

And for the first time in his life, he felt genuine panic.

Chapter
Twenty-five

FIRST THERE WAS a flash of light.

Then there was an explosion.

Holbrook's feet flew out from under him. He toppled sideways, from the fourth landing to the third landing, coming to a full stop against the front door of the flat just under his.

The door opened and the old woman who lived there stared down at him.

Stunned, he told her, "Somebody just tried to kill me." He looked at her electric-blue jogging suit that said "Training," and furry pink slippers. "Somebody just tried to murder me," he said, and then started to laugh.

It was uncontrollable.

He laughed. And he laughed. And that made him laugh even more.

Somebody wanted to kill me.

He couldn't stop laughing.

Tears rolled down the sides of his cheeks.

She watched him, confused, then glanced up the stairs. "I heard an explosion." Then she shrieked, "My God, there's a fire."

Screaming, she ran to her phone to ring 999.

He tried to calm down. He wanted to stop laughing. Someone just tried to kill me. There's nothing funny about that. But he couldn't get himself under control.

The fire brigade showed up within minutes. Sirens blazing. Red light spinning. Firemen clomped past him in their heavy boots and rubber coats. They barged into his flat, yelled down orders for a hose, shouted that the fire could spread and that they would have to evacuate the building.

And through it all, Richard Holbrook kept laughing.

The firemen escorted everyone outside. They rushed people down the stairs and into the evening's rain. Someone threw a blanket around his shoulders and took him into a large white van that had some cots in it.

He was still laughing.

"Let's try and calm down," an attendant said, giving him a small paper cup with a red liquid in it. "Drink this. Come on."

He somehow managed to swallow it without ever tasting it.

His sides hurt. And his face hurt. But eventually his laughter slowed. Like music on a stereo when you shut it off without first lifting the needle away from the record, his hysterics wound down, slower and slower until the laughter simply ground to a halt.

"You'd better lie down here," the attendant said.

Holbrook put his hands against the cot to steady himself. "I'm all right." He kept trying to catch his breath. "It's okay. I'm all right now."

A fireman climbed into the back of the van. "You the owner of the flat, sir?"

He nodded several times. The medicine had quickly drained him and now there was no laughter left. "Yes . . . I mean that I live there."

"I'll need some information," the fireman said. "We've pretty well got it under control. We think it might have been a gas leak. Did you smell anything? . . ."

"A gas leak?" He felt very tired so he sat down on the cot. "No. The last thing it could have been was a gas leak. It was a bomb."

The fireman stared at Holbrook. "What makes you think that, sir?"

"It was a bomb," Holbrook told him. He tried to think of what he should do or what he should say. "I don't . . ." The medicine was making him dizzy so he lay across the cot and thought to himself that it might be best if someone else was there with him. "I'm an officer in the United States Navy. I think I'd better have my people here. I think they should be notified."

The fireman said, "Just a minute," opened the door and shouted to someone. A police officer stepped into the van. "How are you feeling, sir?"

Holbrook repeated who he was and that he wanted someone from the Navy to be present. "Ask for the OOD. He'll know what to do." The policeman took his two-way radio off the clip on the front of his jacket and spoke into it.

Holbrook mumbled to the attendant that he was very tired.

He said his limbs were starting to feel heavy.

He said his eyes were beginning to blur.

Firemen came into the van and left again. Policemen came into the van and left again. And all the time Holbrook lay thinking to himself, I feel so tired.

Then there was a knock on the van door. A policeman was standing there with someone in a U.S. Navy uniform and three fellows who looked like U.S. Marines.

Holbrook steadied his eyes on the man in the Navy uniform. He looked at the man's face and mumbled, "Ah shit."

It was Wagner. "I just got back from up north and they rang me that you got into some sort of trouble. What's this all about?"

Holbrook wanted to shake loose the fuzziness inside his head but it wouldn't go away. "I thought I should have someone here when I made my statement to the police and fire department."

"Just tell the man what happened," Wagner said to Holbrook, then turned to the police officer. "I'm Captain Wagner. Head of security for U.S. Naval Forces Europe. Commander Holbrook here is one of my men so I would appreciate any consideration you might be able to show him . . ."

I am not one of your men, he wanted to say. "If the light-timer switch hadn't been off I would have gone inside the apartment and I would have been killed."

"We suspect a gas leak," the fireman said to Wagner.

Holbrook shook his head. "It wasn't a gas leak."

"Let the man talk," Wagner said.

"It wasn't any gas leak," Holbrook protested. "It was a goddamned bomb!"

"What makes you think that?" the police officer asked.

He was fighting to stay awake. "When I came home tonight I rang for the elevator. Except it was on my floor. Except my apartment is the only one on the floor. It means someone went up there in the elevator and came down by the stairs. I didn't take the elevator upstairs. I walked. And then the bolt lock wasn't right."

His vision was fuzzy. Everybody was out of focus. "I always bolt-lock it. But it wasn't bolt-locked tonight. So I opened the door and the light-timer switch wasn't on. I bought it the other day at Selfridges. The fellow there had two. One was this one and the other one . . . the other one was another one . . ."

He was having trouble getting his tongue around his words. They didn't even sound right inside his own head. "The other one had batteries which meant that it would always work even when the lights didn't . . ."

No matter what he did his eyes wouldn't stay open. "It was a bomb, because someone tried to kill me . . ."

"I'm sorry to say"—Wagner's voice was loud—"that our Commander Holbrook here has been under considerable personal strain for the past several months. Regrettably he has a drinking problem. I wonder . . . would either of you be terribly inconvenienced . . . ? What I'd like to do is take Commander Holbrook back to our building. I'll see that he gets a night's sleep and that he reports back to you in the morning. I'll see that he makes a real clear statement then. I'd appreciate this as a personal favor."

The policeman said to the fireman, "It's all right with us if you don't mind. Considering that he is with the American Navy."

"He's been given something to calm him down," the fireman explained. "We found him laughing. He was sitting on a landing laughing like a madman. Completely hysterical. He might have been drunk. We probably should put that somewhere on the report.''

They're talking about me as if I were dead, Holbrook thought. "I wasn't . . .'' He couldn't make the words come out right. "I wasn't . . .''

"What we do in a case like this,'' the fireman went on, "is go back in with our investigators after the place is made safe. So we'll know for certain in the morning. But when we were heading upstairs someone in the building reported to one of my men that he smelled gas and was just about to ring us. We'll have to check with him again.''

The policeman pulled out a notebook and pencil and asked, "Have you got his name?''

"I haven't but he said he lives in the building and he won't be too hard to find because he's Chinese.''

"Chinese,'' Holbrook said. "Chinese guy in a baseball jacket.''

The fireman said to Wagner, "Maybe we should send him to the hospital overnight to be looked at.''

Wagner gave the fireman a friendly tap on the shoulder. "For all sorts of security reasons I'd much prefer to have our medics check him out.''

"Well . . .'' The fireman shrugged. "Like I said, it's all right with me as long as we can get a full report from him tomorrow.'' He asked the policeman, "Any objections?''

"We know where to find him if we need him,'' the policeman said. "That's all right.'' He nodded to Wagner. "You people go ahead. We understand.''

Wagner opened the van door and called to the three Marines. "Y'all want to give me a hand with the commander. Get the car up here. Come on. Pronto.''

Wagner helped Holbrook stand up. "Let's go, buddy.'' Then the Marines walked him to the car. "Nice and steady.'' They bundled him inside. "That's it. Watch your head. Easy goes.'' Wagner sat next to him in the rear seat as a Marine drove them the one block back to North Audley Street. "I really don't know how a fuck-up like you can be allowed out in the world . . .''

Holbrook said nothing. Through the cobwebs in his mind

he kept thinking to himself, a Chinese guy in a baseball jacket just tried to kill me.

The Marines took him inside, to the medics station, where a Navy corpsman undressed him and put him into a bed.

The corpsman talked to him. "Are you in any pain? Have you been drinking? Can you feel me moving your leg?"

"I'm all right," Holbrook heard himself saying . . . but every time he looked at the corpsman it was as if the corpsman hadn't understood what Holbrook was telling him. "I'm all right. I just want to go to sleep. I'm okay."

Holbrook shut his eyes.

The corpsman's voice grew fainter and fainter.

Eventually the corpsman's voice was gone.

The next thing he heard was someone shouting, "Lookey here, boys and girls, it's the boss. I said the boss. It's Springsteen!"

And then there was music.

He opened his eyes.

He found himself lying in a single bed, in his underwear, in a small room with white walls. There was a washbasin at one end of the room and a door at the other.

He got up and washed his face. Then he rinsed out his mouth.

Springsteen was still singing.

He opened the door and looked out.

It was the medics station. There were shelves filled with bottles of pills, and an examination table, and a scale, and the air smelled of rubbing alcohol.

A Navy corpsman was sitting at a desk, with his back to the door.

"What time is it?" Holbrook asked. "And what do you do around here for coffee?"

The corpsman, dressed in a starched white uniform, swung around. "Oh." He snapped off the radio. "Morning, sir. How do you feel?"

"Surprisingly, not too bad." Holbrook stretched. His head was amazingly clear. "Can I have my clothes?"

"Yes, sir." The corpsman—who couldn't have been more than about twenty—jumped up, reached for a hook behind the door and gave Holbrook a hanger with the suit and shirt.

"It's almost nine. I've got some coffee, sir, if you really feel up to it. And Doc Glass will be right back. He said he wants to see you before you think about going anywhere."

"Yeah, sure," he said. "What was that stuff they gave me last night? I feel like I slept for the whole night." He put his clothes on. "I need a razor and a toothbrush, if you've got anything like that."

"Yes, sir." The corpsman gave him a throwaway plastic toothbrush with the toothpaste already squeezed along the brush, and a plastic throwaway razor. "Don't have any shaving cream or anything. But the soap lathers real good."

Standing at the basin, Holbrook shaved and brushed his teeth. "Where's that coffee now?" he asked when he was finished. "Easy on the milk. No sugar."

The corpsman handed him a cup.

That's when a good-looking fellow of about thirty-five came into the room. He was wearing a white coat and a stethoscope. "Hi. We've never met." He extended his hand. "I'm Dave Glass. Chief pill-pusher. How do you feel?"

"Yeah." Holbrook shook his hand. "Fine. I don't think I've slept as good in a long time."

"No hangover or anything?"

"No," Holbrook said. "No. I really did sleep."

Glass shrugged. "I wish I could get up feeling good like that after a night of drinking. I always get the worst hangovers."

"Drinking?" Holbrook stared at him. "I wasn't drinking."

"That's what the report said."

"What report?" Holbrook demanded. "There's a report that says I was drinking? Let me see it."

Glass found it on the corpsman's desk and handed it to Holbrook.

"Firemen located Commander Holbrook inside the building, one floor below the apartment on fire. They said he was inebriated and hysterical. When I was asked to come to the scene by the police, I found Commander Holbrook in a fire department vehicle, in a total state of intoxication. His pupils were dilated. He was unable to speak coherently or walk without assistance. Both the police and the firemen at the

223

scene have reported the same state of inebriation in their official reports.''

It was signed, Robert A. Wagner, Captain, USN.

"You son of a bitch," Holbrook said. "You rotten son of a bitch."

Under Wagner's report was a paragraph written by the corpsman who had been on duty the night before. He explained how he had to put Holbrook to bed because he was too drunk to help himself.

"I wasn't drunk," Holbrook told the doctor. "They gave me something. Red stuff in a little paper cup. It knocked me out."

"What about before they gave you the red stuff in the little paper cup?" Glass wanted to know.

"It was weird. Really weird. When the bomb went off, I started to laugh. I just couldn't stop laughing. That's why they gave me the red stuff."

"I'm not worried about the laughing," he said. "That's par for the course. I'm looking to find out if you were drinking before that."

"What do you mean, par for the course?"

"The hysterics? No problem. Happens a lot in wartime. Guy sees his buddy shot and he starts laughing. The brain gets overloaded. The circuits flood. Triggers off a reaction in the nervous system. There's a medical term for it if you want me to look it up. Somebody-or-other's syndrome."

"So at least you believe I wasn't drunk."

"Wait a sec," Glass said. "I believe that when the explosion happened your brain was so relieved that you didn't get killed, it overloaded the circuits to your entire nervous system . . . the whole thing went tilt . . . and manifested itself as laughter. Sometimes it comes out as amazing strength. People see their kid roll under a car, they panic and lift up the car. Same people couldn't pick up a bowling ball otherwise. Sometimes it comes out as total helplessness. Can't move. A hundred percent catatonic. You know, just like shock. Sometimes it comes out the other end and only your laundry knows how scared you really were. No, not to worry about the laughter. I just want to know if you were drinking before the explosion.''

"I wasn't. I was sober. But what about that report? What about that son-of-a-bitch Wagner?"

"I guess," Glass said, "you might have yourself a problem there. Now if you don't mind taking your shirt off, I want to hear your heart thump."

When Glass said he was free to leave, Holbrook went directly to the admiral's office.

Miss Cecilia gave him a nasty look. "He's having orders cut."

Holbrook moved past her desk and reported in. "Sir?" He saluted.

Roth was sitting behind his desk going through the morning read-file. "Dad, that's it," he said. "This was the last straw." He tossed a copy of Wagner's report across his desk.

"Admiral," he begged, "you've got to hear me out. This is total bullshit. I was not drunk. The doc downstairs will tell you that. They gave me some sort of medicine. They made me drink something. Someone tried to kill me last night."

Roth left Holbrook standing at attention. "I'm sitting here with three independent versions of what happened last night. And all three of them agree that you were loaded. Now I've told you, Dad, that you've got to get yourself straightened out. If it was anyone else, I'd see their ass shipped out of this man's Navy. As it is, I'm having orders cut. You're on your way back to the States."

"Damnit," he said, shutting his eyes and taking a deep breath. "Admiral, please, you've got to believe me. I wasn't drunk."

Now Roth glared at him and opened one of his desk drawers. He pulled out Holbrook's bottle of dark Jamaican rum. "What's this all about? Snake bite?"

Holbrook looked at it and sighed. "I wasn't drunk last night."

"Once too often, Dad." Roth put the bottle back in the drawer.

"Please." He looked straight into the admiral's eyes. "Please just listen to what I've got to say."

When Roth didn't stop him, Holbrook told him the whole story. He told Roth about Boston. About how Boston offered him a bribe and about how Boston's name was the only name on all the forms associated with the smeared DoD 3093s. He told Roth how he was followed from Boston's office by a young Chinese guy in a baseball jacket. He told Roth about the light-timer. He told Roth that it was a bomb, not a gas leak.

He told Roth, "I saw the explosion and then I heard it and when I fell down the stairs I suddenly realized that someone wanted to kill me. I realized that someone was trying to murder me. And you know what, sir, I was scared shitless. I explained it to the doc just now and he recognized what happened to me as . . . somebody's syndrome. I laughed because I was hysterically frightened. The guy in the fire department van gave me something to calm me down. It was red and it came in a little white paper cup and if you'd just check with the guy he'll tell you that. I swear I wasn't drunk."

But Roth was relentless. "Sorry, Dad. I'm cutting orders for you. This is once too often."

He started shaking his head. "I'm standing here telling you that a Brit has been stealing Navy PuN and you're telling me that you don't give a shit?"

"Captain Wagner will handle—"

"Captain Wagner, my ass," he blurted.

"Now you listen to me, Commander," the admiral lectured him, "I'm doing you a favor. You don't know this, but the ambassador wants me to bring charges against you. Do you hear what I'm saying? Special Court Martial. The ambassador is all over me about you. So just you consider yourself lucky to be getting off with nothing but a transfer Stateside."

"The ambassador?" Holbrook begged. "Can't you see what's going on? It's all happening behind your back and you can't imagine that anyone would do that to you. It's Wagner. Just tell me how the hell the ambassador could have found out if Wagner hadn't first told Admiral Foster? I don't know why he's got it in for me. I don't know why he's on my case. But can't you see it?"

"I've got a Command to run." Roth saluted. "If you have anything else to say on this subject, put it in writing and give it to Commander Parrot. Unless I see something concrete in writing, as far as I'm concerned, the matter is closed."

Holbrook stared at Roth. "What about the two hundred and seventy grams of missing PuN?"

"Captain Wagner is handling the matter." Roth pointed toward the door. "That will be all, Commander."

With nothing else to do, Holbrook saluted and left the admiral's office.

I don't believe that Roth could be so pig-assed blind.

He went back to his office to find a sailor there clearing out his desk, putting everything in cartons. "Who gave you the order to do this?"

The sailor said, "Chief McIntyre, sir."

"All right. Just hold on a second." He went to his desk and fumbled through the papers there. First he copied down all the log numbers on those nine shipments to and from Harwell. Then he gathered up the nine closed-star DoD 3093s and all the associated forms that were clipped to them, put them into an envelope and walked back down the hall to the admin office. "Who gave the order to clean me out?" he asked McIntyre. The admin chief said, "Sorry, sir. It came from Commander Parrot."

He licked the envelope closed and handed it to McIntyre. "Do me a favor. Put this in your safe. Give me a receipt for it. Put my name on it. Or mark it for Admiral Roth, 'eyes only.' Just for Godsake please make certain that no one else gets to it."

"No problem." The admin chief took the envelope, opened his safe, logged it in, shut his safe and wrote out a receipt.

Now Holbrook asked, "Have you got a phone book somewhere with a number for Harwell?"

"Place near Oxford?" He rummaged through a shelf filled with phone books and sorted through a few of them until he came up with the number. Holbrook dialed it and when he had the duty officer on the phone he read off the list of log numbers for the nine shipments. "I want to know if there were access vouchers on any of these shipments."

The duty officer said he wouldn't be a minute because he had to fetch his logbooks—except it sounded to Holbrook as if he was punching information into a computer—and then the duty officer picked up the phone to answer, "You wouldn't mind telling me, would you, why it concerns you? Those are British shipments."

So that's the way he did it. Holbrook understood. Logged into the storage site with the DoD 3093s, and then logged out on a British form. Sent to Harwell, returned on the British form, then logged out of the storage site with the 3093s.

"Trying to check something for the Inspector General," he lied. "In the midst of a surprise IG and all of a sudden they've dug into our own logbooks and found some unaccounted-for access vouchers. These were the numbers on them and we were just checking to see if somehow we got them when you should have had them."

"You have our access vouchers?" The duty officer sounded shocked. "But you shouldn't have them if they belong to us."

"That's what I'm trying to tell you. And if the IG finds out about this call, I'll be up the creek. You guys ever get surprise inspections? You gotta know what kind of pressure we're under right now. Look, if they belong to you, I want to get them the hell outta here before someone asks me why I can't account for the paperwork that should go with them."

"Oh, yes . . . yes, now I understand. Hold on, will you." He went away again.

McIntyre whispered, "What's all that about an IG?"

"All functionaries who fudge their books sympathize with other functionaries who fudge their books when the inspectors roll around. It's called Holbrook's Law of Them Against Us."

The duty officer at Harwell came back on the line. "I don't understand. I've got the access vouchers here for those shipments. How can you have them as well?"

"I've got vouchers for . . ." Holbrook made up a name. "Mr. Tiznar."

"Tiznar?"

"Yes, Mr. S. Tiznar."

"No, no." The duty officer was categorical. "Wrong vouchers. Something isn't right at your end. Nobody here by that name at all. The access vouchers here are all in the name of N. Boston."

A big smile swept across Holbrook's face. "I see . . . well, sorry to trouble you. Thanks anyway."

The duty officer started to say, "Perhaps you should . . ."

But Holbrook hung up. "Bingo. Gotcha. And double bingo." He pointed toward the safe. "Take care of that envelope in there for me. And thanks."

"What do you want me to do with the stuff from your office?"

"Hold on to it. I'll be back." He started out of the office.

"Where are you going?" the admin chief asked.

He said, "To save my own life." And he left the building.

Now he didn't care if there was an entire team of Chinese guys in baseball jackets. He walked out to North Audley Street, hurried through the drizzle along Grosvenor Square and turned left into Duke Street. A red Ford with London Fire Brigade written on the side of it was parked in front of his door. He took the lift to the top floor and found a fireman in his apartment.

"Can I come in?" The hall was black with soot. The air stank of smoldering. The living room was a wreck. His bedroom seemed to be all right. The kitchen and bath were all right too. Except that soot was everywhere. Everything was covered in a thin film of soot. The grimy black dust was inside his dresser drawers and inside his closets. Everywhere that air could have gone, there was soot.

"U.S. Navy, isn't it?"

"Holbrook," he said, coming into the living room.

"Longstaff. I'm with the fire investigation unit."

The two nodded at each other.

"Some mess, huh?"

"Living room ceiling spawling," Longstaff mumbled as he jotted notes down on a clipboard. "Fire started here."

"Last night you were saying it was gas. Changed your mind?"

"Have I?"

"Hope so. For your own sake. 'Cause there is no gas in the apartment. Everything's electric. I tried telling you last night that it was a bomb. But no one wanted to listen to me."

Longstaff shook his head. "We never make final judgments until we come here and go through the scene with a fine-tooth comb."

"How do you know the fire started here?"

"Fire burns upward," Longstaff explained. "So we start by looking at the walls and the ceiling. No real damage to any walls or ceilings except in this room. So I ask myself, did it start here? The trick is never to make suppositions. Just keep asking questions and hope that they'll lead you to other questions. Now look at that ceiling."

Holbrook did. "Totally black."

"Not quite." Longstaff pointed to the corner. "Flames burn up. Heat rises. Hottest part of the flame is the tip and the ceiling touched by the tip will show the most damage. Look closely here." He indicated a point where some of the ceiling seemed to have bubbled. "When you know what to look for it's easy. That's called spawling and if you check the rest of the ceiling, you won't find it anywhere but here. Now look again at these walls. Look how the pattern of the burning is heavy here, thinning out here. It usually shows which way the fire traveled. Now start checking the floor directly under the spot where the ceiling spawled."

Looking down, Holbrook saw nothing but a charred pile of rubble. "I had a lamp here."

"Most of it is still recognizable." Longstaff knelt down. "But what was it attached to?"

"A light-timer."

"One of those electric things that switches the lights on and off at a preset hour." He was talking as much to himself as he was to Holbrook. "Lamp plugged straight into the light-timer and the light-timer plugged straight into the wall. That right?"

Holbrook said, "That's right."

"Well, then, if that's the case"—Longstaff showed Holbrook something in the rubble—"what have we got here?"

Holbrook bent down to have a closer look.

With the tip of a pencil, Longstaff pointed to a small, almost totally melted plastic box with wires sticking out. "And this is what?" He pushed the pencil through the rubble to reveal what looked like several short strips of electrical tape.

"I don't know what any of that is," Holbrook said.

Longstaff asked, "What happened when you came home last night?"

"Like I told you last night, when I rang for the elevator I was surprised to find it was already on my floor. That was the first thing that struck me as being strange because this is the only apartment on the floor. Then the bolt lock. I always double-lock it. Last night it wasn't locked at all. That was number two. Then when I opened the door the light-timer hadn't turned on this lamp here. The whole place was dark."

Longstaff asked, "How much time was there between opening the door and the explosion?"

He tried to remember. "Maybe a minute. Maybe two minutes. I don't know."

"Hmm." Longstaff thought for a moment. "As I said, what you do when you investigate a fire is never make your facts fit your guess. You've got to have a totally open mind. Now, if I came in here seriously looking for a gas leak I could probably just about find enough facts to match my theory."

"But there's no gas," Holbrook reminded him.

"That's why it's dangerous to start drawing any conclusions before you've got all the evidence and can ask all the questions. So you see that stuff there . . ." He pointed to the rubble. "That piece of plastic and those wires and that tape. The reason I find that so interesting is because it's not an electric light-timer device. In fact it looks to me as if it could be something that's not supposed to be there, something that appears to have been hooked up at one time to the light-timer switch. So I want to know what it is and why it's there."

"How about," Holbrook suggested, "if it doesn't look like a light-timer, and it's not supposed to be there, and if this is where the fire started, then maybe it is part of a bomb that someone hooked up to the light-timer to use the clock like some kind of detonator."

"Let's call it a possible explosive device," Longstaff said. "But I've got to keep looking."

"You do that," Holbrook said and walked over to see what there was of the sweatshirts and the food and the Stevie Wonder record he had left on the couch.

Everything there was charred and, like the couch, just a pile of rubble. He sifted through it. Part of a Twiglets box had somehow survived. And so had the can of spaghetti sauce. He tossed them aside.

The Stevie Wonder record was now nothing but a shriveled ball of plastic.

He took it with him into his bedroom, picked up his telephone to find that it was still working, ripped the sooty duvet back from the edge of his bed, sat down on the clean sheet and dialed Florida. "It's me," he said when Millicent answered.

"What time is it?" She sounded still asleep. "I've got to get the kids up for school. Why are you calling so early?"

He hesitated before he said to her, "Because someone tried to kill me last night."

"Oh my God." She was awake now. "Are you all right? What happened?"

He told her the story.

"Oh my God," she kept saying. "Did you call the police? Was anyone hurt? Did you tell your admiral? Who would want to do this to you?"

"I'm all right," he said. "I just . . . well, you know how people talk. What did we call it in Italy, the Arab telephone? I figured someone here might tell someone in the States and you'd hear about it somehow. I was afraid the kids would hear about it. I figured I'd better be the one to tell you."

"I don't know what to tell the kids. I can't tell them someone tried to murder their father."

"Well . . ." He came up with, "Just tell them there was a fire. Tell them I'm fine, I wasn't even in the apartment and that I'll call them Saturday. Or maybe I'll call tonight and talk to them. No, don't tell them anything about a bomb."

"All right. But . . ." She asked, "The police haven't found anybody yet, have they?"

"Not yet. But I'm working on it."

"For Chrissakes, Richard, don't play the hero. I mean, what happens if he tries again?"

"He'd better hurry." Holbrook chuckled. "He's not gonna have a lot of time for a second shot. I told you how I didn't keep my ass covered. Well, when this place blew up, so did my career. Roth's shipping me back to the States."

There was a long pause. "Where will you go?"

"Dunno," he said.

"Will you fly again?"

"I can't fly."

"What will you do?"

"I don't know."

Now there was a longer pause. "Will you come to Florida?"

He said, "I don't know . . . Millicent, I've gotta get my head together. I've got to save my own life first. Maybe then."

She told him, "I think the kids would love to see you."

"And . . . what about you?" he asked.

"I don't know about me," she said. "I kinda think it's really up to you."

He suddenly didn't know what to say to her. He settled for, "I'll try and call tonight. Tell the kids I love them."

Hanging up, he put the melted record next to the phone, went to his dresser, opened the top drawer and pulled out his second wallet. It was covered in a thin layer of soot. So he took it into the bathroom, wiped it off with a towel and checked to see that he had enough British money for a taxi.

Back in the living room he asked Longstaff, "Do me a big favor, will you, please? When you've got something ready, when you can prove beyond any doubt that it was a bomb, will you please ring the Navy, insist on speaking with Admiral Roth and tell him what you've found? Have you got the number?"

Longstaff reached into his shirt pocket. "Let's see. I've got this name and number . . . fellow last night wanted the report . . ." He pulled out a card. "Wagner?"

"No." Holbrook took the card from him and ripped it up. "That's what we call no longer operative. The only guy who counts is the admiral. Please. Don't speak to anybody but him." He reached for the pad that Longstaff was holding, and wrote down Roth's name and phone number. "Please. It's really my ass on the line."

He left the flat, went across the street to the Marriott and got into the first taxi on the rank. He told the driver, "Storey's Gate."

The commissionaire at the front door of Chappell House asked if he had an appointment with Mr. Boston. Holbrook lied, "He's expecting me." The commissionaire told him to go on up. "Fourth floor."

In the lift, Holbrook psyched himself. No beating around the bush. I'm gonna give it to him with both barrels.

The lift door opened, he stepped out and turned into Boston's office.

And it was empty.

That stopped him. He'd expected to find Boston sitting

there. Maybe he's in the john. But the W.C. at the end of the hall was empty as well.

He went back to Boston's office, determined to wait.

He sat down, crossed his legs and let his eyes wander over Boston's desk.

Some letters appeared to be unopened. The thought crossed his mind, maybe he didn't come in today. But other letters were open and some telexes were scattered across the desk. If a secretary put them there for him she would have put them in a neat pile. So he's here somewhere. I'll just wait.

He looked across the street at the Conference Center.

He looked back at Boston's desk.

He uncrossed his legs and then he recrossed his legs.

His eyes fell on Boston's telephone. He looked at the "R" button and thought to himself, what a dangerous little invention. What happens when a husband has been fooling around and his wife suspects that he's been phoning some dolly? All she has to do is push that "R" and the phone automatically dials the last number the husband has called and when the dolly picks it up, the wife is all the wiser.

He stared at the "R" button.

Who was the last person Boston had phoned?

He even thought about pushing the button to find out.

But he didn't.

Instead he reached for the newspaper sitting on Boston's desk. Today's *Telegraph*. He opened it and paged through it.

Nothing was of any interest to him.

He put it down and uncrossed his legs.

"May I help you?"

He spun around to see Boston's secretary. "Hi. I thought no one would mind if I waited."

"Waited?" she asked. "You're from the American Navy, aren't you?"

"That's right."

"And you're waiting for Mr. Boston?"

"That's right."

"Well," she explained, "I'm afraid he's gone out. I'm sorry, but did you have an appointment with him? I didn't see your name in his appointment book this morning."

"Yeah, well, you see, I was supposed to meet him . . ."

"Oh," she said, putting her hand in front of her mouth, looking a bit upset. "Oh, my goodness. You must have misunderstood. You're having lunch with him, is that correct? I'm sorry. I didn't realize it was you with whom he was lunching. Well, he's already gone off to the Reform Club. That's where you were supposed to meet him. Not here. I'm terribly sorry. Do you know where it is? In Pall Mall. But I believe you'll need a tie."

"A tie . . . yes, of course." Holbrook thought quickly. "You see, I understood that I was supposed to meet him here." He pretended to check his watch. "I'm going to be late, then."

"I really am very sorry," she said. "I went out this morning, to the dentist, and when I came back I found a note saying that he had already gone."

"No problem." He stood up. "Thank you very much. The Reform Club on Pall Mall." He told himself, it sounds like as good a place as any.

She showed him to the lift.

"Tell me something." He looked at her. "Mr. Boston's first name is . . ."

"Matthew."

He snapped his fingers. "That's right. Matthew. With an M."

On his way downstairs he tried to remember exactly what the duty officer at Harwell had told him. I thought he said, N. Boston. I thought . . .

The lift doors opened and he left the building.

No . . . he must have said M. Boston and I got it wrong.

He had to ask a cop in Parliament Square how to get to Pall Mall. Top of Horse Guards Parade, other side of the Mall and up the steps. He wanted to ask, why do you Brits always say go to the top of the street or to the bottom of the street? How the hell can you tell which is top or bottom? But he didn't want to get into a conversation with the cop. He had other things to do. First he had to buy a tie. So he now asked if the cop knew where the nearest tie store might be. Yes, sir, you should find one at the bottom of Victoria Street. Top. Bottom. I'm glad there are only two choices. He said thanks and walked quickly through the rain and along Victoria Street until he found a small men's shop. You sell ties? The young West Indian sales assistant corrected him, we sell neckwear. Top of the street. Bottom of the street. I want a tie. The young man led him to the rack of neckwear. You take plastic money? We accept credit cards. Even for a tie? Even for neckwear. He bought a tie, put it on and hurried back up Victoria Street . . . if that's the bottom, then, baby, you're the top. Thanks, Cole Porter.

He passed a shop that sold radios, stereos, watches, cameras and computers.

Suddenly he had an idea. He went in and found a tiny pocket microcassette tape recorder. "You take plastic money? You know, credit cards?" The Pakistani salesman said they did. "I'll need some of those mini-cassettes. And . . . you got anything like a microphone on a long cord?" The salesman pulled out a box of microphones. Holbrook spotted a very tiny one with a clip-on device. "Will this work?" He plugged it into the cassette recorder. The salesman loaded the batteries. Then Holbrook turned it on and started talking. "One, two. Testing. One, two, three." He shut it off and played it back. It was perfect. "I'll take it."

The recorder fitted his inside jacket pocket. He ran the cord down his left sleeve and clipped the microphone under his cuff. No one would be able to tell that he was wired for sound. He practiced turning the machine on and off without taking it out of his pocket. When he had that right, he stashed the extra cassettes into his pants pocket, and went to meet Matthew Boston.

The porter at the Reform Club asked, "May I help you, please?"

"Mr. Boston is expecting me."

The porter said, "Yes, sir, please follow me."

Chapter
Twenty-six

THE PORTER ANNOUNCED QUIETLY, "Your luncheon guest has arrived, sir."

Boston swung around.

Richard Holbrook was standing there.

And for the first time in Boston's life he felt genuine panic. "Oh, my God."

Holbrook said straightaway, "Someone tried to kill me last night."

Boston managed to ask, "What are you doing here? What do you want? Kill you? Who would do anything like that?"

Holbrook said, "You."

"Me?" He was horrified.

Holbrook's voice was calm as he explained, "I was followed yesterday after I left your office. And last night someone planted a bomb in my apartment. I'm not sure I always believe in coincidences."

Oh, my God. Boston could hear Li'Ning's voice assuring him, I will handle Mr. Holbrook. "Oh, my God," he said out loud. "Your family? Was anyone hurt?"

"No," Holbrook said. "But I think you know something about this. I think this has something to do with the PuN missing from those DoD 3093 forms that I came to see you about yesterday."

He stammered, "This is preposterous. I have never . . ."

"I was followed when I left your office. Someone knew I was coming to see you. And the only person who could have known was you."

"Who . . ." he asked, "who followed you?"

Holbrook said, "A young Oriental guy. Probably Chinese." Then he corrected himself. "Almost certainly Chinese."

It had all gone wrong. Suddenly everything was wrong. It wasn't supposed to end like this. Oh dear God in heaven, now what? "Perhaps," Boston said, pulling himself up to his full height—the time has come, he told himself, for some good old-fashioned British dignity—"perhaps, Commander Holbrook, you will do me the honor of joining me for lunch."

"Lunch? You try to kill me last night and today you want me to have lunch with you? Are you out of your fucking mind?"

"Please. I haven't tried to kill you." His throat was totally dry. "But I must admit I know who has."

"Yeah, I'll bet you do." Holbrook faced him. "No one believed me when I discovered there was thirty grams of PuN missing per shipment. Nine shipments. Two hundred seventy grams total. Half a pound. No one would believe me. Then last night I started checking log numbers and shipment sites and dates in and out. I also decided to find out if any one name appeared on every form related to those nine shipments. You, Mr. Boston. You came up trumps."

Boston didn't know what to say. No, it wasn't supposed to end like this.

"It took me ages to check all those forms and make all those lists. I didn't know where the trail would lead me . . . but it took me to Harwell. And it took me to all the access vouchers."

He spoke slowly and deliberately. "My wife. My son. What ever will become of Denise if Nigel and I can't help her?"

"Nigel?" Holbrook stopped short.

Boston nodded. "My son. But we only did it for Denise. You must believe me. If only there was some way to undo . . ."

It took a moment for Holbrook to understand that. "Your son's name is Nigel? He works at Harwell? N. Boston? N . . . not M?" He started to laugh. "Your son Nigel works at Harwell!"

"Yes," he muttered. "But I don't see any humor in that."

"You probably wouldn't," Holbrook said. "N. Boston, not M. Boston. Who would have guessed."

Boston stared at Holbrook for a moment, then turned away to glance around the room. Dignity, he reminded himself. This must be done with dignity. "Have you ever been here before? A splendid setting, isn't it."

Holbrook gave him a strange look. He wasn't laughing anymore. "I don't think you really understand what I'm saying to you. You've been found out. You and Nigel. It's over."

Boston tried to think of something dignified to say. "Did you notice the main hall. The rotunda." He took Holbrook's arm . . . "Please . . ." and gently led him out of the library. "Please . . ." He escorted Holbrook toward the dining room. "It was in the rotunda where Phileas Fogg made his bet to go around the world in eighty days."

"Mr. Boston?" Holbrook kept shaking his head. "You tried to murder me . . ."

"Please," Boston begged him. "I am going to tell you everything. But it truly would be pleasant to have lunch. Do me this favor. It would . . ." His voice cracked. "Everything would be easier over a bottle of wine. And I sincerely would like to make my apologies."

With an incredulous expression on his face, Holbrook allowed Boston to lead him into the dining room.

The waiter showed them to a corner table.

The room was long and narrow, lined with windows that looked out to a garden. The table was covered in white linen. Boston suggested the fish. "It's quite good and quite fresh."

"I don't believe this," Holbrook said.

Boston took a pencil and wrote on the order chit, "Two Dover soles." Then he offered Holbrook, "Melon to start? And may I suggest a Sancerre?"

Leaning forward, Holbrook reminded him, "You tried to kill me last night . . ."

"No," Boston said softly. "No, I didn't. But if you will have this lunch with me, I shall tell you who did."

Holbrook sat back.

Boston handed the chit to the waiter.

Nothing was said until the Sancerre arrived. The waiter opened the bottle and poured a little for Boston to sample. "Yes, it's fine." Then the waiter poured a glass for Holbrook but he didn't touch it. Boston raised his glass and said, "I am very, very sorry. I truly am."

Holbrook watched Boston take a sip.

It's over, he told himself as he swallowed the wine. He took a second sip. It's over. "I didn't expect to see you here. I was waiting for someone else." An odd sensation swept over him. He toyed with his glass. It was almost a feeling of relief. "I should have known you weren't going to give up as easily as you made me believe."

Still Holbrook said nothing.

"It was because of the missing Navy van, wasn't it?" He sipped more wine. "Odd how life can be sometimes. How cruel its tricks. How nasty Fate can turn." He said to Holbrook, "I read once about a book based on the idea, what if? You know, what if George Washington had lost the American War of Independence? Or, what if your John Kennedy had not been assassinated? It wasn't exactly that, but that was the basic idea. And now I can't help but wonder, what if that Navy van of yours hadn't been hijacked? Of course I know the answer. You would never have started looking into the shipments attached to those forms. You wouldn't be sitting here now."

Holbrook folded his arms on the table and didn't take his eyes off Boston.

"On second thought, more to the point of irony perhaps, the question might be, what if my wife had never been taken ill?" He stopped when he saw the waiter bringing the melons. "Please," he said to Holbrook. "Please start."

But Holbrook didn't budge.

"Forgive me." Boston tasted the melon. "It's quite good, you know." He looked at Holbrook, who merely stared back at him. Suddenly the need to apologize became an overwhelming urge to justify this luncheon. "An eccentricity, perhaps. But I wish you would understand that I so want to be dignified about this. I'm concerned that soon I shall have nothing else left save my dignity. And even that may desert me, or worse, be taken away." Again he gestured toward Holbrook's melon. "Please."

Holbrook shook his head. "I'm not hungry."

Boston finished his melon. "My wife was taken seriously ill over twenty years ago. We were living in Hong Kong. Such an illness can put a terrible strain on one's family life. At times, unbearably so. Not our marriage, you understand. I could never abandon her. But it's meant we've always had to have someone in the house to help her. It's meant that I've always had to consider her needs before anything else."

Holbrook continued to stare.

"At first she was much too ill to travel which necessitated our remaining in Hong Kong. It was another eight months before the doctors felt she could return to Great Britain. Do you know Hong Kong, Commander?" He didn't wait for an answer. "It's a wonderful place. Like no other place on earth, really. I loved every minute of our stay there." He motioned for the waiter to take the melons away and bring the fish. "There's something about the way that Hong Kong smells. It's an odor you don't find anywhere else in the world. It's the smell of something so terribly exotic. Foreign spices. Intrigue. The East."

The waiter arrived with the fish and a platter of mixed vegetables.

Boston offered the vegetables to Holbrook.

He refused them.

"Please," Boston said, picking up his knife and fork.

Holbrook still didn't move.

"In Hong Kong," Boston went on, balancing small pieces of sole on his fork, looking at each one before eating it, "I met a man who loved cricket. Oh, perhaps I didn't mention that I played cricket in those days for the office team. I was working at Government House. Well, this man loved cricket probably more than anyone I've ever met in my life. His name was Joseph Li'Ning."

241

Holbrook listened.

Boston's voice was sadly nostalgic. "He was a banker in Hong Kong and he had a young son who used to come to the cricket matches with him. Joseph Li'Ning was a wealthy and powerful man in the local Chinese community. We never mixed socially. The Chinese in Hong Kong remain somewhat aloof, especially aloof from British civil servants who are hardly their peers. Yet when my wife became ill, Joseph Li'Ning personally saw to it that she was looked after by the finest doctors in the Colony. Thanks to Joseph Li'Ning . . ." He stopped for a moment, put his knife and fork down and looked directly at Holbrook. "Due to the severe nature of her illness . . . I have often believed that it is thanks to Joseph Li'Ning's concern that she is alive today. It is therefore perhaps not so surprising that when his young son grew up and became a banker and started doing business in London, I should feel somewhat obliged to him." Boston took a deep breath and shook his head. "No, Commander, I did not try to kill you last night. It was Christopher Li'Ning who did."

Holbrook demanded, "The banker's son? But why?"

"Because he feared that you would find out about him." Boston pushed his plate away. His appetite was gone. "The weather in this country is killing my wife. Christopher Li'Ning knew what I did for a living. He said he always wanted to help us. When his father died he said he now felt responsible in a way to help us with Denise . . . with my wife. Of course he knew that Nigel was working at Harwell but when he realized that we both had certain access to fissile materials . . . well, one evening over dinner in an innocent conversation . . . we were talking about spy novels . . . and he suggested we construct a plot. It was a party game. Talk across the dinner table. It was never supposed to be anything more than that. I said that alone neither Nigel nor I could do much of anything, but that . . ."

"You and your son?" Holbrook said. "For Christ's sake, man, do you know what you've done?"

Now Boston couldn't look at Holbrook. But he wanted to explain why. "It was never for me. It was never for Nigel. It began as nothing more than a plot for a book none of us would ever write." His voice choked and he had to stop to drink some more wine. "Christopher Li'Ning was supposed to meet me here this afternoon at twelve-thirty with numbers for a bank account in Zurich. Please understand . . . I beg you to understand that the money in that account was only to pay for an apartment in Spain where the weather would be much less harsh on my wife. The money was to give her a new lease on life."

"And what was Li'Ning doing with the PuN?"

Boston shrugged. "You may never believe this, but I never asked. Although I suppose it's obvious. He has given it or is planning on giving it to the Chinese."

"Shit," Holbrook said. He leaned forward. "Do you have any idea . . ."

"Of course I do," Boston snapped. "Do you think I'm a total fool." He stopped short and reminded himself, calm down and be quiet. "Yes," he said, more softly this time. "Yes, I do."

"Where did you get the DoD forms?"

"I had them printed. We only planned to use one or two . . . this was only going to happen once or twice . . . but you can't just have a couple of forms printed, you've got to order a whole batch. Actually it was odd how the printer never once questioned me. As far as he must have cared it was just another job. I offered him cash. Funny how blinkered we can all be sometimes."

"Yeah." Holbrook raised his eyebrows. "Real funny."

Boston let the remark slip by. "I had to have the forms printed myself in order to make the accounting procedures work. Otherwise it would have been too obvious that something was wrong." He stopped and looked at Holbrook for the first time in several minutes. "Please, do tell me, was there something about the forms that made you suspicious?"

"Someday I'll explain to you about closed stars and open stars."

"I don't understand."

"It doesn't matter," Holbrook said. "It's more important that you tell me, how difficult was it to actually get to our PuN?"

"Nothing could have been simpler," he admitted. "Controls are lax. I was able to borrow your stored shipments for a day or two, send them to Harwell under British orders where Nigel received them, took just an ounce, and returned the rest. It worked so easily the first time that we did it a second time." He refilled his glass. "It seemed the most sensible way of doing it. I'm afraid that our physical controls of fissile materials are not as sophisticated as we would have others believe."

Holbrook took a deep breath and said with some irony in his voice, "And because it worked so easily the second time you did it a third time and a fourth time and nine times."

"It's just that . . ." Boston wanted him to understand, "it was never supposed to happen a second time or a third time."

"Or a first time," Holbrook reminded him.

There was nothing Boston could say to that.

"This Christopher Li'Ning . . ." Holbrook asked. "Where is he? How do I find him?"

Boston shrugged. "He was supposed to meet me here at half-past twelve. The newspaper this morning said he left yesterday for New York. Did you see in the *Telegraph* today that he bought a very expensive piece of Chinese ceramics this week? It's to be a gift from his bank to the Chinese government. When I read that he was in New York, I rang his bank in the City. But he answered. I spoke to him at ten-thirty this morning in his office. He promised to meet me. He never showed up. I would suspect the reason is because he's already left the country with the plutonium nitrate."

"Shit," Holbrook said. "How can you be so fucking calm about this? Don't you understand what's happening? Don't you understand what you've done?"

Boston signaled for the waiter. "I am trying, Commander, to maintain my dignity."

"Dignity?" Holbrook said directly into Boston's face, "Fuck your dignity."

Boston stared into his wine glass and tried to think of something to say. "I don't suppose," he came up with, "that you would care for some pudding or a coffee?"

"And I don't suppose," Holbrook asked, "that you'd mind if I called the police."

Boston waited for a few seconds before he wondered, "Is it that time yet?"

Holbrook reached for his left cuff, pulled it forward and made sure that Boston could see the microphone. "It's that time." Then he snapped off the tape.

Trust an American, Boston thought, to play by rules like that. Hah. I should have known. But . . . well . . . He straightened up. "Commander, would you mind terribly if I rang them instead of you?"

"What?"

"That's what I'd like to do." He stood up and said to Holbrook, "Would you please come with me?"

Holbrook followed him out of the dining room, through the rotunda and down the steps to the telephone booths opposite the porter's desk.

Boston put a coin in the box and dialed. "I'm ringing the Assistant Chief Constable of the Atomic Energy Authority's Constabulary," he told Holbrook who simply stood there watching him. When Wooldridge answered, he said, "Derek, this is Matthew Boston. I'm at the Reform. Would you mind coming here right away." He paused only long enough to glance toward Holbrook before he said, "Derek, my son and I have, for nearly three years, been deeply involved in a serious crime against Her Majesty's government. If you wouldn't mind, I would like to give myself up."

"Buster?" Wooldridge was shocked. "Buster . . . are you telling me that . . . Buster, I shall be right there."

"Thank you, Derek." Boston put the phone down. "Excuse me," he said to Holbrook and called to the porter, "I am expecting a Mr. Wooldridge. He will be here shortly. Will you please bring him into the library." Then he motioned to Holbrook, "He won't be long," and walked back up the stairs to the reading room. "Please." He offered Holbrook a chair.

"I want Christopher Li'Ning."

Boston took a seat. "I don't know where he is. Honestly I don't. Hong Kong? China? New York? As I've said, I fear he may be well away by now."

"What's the bank called and where is it?"

"The Mandarin Commerce in Threadneedle Street," Boston said. "Yes, perhaps you might try there first. Please excuse me if I don't come with you." He looked at Holbrook and for the first time he felt himself losing control. What will become of Denise? "Please excuse me if I sit here and wait for Mr. Wooldridge." His throat tensed. "Please excuse me if I . . ." His eyes welled up, his head fell into his hands and he started to cry.

Chapter
Twenty-seven

NOW HE FELT STRANGE.

Slightly uncomfortable.

As if he was an intruder.

So he quietly backed away, leaving Boston to his fate.

The day's newspapers were spread out across the polished top of a long mahogany table in the center of the reading room. He didn't know if anyone would mind, but when no one asked him what he wanted, he opened the *Daily Telegraph*, found the story and the two small pictures on page three and ripped it all out of the paper.

Okay. Now I know what Li'Ning looks like.

Okay. Now I'm going to find him.

He left the Reform Club and jumped into the first empty cab that came along. A bank called Mandarin Commerce. It's on someplace called Threadneedle Street. The taxi driver got him there.

The guard at the desk downstairs asked Holbrook's name.

He almost told the truth. But then he thought, if Li'Ning was the one who tried to have me killed, telling him I'm here might not be such a good idea. He told the bank guard, "Tiznar."

The guard called upstairs to speak with someone before hanging up and saying to Holbrook, "I'm terribly sorry, sir. I was afraid this would be the case. But Mr. Li'Ning left for New York yesterday."

"I see . . ." Except that Boston told me he spoke to Li'Ning this morning. "I need to see him about something . . ." He reached inside his pocket for the newspaper cutting. "It's about this article. I'm a journalist . . ."

"Just a moment, sir." He called upstairs again, spoke briefly to someone, then said to Holbrook, "This is Mr. Peter Kan, Mr. Li'Ning's personal assistant."

Holbrook took the phone and explained, "I was looking for Mr. Li'Ning. It's important that I get in touch with him."

"He's left for New York," Peter said. "He went yesterday."

"That's strange." Holbrook decided it was worth a shot. "Because I spoke with him in his office at about ten-thirty this morning."

There was a pause. "Your name, sir?"

"Tiznar."

"And would you mind if I asked what this was in reference to? Perhaps if I speak with Mr. Li'Ning in New York."

"The article in the paper this morning. I'm a journalist with the . . ." The first paper that came to mind was *Stars and Stripes* but he knew that wouldn't work. "The *National Enquirer.*" Millicent always read that in the States. How would anyone in England know what that was. "I told Mr. Li'Ning on the phone this morning that I wanted to drop by and interview him about the piece of ceramics he just bought. But if you're telling me he went to New York yesterday when I know he was here only a few hours ago . . ."

"Yes, well, actually he was supposed to go yesterday and I thought he must have. I didn't see him this morning so I merely assumed . . ."

"Where can I reach him?" Holbrook asked.

"I don't exactly know, sir. There are a number of places he likes to stay in New York. Perhaps if I could take your number and have him reach you . . ."

No, he wanted to say, Li'Ning hasn't gone to New York. This guy is too vague. This guy is hiding something. Li'Ning is still in the country. "What about my interview?"

"As far as I know, sir, Mr. Li'Ning won't be giving any more interviews about the ginger jar. In any case, we shall be releasing a press communiqué to say that the planned official ceremony has been canceled and that Mr. Li'Ning will present the gift himself at a private ceremony.''

Holbrook hadn't the faintest idea what this man was talking about. All he knew was that if Li'Ning was still in Great Britain, he'd have to get to him before Li'Ning found out that Boston was being arrested and had confessed everything . . . ''Yeah, well, thanks anyway.''

He found a taxi and went back to North Audley Street.

I'll play the tape for Roth. Then he'll believe me. But what do I do if he insists on Wagner being there? I'll kill that bastard. Someday. Somewhere. Somehow. I'll get him.

Grabbing his badge from the Marine at the front entrance, he rushed up to the admiral's office. ''I've got to be in there,'' he told Miss Cecilia.

''He's out,'' she said in a very chilly way. ''And you owe me an apology.''

''He's out?'' *How the hell can he be out now? Why now?* ''Where is he?''

''I'm sorry, Commander, he's out. And until I get an apology from you for the last time you barged in here . . .''

He turned and went into Camille Parrot's office. ''When is the old man back?''

''Did you know he's having orders cut for you?'' Parrot said. ''And trying to talk him out of sending you to the States won't do you any good.''

''Camille, when is he due back?''

''I wouldn't concern myself with that if I were you, Dick. First we've got to arrange some temporary quarters for you. I've had someone trying to find a hotel room for tonight. Then, you've got to go to the police and make out a statement for them and one for the fire department . . .''

He left Parrot in midsentence and went down the hallway to his office.

It was empty.

The desk was still there and the phone was still there and so were the chairs facing the desk. But nothing else was there. The room had been picked clean.

''Rumor has it that you're on your way out, boy,'' Wagner sneered at him from the doorway. '' 'Bout time.''

Someday. Somewhere. Somehow. Holbrook thought fast.

"Tell me something, shithead, how come you're not out kissing somebody's ass? Probably the only thing you're any good at.''

"Hey?'' Wagner barked. "You want to try that on me again? I'd just love to throw your ass into a Special Court Martial for that insubordinate remark. You got the balls to say things like that in front of witnesses?''

Keep coming, he said to himself. Please keep coming. "Seems to me with all the ass-kissing you do, somebody along the line would have given you a command. Thank God for the Navy they didn't. I guess maybe you're not even good at ass-kissing.'' Holbrook casually turned his back on Wagner.

"Any time you want to step outside.''

"You wouldn't have the balls to take me up on it.'' He reached inside his jacket. " 'Cause when it comes right down to it, Wagner, you're nothing but a loudmouthed coward.'' Now he snapped on the tape recorder.

"Coward, huh?'' Wagner shouted. "Damn but you're dumb, Holbrook. I thought arranging to have you shipped back to the States might be enough. But you're such a loser that maybe I just gotta make a few phone calls, use up a few markers, and see if I can't get you drummed the fuck outta the Navy. And nothing would please me more.''

Holbrook sat down on the edge of the desk. "What would you say if I told you that Admiral Roth has changed his mind. That he's not sending me back to the States. That he knows all about how you've been going behind his back to Foster.''

"Don't you worry about that admiral friend of yours.'' Wagner said right to Holbrook's face, "Fact is you're chickenshit and not even an asshole like Roth can save you this time. Washed out of flying. Drunk half the time. Official report is gonna say that you torched your goddamned apartment 'cause you were tanked. If I have to pay off the entire London Fire Brigade with my own money, you're going to sink with this one.''

"An asshole like Roth? Strong words for an officer and a gentleman.'' Keep going, he wanted to beg. Don't stop now. "And then to admit that you'd be willing to bribe the fire department to lie about me. Sounds like conduct unbecoming.''

"I want you out of the Navy. You are my number-one project." He pointed his finger at Holbrook. "And this is no threat, this is a promise. If the fucking admiral insists on protecting you, then I guess I've gotta pull a few more tricks outta the bag. My warning to you, boy, is don't look back, 'cause no matter where you are, I'm gonna be gaining on you. If that transfer to the States doesn't come through, you're sure as hell gonna wish it did."

"A personal vendetta?" Holbrook gave him a big smile.

"What are you grinning about?" Wagner demanded.

"I guess this means we can't ever be friends."

"Bet your damn butt we can't." Wagner spun around and left.

Last of the ninth. Three and two. Bases loaded. Here comes the pitch. The kid swings and . . . wham! I just hit me a grand slam.

Holbrook snapped off the tape recorder.

Boston. Now Wagner. Two birds with one stone. Talk about stepping in shit. Someday. Somewhere. Somehow. Right now. Right here. Right on. Captain Wagner, that's one straight up your tailpipe. Zap.

Feeling almost high, Holbrook pulled that tape out of the recorder, reloaded it with a fresh tape and said to himself, this has got to be the best toy I've ever had. Then he went back to the admin office, put the tape inside an envelope and sealed it. He wrote across the front of it, "Admiral's eyes only."

"Do me a favor again," he said to McIntyre. "Stick this in your safe with the other envelope and let me have a receipt for it. Don't give either envelope to anyone else. No matter who says it's all right. No one. I've personally got to take it to the old man tonight or tomorrow." Then for some strange reason he felt the need to add, "And if it's still there tomorrow night, you personally take it to the old man. Make him open those envelopes while you're standing in his office. Please. I'm begging you. My ass is riding on it."

The admin chief said, "Sure," wrote out a receipt, opened the safe, logged the entry and closed the safe. "Is this the beginning of a collection?"

"Nope, it's the beginning of how Richard Holbrook saves his own life."

He returned to the empty office. Got him. I got the bastard. I just blew him outta the water. But, he reminded himself, there isn't time to gloat. We'll celebrate tomorrow. Two down and one to go. On my way to a hat trick.

He reached into his pocket for the newspaper clipping, read it, then got on the phone to the journalist who wrote it. "I saw your story this morning. I'm about to become a collector of Oriental ceramics and I wanted to get in touch with Mr. Li'Ning but didn't know how to reach him outside banking hours and I was wondering . . ."

"Beats me," Pantucci said. "I tried him this morning but the bank said he'd left."

"Yes," Holbrook said. "I got the same response." An idea crossed his mind. "Tell me something about ginger jars. There's an opening on the top. About how wide across would it be?"

"Six or eight inches. They vary."

"Thanks," Holbrook said. "Sorry to bother you." He put the phone down and re-read the article, especially the part about the ceremony along Gerrard Street.

The guy at the bank said something about canceling the ceremony. Li'Ning was going to present the ginger jar himself. Now it's canceled. So . . . the voice inside his head told him, maybe Li'Ning is still going to present the jar himself, but this time in China.

The guy who wrote the newspaper story said the opening on the top of the ginger jar is six or eight inches across. So . . . the voice inside his head told him, that's big enough to pass a cigarette package through. Or several cigarette packages. Or several lead containers the size of a cigarette package.

Son of a bitch!

He grabbed the phone and rang British Airways. "I'm sorry to bother you with this, but I've screwed up my agenda and I've gotten all my appointments wrong. My secretary should have booked me through to Beijing but it might have been via New York . . ."

"Your name, sir?"

"Li'Ning." He picked up the article to spell it for her. "You see my secretary is out . . ."

"Just a minute, please." He could hear her clicking the letters into her computer. "Mr. Christopher Li'Ning? Or Mr. C. Li'Ning?"

"Both," he said right away. "With my secretary out . . ."

"I don't understand . . ." She kept clicking her computer. "I show a reservation for Mr. Christopher Li'Ning on this morning's B.A. 193, Concorde service to New York. And also one for Mr. C. Li'Ning on B.A. 5612 at thirteen-fifteen. If these were for you, Mr. Li'Ning, you've missed them both. You know, sir, we do ask passengers when their plans have changed and they're holding reservations to please advise us . . ."

"It was my secretary who made these reservations and she's gone home ill and you can imagine what the office is like without her. I'm only afraid the temp filling in for her might have made some other reservations. You do fly to Beijing? Or perhaps Beijing via Hong Kong?" It was worth a try.

"No, sir, that's all I'm showing for you. Exactly where would you like to go?"

"Ah . . ." Something he once saw in a movie flashed into his mind. "You know what happens sometimes, because my name is a little hard to spell, sometimes it gets turned around. Perhaps you've got something under L. Christopher."

"L. Christopher?" She put that into the computer, waited for the answer on her screen and came back to him with, "No, sir. Nothing under that name."

"Oh well . . ." It worked once for Clint Eastwood. "Now, that second flight you mentioned . . ."

"Yes sir, B.A. 5612 . . ."

"That's right, B.A. 5612." He wanted to know where it was going but he was afraid if he asked and aroused her suspicions she would realize he wasn't Christopher Li'Ning. "Obviously I missed that one. Is there anything later this afternoon?"

"I'll check, sir . . ." There were more clicks and then there was a pause. "There's another flight at fifteen-thirty, sir, arriving at sixteen forty-five. But I'm showing full for that one. Our next service is seventeen-forty-five and that arrives at nineteen-ten . . . and again, I'm sorry, sir, but I'm showing full.''

"Full," he said. "That's really too bad. But tell me, how else can I get there?''

"You might want to try standby, sir. But your chances would depend on no-shows. And it doesn't look too good. I see there are waiting lists for both flights. Unfortunately, there is no other service from Heathrow, sir.''

No other service to where? "Well . . . who else flies there? B.A. can't be the only one."

"Let me see . . . there is Dan Air but that's out of Gatwick. You might try them. It's unfortunate, sir, because we do run seven flights a day to Aberdeen so . . .''

Aberdeen! "Yeah . . .'' he said. "Well, I'll have to think about it . . . my secretary will be back tomorrow. Thanks very much . . .'' Aberdeen? Why Aberdeen? Now he asked, "Could you tell me one more thing. If I wanted to make a connection out of Aberdeen on an international flight . . .''

"International flight? To where? There are no international flights out of Aberdeen. You'd have to connect through Glasgow. Or Manchester.''

"That's all right. Thanks a lot.'' Aberdeen. Where the hell is Aberdeen? He went back to the Admin office. "Chief, you got an atlas?''

McIntyre pulled a large, old, green book down from a shelf.

"Where's Aberdeen?''

"Scotland.''

"Scotland?'' Holbrook ran through the atlas until he found a map of Scotland and sure enough, there was Aberdeen on the east coast. "What the hell is there to do in Aberdeen?''

"North Sea oil,'' the admin chief said. "It's a port.''

A port. No international flights. Just a port. "How do you find out in this country what ships are going in and out of someplace like Aberdeen?''

The admin chief shrugged. "Beats me. Phone the port, I guess.''

"I guess.'' He went back to his old office and asked information for the Aberdeen Scotland Port Authority. Information came up with the number for the Aberdeen Harbor Board. He dialed it and told the operator there that he wanted the harbor master's office. She put him through to the harbor engineer's office.

"My name is Holbrook," he explained to the man who answered. "I'm with the United States Navy in London and we're trying to get some shipping information. This may take some time but I'm hoping you can help me. You have freighter traffic in and out, I suppose."

"We do," the man replied.

"Any passenger vessels? You know, cruise ships or something like that?"

"We don't normally."

"You don't normally? Does that mean you've got something in port now?"

"We don't."

"Well, sir, have you got any foreign-flag freighters in at the moment?"

"We do."

He knew he was on to something. "What flags?"

"Don't know offhand. Norwegian? French?"

"Sir . . . are you asking me or telling me?"

"Norwegian. French."

His heart sank. "Well, how about tankers?"

"We do."

This guy's a lot of help, he thought. "I was wondering . . . what have you got in port now that's scheduled to ship out this afternoon or tonight?"

"Norwegian, maybe. French, maybe."

"That's all?"

"No," the man said, "you asked me what's sailing today that's already in port now. But that's not to say there's nothing due in that's also due out."

"All right," he tried, "what's due in?"

"Maybe three."

"Three ships are due in?"

"Maybe three. Maybe two."

Great conversationalist, this guy. "Is anything due in today that is also due out today?"

"Maybe one."

"Which one?"

"*Dragon Empress* from Rotterdam—no, London—she

skipped Rotterdam. Due in right about now. Sailing to-night.''

His pulse rate clicked into second gear. "What flag?"

"Chinese."

That's it. "Where is she going?"

"Originally Riga and Tallinn. Now that's been changed to Tianjin."

"Where's that?"

"Don't know."

Tianjin. Sounds Chinese. "What time is she due out?"

"Got it down here for three to four hours refueling time."

That's gotta be the one. "Is she off-loading?"

"Nope."

"Is she on-loading?"

"Don't know."

"Thanks." He hung up and returned to the admin office. The atlas said Tianjin was a small port not far from Beijing. "Bingo." He ran to Camille Parrot's office. "Can you get me in touch with the admiral?"

"You don't believe me when I tell you that he doesn't want to hear from you."

"Camille, we don't have a lot of time. It would take too long to explain but there's at least two hundred and seventy grams of U.S. Navy plutonium nitrate on its way to China in about three hours."

"Come on, Dick." Parrot made a face. "You're not still harping on that, are you?"

"For Chrissake," he yelled, "don't you hear what I'm tell-ing you? There's a freighter called the *Dragon Empress*—a Chinese freighter—and there's a banker named Christopher Li'Ning who is on his way to Aberdeen, or already in Aber-deen with a ginger jar full of fissile materials . . ."

Parrot stared at him. "What's a ginger jar?"

He pleaded, "It doesn't matter what a ginger jar is. Just listen to what I'm telling you."

"I don't know why you're even bothering to talk to me about this," Parrot said. "There's nothing I can do about it. If it's a matter for security, then Captain Wagner . . ."

"Camille." He kicked the side of Parrot's desk. "Camille, let's pretend we haven't had this conversation yet. I'll start all over again. Hi, where's the admiral? Camille, we've got to stop a Chinese freighter from leaving Aberdeen.''

Parrot folded his arms. "The admiral is very angry about you right now. Maybe if you wait a few days until he calms down . . .''

"A few days? This can't even wait a few hours." He took a deep breath, looked at the ceiling and shook his head. "Fuck it. I'll go to Aberdeen myself.''

Parrot said right away, "Without the admiral's permission I won't authorize any TDY expenses . . .''

"TDY, my ass. Nobody wants to know so I'll stop the bastard myself. Maybe then somebody in this shit-house will believe me." And now he said to Parrot, "I need an airplane.''

"Right now you need quarters for tonight. That is much more important than this continued raving lunacy about Chinese ships and missing PuN.''

"Camille, this is an emergency.''

"No, it is not," Parrot protested. "It is something gone haywire in your head. The admiral is not going to authorize a plane for you." He stood his ground. "And neither am I. Right now you are the last person on earth the admiral wants to talk to. Can you possibly imagine how disappointed he is in you? Really. You are the last person on earth he wants anything to do with.''

"Shut up and get me a plane, Camille.''

He was immovable. "No. Negative. N.O. I am not going to cut orders for you to go somewhere just because you've got this cockamamie idea—and anyway, you can't fly it yourself because you're no longer current.''

"Shit." He stormed out of Parrot's office and went back to see the admin chief. "Where did I hear that there's some sort of flying club around here?''

Chief McIntyre started to say, "Yes, sir . . .'' when Holbrook remembered seeing a VFR textbook. "Wait." He tried to picture it again in his mind. Someone showed me a VFR textbook. Where did I see it? *A Manual For Flight*. Ben. Patrick Ben. "Thanks," he called to the admin chief and ran downstairs. "Where's that flying club of yours?''

"Huh?" Ben looked up from his desk. "Oh, hi.''

"The flying club," Holbrook insisted. "Where is it? Have you got a phone number for them?"

"Sure." Ben seemed confused. "But why do you want to know?"

"I don't have time to explain. Just get someone on the phone right now."

Ben searched through his desk until he found the number. He dialed it and asked for someone called David Edgeware. When he had Edgeware on the phone he said, "Hold on a second. This is Pat Ben calling from the U.S. Navy in London. A friend of mine wants to speak with you." He gave the phone to Holbrook. "All yours."

"Mr. Edgeware? My name is Commander Richard Holbrook. I need a very big favor and I need it fast. I need a plane to get to Aberdeen."

"No problem," Edgeware said. "We're a licensed flying school so we've got planes. That is, as long as you've got a valid license."

"I'm a Navy pilot. I've been rated for, I don't know, seventeen or eighteen years. I used to . . . until I came here I was flying jets off carriers. But right now I'll take anything with wings, a motor, baling wire and enough fuel to get me there."

"Ah . . ." Edgeware said, "not quite the same thing. U.S. military license isn't valid here. Are you telling me you haven't got a civilian license?"

"No, sir, I don't," Holbrook admitted. "But you might say this is an emergency."

"Commander, I really would like to help . . ."

"Please," Holbrook said. "Mr. Edgeware, this truly is an emergency situation."

There was a pause until Edgeware said, "Aberdeen? You're going to need something with a bit of range. And the weather's pretty soupy." There was another pause. "Listen . . . I'm going to give you a name and address. But don't you dare tell anyone where you got it from, all right?"

"All right."

"We're at the Denham Aerodrome in Uxbridge. You know where that is?"

"No, but I'll find it."

"You know where Northolt is? RAF base?"

"No, but I'll find it."

"Middlesex. About twenty-five minutes from London."

"Mr. Edgeware, just tell me where the plane is, please."

"It's here. On the other side of the field. Small operator named McCauley. A one-man flying school. He hires out a couple of Piper Aztecs. They'll get you there. I've got a number for him but don't bother ringing him because he won't answer. You'll just have to show up and take your chances with him."

"How the hell do I know if he's got any airplanes available?"

"He's got planes. I can see that from here. And . . . I'll even go over there to tell him you're coming. But if he lets you have a plane, for God's sake, man, don't ever tell anyone I had anything to do with it."

"We're on our way. Thanks." Holbrook hung up, then told Ben, "You must know the way out there. Let's go. Come on." He dragged Ben out of the office and down to the guard desk at the entrance. "We need a car. Fast."

The Marine on duty checked a clipboard and said, "I think 4111 is out back." Holbrook went to the OOD's station, grabbed the keys, slapped them into Ben's hands, and tugged him outside. "Drive."

"I don't even have my cover," he said, showing Holbrook that he had forgotten his hat.

"Drive," Holbrook said.

Ben got behind the wheel of the blue Chrysler, Holbrook got in next to him and they headed for Denham.

Traffic was heavy, but once they got out of town Ben made good time. He pulled up to the main office of the Denham flying school. "Not here," Holbrook said, looking toward the other side of the field. "There. McCauley's place."

Ben started around the bottom of the single 2,400 foot tarmac runway.

"Come on." Holbrook grabbed the wheel. "Nothing's coming. Take the short cut."

"You're outta your skull," Ben said, looked into the sky both ways, saw the runway was clear and shot straight across it.

He pulled up next to a large hangar and Holbrook jumped out. "Mr. McCauley?" There were two Piper Aztecs sitting inside the hangar. One blue. One red. "Mr. McCauley?"

"Who's looking for him?" a man asked, coming from the rear of the hangar, wiping his hands on the sides of his already filthy overalls. He stared at Holbrook. "Who are you?"

"My name is Richard Holbrook. I'm a United States Navy pilot and I need to hire a plane. This is kind of an emergency."

"Kind of an emergency, eh?" McCauley wasn't going to be rushed. "Got a ticket?"

Holbrook dared, "You want to see it?"

"You got one? I mean a civilian ticket?"

He studied McCauley and almost said yes. But something in the old man's eyes told him not to. "No."

"You current?"

This time Holbrook lied, "Yes."

McCauley stared at Holbrook, then looked at Ben, then looked back at Holbrook. "What do you want and where are you going?"

"An Aztec is fine," he said. "I've got to get to Aberdeen."

McCauley leaned against the red plane's wing. "So, you want an Aztec." He pointed his thumb at Ben. "He qualified?"

"I'm alone," Holbrook said.

"How come . . ." McCauley wanted to know, "you being in the Navy and all. How come they're not giving you something to fly?"

Holbrook answered, "We don't have a lot of planes at Grosvenor Square."

McCauley thought about it for a long time. "They could shut me down if they ever found out I hired out to someone like you."

"Yes, sir," Holbrook agreed. "I understand."

"You know the weather is closing in."

"Yes, sir," Holbrook said.

"It's a long leg all the way up there to Aberdeen."

"Yes, sir," Holbrook said again.

McCauley stared at him, then tapped the red wing. "I'll

let you have Juliet Romeo here for £160 an hour." He shrugged. "I mean, I know who sent you. Just wanted to make sure you could keep your mouth shut. They told me you didn't have a ticket. Just testing you." McCauley nodded several times. "Come with me and we'll get you some maps and a flight plan."

Holbrook and Ben followed McCauley into the small office at the side of the hangar where McCauley handed Holbrook a couple of radio navigation charts for sectors Eur 1-2 and Eur 3-4. He also gave Holbrook a headset. "Can't keep 'em in the planes anymore or the kids will steal them." Then he called the weather office. "It's not so good." And then he filed a flight plan. "You got full navaids on Juliet Romeo. She'll get you there. Does about one-sixty. We'll send you out at 8,000 feet and maybe that will put a little wind on your tail. It's pretty straightforward flying. Time into ADN should be two, two-and-a-quarter hours. We'll use Edinburgh as an alternate."

Holbrook studied the flight plan. From BNN to DTY, LIC, POL, TLA, ANGUS and into ADN. He marked those points off on the charts. "Yeah . . . pretty straightforward. Let's see the plane." They went back into the hangar.

"Hey." Ben grabbed his arm and said in a very low voice, "Why don't I come along? I can't help you fly it but I know what happened and why you're not flying anymore . . . and maybe it would be easier if there was someone with you."

"Thanks anyway." He moved around Ben. "I've gotta get going."

He inspected the tires. Then he looked at the flaps. Then he surveyed the deck under the plane for any possible oil leaks. He walked all around the plane. Everything was battened down. Everything looked okay.

"I just serviced it," McCauley said. "Plugs are fresh."

"Thanks." Holbrook climbed into the cockpit and ran his eyes over the instrument panel.

"All those dials and buttons make sense to you?" Ben peeked over his shoulder. "I keep reading my damn books and they all look alike."

Holbrook disregarded him.

"She's got five hours of fuel in her," McCauley said.

"Should get you there but you'd better do something before you come home. Now . . . you going to leave a deposit?"

"You take plastic? You know, credit cards?"

"I take anything."

Holbrook handed McCauley his American Express card. Might as well put something on it, besides espresso machines. "I'll leave this with you." Then he pointed to Ben. "Him too. They know him across the field. If you don't want the card he'll give you a check."

McCauley nodded okay. He and Pat Ben backed away from the plane.

Holbrook shut the door and locked it.

He pulled off his tie, unhooked the cassette recorder from his shirt cuff, took off his jacket, and rolled up his sleeves.

In the back of his mind he could hear Ben saying, I know about what happened and why you're not flying anymore.

This is different.

He tried to push that out of his mind.

This isn't a real plane. This is a toy. This isn't the way it was with Bean Bag.

I know about what happened and why you're not flying anymore.

He strapped himself into the left seat and fired on the electrical system. Lights flickered and dials jumped. He watched the panel, saw all the needles come up to full, saw that his navaids were working, plugged in the headset, made sure McCauley and Ben were clear, and fired up the engines. They coughed and sputtered for a second, then the props started spinning. He motioned a thumbs-up to McCauley who kicked the chocks from in front of the wheels. Then Holbrook lifted his feet off the brakes and the Piper Aztec moved forward toward the bottom of the airstrip.

"Denham Tower, this is Juliet Romeo 5-1-2. Denham Tower."

"Juliet Romeo 5-1-2, this is Denham Tower. You're clear to taxi."

He drove the Aztec through the drizzling rain to the bottom of the runway where the tower called down to him, "Roger, Juliet Romeo 5-1-2, this is Denham Tower and you're clear now for takeoff, heading 334. Contact BNN at 112.3 when passing through 1,500 feet.''

"Roger, Denham Tower, Juliet Romeo 5-1-2. Into my roll. Thanks a lot.'' He steered the plane from the taxi strip onto the runway, aimed it straight down the middle, checked his engine revs, gave it some throttle, put both hands on the stick and pushed it forward.

The little plane started to run and bounce along the tarmac.

Okay, Bean Bag, straighten 'em out.

He watched the red and blue runway lights go by.

I know about what happened and why you're not flying anymore.

He kept an eye on his ground speed.

Nose up, Bean Bag . . .

He drove the little plane faster and faster.

Bean Bag, get your fucking nose up. Bean Bag!

He pulled on the stick and the nose of the plane lifted—just a little, then more—tilting him back in his seat as the tires left the tarmac.

And for the first time since Bean Bag had been killed, Richard Holbrook flew an airplane.

A cross-wind started to belt the little plane.

He gave it more throttle, added some left rudder, pulled the nose high up and banked out of the takeoff pattern, setting her into a 334 heading. Then he straightened her out and trimmed the tail. He left the nose up at a gradual slope, and watched the ground fall away from under him.

At 1,500 feet he contacted the next radio along the route. They told him that the sky was clear and that he could now climb to his cruising altitude of 8,000 feet.

The little plane flew easily.

He headed for Aberdeen.

The sky was closing in on him.

He reached 8,000 feet.

By the time he passed Daventry, rain was pounding off his windshield.

He radioed down, asking permission to change his altitude. He said he wanted out of the weather. But Birmingham radio said there was commercial traffic above him and anyway, the weather was pretty bad all the way down to 800 feet so he was better off staying where he was. He said he wanted to go higher but they refused permission.

The little plane bounced through the rain.

He followed his flight plan to Lichfield, then came starboard onto a 354 heading. But he couldn't get out of the rain. And every now and then the plane would cough to tell him that she didn't want to stay in this weather either.

When he passed Oxenhope, he came port a few degrees, to a new 345 heading.

The rain stayed with him.

Now the skies went from dark gray to pitch black.

He radioed down, "Talla, this is Juliet Romeo 5-1-2 . . . just passing Margo at 8,000 feet on B4. I'm in the middle of some pretty soupy stuff here. Requesting permission to climb to 10,000 feet."

"Juliet Romeo 5-1-2, this is Talla . . . we've got you on B4, just passing Margo at 8,000. Sorry, Juliet Romeo 5-1-2, but it's no better at 10 than it is at 8. First break comes at 14."

"All right, Talla. Requesting permission to climb to 14,000 feet."

And Talla said okay.

He nosed her up.

Now the winds tore at the little plane and as he climbed the rain turned to sleet.

He got her through 10,000 feet, then 12,000 feet, and finally found a break in the weather at 14,000 where he leveled her off and continued along on his 345 heading.

But now the starboard engine was coughing.

And now the cabin was getting very cold.

I should have brought gloves.

He slipped his jacket over his shoulders.

That tailor is gonna kill me.

Goddamnit, why doesn't the heater work right?

He didn't like the sound of that starboard engine.

The skies were dark here too but, he told himself, at least it isn't raining.

Ten minutes later the weather closed in again.

I spoke too soon.

He flew straight into the middle of a front.

Sleet started pounding off the windshield.

He had to keep taking his hands off the wheel to flex his fingers.

And now the starboard engine was coughing very badly.

"Talla," he radioed down, "this is Juliet Romeo 5-1-2 . . . you guys got me right back in the weather . . ."

They told him to come starboard, heading 015 and to contact Edinburgh Center.

He radioed down to Edinburgh that he was having starboard engine problems and wanted to get the hell out of the weather.

Edinburgh said he could come in to land there and they started to give him a new heading. But he said no, he had to get to Aberdeen. They told him to stay on B226, heading 015. He repeated that he wanted out of the weather. They gave him permission to climb to 16,000 feet.

He pulled back on the stick and brought the nose of the little plane up, making her climb higher.

And all the time the engine coughed and spat.

And all the time the cockpit got colder and colder.

He watched the altimeter's hands swing around the clock face going up to 16,000 feet.

Because the cockpit wasn't pressurized he knew he couldn't go much higher without oxygen—17,500 was the usual limit —but already at 16,000 feet he could feel a certain lightness in his head.

The sleet stopped.

But now the wipers were frozen to the windshield.

The plane felt sluggish to him. She wasn't responding well. The stick felt heavy. The starboard engine spattered.

And then it ripped.

A flame shot out of the cowling.

He saw the flash.

Bean Bag.

The back canopy blew and Bear was gone.

Christ, Bean Bag screamed on the radio. Holy shit . . .

Bean Bag, straighten it out . . . what the hell happened? . . . level off . . . Bean Bag.

The little Piper Aztec rolled sharply right.

Holbrook yanked the small red handle for the starboard

engine's fire extinguisher. He cut off the fuel to the engine and feathered it. And all the time he had to fight to keep the little plane from banking right.

The cockpit was freezing.

His head was spinning. He was dizzy.

Bean Bag, straighten it out . . . what the hell happened? . . . level off . . . Bean Bag.

His eyes were closing.

Bean Bag . . .

The Piper Aztec nosed down.

Bean Bag . . .

He fell through 15,000 feet.

Bean Bag, straighten it out . . .

He fell through 14,000 feet.

Bean Bag . . .

And then someone was yelling at him in the radio. "Juliet Romeo 5-1-2, do you read me? . . . Juliet Romeo 5-1-2."

Holbrook opened his eyes. One split second passed. Then he screamed, "Bean Bag," as his heart pumped adrenaline through his body. Instantly he grabbed the stick and yanked it back, pulling the little plane out of its dive, straining the wings, pushing himself down into his seat, finally leveling her off at 13,500 feet.

"Juliet Romeo 5-1-2 . . . Get the hell out of there," they shouted. "You're in commercial airspace." It was Edinburgh Center. "Juliet Romeo 5-1-2, come starboard to 050. There is traffic in your eleven o'clock."

"Coming starboard to 050," he acknowledged Edinburgh Center. "I've blown an engine and want to come down to 4,000 feet."

They told him to get the hell out of 13,500 fast, and gave him permission to come down to 12,000. Then they asked him if he wanted to declare an in-flight emergency.

He knew enough to say no. If he went IFE they'd force him to land at Edinburgh. "No, I just want to come down to 4,000."

They talked him down to 12,000 feet and told him to contact Dundee radar.

His fingers felt like they were going to frostbite.

The sudden loss of altitude like that made him feel nauseated.

The wind and the rain were fiercer now than before.

He informed Dundee that he had blown an engine and needed to come down to 4,000 feet.

They radioed back that B22 was weathered out from the 500-foot ceiling at Aberdeen all the way up to 12,500 feet.

"I'll take 4,000 feet," he said, feeling very sick. "Just get me down there."

"All right," they said. "But why don't you go into your alternate at Edinburgh?"

"No. I've got to get to Aberdeen."

He didn't know how much longer he could fight the freezing cockpit and his own nausea.

"Roger, Juliet Romeo 5-1-2, come port now, to 042, and you're clear down to 8,000 feet. Hold there."

He nosed her down—straight down—then he banked her sharp to the right and brought himself onto the new heading.

With only one engine he could feel the little Piper being pushed to its limits.

And again he was hitting the weather straight on.

The sky was pitch black.

There was absolutely nothing to see beyond the windshield.

His hands felt frozen onto the stick.

Winds buffeted the plane, shaking it violently.

He battled to keep the plane on course.

He came through 10,000 feet.

Sleet bounced off the airframe.

He fought to keep his eyes from closing again.

"Take me out to the ball game," he sang at the top of his lungs. "Take me out to the park. Buy me some peanuts and Cracker Jacks . . ."

He wanted to take his hands off the stick, just for a few seconds, to shake them, to get some circulation back into his fingers. But he didn't dare.

". . . I don't care if I never come back. And it's root, root, root for the home team, if they don't win it's a shame. And it's one, two, three strikes you're out at the old ball game."

He started again, "Take me out to the ball game . . ."

He held the stick tight, with both hands, pulling at it, pushing it, working the rudders with his feet, battling with the weather, flying the little plane. And singing to keep from passing out.

He leveled off at 8,000 feet.

The lightness in his head started to fade away.

But the winds still tore at him, shaking the wings.

". . . And it's one, two, three strikes you're out . . ."

He held there at 8,000 feet until Dundee radar told him that he was free to come down to 4,000 and to contact Aberdeen Center on 114.3.

Again he nosed her straight down.

The sheer violence of the wind and the force of the rain rocked the little plane.

"Take me out to the ball game . . ."

He came through 6,000 feet.

McCauley, if I ever get out of here alive I'm gonna take your fresh spark plugs and jam them down your throat.

Forty miles to Aberdeen.

He leveled off at 4,000 feet.

The winds kept up. And the rain kept up. But now his head was clear and now the nausea was gone and now he could rub his hands together to get some feeling back into them.

He fought with the cabin heater and located a closed vent. He opened it and suddenly heat rushed into the cockpit. Son of a bitch.

Then he reached across the instrument panel and found another vent for the de-icer.

Hot air shot across the windshield. After a few minutes the wipers rattled, broke through the ice and cleared the windshield.

But it was still black outside.

Now there were only thirty miles left to Aberdeen.

He radioed down and told them he was on his way in.

They radioed back and told him the field was closed.

"Closed?" He couldn't believe it. "What do you mean the field is closed? It can't be closed."

"Sorry, Juliet Romeo 5-1-2, we've just gone below minimums and we're shut down. We'll give you a course back to Edinburgh."

"No," he screamed at the top of his lungs. "Listen, Aberdeen, I've got to get in there."

They said, sorry, but no.

He said he absolutely had to.

They said, sorry, it's impossible. They told him, proceed to your alternate destination.

He stayed on course.

They gave him a new heading, ordering him to turn around for Edinburgh.

He looked at his feathered starboard engine.

"Aberdeen, this is Juliet Romeo 5-1-2." He knew how to handle them. "I've got my starboard engine down and," he lied, "I'm fast losing pressure on my port engine. I'm declaring IFE and requesting an approach into Aberdeen."

"IFE?" The voice from Aberdeen crackled over the radio, "Juliet Romeo 5-1-2, is this a real emergency?"

"I repeat, Aberdeen, I've blown one engine and I'm nursing pressure on the second one. Now, I'm not asking you, I'm telling you, this is an IFE. Repeat, IFE. I'm requesting approach instructions into Aberdeen."

The air controller at Aberdeen asked, "Have you got the fuel to get you back to Edinburgh?"

He lied again. "I doubt it." Then he added, "I'm not sure I've even got enough airplane here to get me to Aberdeen. But do you understand what an IFE is? The sky is mine. You clear everybody out of the way and get me the hell into Aberdeen."

"But Aberdeen is shut."

"You get me there, I'll reopen it."

The controller told him to maintain his heading but to come down to 2,000 feet.

He nosed the little plane down.

The wind and rain were no better at 2,000 feet.

But now he was only twenty miles from Aberdeen.

Another voice came onto the radio. "Juliet Romeo 5-1-2, this is Aberdeen Center. Have you declared IFE?"

"That's affirmative," he said.

"What's the problem?"

"I don't believe you guys," he shouted. "I'm sitting up here with one engine down and one on its way . . .''

And now they gave him permission to come down to 1,500 feet.

He was ten miles from Aberdeen.

"Juliet Romeo 5-1-2, are you requesting an ambulance and fire trucks? We've got foaming equipment . . ."

"No, man, I'm just requesting you talk me into Aberdeen."

"Juliet Romeo 5-1-2, Edinburgh reports that you lost your starboard engine sometime between Talla and Angus. We'd like to know why you didn't declare IFE back there . . ."

"For Chrissakes, man, this is an IFE. Will you get off my ass so I can get down on the ground?"

He was five miles out of Aberdeen.

Aberdeen Center passed him over to Aberdeen Tower. They adjusted his heading for a final approach into the field.

He was two miles out.

He knew they were right in asking why he hadn't declared IFE sooner and go into Edinburgh. And it dawned on him that someone might start asking him point-blank questions once he got on the ground. That could lead to someone wanting to see his license. And that was the last thing he wanted. There wasn't going to be time for any discussions once he touched down. So just to make it look really good, he started changing his fuel mixture into the port engine.

Now he was down to 1,000 feet.

And now he was one mile out.

"I'm losing pressure on my port engine," he told the tower. He figured McCauley would get into a lot of shit for hiring out a death-trap like that. But that was McCauley's problem. Right now he was still flying in clouds, and it was still raining, and his wings still shook. Aberdeen Tower warned him that visibility was down to just 250 feet. That meant he wouldn't see the runway until he was almost on top of it.

He held onto the stick with his right hand, and lifted off the throttle with his left hand. He worked his rudders to tack into the wind and lowered his flaps.

It would be just like a carrier stalled landing.

Nose up.

Bean Bag, you're gonna make it. 1,000 feet. Keep 'em steady. Okay, Bean Bag, straighten 'em out. 500 feet. Bring it down, level off and bring it down. You're doing fine. 250 feet.

The clouds broke.

The runway was right there in front of him.

Throttle down.

Goose the nose up.

Stall.

He cut the port engine.

Nose up.

Level off now. You're high left. Bring it down just a skosh. Okay, you're doing fine. Hang in there, buddy. 100 feet. Coming in straight. Keep your nose up. Nose up, Bean Bag. Get your fucking nose up. Bean Bag!

Holbrook glided in, silently, perfectly, with no engines at all. He touched down and rolled about five hundred feet before starting the port engine again, and getting behind a Follow-Me truck which led him down a taxi ramp to a hangar.

The driver of the Follow-Me jumped out and showed Holbrook where to park.

Cutting the engine, he snapped off the electricals. The needles and dials simply fell over dead.

He sat right there.

For the longest time he didn't move.

He kept thinking to himself, I just flew an airplane. Goddamn, did I just fly an airplane. He took a long deep breath and said to the empty seat on his right, thanks, Bean Bag.

The driver of the Follow-Me banged on his wing.

Holbrook unlocked the door, grabbed his jacket, and jumped out of the plane.

"Jimmy?" The driver of the Follow-Me gave him a hand down from the wing. "Jimmy, where did you ever learn how to fly a plane so sweetly?"

Holbrook looked at him. "Where can I get a taxi? Don't bother servicing the Aztec 'cause it won't get me home. I'll worry about it later. Can you please just get me to a taxi? I've got to get to the port. Fast."

"Jimmy, I've been listening in on the radio since you declared your IFE. Weather like this in a tin bucket like that. I've been here for fifteen years and I've never seen anyone land a plane like that. Jimmy, you're one helluva pilot."

He nodded. "Yeah, thanks. We're standing out in the rain. Can you please get me to a taxi?"

"Sure, Jimmy. Pile in."

Holbrook got into the Follow-Me and the driver took him around to the front of the airport, to the passenger terminal. "Sweetest job of landing I've ever seen . . ."

"Thanks." Now he raced over to a Ford with a taxi sign on the roof and told the driver, "The port of Aberdeen. And fast."

The cab driver half turned around and asked over his shoulder, "Where in the port do you want to go? It's pretty good-sized now, you know. Not like it used to be before the oil and all . . ."

"Just drive," he said. "Please. Step on it."

"Okay. Okay." The driver started the motor and headed out of the airport.

Holbrook checked his watch. The harbor engineer told me the *Dragon Empress* was scheduled for three to four hours in port. Three minimum. Four maximum. Count on the minimum. She wasn't in yet when I spoke to the guy so say it took her fifteen minutes. I was twenty-five minutes from North Audley Street to McCauley's. I was two hours and forty minutes to here. That's three hours and five minutes. Minus fifteen. That's ten minutes under the three-hour minimum. She's still there.

"Can't you drive this thing any faster?"

The driver said he had to obey the speed limits.

Holbrook reached into his pocket and pulled out a five-pound note. "Here. This will help if we get a ticket. How much further is it?"

"You see," the driver explained, "this is what we call the Great Northern Road. This will lead us into Powis Place and from there we take West North Street . . ."

"Just how much further is it?"

"Maybe five, maybe ten minutes."

Holbrook closed his eyes. Please keep that ship in port. The taxi stopped.

"This it?" Holbrook looked up.

"King Street," the driver said. "Always traffic."

"Come on," he begged. "Come on."

They had to wait for several minutes until they could get across King Street. Then they headed down East North Street. When the driver turned right along Commerce Street, Holbrook leaned forward with his arms draped over the seat in front of him so he could watch where they were going.

Now he saw the cranes and warehouses and now he saw the docks.

They came into the port.

"Go left here," Holbrook ordered. "Go out that quay."

The driver turned left on Waterloo Quay.

Victoria Dock was empty.

Holbrook told the driver, "Go all the way out, past the jetty. There, follow that road around."

They went to the end of North Pier. Holbrook got out of the car. The navigation channel was empty. But he could see other docks and there were ships in other docks, so he climbed back into the taxi and told the driver, "We've got to go all the way around to the other side."

The driver took him along Waterloo Quay, to the bottom of Victoria Dock where Holbrook spotted the harbor office. He shouted, "Stop here," threw another five-pound note on the front seat and jumped out.

A man was just going inside the office.

Holbrook called to him, "Where would the *Dragon Empress* be?"

The man pointed and shouted back, "Albert Quay."

It's here.

"Call the police," he screamed. "This is an emergency. Call the police and get them over there right away. It's a matter of life and death. Call the police quickly."

It's here.

Now he ran as fast as he could along the street, through the light drizzle, in front of the fish market. "Where's Albert Quay?"

A man told him, "Left here."

He tore around the corner.

Some ships were docked further up.

He ran past the pontoon docks.

Lorries were loading and unloading. Forklift trucks were

hurrying along the quay. Boxes and crates and cartons were scattered all over.

He ran past lorries and forklifts and in between crates.

There was a ship at dock four.

It was a tanker.

He kept running.

There was a ship at dock three.

It was a Norwegian coaster.

The light rain trickled down his face.

He kept running.

Dock two was empty.

But there was a freighter at dock one.

It's here.

A ship's horn sounded.

He ran as fast as he could. His legs hurt and there was a slight pain in his left side. But he didn't stop running.

There was a siren behind him.

The police.

He kept running.

The ship's horn sounded again.

The siren grew louder.

He looked over his shoulder and saw a police car just turning into Albert Quay.

He passed the empty number two dock and got close enough to the freighter in number one . . .

The police car raced up to him.

The ship's horn blasted one more time.

And then he stopped dead in his tracks.

Dock one . . .

The two cops got out of their car.

Panting and holding his side, he stared at the freighter in dock one.

"What's the problem, sir?"

He couldn't believe it.

"What's the problem, sir?" one of the policemen asked again.

The freighter was pulling out.

And on its stern it read, *Ma Jolie*, Le Havre.

"Sir?"

He spun around and looked at the other ships in dock.

"Sir?"

He didn't want to believe it.

"What is the problem, sir?"

"The *Dragon Empress,*" he said. He turned around again. He turned all around. There was a forklift coming by and he shouted to the operator, "Where's the *Dragon Empress?*"

The fellow on the forklift raised his right hand and motioned with it to show him that it sailed away. "Two hours ago," he called back. "Long gone."

"Sir?" One of the policemen tapped him on the shoulder. "Sir, would you mind telling us what's happening?"

Two hours ago. Long gone. He moved up to the front of the police car and put both his hands on the roof. He was breathing deeply. Two hours ago. Came into port just long enough to pick up Li'Ning and the ginger jar. Now it's gone. Long gone.

"All right, sir." The policeman was getting upset. "If you don't tell us what this is all about, I'm afraid you'll have to come with us."

"Long gone," he said, with his back still to them.

"What's this all about?" the other one wanted to know.

"It's about being the only one who believed." He tried to get his breathing back to normal. "I'm sorry to have bothered you. I'm sorry. I really am."

The policemen whispered to each other. Then one of them said sternly to Holbrook, "Listen, sir, you sound like an American. Maybe it's different in America. But around here we don't go crying wolf. We don't go claiming something is an emergency when it isn't. Now if you were from around here we'd nick you for wasting our time. But seeing as how you're an American we're going to let you off this time with just a warning. But if it ever happens again . . ."

"I'm sorry," Holbrook kept apologizing. "I'm sorry."

"Is that understood?"

"Yes, sir," he said. "Yes, sir."

The cops got back in their car.

Holbrook stood up and watched them drive away.

Two hours, he said to himself.

Long gone.

There was a clap of thunder and the drizzle turned into a storm.

He pulled the collar of the jacket closer around his neck and walked back toward the bottom of the quay.

The rains came down.

He got soaked.

Two hours. Long gone.

He walked to the bottom of the quay where he saw a bright red telephone booth.

He stared at that for several minutes, almost as if he was totally oblivious to the rain.

Two hours. Long gone.

Then he stepped inside the phone booth.

It's about being the only one who believed.

He dialed the overseas operator and placed a collect call to Florida.

And when Millicent answered he said to her, "I think I'd like to come home."

SUSPENSE, INTRIGUE & INTERNATIONAL DANGER

These novels of espionage and excitement-filled tension will guarantee you the best in high-voltage reading pleasure.

___**FLIGHT OF THE INTRUDER** by Stephen Coonts 64012/$4.95

___**NERVE ENDINGS** by William Martin 50458/$3.95

___**DEEP SIX** by Clive Cussler 64804/$4.95

___**ICEBERG** by Clive Cussler 63255/$4.50

___**MEDITERRANEAN CAPER** by Clive Cussler 63256/$4.50

___**RAMPAGE** By Justin Scott 64852/$4.50

___**THE SHATTERED EYE** by Bill Granger 47756/$3.95

___**THE ZURICH NUMBERS** by Bill Granger 55399/$3.95

___**SHELL GAME** by Douglas Terman 53291/$4.50

___**FREE FLIGHT** by Douglas Terman 50925/$3.50

___**BLACK MARKET** by James Patterson 63921/$4.50

___**WARLORDS** by Janet Morris 61923/$3.95

POCKET
B O O K S

Simon & Schuster, Mail Order Dept. SUS
200 Old Tappan Rd., Old Tappan, N.J. 07675

Please send me the books I have checked above. I am enclosing $_____ (please add 75¢ to cover postage and handling for each order. N.Y.S. and N.Y.C. residents please add appropriate sales tax). Send check or money order—no cash or C.O.D.'s please. Allow up to six weeks for delivery. For purchases over $10.00 you may use VISA: card number, expiration date and customer signature must be included.

Name_____

Address_____

City _____ State/Zip _____

VISA Card No._____ Exp. Date_____

Signature _____ 318B-01